Acknowledgments

I can't express how wonderful Robert DeLuise (literary development agent, Page Publishing) has been for myself through our correspondences. Hearing his voice on the other end of the phone and understanding his belief in my work created a smooth process from a rough manuscript to publication. Gretchen Will's (publication coordinator) dedication to my work and guidance through the process of the continuing editing process must also be acknowledged and recognized for all her demanding work for my dreams. I must express my enormous thanks also to the dedicated and amazing editors, cover designers, layout, and printing staff of Page Publishing as well. The work they accomplish behind the scenes is nothing short of incredible.

The fabulous cover illustration for my novel was created and designed by the ever-so-talented fourteen-year-old Sahs (Samantha Hancock-Simon). The moment I viewed her artwork, I immediately desired to use it for my cover. Sahs graciously allowed me the privilege to apply her stunning concept (that so happened to flow with the manuscript's content perfectly) as my cover design. Thank you so much, my friend.

I can never express enough gratitude toward my family, Brian, Aidan, and Dalon, for believing in me and giving me the time I need to be absorbed into my world of make-believe.

Cheers.

1

"Am I changing color yet? I am, aren't I?" Lisa shouted her question toward Bree as she came back from the living room to the kitchen where Bree was sitting at the table trying to enjoy her cup of tea. "I am definitely changing color! I am glowing green with envy right now. You received a sought-after invitation to the grand opening of the American Museum of Natural History's special exhibition tonight, and you are acting like it is no big deal. You are just sitting there, calmly drinking your tea like everything is normal. Everyone who is anyone will be at this gala, and you don't even care. I am so jealous I could rip my hair out right now! Do you even know what I would do to get my name on that guest list?" Bree opened her mouth to answer Lisa, but she held up her finger and shook it at Bree. "Don't answer that. I know, and you know that I would sell my soul to the devil to go." All Bree could do was shake her head and roll her eyes toward her best friend and roommate for the hundredth time this week.

Bree regretted telling Lisa about the invitation to the gala in the first place. Ever since she'd told Lisa that Derrick had invited her to the social event of the year, Lisa had performed on and on about how Bree was the luckiest woman alive, how it wasn't fair that she was going to the "most epic party" of the year. If Bree hadn't wanted to see the exhibit badly herself, she would have certainly given Lisa her invitation to just shut her up about it all. Bree could not give the invitation away though, as someone else had invited her. The invite only held on her going out on a date with Derrick. He had been asking her to go on a date with him for the last two years futilely. The only reason she had said yes to his offer this time was due to the exhibit itself. The invitation for the event was incredibly hard to get one's mitts on and for good reason. The exhibit was for one night only. Then the ancient artifacts would go away forever, according to the proprietor of the relics. This may have only been an advertising ruse in order to sell tickets at ten thousand dollars per person, but if it were true and the artifacts did go into obscurity, then the ten thousand a head was completely worth every penny if one could afford it.

When Bree heard that a certain artifact she had been dying to see was in this exhibit, she knew that she had to somehow get her name on the guest list. She tried in every way she knew possible to gain an invitation; unfortunately, the means to securing entry to this popular showing was for Bree to finally agree to go on a date with Derrick. Bree worked for a private foundation called Artifacts Alive. Derrick's family endowed the foundation to the Museum of Natural History. Bree had been born and raised in Egypt till she was ten years of age with her mother and her father. She moved to America with her mother after her father, who was an archeologist, tragically died on a dig. A boulder had collapsed on him as he had been searching for tombs. As a child, Bree had always loved to listen to her father's tales about his work. Even though he had been in a tragic accident in his pursuit and love of archaeology, Bree was still as fascinated as her father had been with archeology and followed suit.

Bree had her masters in archaeology and was working on her doctorate for her anthropology, so when the opening came up in the museum, she jumped at the chance to receive a position within the anthropology department to further her education and career. Derrick's father, Victor Radcliffe, and the foundation's CEO as well as all the board members interviewed her for the opening within their foundation two years ago. After her interview, Victor Radcliffe came to her himself offering her the job personally, telling that she was a perfect fit within his organization. He did not want anyone else but her to fill the position. Victor also delighted in the fact that she spoke fluent Egyptian Arabic, which came in handy for her choice of vocation. The offer to work in the museum for the foundation was an excellent experience for Bree. She would use her experience to help her with her thesis she was working on for her entrance into university for her doctorate.

Bree fell in love with working for the museum. Victor had been right; she did fit in well. She was a resolute member of staff and wanted to absorb everything she could learn from everyone that she worked with. She also got on well with everyone she worked with and had made friends within the museum. The only objectionable consequence about working at the museum was Derrick and his constant pestering of her to go out with him on a weekly basis. Bree heard about Derrick's womanizing even before she had started her job. His family was extremely rich, and Derrick was a high-society circle member. He had social connects and always attended grand events, parties, award shows, fashion shows, and fund raisers in and around Manhattan. He constantly surrounded himself with celebrities and models which instigated his name and photo to frequent articles and gossip columns in local magazines and newspapers.

Bree believed the only reason Derrick continued to pursue her was her constant brushing him off like an annoying fly. Derrick always got what he wanted whenever he wanted it. Bree was just a challenge to him. Sure, Derrick was devastatingly handsome, well-built, and sexy as hell, but despite these facts, Bree considered him to be a spoilt man boy in an exorbitantly priced suit who existed off his family's wealth and nothing else. Derrick, in no way, contributed to society with his own hands, brains, or arduous work. This kind of man was not attractive to Bree in the slightest, no matter how debonair or connected he seemed to be.

Lisa stepped in front of Bree, waving her hands in front of her face. "Did you even hear what I said, Bree? God, I hate it when you zone me out like that!" Bree returned to reality and rolled her eyes again. "Look, Lisa, I understand you are crazy jealous that I am going to this Egyptian artifact soiree. If I were able to have invited you, I would have. You know that, right?" Lisa just stared at Bree with pouty lips. "Besides, I will be fighting off Derrick's advances all night just so I can finally see the priceless stone obelisk. Did you know that the obelisk's hieroglyphs are so old they are unlike any form of Egyptian hieroglyphs ever discovered before? Not one translator who has had the privilege of seeing the obelisk has been able to decipher them yet. It has mystified scientific professionals who have seen it.

I have to see this piece, Lisa. It is the most important find in the last ninety-nine years. Ever since King Tutankhamun Nebkheperure's tomb discovery and excavation, nothing has been more important than this certain discovery."

Bree could see that Lisa's eyes had glazed over as she discussed the importance of the collection that Sir Ashton Cummings had discovered a year ago far beneath the sphynx in Egypt. Bree looked at the blank pout that was on Lisa's face, and she wanted to pull out her own hair now. All Lisa cared about was the social aspect of this event. She wanted to mingle and hobnob with all the celebrities and rich people who would be at the show since she was a struggling and, at the moment, unemployed actor. Lisa saw the artifact attraction as a way to advance her career by meeting and/or sleeping with anyone connected within the film industry. She cared nothing about the "archaic dust collectors," as she called them. Bree sometimes wondered why they were still such good friends with how opposite they were to each other. They had been besties since the sixth grade and had been together ever since. Lisa was Bree's yin to her yang. They balanced each other out. This was the only way she could describe her relationship to her museum friends when they met Lisa.

Lisa inhaled a deep breath and then exhaled with exaggeration as she flopped herself onto the kitchen chair beside Bree. "I know you would have invited me if you could. I am just envious, jealous, pissed that it is you going with Derrick and not me. I am taking it out on you to make myself feel better. I am sorry. I'll stop." Bree sighed in relief. They sat in silence for a moment. Then suddenly Lisa flopped forward onto the kitchen table with her hands in prayer formation. "Can you please call Derrick! Tell him I will blow him for a month, anytime he wants, if he just gets me a ticket for tonight. Please!"

Bree snorted in disgust, put down her tea, shoved her chair back, and exited the kitchen. She entered her bedroom and slammed the door as hard as she could. Lisa followed behind and banged none to softly with her fists on Bree's door. "Hey, why so dramatic? I was kidding, silly. Lighten up."

Bree snorted again and yelled through her door, "No! You were not kidding, Lisa. I know you all too well."

Bree could hear Lisa shuffling her feet outside of her door, and then she mumbled, "Okay, so I wasn't kidding. I just don't understand why you won't call Derrick. I thought you were my soul sister."

Bree sat on the end of her bed staring at the dress she had picked out for her date and thought for a moment. She jumped up, went over to her bedroom door, and flung it open to face Lisa. "I will not degrade myself low enough to ask such a question of Derrick, and I most definitely will not 'whore out' my best friend to him either. Even if you want me to."

Lisa grinned at Bree. Lisa's smile could always cheer Bree up when she was in a mood like she was right now. "It's not 'whoring me out' if it's free and with my permission."

Bree picked up a decoration pillow that was on a chair by the door and threw it at Lisa. "It's not free when Derrick will have to purchase a ten-thousand-dollar ticket for you, you freak!"

The pillow hit Lisa square on the head. As she threw the pillow back with her hair all out of place, she missed Bree entirely and then said, "Damn it, you're right." They both suddenly burst out laughing. "Okay, for truth, I will stop harassing you about tonight. So, what are you going to wear? I know your bland tastes in fashion. I need to inspect whatever piece of garbage you picked out for tonight's event." Bree frowned but knew her friend was correct. She had never been astute in the ways of fashion. It wasn't something that mattered to her. She was always around old dusty objects or out in the field around sand and dirt for her excavations to find artifacts. She had no reason to dress nicely. Jeans and a T-shirt were her go-to fashion. It never mattered how she dressed.

Bree turned to her bed and picked up the simple black dress that was one of the only two dresses that she had in her closet and turned to show it to Lisa. Lisa raised her eyebrows and then pretended to gag. Bree blushed bright red. "You've owned that dress since we were in high school. Why didn't you buy a new dress for this evening?"

Bree blushed deeper red. "You know I can't afford to purchase new clothes right now. I am putting myself through school and trying to pay for everything myself with a part-time job. How can I afford a new dress?" Bree huffed and held the dress back up to herself.

"This will do just fine." Lisa shook her head and stared at the dress she held up. Bree could tell that she was thinking of something, and sure enough, Lisa snapped her fingers, turned on her heels, and left the room. She soon came back with an outfit draped over her arms from her own closet. "Here is what you are going to wear tonight. I always make it a habit for my contracts the choice of keeping the clothing if I choose from my acting gigs. This is absolutely perfect for tonight. It even goes with the theme of the show. It's what I would have worn if I were able to go. Here, try it on."

Bree took the dress and stripped down to her undergarments. She pulled the little black-and-gold number on, turned to look in the mirror, and gasped. *Damn, it's perfect.* The dress fit her like a glove. The neckline came to just below her chin. It had black, gold, and silver beads all down the neck and scooped around the tops of her shoulders all around to the back with beads hanging in a loop down both her shoulders. The dress had long sleeves with beading bands going down the midlower arms and wrists. The length only came down to just below the top of her thighs. *It's so short, though.* She would have to stand for most of the night just to remain decent. The dress had beading on both hips and waist. The circles inside the beading were open. The dress left bare flesh exposed. Bree had never worn anything so daring and yet so perfect for the evening.

"Well, crap! That looks far better on you than it ever did on me. You have such amazing long legs. You need to show them off more. Derrick is going to salivate at the sight of you." Bree almost ripped the dress off when Lisa made that comment, but damn, she did love this dress. Before she changed her mind, she turned away from the mirror. "Thank you, Lisa, for letting me borrow this dress. It's amazing." Bree looked slightly guilty when she blurted out, "You wouldn't happen to have any shoes to go with the dress per chance?" Lisa winked, left the room, and was back in a flash again, this time with a pair of high black platform stilettoes with gold chains and beading on the back of the heels. Bree slipped on the shoes thanking the stars that Lisa and herself had the same size of feet.

When Bree looked in the mirror after she had the shoes on, Lisa groaned, "God, I wish I had your legs. They go on for days. Enough of the envy. Sit at your vanity. Let me style your long black hair in a messy updo, and you will stun everyone." Bree was beginning to get excited. When Lisa finished playing with her hair and makeup, she did not recognize herself in the mirror. Lisa clucked around like a proud mother hen. "No one will care about any of those artifacts once they get a look at you. You are going to be the highlight of the night." Bree thanked Lisa and looked at the time. Derrick would be there within minutes to pick her up. Bree made sure she had important things in her small clutch that would carry her through the night, and just as she finished touching up her lipstick, the doorbell rang. She hugged Lisa, quickly peeked in the mirror for an adjustment, took in a slow, deep breath, and then she answered the door.

Derrick almost stumbled back in shock when he saw Bree. She was always extremely beautiful in her natural state, but now, he stood stunned. Standing before him was the most magnificent woman he had ever seen. If someone had told him that she was an Egyptian goddess, he would have believed them. He had been with countless fabulous women his entire adult life but never was he so attracted to one as much as he was right now. Her large amethyst blue eyes were brilliantly sparkling. Her waist-length silky black hair was piled high upon her head. The dress was short and showed off her lovely long legs and her amazing figure. She stood about six feet tall with the heels she had on. Derrick stood six foot four himself. They would be the finest-looking couple this event, and he would be the envy of all men who caught sight of Bree.

He would turn on all his charm and swag tonight. He would woo her so she would not be able to resist him any longer. She had eluded him for two years now, which had frustrated, dumbfounded, and enraged him. His father had him mind his ways with her, though. He had said she was important to the foundation and their project, so he was in no way allowed to chase her away. If his father had not told him to stay away, he would have been far more aggressive in his pursuit of Bree and would have not taken no for an answer for so long. He always obtained what he wanted, and since he laid his eyes on Bree, he had wanted her. Tonight would be the night he would make her his.

Derrick, as always, looked handsome as ever. He carried himself proudly in his immaculate well-filled out tuxedo. His hair was on the longer side, slicked back with a small piece hanging off to one side of his cleanly shaven, exfoliated face. He had a glorious tan with a perfect manicure. No doubt he made most women swoon with one look at him as Lisa was doing behind her right now. You could almost hear the drool hitting the floor. Before it became too awkward with Lisa, Bree said, "Shall we head out?" Behind her, out of the corner of her eye as she exited the apartment, she could see Lisa holding her hand to her ear and mouth in the shape of a phone, lip-synching the words "Call me" to Derrick with the sexiest smoldering look she could muster. Derrick cleared his throat, but Bree could have sworn she saw him nod toward Lisa ever so slightly. What a true wolf he was. Once a dog, always a dog. Thank God she had no feelings toward this man, or she would have been devastated.

Derrick placed her arm in his and escorted her out of the apartment to the limo that was waiting for them. When they settled into the plush leather seats in the back, Derrick at once poured Bree a glass of Dom Perignon Rose Champagne. When he handed the flute to her, Bree declined. Derrick frowned. "This is an eleven-thousand-dollar bottle of champagne, Bree. You should at least try it."

Bree shrugged a little uncomfortably. "I am a gin and tonic girl myself. I have never been able to stomach champagne. One glass and I have a raging headache the next day." Derrick put the champagne flute down and opened the bar to his right. He pulled out a bottle of Watenshi gin, poured a shot in a glass, then added ice and tonic. He even had fresh lime in the limo bar, and he added a twist to her glass then handed it over to Bree.

Bree took a small sip and smiled. It was the best gin she had ever tasted. "Wow, this is delicious Derrick."

Derrick smiled. "You have good taste, Bree. This is a rare Watenshi gin from England. It only cost me twenty-five hundred dollars for this bottle."

Bree almost choked on the second sip of her drink due to Derrick's comment. "Is there anything you do not own that is ridiculously overpriced, Derrick?"

Derrick laughed and slid back comfortably into the seat, sipping his champagne. "I have very expensive taste, Bree, only the best will do for me." As he said this, he winked at Bree, who could not help but snort at that comment. She turned to watch the city go by as they headed to the museum. They sat for a minute when Derrick broke the silence. "I need to know something Bree, if you do not mind me asking. Why did it take you so long to accept a night out with me?"

Bree turned away from the window and looked Derrick in the eyes. It was too bad she did not find him attractive. He was an exceptionally attractive man to look at. "Do you want me to be gentle and lie, or would you like the truth to your question?"

Derrick clenched his jaw as he watched the beautiful woman sitting across from him. He enjoyed how amazing she looked for a moment. He thought for a minute and then laughed. "You are blunt. I like that in a woman. Everyone skirts around me and kisses my ass trying to please me all the time, as they all want something from me or my family in return. I would like the honest truth, if you would not mind. That would be quite refreshing for once."

Bree raised her eyebrows a little in shock but went ahead. "Okay, Derrick, I will be honest then. I have no attraction to men that live off their family's wealth and do nothing but party, flaunt, and throw money around like water. I see how you go through women faster than I change my underwear and then throw them away like garbage when you finish with them. You have never gotten your hands dirty with a day of arduous work, and you always have someone do everything for you. You are a prodigal son and a rake. I have said no to your advances as I do not agree with your lifestyle. Money, famous people, and parties are not my thing."

When Bree finished her very blunt explanation, Derrick laughed heartily. "How delightful. Everything you said is true. I cannot deny it. So why is it, then, that you finally said yes?"

Bree squirmed uncomfortably for a moment before answering Derrick's question. She pulled at the hem of her dress to make sure she was not exposing anything inappropriate. "To tell you the truth, Derrick, it is the exhibit itself that made me say yes to your invitation tonight. I could never afford the admission to the exhibit. You're the only way I was able to get into the show. I did try every way decently possible to get my own invitation but to no avail. I apologize for using you, Derrick. That was very selfish of me. I completely understand if you have this limo turned around and you drop me back off at my apartment and take someone else."

Derrick sat forward in his seat. "I already knew this is why you accepted my invitation, Bree. I just wanted to see if you would be truly honest with me. You passed. I still want you to go with me to this show. You are ravishing tonight. I believe we will be the talk of the town after this event is over. I want you on my arm tonight as I will be the envy of every male at this party. Oh, and you are correct, Bree. I am a rake." The grin that Derrick produced after that comment shot warning bells through Bree's brain, but she pushed them aside. She had to remember that she worked for his father, and he would not dare do anything untoward to her person, or so she hoped. Besides, they were close to the museum, and there would be hundreds of people around. It was just the ride home that she was worried about now. By the end of the night, he would realize she would not put out for him, and eventually he would get bored and pick someone else to end the night with. Then she would just cab it back home, and all would be well.

2

As they pulled up to the museum, there were limos and fancy cars lined up waiting to have a valet transfer their cars to the designated parking area. Security was swarming the museum and for good reason. The artifacts on display tonight were priceless. There were massive amounts of bling dangling from attending lady's necks and wrists tonight. Bree shook her head, realizing as she watched all the wealthy and famous people exiting their limos and fancy sports cars, looking like they were on an episode of the show *The Rich and Famous*, how glad she was that she was not part of this society. She did not covet what others had. She was happy with her life, her job, her little apartment and having to take the bus to work as she could not afford a car. Her life was simple. That was all she needed. When their limo pulled into the center of the throng of vehicles at the front steps of the museum, it was their turn to exit their transportation and head up the stairs. Derrick's chauffeur opened the door for them. He grabbed the ticket for their vehicle and went with the car and the valet. Bree gladly accepted Derrick's arm to head up the stairs to the entrance. She never wore high heels. So, she was slightly unstable. There were photographers everywhere.

The flashes from the paparazzi cameras were overwhelming. They were all yelling at celebrities to get them to turn in their direction for a photo opportunity. Derrick was all for it. He turned himself and Bree to all that called out his name. He made sure he always had his arm around Bree's waist. One paparazzi yelled out to Derrick, "Who's the stunner you have on your arm tonight, Derrick?"

Derrick only smiled at the reporter, so they turned a question to Bree, "Tell us your name. Are you a model, an up-and-coming actor?

Give us the juice." Bree took Derrick's direction of response and just smiled brilliantly at the reporter but stayed silent.

Derrick squeezed her waist, showing she had done well. He bent down to her ear and whispered, "Well done, Bree, keep the bastards guessing. They will be eating out of your hand by the end of the night for just a snippet of who you really are."

Derrick had enough of the reporters and paparazzi and led Bree the rest of the way up the stairs. At the front entrance, there were four giant security guards and a small man taking the invitations and tickets. Derrick handed him the tickets and went on inside. "Welcome, Mr. Radcliffe and Ms. Sabry, enjoy your evening." Derrick nodded cordially and ushered Bree inside the main lobby. Bree was shocked; she had been in the main lobby hundreds of times, but tonight it was lit up in spectacular abietic lighting. Egyptian decorations, statues, and false pyramids were everywhere. There were Egyptian banners hanging in between the large marble pillars. The main dinosaur display in the lobby had a large white screen hiding it with images projected across them with different ancient Egyptian artifacts that archaeologists found over the past century.

The hall was filled with hundreds of people all dressed to impress and were beautiful. Everyone who was anyone was there. Bree began to feel very self-conscious and nervous. Derrick read her mind as he leaned in once more. "You have nothing to be nervous about. You outshine every woman in the room tonight. Remember you are with me, and I am in my element. Relax and enjoy." Before he pulled away, he let his lips trace the outside of her ear, and it sent warning shivers down her spine. As he led her more toward the center of the room, his hand placed protectively on her lower back. It was a little too close to her buttocks than she liked, but she did not want to cause a scene, so she let it slide for now.

A server came by dressed in full Egyptian attire, like in the Cleopatra movie, with a tray of champagne. Bree declined so Derrick whispered in his ear, and the server nodded. Within minutes, the server returned with a gin and tonic for Bree and a glass of whiskey on the rocks for Derrick. Bree thanked Derrick and the server. That was a nice touch on Derrick's part, but this was a way for him to soften her up, she realized. She had to keep up her watch with him and his subtle ways. She would only sip this drink and make it last as she did not want to become intoxicated and let her guard ease even a little with this particular rake. People were staring in their direction, and others were bold enough to come up and blatantly ask who she was. Bree let Derrick take control of the conversation, and she just smiled and nodded. Her mouth was beginning to ache with smiling so apprehensively. He played her up so much she sounded like she already had her PhD in archeology and was an amazing anthropologist who would be one of the few who would crack the code on the indecipherable hieroglyphs on the artifacts on display tonight. Everyone was impressed.

Bree blushed in embarrassment as she knew all of what Derrick was spewing was an outright lie. She kept her mouth shut with comments here and there that Derrick was overexaggerating. When they had a moment alone, Derrick looked at Bree. "Do not be so modest. Live the dream for the night. No one will remember anyway."

Bree snorted. "You are lying about me, and I do not appreciate it. There is no reason to embellish who I am. I do not have a need to impress any of these people, nor is it necessary. I do not need the recognition or the hype that you seem to thrive off of. Please stop it."

Derrick just laughed and slightly shrugged his shoulders at her complaints when she noticed a very charismatic man approaching them.

Bree startled into a moment of silence. She could not help but recognize who it was that was introducing himself, and she was in awe. Here standing before them was the one and only Sir Aston Cummings. This very man was who she wanted to emulate within their field. He had unearthed the now famous Egyptian artifacts that were on display tonight. Bree let her mouth drop open as he introduced himself to Derrick but then ignored him completely and turned to Bree. "I have heard about you in the last hour as I have been mingling. I am—" Before he had a chance to say anything more, Bree grabbed his outstretched hand and shook it with enthusiasm as the words just fell out of her mouth.

"Sir Aston Cummings, I know all about your work. I have studied and followed every single excavation project you have been involved in. You have a keen intuition of where to look and you have never come up empty-handed. You have discovered the most famous recent finds, including the artifacts here tonight. You are my mentor and my idol, sir. I would love it, one day, to be able to go with you on a location on which you are working, even if it is to watch your ability at work. I would be honored to one day aid you, Sir Aston. I am Bree Sabry, and I cannot even say enough about how delighted I am to finally meet you. I am working on my doctorate at the moment and would love to learn from you in any way possible."

Sir Aston was delighted and flabbergasted at the woman before him. Never had he met someone so gratified to meet him before for his work, nor by one so shockingly beautiful. She looked at him with admiration for his achievements and not for his wealth. He made a hasty decision and proceeded to place Bree's arm in his and then turned and stated to Derrick, "I am stealing your very appealing date for a minute if you do not mind. We need to talk privately."

Irritated, Derrick nodded curtly. This man gave off a type of persona that said "do not trifle with me." He did not have a clue who this man was until Bree had slobbered all over him with her introduction. Of course, Bree would be into this guy. He was the one that brought this show to the museum and was in the same line of work that Bree loved. Now he had the nerve to steal her from him.

Bree seemed thrilled to be in this man's company, and for the first time in his life, Derrick felt jealous and rage wash over him. Usually, women fawned over him, and it was he who stole other men's dates, but with the tables turned, he did not like it one bit. Even though Sir Aston's name sounded like he was an old retiree, he could have not been more opposite. Sir Aston was tall and well-built with sandy-blond shoulder-length hair that he left loose and waved over the shoulders of his tuxedo. His bow tie was hanging loose on his shirt and buttons opened, showing off a bit of his chest hair. He had a good tan with leathery skin that made him appear like a hardened Indiana Jones-type character. He had a chiseled handsome face with a strong cleft chin. Derrick guessed that he could not be a day over forty. As Derrick watched them walk away, he said, "Just remember who she came with, Sir Aston." Bree looked back, looking a little embarrassed, but Sir Aston ignored him completely and led Bree off through the very crowded main hall.

Bree was over the moon. Never in her wildest dreams had she thought she would ever meet Sir Aston himself. He was a very private man that kept to himself, like a lone wolf. He never attended the showings of his finds. He was always involved with some kind of adventure, looking for ancient artifacts all over the world, and just had his personal aide travel to the shows, but here she was, with her arm laced through his walking through the crowd to a more secluded spot so they could talk more privately. People tried to stop and converse with them as they exited the main hall, but Sir Aston just waved them aside and kept leading Bree with him out of the hall. Sir Aston veered over to the bar and ordered a couple of drinks. After he was handed the drinks, they went ahead over to a room that had two menacing-looking security guards blocking the door. As they approached, the guards just nodded and let them pass without a word. They entered an office with an old antique desk in the center with an array of artifacts, bones, rocks, and books piled strewn everywhere. Pieces were in glass cases or just lying about or discarded on a shelf.

Sir Aston handed Bree her drink, and she took it with a thank-you. She noticed he had ordered a gin and tonic and was impressed with his observation. He himself ordered a beer and just had it in the bottle like a normal, regular guy. Sir Aston gestured for her to sit at the chair by the desk, and he himself leaned on the desk in front of her instead of sitting behind it like he was the boss. This gesture made Bree relax. She realized he wanted her to be comfortable with his presence. She was thankful for that as her anxiety level was on high alert being as she was in the presence of Derrick. She could not relax around that man, but she found that she instantly relaxed with Sir Aston.

Sir Aston broke the silence first. "I hear that you think you can translate the obelisk that I have brought to the show tonight—the very obelisk that no one has been able to decipher as of yet."

Bree choked on her drink and sputtered a little as it went down her windpipe the wrong way. "You can blame my date for that. He has bolstered lies about me to everyone he has talked with tonight—against my wishes, I may add. I am but a mere employee here at the museum. I work for the Artifacts Alive foundation. I earned my degree in archaeology at the University of Cambridge. I am working on my thesis right now in hopes of entering Harvard in Massachusetts for my doctorate in anthropology. Hence my two-year sabbatical here at the museum."

Sir Aston raised his eyebrows as he listened to Bree explain why he had heard so much about her in the last hour, and then he laughed. "Your date seems to have caused some embarrassment for you then."

Bree nodded and then sighed. "He is Victor Radcliffe's son. Victor Radcliffe is the founder and CEO of Artifacts Alive here at the museum. Derrick Radcliffe is a spoiled socialite that lives off of his family's wealth and nothing more. I tried to get access to the show but to no avail. The only way to get in tonight was to finally accept a date with Derrick, who has been pestering me to go out with him for two years. I broke down and agreed to a date with him in order to be able to see these special artifacts, since they may never be able to view again. I know it sounds horrendous on my part as a person, but I was desperate to be able to see these particular specimens before they go underground, and well, the amount it cost per head to enter this show was way above my pay grade. Unfortunate, I went against my better judgment, and well, here I am." Bree was blushing a little as she realized she was babbling.

Sir Aston stared at the exceptionally beautiful woman sitting in front of him and made a hasty decision for the second time tonight, which was very unlike him. He never made hasty decisions and thought thoroughly about everything he ever decided on. He was a very precise man who thought about every angle before he ever decided. Here he was twice in one night not thinking through anything when it came to this gorgeous woman. He would have to be incredibly careful around her, as he threw all his caution to the wind where she was concerned. There was something special about this woman who seemed so very enthusiastic about the show's artifacts tonight. His gut was 99 percent right. He cleared his throat before he bent down to her level and looked her in the eyes. "What would you say to a private viewing of my artifacts when the show ends? Just you and me, after everyone leaves. I would give you the rest of the night if you would like just to view my pieces that I will never display again. I would be very interested in your educated opinion about the hieroglyphs on the obelisk. I have nothing to lose by showing you my collection before I put them away from prying eyes after the show." Bree felt extremely honored. To be able to have a private viewing of the artifacts would be a dream come true. She was suspicious though about Aston's intentions and decided to be honest with him. "I am extremely wary of this offer right now, Sir Aston—"

Sir Aston interrupted her as she began to speak. "Please stop with the sir. It is just Aston."

Bree nodded and cleared her throat. "Okay, Aston, what I was trying to say was I would absolutely love to take you up on your offer. I am, however, suspicious of your true intentions as to why you would give me the distinction of viewing your collection privately when you are only willing to share these artifacts this one time only to the public. I have already come to this event with one rake. I do not need to dispose of one just to acquire another."

Aston burst out laughing, and when he caught his breath, he looked at Bree with appreciation. "I have to say, you are extremely refreshing to all the other women that I have met in my past. No one has ever been so upfront and honest with me. My wealth has something to do with this, obviously, but here you are throwing me your true thoughts right at the get-go. Yes, I do find you the most attractive and beautiful woman that I have ever met. Yes, I find you very sensual. You have the most amazing long legs on a woman that I have ever seen. You have an exotic look with the most beautiful alluring blue eyes combined with your lustrous black hair. Your look is unique.

"Everyone in the room tonight had their eyes on you. Everyone is wondering who you are and where you come from. I must admit I was one of those people as well. Your beauty is not what I am after, however. What interests me about you at this very moment is to see if you truly can translate what is on my obelisk. I will not lie and tell you I would not love to take you to dinner sometime in the near future to get to know you better, but right now, it is my artifacts that I need you for."

Bree was now the one impressed. He was just as refreshing to her as she was to him. Bree thought for only a moment before she spoke. "I want you to swear on your prestigious name that you are not doing this to get me into your bed."

Again, Aston laughed and nodded his head as he lifted his glass toward Bree. "You have my word that I do not have a motive to get you into my bed by showing you my collection, Bree. If I try, you may have the obelisk in this collection as your own."

Bree sucked in her breath as he said he would give her the obelisk if he tried to bed her. This was serious, and she knew that he was telling her the truth. The obelisk was worth at least twenty million dollars on its own, if not more. That sealed the deal. Bree stood up and approached Aston. "You have a deal. I would love the chance to see the collection after the show ends. I can or I cannot deduce what hides within the hieroglyph's secrets, but getting the privilege to try is worth much to me. Thank you, Aston." Then they shook hands.

Aston slugged back the rest of his drink. "Well, it is about time for the show to begin. I will take you back to your date for now. I will meet you back here in this office after the show. It will be late as the show goes until midnight." Bree's heart was pounding in her chest from excitement. The late hour did not matter in the least, and she agreed to meet Aston back in the office at midnight.

When Aston dropped her off back with Derrick and wandered away to start the show, Bree could not help but look at the large clock on the wall with the countdown. There was only three minutes left on the timer. It was almost eight o'clock. Four hours until she could have her very own hands and eyes examine the collection that was on display tonight. Bree knew the time would drag. Against her own promise not to get drunk tonight, she grabbed another drink as the server passed by. It was champagne, but she did not care. She had to calm her nerves somehow. Sir Aston jumped on the temporary stage in front of the screens surrounding the dinosaur display and tapped the microphone.

The room became silent except for Derrick as he leaned in toward Bree's neck and whispered, "So I have competition. Just so you know, I always win." Again, he let his lips caress the side of her neck as he spoke. Bree stepped ever so slightly away and shivered. The shiver was not a pleasant reaction to his lips caressing her neck. It was a threat, and she did not like it one bit. Bree sighed. What was it with men and their egos. It was as if Derrick were about to take out a measuring tape and measure his cock so he could boast to her that he was the biggest in the room. It made her a little nauseous, and she exchanged her already empty glass for another full one off the tray as another server roamed by.

Bree could not take her eyes off Sir Aston as he introduced himself to everyone and had a brief speech prepared as he slipped a folded paper from his pocket. He was even more devastatingly handsome than he was in his articles and pictures. Everyone's attention turned to the stage as they all clung to every word that he spoke. Derrick took this time to place his arm around Bree's waist. She did not pull away or really even notice that he pulled her closer due to her being enraptured with Sir Aston's speech. He was explaining about how he came across the artifacts deep down in the bowels of the Egyptian sphynx. He explained how he had been allotted this privilege by the Egyptian government and how they worked together privately and quietly to find the artifacts on display tonight.

Sir Aston went on with his speech, and as he did so, Derrick's fingers began to lace into one of the sides cut out on Bree's dress. He then began stroking her skin softly. He was not even listening to the speech as he leaned in and smelled Bree's hair. His fingers lingered lower into the front of her dress and were close to the top of her hip bone. He then boldly slipped his hand even lower. Bree swallowed hard as she realized what Derrick was doing. She tried to step away, but he held on to her at her waist with his fingers digging into her flesh. She turned to Derrick and hissed quietly so no one could hear, "What do you think to gain with touching me this way in public?

It is only making me upset with you, and I am about to walk away, Derrick."

Derrick leaned in closer to her again. "I told you I am a rake, and when I want something, I take it."

Bree could smell the liquor wafting off his breath. She realized he must have pounded back drinks when she was in the company of Sir Aston. His touch was becoming aggressive, and it was hurting her hip as his fingers dug into her soft flesh. "Derrick, you're hurting me."

Derrick snickered at her. "I will do more than that when the night is through. Stay away from that Aston character if you know what's good for you. I brought you here, and it is I that will be taking you home."

Bree instantly became angry and turned fully to face Derrick. He had to let go of her hip but moved his hand so he could hold on to her arm. Bree looked down at his hand as he squeezed her arm and then looked back up at him. She said coolly but with venom, "As a matter of fact, Derrick, Sir Aston has invited me to privately view his collection after the show is over, and I have taken him up on his offer." Derrick leaned back angrily, and Bree took advantage of his stepping away from her to yank her arm back, but he was quick and snaked his arm back around her waist and stepped even closer to her. Bree stood her ground at his boldness. "I must thank you for bringing me this evening, but I am now saying good night to you. You seem to think that I am your property for the evening. I am telling you right here and now that I am not. I warned you that I will not sleep with you now or ever. So let go of me, or I will make sure everyone in this room will hear me scream bloody murder if you do not."

Derrick held her for a second more as he slowly looked her up and down trying to decide if he believed what she had threatened. Before he let her go, he said menacingly, "You're going to fuck him, aren't you?"

Bree snorted with disgust and wrenched herself away from his hot grasp. "How dare you. I am not going to lower myself with an answer. Aston wants my professional opinion on the artifacts and nothing more."

It was Derrick's turn to snort. "He wants to bed you as much as every man in this room does tonight, believe me, Bree. A heads-up, you will be leaving with me tonight." Bree just shook her head at Derrick and turned to walk away. Derrick grabbed her and quickly turned her back to him as he planted a hard, bruising kiss on her lips. When Bree pushed away, he grabbed the back of her neck and held her close to him. "Do not assess me, or you may force me to do something you may regret later." When he let her go, it was Derrick that walked away. Bree stood rooted to the spot for a moment, shaking. She noticed people had turned to watch her. She tried to casually tuck her hair that was hanging on her face back behind her ear. She even smiled at the few that were staring at her. She wanted them to think nothing untoward had just happened between herself and Derrick and that everything was peachy.

Bree did not stay in place for long, as she became terrified that Derrick would come back and try to drag her out of the museum, back into the limo with God knows what plan. She knew that she would have to fight him off a bit tonight, but this had gone much too far. Derrick was acting possessive since her meeting with Sir Aston. It was like a switch had turned on inside of Derrick. He was really showing what kind of man he truly was. She decided to go back to the office Aston had taken her to earlier and wait inside till midnight. She was not really interested in seeing the show since she was going to have a private viewing of the artifacts later. The security guards let her enter the office without question. She figured Aston had told them that they would be meeting here later, so they were prepared to have her come back.

She contemplated locking the door and then decided there was no need due to the large guards outside the door. The two security guards would not let Derrick enter anyway, and it would be awkward explaining to Aston why she had locked the door if he tried to come in after his speech ended. She was upset and still slightly shaking. Derrick was determined to ruin her night. Men with that kind of money expected everyone to hand them whatever it was they wanted. She would not be one of those people. Derrick would be leaving without her tonight; she would see to that. In the morning, she would have an incredibly open talk with Derrick's father and demand that he made Derrick stay away from her from now on.

Bree passed the next couple of hours examining the books, stones, bones, and other things in the office to kill time. The items were impressive, and she wondered why they were not on display yet. Before she knew it, the door opened, and Aston entered the office. He was a little startled that she was already there. "Bree, I wondered where you had wandered off to. Your date is also looking for you. He looks quite put out. Did you two have a disagreement?"

She snorted very unlady-like. Snorting was becoming a bad habit for her tonight. "Let's just say that I regret coming with him tonight. I wish I would have been able to obtain entrance to the show without having to lower myself to accept his invitation. That man is a wolf in sheep's clothing, and tonight I was the sheep."

Aston came close to Bree with concern in his eyes and gently clutched her hand. "Did he hurt you? I can have my security escort him off the property if that would make you feel secure."

Bree slid her hand out of Aston's kind but firm hold and leaned against the desk. The champagne she had consumed was making her wobbly. "No, he didn't hurt me. He did suggest something worse when the evening ends, though. I am not that kind of woman for any man. To be honest with you, I would not mind if your security team made sure Derrick leaves without me when the show ends, if that would not be too much trouble."

Aston turned to the door of the office and opened it. He stepped out for a moment and was soon back in. "It's done. When the show ends, you will no longer have to worry about your date. He will leave without you." She visibly relaxed with gratefulness and thanked Aston for his kindness.

3

Aston slipped a flask from his inner suit pocket and poured both of them a shot of whiskey. When he handed it to Bree, he apologized that it was not gin, and she laughed. She was already tipsy from the champagne, so her inhibitions relaxed, she accepted the drink from Aston, and they clinked glasses. "To trying to decipher the obelisk." Bree drank to that. She was beginning to get excited again, not having to worry about Derrick for the rest of the evening. She was looking very forward to examining the artifacts. She was feeling relaxed around Aston, so she asked a very straightforward question. The amount of alcohol that she had consumed was also playing a factor with her sudden boldness as well. "Aston, if I may ask a question?" Aston nodded and tipped his glass toward her for her to continue. "This question has been plaguing me since I heard about these artifacts. How did you convince the Egyptian government to allow you inside the Sphynx's passage? Even Mark Lehner couldn't enter the passage, and he was the one that found the passages in the first place using their remote sensing equipment in the late 1970s. He also found and excavated the lost city and the Sphynx temple! Still, the Egyptian government denied him entrance into the passage of the Sphynx."

Aston raised his eyebrows, and then with a serious look, he only said, "If I told you, then I would have to kill you!" Bree laughed at Aston's response and waited for him to truly answer her. She soon realized, as they stared at each other, that Aston was deadly serious. Bree squirmed a little uncomfortably. For the first time that evening, being in Aston's presence, her spider senses were beginning to rise up the back of her neck. Bree sensed that there was something suddenly off about Aston and his manner since he had entered the office this time. It was the way he was staring at her, or it was the sudden dopey feeling that was quickly beginning to fog her thoughts.

As they both continued to watch each other, Aston was slowly becoming blurry; her limbs began to feel very heavy, and she tried to shake her head and blinked to clear her vision to no avail. When she did this, Aston pushed himself away from leaning on the desk and bent down in front of her. "How are you feeling, Bree?" She blinked again and found Aston leaning in front of her with an unpleasant smile on his lips. He swiftly looked like a predator, ready to pounce on her at any moment. She realized that she had jumped from the frying pan into the fire. Derrick's antics seemed like child's play to her now as she could sense something bad in Aston as he knelt in front of her. She tried to stand up to leave. Aston laughed a little as he placed his hand on her shoulders and pressed her back down into her seat. Aston stood up then and stated, "I don't think so, my dear. You are smarter than I thought you would be. Beauty and brains. Unusual combination in a woman as beautiful as you. Your assumption about me is correct, but sadly, it has come a little too late."

She glared at him. *Why are men so wrong about women? Men always underestimate a woman's abilities. It has nothing to do with their looks. What an asshat.* Her gaze landed on the empty glass still in her hand. A thought suddenly popped into her head. She looked back up at Aston. "Did you drug me?"

Aston turned away from her and went back toward the desk before he answered her. "Yes, Bree, I did." Aston pushed an intercom button that was on the desk. "You can come in now." Bree turned her head slowly toward the door. To her horror, she watched as Derrick sauntered into the office. He looked at Bree with a brilliant evil smile. She tried to stand up again, but whatever drug she had consumed in her drink was acting fast. She had no control of her limbs. Derrick walked over to Aston, and they shook hands. "You played your part perfectly, cousin. Chased her right into my arms." Aston slapped Derrick on the shoulder, and they both turned to look at Bree. Bree was terrified. She wanted to scream at them, but she could not even make her tongue move to speak now. She was utterly and completely helpless. They could take turns assaulting her and she would not even be able to scream. What were these two despicable men planning? Bree's mind was working simply fine except for a slight fog, but her motor control was totally incapacitated. She was at the men's mercy. A hundred thoughts slammed into her head at once as she tried to figure out what the two men were going to do with her and why. The two men poured a drink and conversed quietly with each other as she sat helpless in her chair watching them. They did not offer her any explanation and ignored her until there was a knock on the office door.

To Bree's utter astonishment, Victor Radcliffe entered the office and walked over to her. *Victor's involved as well.* Bree was very hurt. He had treated her like a daughter ever since she had started working for his foundation. Victor looked her over to make sure they had not injured or hurt her. When he noticed she was okay, he turned to his son and nephew, "Other than the effect of the drugs, she is okay, right?"

Both Derrick and Aston nodded. "The drug will not alter any of the ritual for tonight if that is what you are worried about, Uncle. Her mind is still intact. She just can't run away or scream," Aston stated.

Victor nodded. "Good, good! We will do the ritual within the hour. Just a couple of stragglers leaving the show, and then we can get to opening the portal. You are sure you have the translations correct? We can't afford for anything to go wrong. Tonight is the summer solstice—it is the only night we can do this. If it does not work, we will have to wait another year. This is not an option, gentlemen."

Bree listened to the men talking, and she was extremely confused. *Ritual? Portal? Was she now in the company of Satanists and they were about to have a Satanic, demonic seance? She wasn't a virgin, so why was she being involved in this? Did they not need a virgin to sacrifice or something for these kinds of things?* She tried to clear her head and concentrated with everything she had to get her body to obey her. All she was able to produce was a violent jerk of her entire body, and *God, did that hurt.* The glass that she was holding fell and shattered on the floor of the office. The three men looked over at her. Aston walked over to her and knelt in front of her once more. "Bree, my beauty, do not try and move. The drug that is in your system will last for hours with its paralysis effects. If you fight it, you will only cause yourself extreme pain. Don't fight it. Without you, we would not be here in the first place. You are the final piece to the puzzle." Aston then traced his finger slowly down Bree's arm, and Derrick glared at his cousin but remained silent.

If Bree could spit in someone's face, now would be the perfect time, but unfortunately, she was unable. All she could do was glare at Aston. Aston sighed. "If we could have done this any other way, we would have. I guess we do owe you an explanation for what we are about to do with you tonight." Bree's eyes showed terror, and they began to tear. She could not blink very well, so her eyes were watering. Aston took her watering eyes as crying, which made her cringe internally. "No, no, we are not going to harm you. We are not here to hurt you or take advantage of you."

Derrick interrupted Aston as he was talking to Bree, "Speak for yourself, cousin. I have laid claim to her, remember that. She is mine to do with when we are finished, which my father promised me. I have waited two years. My patience is wearing thin."

Aston turned and growled at Derrick as he spun on his heels to reach for him, but Victor intervened. "Boys, calm down. No one is to touch Bree. She is here to get us in. She is not to be man managed or devoured by the likes of you two," Victor ground out in frustration. Aston turned back to Bree and pulled his hand through his long sandy hair in frustration. Derrick just snickered. "Like I was saying, Bree, we are not going to hurt you. You will open the portal for us so we can get to the other side. You see, we have deciphered the obelisk. I marketed that it was indecipherable. Victor knew this would lure you in. We know the meaning of the hieroglyphs."

Aston was getting enthusiastic as he began explaining why they needed her for their plans tonight. "The obelisk is not Egyptian hieroglyphs, Bree. This obelisk is of the Sumerians. The writing on the obelisk is cuneiform writings from the age of Mesopotamia, approximately 4400 BC. The obelisk refers to the *Anunnaki* gods that came to earth from the planet *Nibiru*. They came to earth because their planet was dying. Their atmosphere had become unstable, making it difficult for them to survive. The Anunnaki came to earth when they realized the abundance of gold they could harvest here. They needed massive amounts of gold to reverse their planet's deteriorating atmosphere. They had already depleted their planet of gold. They needed to build massive gold domes to cover their cities to withstand the cosmic rays that penetrated their planet. As Nibiru came close to earth on its three-thousand-year rotation around the sun, they boarded their ships and came to earth.

"Their technology was far more advanced than humans are even capable of to this today. The Sumerian text state that the Anunnaki came to earth around four hundred forty-five thousand years ago. They were the first extraterrestrial inhabitants to colonize earth. When they arrived on earth, there were no humans yet. Earth was uninhabited by any truly intelligent bipedal species. They built a city when they arrived. They called the new city *Edin* within a city-state they set up called *Eridu*. The Anunnaki had brought along with them an alien species they had captured before their arrival on earth to use as slaves to mine gold. The Anunnaki called this slave race *Igigi*. The Igigi rebelled after years of hard labor and revolted against their captors. They lost the battle and, in the process, were killed off entirely."

Bree listened to Aston. She was already aware of these stories depicting the Anunnaki and the Sumerians. In spite of her demise at the moment, she was intrigued. She was wondering where Aston's story would begin to explain why they thought they needed to drug and abduct her and how she was important to a story that had these ancient beings. Aston continued, "The Anunnaki needed a new slave to do the challenging work for them. They needed slaves that were not as hospitable as the Igigi. They needed a docile, agreeable, strong, and healthy slave. With highly advanced technology and knowledge, they began to tinker with creating another species. In the beginning experiments, they created the *Nephilim*. The Nephilim were giants and were extraordinarily strong, but they were violent and devoid of the kind of intelligence that they needed in a slave to be able to command them and for them to understand and willingly work for them.

"The Anunnaki were unable to control their new creations. They decided the Nephilim had to go, but that is another story I will not get into at this time. The Anunnaki played and manipulated with creation again, and they finally created humans by fusing *Homo erectus* DNA with their own, thus creating the *Adama* prototype. Our ancestors were submissive and diligent workers. The Anunnaki developed kinship with their new human slave creation. They enjoyed what they had created. The Anunnaki males also developed a lust for human females and found them to be incredibly attractive. They took human females on as their concubines.

"This, of course, produced children from these unions. Unfortunately, after the great flood caused by Nibiru coming back around near earth's orbit, the Anunnaki decided to abandon earth and return to Nibiru. They finally had enough gold to save their planet anyway, and with all the battles between their two factions, they decided to leave. Before they left, the Anunnaki's chief scientist, *Enki*, and his order, gave their favored humans the knowledge to survive without them. *Enki* only gave this knowledge to, of course, the ones that were half Anunnaki. He taught the human hybrids the knowledge on how to create a Monache system as well as a sophisticated system of what we would call *propaganda* today in order to manipulate and control what his hybrid humans created.

"These hybrid humans had to keep all these teachings a secret in order to obtain structure and organized ruling for only them. Enki and his order taught them leadership without protest from the regular humans. These select few supplied the knowledge on how to create new species and manipulate and control genetics and DNA. They were not to divulge this information to anyone. They passed their knowledge down to their own bloodline. They obtained the technology and the resources to create their own slave races to work for them so they could enjoy life and reap the benefits without having to do the arduous work in life after the Anunnaki left earth."

Aston was on a roll as he excitedly explained his tale to Bree. Then to her astonishment, Aston leaned in. He was so close to her face as he whispered, "This is where you come into the story." If she could have widened her eyes in shock, she would have. Aston stood and strolled around her chair. He bent back down behind her and quietly said, "The most dominant, influential, and important

Anunnaki was named '*Anu*,' and you, Bree, are a direct descendant of his bloodline." Bree could feel his hot breath on her neck. What he had just said made her shiver. *Did they really think that she was of an ancient alien bloodline?* As suddenly as he was at her back, he was in front of her again, continuing his story. "Anu was the oldest and wisest of the Anunnaki. He was their leader and king. His lineage flows in you. Anu had human concubines too. His favorite concubine he named after himself and his Anunnaki wife, *Antu*. He called her *Tuanu*. Bree, you are a direct descendant of Anu and Tuanu. My colleagues and I have been trying to find your bloodline connecting a human to the greatest Anunnaki god, Anu, for years. This quest started before my time. Through my uncle's father's father's father. This is why I, too, fell in love with archeology. It is in my blood, my family's history. My family's passion has finally led me to you. You are a descendant of true heaven and earth.

"My families' foundation, which you are privileged to work for, has been looking for this ancient DNA, first discovered by the young archaeologist Zahi Hawass. Zahi worked with Lehner on the Sphynx. He discovered an ancient Sumerian tablet that explained the genetic line of Anu. Uncle Vincent here was able to buy that same tablet. Vincent has his fingers involved in everything you can imagine. My family and our bloodline are also ancient but sadly not as direct or as ancient and royal as yours is. Because of our wealth, we are able to obtain most items or information we want or need. If we are unable to obtain things we need, well, you get the picture. We are willing to do whatever it takes to obtain the things my family wants. Right now, what we want is to open the portal, and you are our key."

If Bree could have snorted, then she would have. DNA was a fairly new process of technology only truly recognized since the early '80s. Here, Aston was trying to convince her that she was related to the Anunnaki. If she could have laughed aloud, she would have. Being a direct descendant to the Anunnaki was as impossible to detect as being a direct descendant of Christ. There was no way they could have been able to follow a bloodline that far back. These people were radicals, yet here they were saying that she was related to an ancient alien god Anu and his human concubine Tuanu. Were they going to drain her of all her blood for ritualistic sacrifice to open a fictitious portal? She was still looking at Aston, and her heart was pounding in her chest so hard that she was sure it was making her rock back and forth in her chair from the strength of its hard beating. Aston continued as he looked at Bree with a surreal crazy look in his eyes. "Do you realize how important you are? When you look in the mirror, how do you not see how perfect and special you are? Your beauty and perfect health alone should have been a sign to you that you are special." Bree wished so much that she could shake her head and laugh at these three fools. Beauty and health just meant she had good genetics, ate healthy, exercised, and took care of herself. It did not mean she was related to a mythical god.

Aston stood up. His legs were giving out from squatting for so long. Aston moved away to pour himself another drink. Victor stepped in and took over Aston's spot and continued with their bizarre story. "Bree, my dear. I adore you. You know this. Please do not think that we are going to harm you. You must understand this. We know that you would have never believed us if we told you what we know. We had to concoct this scenario for you to trust Aston enough to be alone with him. This entire exhibit is actually in order for us to have all the artifacts in one place. The obelisk, a translator, you, and the eve of the summer solstice—you are our key. The obelisk states specifically that in order for this to work, we have to conduct the ceremony during the summer solstice, and the obelisk has to be in your hands as a direct descendant of Anu. We are going to open the portal to the plane of existence that all the known creation of the gods of Egypt moved to.

"The first pharaoh of Egypt, who was known as Narmer or also as Menes, in the year 3200 BC, had the knowledge handed down from his Anunnaki descendants to create a slave race for his people. This way they did not have to do laborious tasks that they felt were beneath them. They created species that have been widely known in all the history of hieroglyphs, writings, and carvings throughout Egypt. They created these beings to work at different tasks. In time, these creations began to be known as *'representative gods'* of Egypt. The everyday Egyptian began to worship these manufactured creatures, but they created these beings as slaves, not as gods. They were so unique and unlike any other creature that the Egyptians began to worship these creations as gods. In the year 1348 BC, the pharaoh *Akhenaten* became jealous of these creations.

"Akhenaten became threatened by the hybrids when his people began taking them on as their gods and worshipping them. I am speaking, of course, of the combination of humans with the falcon, cobra, lion, jackal, cat, bull, crocodile, and crane." Bree now knew that the three men in the room were literally batshit crazy. Did they really believe that these creatures depicted in ancient Egyptian hieroglyphs were actually real creatures? If she could have laughed, she would be in hysterics right now. She could not wait to hear the rest of this weird story. If she believed Victor and got out tonight alive, she will have to author a book about her experience. So, she listened intently when Victor continued.

"Akhenaten ordered his soldiers to exterminate all the hybrids. With the hybrids gone, he would protect his rein and power as the pharaoh of Egypt. The next in line to be pharaoh was *Neferneferuaten* or commonly known as *Nefertiti*. Before Neferneferuaten came to the throne as pharaoh, she went behind Akhenaten's back. She despised the orders to kill off their creations. She was sympathetic toward her ancestors' hybrids. Nefertiti wanted to save these special lives from annihilation as she had become attached to them. She realized that the Egyptian people revered these diverse species of man and animal hybrids as gods. She came to understand that this helped the people of Egypt cope. It also balanced their religious beliefs with the ancient teachings of her ancestors, the Anunnaki. Nefertiti decided to do something about the annihilation orders.

"Nefertiti went to her personal mystics, and together in secret, they used the ancient secrets of their relatives' advanced technology. They created a portal that was able to open up another plane of existence right here on earth. They sent all of Nefertiti's beloved ancestors' creations into a new plane of existence to live without the threat of complete annihilation. Nefertiti had enabled her ancestors' creations to be safe once more. Akhenaten's soldiers seemed dumbfounded with the disappearance of all the hybrids they had been ordered to eliminate. In fear, they decided to tell Akhenaten that they had destroyed them all and burned their corpses to keep themselves from execution. Thankfully, Akhenaten believed his soldiers' lies. The only way to open the portal is through four ways. We have all four ways now, and my beautiful Bree, it is time."

4

When Victor finished his story, he rubbed his hands together in delight. He turned to Aston and Derrick. "Let's get this show started, shall we, boys." Aston put down his drink onto the desk and went over and opened the office door. The two large security guards entered the office. Bree snickered inwardly. *So, they're involved as well! Bastards!* No one said anything as the two guards came over to Bree. With one guard on each side of her, they picked her up, chair and all, and carried her out of the office. They continued into the Mignone Halls of Gems and Minerals, where they placed her down in front of the twelve-thousand-pound oblong amethyst. In front of the amethyst display was a stand with an ancient-looking rectangle box sitting upright on a small table. Victor, Aston, Derrick, and another small man that she had not seen before now entered the room. Victor came from behind Bree and leaned down from behind her to whisper in her ear, "Are you ready to make history?" Bree was becoming apprehensive. What were they expecting her to do for them, and better yet, what if what they were saying was actually true? Was she an actual descendant of *Anu*? Would she be able to open an ancient portal created by *Nefertiti*? *Oh god, now I'm sounding as crazy as they are!*

Aston approached the small table in front of the amethyst and opened the box. He delicately reached into the box and removed the obelisk. It was approximately fourteen inches in height and seven inches in diameter. Aston turned, approached Bree, and placed the ancient obelisk in her lap. He then maneuvered her hands so that she was holding on to it. He stepped to the left side of her, while Derrick stepped up and stood to the right side of her. Aston then asked the small man to come forward and stand in between the amethyst and Bree. The man opened a scroll he was holding and cleared his throat. Bree's heart started to pound in her ears as she realized that she was beginning to regain feeling in her body. It was like pins and needles all over her body at once. She tried to move her fingers and found that they twitched in response. The drug was wearing off, and she was not experiencing mental fog anymore. The man holding the scroll nervously cleared his throat once more. Aston impatiently motioned with his hands for him to start the translation that they had transposed onto the scroll.

No one notices Bree's slight twitches as she regained the use of her limbs. The man began to read from the scroll with Aston and Derrick standing beside her. They were both looking in the direction of the man as he recited the words on the scroll. Victor was off a little to their right, smiling like a gleeful evil child that stole all the Halloween candy as he, too, intently listened to the little man reading from the scroll. Bree started to feel static electricity in the air. Her hair began to lift from her scalp. Was she imagining this? Bree ignored the strange sensation of a small electrical current that was passing through her body. She concentrated on not dropping the obelisk when she felt the strong buzzing sensation in her arms and hands, showing that the drug had also begun to wear off in her upper torso as well. She assessed her ability to move her hands by adjusting her grip on the obelisk. It worked. Her movements were now her own again, if not slightly slower than normal.

The interpreter continued his speech in ancient Egyptian, but she could hear the nervous panic starting to rise in his voice. She noticed that his hair was lifting from the static electricity as well, and there seemed to be a slight glow and heat emanating from the obelisk in her lap. Bree was becoming a little frightened. She hastily decided that this was enough. She would not allow these three men to dictate what was real and what was fantasy. She had to stop this ridiculous ruse now. These men were living in a fictional world, and she would not be a part of it any longer. They had tricked her. They must be using some kind of illusions or magic to make her see things. They used her and made a fool of her in order to fulfill a diabolical ancient dream they believed in. She would not give them the satisfaction of her being a part of it for one second longer.

Thank God they didn't tie me to the chair, Bree thought as she put her small plan into action. It was not an amazing plan, but she could only try. Just when she thought the man translating the scroll was close to the end, Bree lunged out of the chair with the obelisk still in her hands. She knocked the small man backward into the giant amethyst display. When Bree lunged out of the chair, the translator had completed the translation of the scroll. There was an enormous electric burst that developed around herself, Aston, Derrick, and the translator. When the two men realized what Bree was doing as she vaulted out of her chair, they instinctively grabbed ahold of her. Bree's velocity in the forward direction made the three of them catapult into the tiny translator just as he finished reading the end of the scroll. The poor translator grabbed on to the woman that came flying at him, and he dropped the scroll. Within a millisecond, there was an ear-shattering boom combined with a blinding flash of light. They all landed with a hard blow onto the floor in a pile of entangled arms and legs. Bree was sandwiched between the men with the poor miniature translator at the bottom of the heap.

There was no pain, gashes, wounds, or scratches from flying into the amethyst where there should have been. Bree couldn't hear anything except a loud ringing in her ears. The boom and flash had been so loud and bright that it was like a flash bomb had detonated. She became temporarily blinded by the immense burst of light that had flashed just before she made full-body contact with the translator. Bree lay on the hard, cold floor with the translator squirming underneath her. She tried to get orientated to her surroundings. She could feel Aston still holding on to her left arm and was sure it was Derrick's arms wrapped around her waist. She tried to shrug them off. They were in a tangled mess. Aston's weight was suddenly removed from her. Then Derrick's was as well. This enabled her to be able to remove herself from being on top of the translator. This was no easy feat. She could not see anything but intense fractured white light in front of her vision. As she struggled to get up, she suddenly felt a cold sharp object pierce into the back of her neck. *Damn it.* She had made the men truly angry with her. They were sticking a knife to her neck to get her back in the chair so they could start the ritual over again. Bree cursed herself for such a foolish tactic by lunging at the translator. What did her attack conduct except for making her captors furious with her? What had she been thinking? *Please do not let them drug me again*, she worried.

When Bree did not move quickly enough, the sharp point pressed into her neck firmer than the first time. This made her yelp loudly. "Ouch! Okay, okay! I will get back on the chair. Just let me get my bearings please." All she could hear from her own voice was a muffled sound like she was trying to speak underwater. Whatever they had against her neck was being forced into her flesh painfully. She could feel blood starting to trickle from the point of the knife. "I thought you said you weren't going to hurt me. Well, you're hurting me!" The knife pierced deeper. She realized they were serious now, so she stood up as fast as she could without any more argument. She realized that she had made a noticeably big mistake. They were obviously willing to hurt her in order to have their ridiculous fantasy realized. When she stood up, they forced her to walk. Instead of sitting back onto the chair, one of the men forced her to kneel on the hard floor with the sharp steel still in her neck.

Bree was frightened now, so she started to babble, "I am sorry if I destroyed the amethyst. You had it coming, you must admit, taking me hostage as you did. Did you ever think that if you came to me and asked me to help you, I would help you to do this, with my consent? Jesus, all you had to do was ask!" The knife poked in deeper yet again. Now she was mad. "Get that goddamn knife off my neck." She tried to swipe the weapon away. She received a hard smack to her hand, and the knife cut in again. *Wow, that hurts*. She could now feel that the blood was soaking into the neck of her dress. "Listen, gentlemen. It is four of you against me, plus you have your stupid gorilla-sized security guards standing by. I'm quite sure you can make me do this stupid ritual with all of you against little ole me." The knife wedged deeper again, and she hissed at the pain. "Fine, I will help you willingly if you just get that knife out of my neck. I get it, I pissed you off. I promise, no more fighting. Just stop hurting me." The knife stayed where it was. So, she decided to just stop talking.

Bree's eyesight was beginning to return, although it was still blurry. She could only make out large blurry figures standing before her. She assumed that they were the security guards due to their size. *So, who's sticking the knife into my neck? It has to be Derrick to get back at me for turning him down*, She thought. Bree turned slightly, looking to her left. She could blurrily see that Aston was beside her on his knees as well. It also looked like he had something held to the back of his neck too. This confused her. She looked to her right and realized that Derrick and the translator were kneeling with something held to their necks too. *What?* she thought. *Why is Aston, Derrick, and the translator on their knees also? Is Victor taking over the ritual all for himself? Did I hit my head hard enough by the amethyst falling on my head? Am I hallucinating all this in a stupor of a comatose nightmare?* The pain that she was feeling was far too real for this to be her dreaming, though. Bree wiped her eyes and gently shook her head to clear her vision. The blasted ringing in her ears was disorientating, but it was becoming quieter by the second.

As the ringing in her ears began to ease, she could make out someone speaking in a deep, booming voice in what sounded like Egyptian, but it was slightly different somehow. The voice was authoritative, as if it came from an excessively big man. She realized that she was still somehow holding on to the obelisk. The reason she understood this was someone suddenly ripped it out of her grasp. The man with the booming voice that held such an authoritative nature began to laugh. After blinking for what seemed to be a hundred times, Bree's eyesight returned. She looked up after clearing her eyes. What she saw before her dumbfounded and shocked her. *I must be dreaming.* She grasped that she must have truly knocked her noggin hard. She was definitely hallucinating now, or it was something much worse. *Oh my god! I am dead, and I have gone to hell for my sins.* She blinked a couple times more in complete and utter disbelief. *Satan looks nothing like I thought he would.* She internally rolled her eyes at herself for her absurd thoughts. She took a better look at her surroundings, and then she had a creeping dreadful thought occur to her about what had actually occurred.

She could not believe what she was letting her mind comprehend. *Those idiots had really accomplished it.* The men had opened the portal. *It worked?* Her abductors were not absolutely nuts after all. She slowly looked around and took in her startling surroundings. What she was seeing was surreal. The room was warm and slightly smoky. She could smell incense burning and the scent of the oil in the flaming lamps on all the pillars in the hall. She could scent animal odors like she was in a barn as well as sweaty bodies one would meet when in a locker room full of men that had just played a robust sport. She was kneeling on smooth, cold marble. The large pillars were of black marble, and they supported a high ceiling at least twenty feet high.

The hall they were in had an echo to it due to its size. She did not dare turn around too much so she looked slightly over at Aston and could see that it was a long spear that pointed into his neck. She dared not turn anymore. She could not see the persons that were staffing the weapons. She had a nauseating feeling she truly did not want to know who it was and what they looked like just yet though. Aston was also looking around in awe, but instead of looking concerned, he looked elated. Looking to her right, Derrick did not look so happy with the spear that was in his neck. He had a look of ire on his face. Bree could tell that he was holding his temper, but just barely. The small interpreter looked absolutely terrified, and he was trembling uncontrollably as he whimpered like a terrified child.

Before them was a step up to a dais. On the dais, there was a massive throne. Sitting on the throne was the largest beast, which was still so unbelievable Bree had to stare in order for her brain to fully grasp what she was seeing. Her brain wanted to push the truth aside; she almost wanted to laugh in hysterics, but she knew that it was due to being utterly shocked with fear. The beast on the throne had the body of a large muscular man from the chest down to the thighs. His lower legs were that of a beast with hooves. He had the arms of a man, but his shoulders, neck, and head were that of a bull. The horns on his head were sharp and deadly looking. His horns had decorations of golden rings, two on one side and three on the other. The beast had a large golden ring pierced through his snout. Its immense chest was bare except for an extravagant heavy golden necklace with a heavy emblem of the all-seeing eye hanging from it. He wore a white-and-gold Egyptian sarong whose length was above its knees. In the beast's hands, he held the obelisk, which the guards had taken from her. The object looked tiny in his huge boulder-sized hands. He was chuckling as he looked at the artifact. As if he suddenly remembered that he had guests, the beast looked up and stopped laughing. For the size of him, he moved gracefully as he stood up. Bree thought he was massive sitting on the throne. Now he stood, he was even bigger, at least nine feet tall. *Oh god.* Bree choked on her own spit in fright as he began to come forward.

His hooves clunked heavily on the marble floor, and Bree swore she felt the vibration from his weight as he walked. The poor translator was beginning to sob louder. The massive bull man had his attention and direction on Aston, but on hearing the sniveling coming from the translator, he turned his attention and his direction toward him. This had the translator panicking and shrinking to make himself smaller. The beast stopped before the translator. He shifted the obelisk to one hand, and to Bree's horror, the beast swung his immense arm and smashed the back of his hand into the side of the translator's head. The translator's body flew off the floor, into the air, and slammed into one of the large marble pillars. Bree could hear his back snap as his body shattered into it. The translator flopped in a grotesque manner to the floor, dead. She held in a scream; it was so close it boiled on her tongue, but she bit it so hard she could taste blood holding the scream back. She did not want to end up like the translator had. She looked away from the broken body and swallowed hard. She was feeling the panic well up inside her chest, and her eyes began to water. She closed her eyes and willed it away.

Derrick growled beside her under his breath but did not move. She could see that he was shaking slightly. She did not know if it was from anger, disgust, or fear. Suddenly Aston spoke up, speaking Egyptian, "Oh, Great Pharaoh, may I be permitted to speak in your divine presence?" The beast turned his attention back to Aston, eyeing him curiously. Then with startling speed for the size of the beast, he moved in front of Aston in moments. The beast lowered his head down to Aston's height then snorted hot hair out of his snout in Aston's face. Aston's hair blew back by the force of the breath, but Aston never moved and then bowed, still kneeling to the beast. The beast stepped back, snorted loudly out of his snout, then laughed loudly.

Then the beast's voice boomed throughout the hall. "This little ape calls me Pharaoh." The beast laughed again with a chorus of low-pitched laughter joining him from the guards behind them. "I may have my people call me Pharaoh from now on instead of King Senepol. It has a quality to it, does it not?" The beast laughed again as he reached forward and smacked his large fist atop Aston's shoulder. The tap was not that hard, but Aston struggled to stay up and not crumble to the floor from the strength of it. "Little ape-man, you show courage even though you are tiny, unlike that sniveling shell of an ape over there." The beast referred to the poor dead translator. "Stand up. You hold my attention for now, little ape, only because I am bored. You have interested me with your sudden uninvited arrival into my palace, and you have brought me a most unexpected gift with you."

Aston stood and bowed again; he was about to speak, but Derrick stood up. "We, Your Grace! We have brought this wondrous gift to you… Your Majesty."

The bull king turned his large head in the direction of Derrick and snorted. "*Silence!*" The room shook with the power of King Senepol's tone. "Little ape, you speak out of turn and with condemnation in your voice." The king slowly stalked to Derrick and lowered his head once more to the height of Derrick. "Interrupt me again and I will have your head as the centerpiece on my banquet table tonight." Derrick physically blanched but kept his mouth shut and bowed slightly with a nod. King Senepol growled at Derrick. "Lower, little ape." Derrick swallowed hard and turned a deep shade of red but did the bull king's bidding as he bowed lower. He held the bow, then the king smacked the side of Derrick's arm hard enough to send him off his feet, flying to the floor. The king erupted into laughter again as he muttered, "Stay, ape." Derrick glared and was red with embarrassment and suppressed anger, but he stayed where he was on the floor. The king returned his interest back to Aston and motioned with his hand for Aston to follow as he walked back up to his throne and sat down. Aston knelt on one knee in front of the bull king as he huffed his appreciation at the respect that Aston was showing him. Bree was disgusted. This beast had just killed the interpreter without a second thought, and here Aston was slobbering all over him as if he worshipped the very ground he walked on. It sickened her. She kept silent. Everyone seemed to have forgotten about her after the spear came away from her neck.

"Your Eminence, my entourage and I have brought the obelisk you hold as a gift. This gift is to show Your Highness that we come in peace. The obelisk holds a power that I would like to discuss with you. This power is of a secret that only Nefertiti and her priests knew about and kept locked away for thousands of years, until now."

King Senepol stood up fast, still holding the obelisk. He was angry at something Aston had said. "It is Goddess Neferneferuaten to you, ape." And then it was Aston's turn. The king laid Derrick out on the floor with a severe backhand. The king was breathing heavily and snorting. "Blasphemer. Never say the goddess's name without extreme reverence and only while in her temple, giving a blood sacrifice." The king was stalking toward Aston. Aston had fallen back near Bree, and he kept backing away on his haunches as the king was closing in on him with murder in his eyes. Suddenly Aston had an idea, and he looked quickly toward Bree, who was trying to stay ignored. *What is he up to?* Bree was terrified. Why was he crawling back toward her? Bree tried to scramble away, but her knees were so numb from kneeling for so long she was too slow.

Aston grabbed onto Bree's arm. "Great King, I have another gift for you." The king slowed slightly. Aston stood up behind Bree and pulled her up with him. "I have with me the goddess Neferneferuaten in the flesh, just for you, oh powerful King. She has asked us to bring her in secret to see if you truly still worshipped her properly." The king slowed even more. Aston took advantage of this and grabbed Bree and pulled her messed-up hair back so the king could see her face. King Senepol stopped completely, and his black eyes grew large with surprise. When he looked at Bree for a moment, his surprised look turned to awe. All one could hear in the room at that moment was the crackling of the fire in the burning lanterns. The king's guards came forward and surrounded Aston and Bree. For the first time since they arrived, Bree could see the guards. They, too, were enormous man-bull hybrids. They looked vicious with their bulging muscles, pointed horns, and long spears steered in their direction. When the guards had a good look at Bree, they dropped their spears to the floor. They all dropped to their knees and bowed with their bodies close to the floor and their arms stretched out in front of them. King Senepol slowly and with reverence moved closer to Bree and looked at her closely. Aston was using her as a shield with Bree facing the king. All she could do was stare back at King Senepol and prayed that she was not next on the kill list. Aston realized that the king was believing his lie for the moment and felt slightly safer for the time being. The king spoke directly to Bree, "My queen, my goddess, you have finally returned to us." Then the immense king bowed low.

5

Derrick took this opportunity to stand up and move to stand beside Bree and Aston. He was still red with anger and embarrassment, but he understood that they had an opportunity to make this work to their advantage and save their lives. Bree, however, was terrified. She was not Nefertiti in the flesh, reborn. She knew the king would soon discover this terrible lie as well as his guards, but at the moment she had no idea what to do about it. *Do I just go along with this ruse?* Bree already knew the answer to this inner question before she was even fully aware she asked herself the question. *Of course I will go along with this. What other choice do I have?* This would give them enough time to discover a way out of this terrifying situation and get back to their reality. She was in survival mode. She wondered why it was that these beings believed Aston's lie in the first place. Yes, she was of Egyptian descent, and she was a woman, but that alone could not be the only reasons.

Something these beasts saw in her must have been the reason, but she could not figure out what it was. The bull king stood from his bow and looked at her with reverence and a bit of dread before he spoke with great gentleness, "Goddess, I apologize for my treatment of you and of your entourage. I beg your forgiveness, oh wonderous divinity. If I had been prepared for your coming, I would not have treated you with any such malevolence. I take full responsibility for my significant actions against you. I understand if you must punish me for my actions against your small priest. Please, my goddess, let me make my behavior up to you, as I have something to show you. You must know that we have not lost our faith in you, that we knew you would return to us as promised. We have kept your temple sacred and prepared for your return for thousands of years. Please come. See with your own divine eyes that we have kept our allegiance active and our belief in your return alive and well." Bree could not believe this massive violent beast spoke with such reverence, gentleness, and devotion toward her of sudden. The beast's entire demeanor had changed to one of adoration of her. This would only lead to their deaths. But for now, all she could do was slightly nod to the king and try not to show her panic at the grand falsehood that they were trying to pull over on these creatures. If their ruse was discovered, then they would surely pay the price with their lives.

Bree cleared her throat and mentally willed her body to stop shaking. She had to say something to break the severe tension that was building in the beast before her. So, she decided to wing it and prayed that it worked. "I am willing to overlook the violent and unnecessary death of my priest. That death is on my hands, King, not on yours." Bree could see the huge bull king relax with his posturing. Aston and Derrick visibly relaxed as well, with the realization that she was going to go along with the story for the time being. "My arrival was purposely unannounced. I planned it this way so there could be no false preparation by the foretelling of my arrival. I needed to see for myself that my forefathers creations were still holding me in their graces, even after a millennium. My grand king, I forgive your actions due to our surprise arrival. I saw true allegiance to me when my consort said my common Egyptian name to you. Your response to his comradery of my person proved to me your devotion. Let us move forward from this. You may now show me how you have kept your faith in me alive." Bree tried to stand tall, straight, and regal. How was she supposed to know how to act or behave? King Senepol accepted what she had said and after bowing low, now eagerly pointing for her to follow him.

Bree swallowed hard. She had to prove to these beasts that she respected and loved them as a goddess would toward her devoted followers, so she walked right up beside the king and looked him in the eye. His immense size terrified her. He made her feel like a small child as she walked beside him. The king nodded silently and led her down a wide marble hallway that were lit by flaming pillar lanterns. It was dim, smoky, and felt claustrophobic even though the hallway was tall and wide. Aston and Derrick followed behind staying silent, but she could feel their intense excitement and interest rolling off them as they were now safe. The king's guards were flanking the men in two lines of four, marching silently as they all turned down yet another large corridor. As they continued, each hall became brighter. They passed large doorways leading to other rooms and such, but they were all closed tight with solid thick wooden doors that were beautifully carved with intricate designs on them all. She would have loved to examine the carvings but figured if everything worked out, they would be able to see them later. They approached the end of the hall in front of two extremely tall wide doors. This foyer was well lit as two massive openings in the wall were letting natural light shine in. Two guards posted at the doors opened them without question as the group approached.

The doors opened up to a beautiful aired hall. The cool breeze that welcomed her as she entered was a wonderful relief after the dark smoky throne room. Bree gasped in surprise, for the room was lit with natural sunlight from the large windows lining both sides of the large room. It was not the bright room that had Bree gasping. Bree had never seen such large living quarters. Giant golden statues littered the room; surrounding the statues were lounging benches and tables. Seated all around the golden statues lounging with fruits, vegetables, pastries, and sweets loading the center tables were cow hybrids in flowing white gowns. Wandering around the room, serving, and doting on the cow hybrids were female jackal hybrid servants. They had the same body as a human, but these beings have the head of a jackal and lower legs of a dog. They wore shorter gowns, which were cream in color, not like the bright crisp white that the cows wore. The bull king interrupted Bree's intense studying of the servant as he walked proudly before her, stopped, and swept his arm across the room. "These are my wives. This part of the palace is their day quarters."

When the group entered, the hall became silent. All activity ceased, and everyone just stared in startled awe. The female cow hybrids gasped and huddled together or moved closer to one another as they gaped at the strange creatures standing before them.

In a booming voice, the king announced, "Women, bow and show respect. Humbly welcome Goddess Neferneferuaten into our midst, our hearts, and our home. She has finally returned to us as promised." Suddenly the room was aflutter with screams, cries, gasps, whispers, dishes smashing, and food tossed and thrown to the floor. For their size, again, Bree became stunned at how fast they could move. The wives all lined up in front of the group and bowed low to the ground. The servants threw themselves to the floor and did not look back up. Bree could see that the servants were all shaking with fear, but the wives were not as they were peeking curiously up at Bree, Aston, and Derrick. This angered Bree. She sensed the servants received abuse. She could see ribs sticking out from under the skin of all the servants closest to her, where the wives seemed well nourished, corpulent, and full of life.

Aston and Derrick gasped behind Bree, though they were gasping at the pure gold statues and dollar signs were dancing in their eyes. Aston and Derrick slightly turned to one another and quickly nodded at each other with half grins on their faces. If Bree would have seen this interaction, it would have made her extremely suspicious of the two men's intentions of why they really wanted to open the portal in the first place. King Senepol spoke again and called out a name, "Thema, come." The center wife stood up and approached her husband. Thema, even being a cow-human hybrid, was beautiful in a beastly sort of way. She had a cow's face, but her muzzle was shorter than a full cow's.

She had a long caramel-colored mane that was swept back behind her horns and held in place with a beautiful jeweled comb. Her eyes were human eyes, but larger. They were soft, golden brown, and her eyelashes were incredibly long and dark. She had horns, but they were much smaller than the king's. They faced forward and upward, not off to the side. Her cow ears were smaller as well and tucked downward under her horns toward her shoulders. Her neck was not as thick as the bull king's, and her figure seemed more delicate. She had the coloring of a Jersey cow with caramel spots that were a little darker on her hide than the rest of her Jersey coloring. She was very feminine-shaped in physic. She even had humanlike breasts under her gown instead of an utter. She had human-shaped arms like the king's. This is when Bree noticed that they only had three fingers and a thumb. Through the gown, she had normal legs to the knee, but then they bent backward like a cow's did after the knees and then went into hooves instead of feet. Thema also had a tail like the rest of them. It was swishing back and forth as it poked out through a small slit in the back of her gown. She dripped in jewels on her fingers and her neck. She had decorations on her horns and jeweled straps on her upper arms.

The king introduced the group to the female beast standing before them. "This is my first wife, Thema. She is the head of the household above all my other wives." Thema bowed low to Bree. Bree almost bowed back as Thema looked and acted regal, but she caught herself just in time. "Thema is in charge of your temple, Goddess. You will see the glory that she had kept it in in your honor." The bull king turned to his first wife and gave her a direct command. "Lead us to the temple, woman." Bree cringed at the title and the way he spoke to Thema. *I wouldn't be married much longer if my husband spoke to me that way in the presence of others.* But Thema seemed unfazed. She actually seemed the opposite. She was incredibly pleased that her king demanded her to do this task for him. Bree inwardly shrugged it off as it was not her business how this king beast spoke to his wives. Thema bowed low and without a word headed toward the back of the large hall to another set of doors. The group followed quietly behind the first wife of the bull king. Following close on their heels were the king and his entourage of guards. They found themselves led through more massive hallways. This palace was colossal.

The group went down yet another hallway, but this one ended with a massive white door at the end that looked like the entire door was ivory. How was this possible? Were they able to somehow melt the ivory in order to meld it together into two massive slabs? The door also had beautiful carvings on it, and this time Bree stopped just before it so she could at least see the intricate art and symbols that were on this door. She was in awe. In front of the door stood six guards, and when the group stopped before them, the bull queen whispered something in one of the nearest guard's ears. The guards turned and went to the edge of the door with two large cranks on each side. It took three guards on either side to turn the cranks in order to open the extremely heavy temple doors.

With a loud groan, the doors began to open. What lay behind the doors was astounding and beautiful. Bree gasped in unison with Derrick and Aston. "All that glitters is gold," Bree heard the hushed whisper from Derrick to Aston. She inwardly cringed. She was beginning to have a truly clear idea as to why the men wanted to have the portal opened. It had nothing to do with discovery, exploration, or education. These two men were nothing more than thieves. The poor little translator had died a horrible death due to Derrick and Aston's greed. They all had almost died because of their greed. Angry, hot bile rose in her throat with this realization of the men standing behind her, and she began to choke with rage. Thema turned to Bree with concern when Bree began choking. "Does your temple not please you, my goddess?" The disappointment in Thema's voice had her choking again.

When Bree was able to clear her throat and get her rage under control, she looked at Thema and played the part of a goddess once more. "It is the opposite, Thema. I am utterly amazed and incredibly pleased with what I have just begun to see of my temple. You honor me more than I deserve with the glory and beauty before me for how long I have been absent from your presence."

Thema's worried face broke into a large smile while her shoulders relaxed. Thema bowed low in respect. "Please follow me and I will show you all." When they entered the temple through the doors, she was able to touch them. They were two large marble slabs, but the carving inlaid within the marble was that of ivory. Bree figured that a vast amount of beautiful animals had to die for this one set of doors. She shook that thought out of her head, continuing to move farther into the temple. *What a remarkable sight,* she thought. It took her breath away. The pillars alone would involve days to inspect for the hieroglyphs and the carvings. The golden statues laden with gems and precious stones would feed a small country for an entire decade.

The aroma of lotus and jasmine was wafting through the entire temple as it was in the incense that was burning in the center of the temple surrounding the largest and most impressive statue. Blue lotuses were floating in the pool around the center statue as well. The center pool and statue were supported on a flat slab of white marble with steps leading up to the center and around the pool. There were large open windows along the outer walls of the temple with thin white cotton curtains billowing in the warm breeze as it entered through the windows. Bree looked closely at the center statue and became shocked to see that it resembled herself in a very eerie way. The hair was different, and the clothing sculpted on her was ancient Egyptian in styling, but the likeness of the face was uncanny. Derrick and Aston were delighted in the similarity between Bree and the statue. This was an amazing plus to their lie.

Bree was so absorbed at the beauty of the temple and the replica of herself in the statue she almost did not notice the small obelisk placed at the feet of the statue. *What the hell...* It was identical to the obelisk that they used to open the portal. The one that the king still held in his meaty hands. Beside the single obelisk, there were three more empty inlays that looked like they were meant for other obelisks. This was at once confirmed as King Senepol walked past her and gently placed the obelisk beside the one that was already there. Derrick and Aston walked up beside Bree and stood with their mouths agape as they stared at the two obelisks now sitting beside each other. Suddenly there was a low humming sound as the two obelisks began to vibrate slightly; the hieroglyphs glowed for a moment, and then a shot of lightning burst out from both obelisks and entered the bull king. Everyone stood in shock. What had just happened?

It all stopped as suddenly as it started. The king snorted deeply, making the three of them look toward him again. It looked as if he was growing and expanding in size. He shook his body like a shiver had run down his spine, and he straightened up tall. The electrical charge crackled around him as he spoke, "Three more. My task in obtaining the other three obelisks is now clear. I can see my rein over the lands. My future, bright. I will retrieve the last three. I will be the rightful leader of this land." The group was not sure if the king was talking to them or to himself. Suddenly the king turned and stalked down the steps before Bree. It took all her willpower for her not to back away as the king was still crackling with electricity. He was now an even more formable giant with the slight growth from the obelisks' magic, but somehow, she managed. She swallowed hard but then felt relieved when the king bowed down and placed himself on one knee. "You have chosen me to be the holder of your personal obelisk. With my stone combined with yours, I have become stronger. I will not fail you in gathering the last three stones, Goddess. Not one life will stop me. With you behind me, I will be unstoppable. If anyone gets in my way, I will kill them in your honor. Thank you for giving me this privileged tribute, my goddess. You have shown me that you have chosen that I be the keeper of the stones, to hold the power over all in this land. You have chosen wisely. I will not fail you, Neferneferuaten."

Bree suddenly wanted to choke again. *What others, living in this land, will fall because of our sudden selfish arrival with one of the missing obelisks? What damage have we caused with our meddling in something we don't understand?*

6

After the display of the temple to them, Bree thanked Thema and the king and said how the temple was up to her standards. Thema was beyond joy. The king nodded in her direction with appreciation, and Thema could not wait to tell all the other wives how well she did. Bree's exhaustion crept up from all the activity of the last twenty-four hours. She was about to collapse from all the extreme violence and activity since she stepped out her door on her date with Derrick. Had it been twenty-four hours since it all started, or had even more time passed? All she knew was she had to find a bed, or they would all see her collapse. Well, if she exuded the aura of a goddess, then she would have to make demands herself, or they would get very suspicious of her sooner than planned. So, she turned to the king as they left the temple. "Now that I have presented you with my gift, I insist on rest. My travels between your realm and mine have been more demanding on my form than expected. Show me where I may lay my head. I also need sustenance for myself and my entourage at once." She inwardly cringed at her bad acting. She had never been good at drama in school. Would they see right through her lie? *Oh god, was I over the top with my demands?*

It must have been believable enough and was not an unexpected demand. It was as if it had been an expected normalcy. It was as if she had kissed their asses all of the sudden, as never had she seen such large beasts hasten in such a manner to please her. Herself, Derrick, and Aston were at once ushered into a beautiful wing of the palace. It was large and open with no wall on the left of the room. Only large white cotton curtains with marble pillars supporting the ceiling were separating the large opening in the wall. Beyond that was a majestic view before them of small pyramids, large buildings, and sand as far as the eye could see covering the land. An eating area was in the center of the room backed by a full pool for bathing. There was a massive bed off to the right of the room with a canopy of more white cotton floating above the bed. Bree briefly worried about the one bed, but right now all she wanted to do was eat and then collapse. At once behind them came a line of jackal servants with tray upon tray of fruits, meats, breads, cheeses, wines, honey, and milk. It was enough food to feed at least twenty people. Again, she found herself looking at the skinny servants and felt herself pause. This would change if she had anything to do with it. These poor beings were starving and forced to serve all this amazing food to a false goddess. *I am so going to address this issue with the king.*

To Bree's utter disgust, Derrick and Aston did not seem to mind or notice the ribs sticking out from under the servants' clothing. If they did, they did not seem to care. They were sitting down, scooping food, and pouring wine into their mouths before it even hit the table. Suddenly she lost her appetite and turned to Thema as she was ushering in the servants, scolding them for being too slow for her liking. "This is unacceptable."

Thema turned toward Bree, looking very chastised. "This is our best guest wing in the palace, my goddess. Please tell me what is not to your liking, and it will adjust at once."

Bree walked toward the large bed and swung her arms out toward it. "What is the meaning of only one bed?"

Thema blushed at Bree's statement. "Forgive me, my goddess. I assumed that your men were brought with you to serve you in your days as well as your nights." Bree almost choked again. This was becoming a bad habit of hers. Derrick and Aston both looked up from stuffing their mouths, smiling at what they had heard but kept silent with the conceited smiles laced across their faces. She could not help but blush with anger and shame, which made Thema look a little closer at her.

A goddess would never show embarrassment about sexual gratifications or anything personal for that matter. A goddess did whatever a goddess wanted. She caught herself quickly so then turned and berated Thema. "Do you think these two miniscule males would be capable of gratifying any of my pleasures? How dare you assume this of these pathetic creatures. I choose your king to be the keeper of the stones. I knew he would be more than capable of my protection. As for personal companionship…" Thema, Bree noticed, after this statement, began to gnaw at her lower lip. "Do not fret, my Thema, your king is not in my sights to please my physical gratifications."

It was Thema's turn to blush. How a cowhide was able to show color in embarrassment was amazing to watch, but it happened. "My divine lady, I must apologize for my petty jealousy. You are a goddess. Any male would fall at your feet to give themselves willingly with just your beauty. They will die for you eagerly. I express my deepest gratitude to you for not choosing my king as one of them. I find in my selfishness it is a strain and has become tiresome to share my king with all his other wives. I do love my husband, and his wandering eye with a goddess would surely have me become unwanted and unneeded." Suddenly Thema realized what she was saying to a goddess about her petty jealousy, and it was her time to choke. "Oh, Goddess, I did not mean…"

Bree walked toward Thema with true compassion. "Do not apologize, Thema. I could never be mad at the being that has kept such vigil for me and my temple. Remember I may be a goddess, but I am also a woman. I do understand jealousy, and I have raged with it myself. You do not need to feel this from me. I promise you as a woman and your deity. My physical desires will not fall on your king, but enough of this talk. Leave us, I need my rest." Thema had tears in her eyes as she bowed low to Bree; she nodded then quickly exited the room.

When the doors finally closed, Bree sighed in relief. Her exhaustion was catching up to her fast. She looked toward the bed with the desire to just crawl onto it and crash. This she would not be able to do with Aston and Derrick in the room. While she stood and eyed the bed with longing, she heard laughing coming from the men that were still stuffing their faces. She turned with disgust on her face toward the men. Aston stood up from the table full of food. As he did so, he brushed crumbs from his clothing and flicked his hair back from his face. "Well done, Bree. I must say you are more impressive than I had ever anticipated." Bree wanted to spit in his handsome face. "The fact that you look exactly like Nefertiti is utterly amazing. We could never have dreamed to be so lucky." As he was talking, he was coming closer to her, who stood her ground as she glared at him. "Had I known about this coincidence, I most definitely would have used that to our advantage immediately."

She just looked intently at Aston. She was just too weary to even argue at this moment. Derrick chimed into the conversation behind Aston. "I wouldn't mind trying out that bed, Bree. I have never had a threesome with one woman and another man, but with all the strangeness that has gone on today, I am willing to give it a go." She could not believe her ears. What a disgusting human being. Derrick made her ashamed of herself to have even agreed to go on a date with him. All she could do at this moment though was snort in revulsion. *What a bunch of selfish pigs, the both of them.*

Bree's anger gave her a little boost of sudden energy, so she accused them of what had been plaguing her mind of late. "Why did you want to open the portal in the first place, huh?" She never expected an answer, so she gave them her assumption before they could respond. "Gold, gems, coins. You both make me sick to my entire being. You are wealthy beyond anyone's imagination, but you and your greedy family come to loot and pillage through a portal into another plane of existence all for deepening your pockets! I hold the murder of the translator onto you both as well as Victor even though he is not here. You may not have been the ones that did the deed, but you are all certainly to blame. I swear to both of you if I see you manage one gem, one statue, one piece of jewelry, or even one coin, I will confess everything to the king, even if it means I will be putting my own life in jeopardy."

This made Derrick furious; he lunged at Bree and caught her by the throat as he brought his face close to hers. "You stupid bitch! You have no idea why we came here! The riches that are here are just an added bonus. We are here for the obelisks. All of them. Did you not witness what happened to the beast when he was near the two obelisks together? We are here for that power. That domination. That control. With those artifacts together in our family's hands, we will be the *new world order*. Everyone will bend over backward for us, or they will all die." Derrick's grip suddenly shifted a little, and he caressed the side of her neck with his thumb. With that, he swooped down and kissed her hard on the mouth.

Aston pulled Derrick off her. "That will be enough, cousin. We need her now more than ever. Your rough movement is not helping matters any." Bree took the opportunity and spit on the floor at Derrick's feet. He went to lunge at her again. She could not have been more relieved when there was a sudden loud knock at the door to their suite. "Enter" was all she had to say to make Derrick break his attack and back away. She glared in his direction and then looked toward the door.

Thema entered with two guards at her back. "I apologize for my sudden interruption, Goddess. If it pleases you, I have made other arrangements for your 'company' to stay in another wing across the hall." Bree inwardly sighed with utter relief.

Derrick stepped forward. "That will not be necessary."

She turned in anger and was suddenly glad they had made her take on the role as Nefertiti. She stalked up to Derrick and smacked him forcibly across his face. *God, did that ever feel fantastic.* "How dare you speak for me as if you know what it is that I desire. Right now, there is nothing more I long for than you both locked in another wing away from my divinity." Bree turned to Thelma and the guards. "I insist a guard posted at their door so they don't get into any mischief whilst I rest. Begone from my sight." Bree pointed at Derrick. "Never speak for me again, priest, or you will not like the consequences."

Derrick was so angry he was purple from it. Thelma indicated that it was time for them to leave. Aston had a huge smile on his face, and he was quietly chuckling. As he passed Bree, he said quietly for Bree's ears only, "Again, you have impressed me." After that, he grabbed Derrick by the arm and dragged him with him as he led them both out of the room with Thema in the lead and the guards behind them. When the door closed, Bree instantly went over to the gigantic bed. With no further thoughts, collapsed on the edge of it, she curled up and fell asleep at once.

When Bree awoke, she had a terrible headache. Her entire body was sore and stiff. When she sat up, she groaned. Before she even had a chance to stretch, there was a knock on the door. She sighed. *No rest for the weary,* she thought before she called out for whoever it was to enter. Thema came in, followed behind with an entourage of servants carrying in food, clothing, and other amenities. Bree was starving but felt guilty about this when she watched the servants again and noticed how undernourished they seemed. Thema had the servants place the food on the table and the clothing on the bed. She smiled at Bree. "Good morning, Deity, I have fresh clothing for you as well as a nice meal. The servants will bathe you and care for you. When you are ready, I am to bring you around to the king's throne room, as he would like to take you around and show you our lands."

Bree nodded. "I thank you kindly, Thema. I must insist that you come along with us on the tour of your lands. I insist that I have a female presence with me at all times. Having all these silly males around can be exhausting without someone of my gender that I can trust being near me."

Thema bowed low, glowing with pride. *Goddess Neferneferuaten personally invited her to be a companion while on the tour of their lands.* She could not wait to brag this up to anyone that would listen. Thema could not wait to remove herself from the room. She did so in a rush after she cracked out more orders directed toward the servants.

When Thema left, the servants slowed their pace just a bit and their bodies relaxed slightly. They were still overly cautious and afraid of Bree, for she was a goddess. She could read from their body language. The servants all showed fear of her as well even though they were trying desperately to hold it in. Bree became saddened by this. She had to make their lives better even if it was just for a moment. "My beautiful ladies, I thank you for such divine servitude from you all. If I could take you all back to my realm, I would do so. I have been so impressed by your remarkable service."

The jackal servants all paused and stared at her for just a moment. Then they caught themselves looking her in the eye. They all dropped their gaze and focused on the floor. They were not sure of what to make of the goddess's compliments. It scared them even more, which was the exact opposite of what she was trying to do. One of the servants even whimpered a little. These poor creatures from so much abuse felt something of a hidden agenda was somehow behind her compliments. They were wary of her. They may receive a whipping if they fell for her compliments.

Sighing, Bree took on another tactic. "I simply refuse to eat alone. Come, all of you, dine with me."

The look of utter horror that crossed the servants' faces would have been comical if not for the reality of it. One of the servants dropped what she was doing and fell to the floor in a low bow with her eyes focused on the floor. "May I be released from your divine presence in order to bring your companions to eat with you, Goddess?"

She could tell that she had to be forceful. This was all they understood. She was very hungry. She could not remember the last time that she had eaten. Her stomach was now vibrating against her backbone with angry growls. "I do not want my companions to eat with me. I want female presence with me right now. I want you all in this room at this very moment to eat with me, right now. Sit with me ladies." Bree walked over to the platform full of every kind of food imaginable and waited. Not one servant moved. She sighed loudly. *I must give this one last try.* She raised her voice. "As your goddess, I command you ladies to eat with me." The servants all looked at each other but still did not move. "I am becoming angry." When she said this, the servants all moved slowly to the table and stood by it. They were shaking slightly in fear and still did not sit down. Bree smiled at them warmly. "That's better. Now, ladies, SIT. Enjoy with me. Do not fear me. This is not a test. You are my ancestors' creations. I did not go against the pharaoh of the time's orders to destroy all your ancestors and create this realm a millennia ago with my priests just to see you starve to death. I love all my ancestors' creations. This includes you ladies as well. I want you to eat with me until sated, then what is uneaten, I want you to take and give to your families and other servants that you come across."

Bree sat down and beckoned the ladies to do the same. The older servant shrugged her shoulders, and she was staring at the food. Bree could tell that this servant was so hungry that she decided, even if this was a test, she no longer cared. She sat down at the table, just too hungry to deny the invitation any longer. When she began to eat, Bree handed the older servant grapes, a hunk of bread and cheese, then began to eat as well. The older servant gladly accepted the food that Bree handed to her and bowed her head in thanks. "I'm Eman. I am the head servant in the palace. I must thank you for your divine kindness, Goddess. This has been the third day we have gone without food. Your kindness will give us a little more energy, and I cannot thank you enough."

Bree almost lost her appetite listening to the words coming from Eman. *Three days without any food.* Bree choked back tears and smiled at Eman. She then turned to the other servant woman and beckoned them to come and join them. The other servants followed Eman's lead as they, too, couldn't resist any longer. They began licking their chops and even started to drool. They eagerly sat down and accepted food from Bree. They ate in silence for a long while, stuffing their mouths full of everything they could stuff in. Bree was happy and sad at the same time. Then after a while, with no repercussions from accepting Bree's invitation, they began to relax. Bree watched and could see the tension leaving the ladies' bodies. With a satisfied smile on her face, she sat back and just enjoyed the moment. After they were all completely full and could eat not one more crumb, Bree let the ladies sit and digest their meal. When the ladies relaxed even more, Bree silently arose and separated herself unnoticed from the table. Without shame, she removed the dress Lisa had lent to her for her date. It had been torn, shredded, and was terribly filthy from all she had been through in the last couple of days. The servants may suspect something if she showed shame or modesty for her nudity, so she sucked it up and stripped quietly then entered the cool refreshing water. It felt glorious.

When the servants heard a small splash, they jumped up in horror at their laziness and ran over to the large bathing pool where Bree was beginning to wash herself with the bowl of *natron* provided at the side of the bath. The oldest of the servants who ate first slightly scolded her. She was to bathe only if the lady servants aided her. This made Bree laugh aloud with joy. Now they began to trust in her and she was not going to punish them. The tension had broken. After an extremely refreshing and relaxing bath, the servants gave Bree a massage; they painted her eyes up with black kohl and green *grepond* eye paint that they made from malachite and copper carbonate pigment. Then they stained her lips red that shimmered, which had the servant explain to Bree that the sparkle came from shiny fish scales.

While the servants were beautifying Bree, she took the time to explain to the servants that how the Apis treated them was against everything that she had taught and had wanted for them. She explained to them that their leader was a tyrant, the king. She told the servants they had the right to stand up for themselves, even if that meant going against everything they had believed. This made the servant ladies quiet and contemplate deep in thought for a while as they finished her makeup. When her face was complete, she dressed in a long white sheath of cotton with one thin strap that went around one shoulder, leaving the other bare. The decorated sari had golden threads and beautiful beadwork around the neckline. The servants brushed out her long black hair, and while doing so, they commented constantly on the beauty of her silken locks. Bree was continuously blushing from their constant compliments. Then the oldest of the servants placed a beautiful headband around the top of her head that had beaded decor dangling from the sides and the back. She stood back and bowed low. "Goddess, you are a vision to behold."

The servants were so happy and relaxed with Bree. They constantly chattered openly as they worked. When the servants finished, they did not want to leave the presence of their goddess. They felt that she was a truly kind and generous deity. They enjoyed their time with her and would all later tell everyone that would listen how amazing their goddess truly was. They also enjoyed laughs and banter between all of them. Bree even teased the youngest of the servants named Safiya of a newly formed relationship that she had begun with a young jackal named Baahir. Safiya had accidentally let this tidbit of information slip out while they were bathing Bree. She said how she could not wait to marry the love of her life. The poor servant girl giggled in delight from Bree's teasing her like a normal friend would tease each other over boyfriends. Bree gathered a large towel from the side of the bath and filled it with what remained on the food trays. She reminded the servants to go and give it to other servants that were hungry, and then she made them understand that this was an order. The servants smiled and did as Bree bid them to do. When the servants finally exited, they took another five minutes with their bowing and thanking her continuously till all made it out the door. They had full tummies and smiles on their faces.

Soon after the servants left, Thema came back to collect her. When she entered the room, she showed her pleasure at how well Bree had cleaned up. Thema was amazed at her goddess's beauty before, but now she looked almost surreal with a glow about her. "Thema, I must thank you for sending me such lovely servants. They need compensation for how well they cared for me. I have never enjoyed such enthusiastic care as I have this morning."

Thema beamed but then said something that incensed Bree. It made Bree realize just how imperial and spoiled Thema truly was. "I am happy you have noticed how hard I have trained my servants. I will accept the compensation for them. It was I that trained them to serve so well, under a hard fist and a firm hand. Thank you, Goddess."

Bree just stared hard at Thema for a moment. *No, Bree, you can't just reach out and smack a queen, no matter how she deserves it.* Bree took advantage of her fake status as a goddess. She calmly asked Thema a serious question. "Is that how your king trained you so well? With a hard fist and a firm hand?"

Thema sucked in her breath slightly and frowned. "I am sorry, Goddess, I do not understand your question."

Bree stood up from her comfortable seat and stalked over to Thema, keeping her body stiff but as tall and straight as she could, her fury rising with every step. "Let me clarify my question to you, Thema. Did your king beat you and starve you so you would be the best wife as you are now?" Thema was thoroughly confused at Bree's questioning, so she decided to just be blunt. "I despise how you treat your servants, Thema. Why are the servants so mistreated, undernourished, and starving?"

Thema looked offended but covered her expression quickly. She then had the audacity to look upset at Bree and her straightforward question on the treatment of mere slaves. "The last couple years, we have been destitute by famine. Our river has been drying up, and our crops are dying. My king has stated this is due to the laziness of the Anubi. If they would toil harder without complaint and pay complete homage to you and pray to you more diligently, this would not be happening. You would continue to bless us as you always used to if not for the laziness of the commoners. They have wavered from their faith. We have had to ration the foods that our servants and our people receive every day in order to sustain everyone. Now the Anubi riot and pillage our royal food stores on a constant basis, stealing from the mouth of their king."

Bree stomped right up to Thema, forgetting that Thema was three times larger than she was. If she wanted to, she could kill Bree with one good hit. Anger made people stupid sometimes. "Do not dare blame me for your lands drying up or your people not praying to me enough. You insult me with even thinking I would be vile enough to destroy the ones that I saved a millennia ago. Yet the king, you, and your own seem to be rich, fat, and happy without lack for the drought you have stated is upon your lands."

Thema stepped back a little. She looked offended. "Goddess, you must understand, being the divinity that you are! Our lineage demands certain entitlements. We were born to a superior life than the everyday commoner. You would not, nor will we, lower our requirements that is our right just so unsavory commoners don't starve."

It took every ounce of Bree's willpower not to jump up and strike this supercilious beast standing so arrogantly before her. She was preaching about her people that were breaking their backs to feed, work, and serve them like they were nothing more than trash. She could not stand Aston and Derrick for this reason, and here was another one who felt like she had entitlement and had absolutely no remorse for her thought and actions. *Why do people that have so much wealth and riches forget that truth, dignity, and the lives of commoners are just as important as their own? If it were not for their commoners, they would die.* She was going to use her falsehood of being Nefertiti to its breaking point now. If she was able to change these creatures' minds even a little, to understand that everyone deserved at least the basics of life like shelter, food, water, and clothing, then it would be worth all of what had happened to get her here. Bree stood tall as she addressed Thema, "I would rather die than let my people starve or fear me. Bring me to your king at once. I feel this tour will be an interesting one indeed."

7

Thema took her to the king, but she was very obstinate toward Bree now. Bree could tell that if it weren't for her believing she was Nefertiti, then she would be dead for the way she had accused her of mistreating her servants. Thema was seething with rage. She wanted to tell the king in private what had happened between herself and the goddess. Thema even tried to get the king's attention before they exited the palace, asking for a private moment with him, but he swept her aside, completely ignoring her as he called for his chariot. As they waited for their transportation to arrive, Aston took the chance to whisper in her ear, "What has happened since you had us locked up in our suit, dear goddess? First wife looks like she would like nothing better than to see your beautiful head on a platter, the way she has been glaring at you."

Bree sighed. "I had a chat with her this morning about the treatment of her servants. She did not like what I had to say."

Now it was Aston's turn to sigh; he became ticked off slightly as well as he hissed harshly back in her ear, "Damn it, Bree, leave it be. Do not blow our cover because you have an issue for something that matters not to us."

Bree was about to retort, but their transportation started to arrive. The arrival of the transportation had her completely forgetting what it was she was about to rasp back at Aston. Now she stood frozen in fear with her mouth ajar and her eyes bulging out of their sockets as the chariots closed in. Pulling the large wooden chariots were horrifying behemoth scarabs. They were at least the size of a half-ton truck. When they pulled up in front of the palace's grand entrance, they hissed and snapped their massive wicked jaws, spread their wings, and flapped them in agitation for having to stop. Bree almost fainted with fear. One of the only things in life that truly terrified her was this very beetle, and her phobia was them at their regular size. These, though, were on a whole other scale. Her fear amplified a thousand times when she saw these massive creatures that were a hundred times larger than normal.

Her eleven-year-old cousin had tortured her one summer when she was four years of age while visiting her aunt with her father in Giza. For the last week of their visit, her cousin tortured her constantly, but his bullying was amped up when he discovered the scarab beetles. He found a dead one in the yard and began chasing her around the house with the scarab carcass. He tossed it at her, dropped it in her hair, hid it in her shoes. Then her malicious cousin, to her horror, had found a couple of alive scarabs. He began to hide them in her bed at night. During the night, they began to bite her. This was what put her over the edge; she had become so afraid of these beetles that even thinking about the beetles would cause a panic attack to start. Even if she saw one years after that summer, she would run away screaming like a maniac. She had thought she had gotten over this stupid phobia, but no.

Bree began hyperventilating. She could not control it. She began to see stars before her eyes, and her legs became weak. She broke out into a cold sweat, and it felt like she had a bowling ball pressing down in the pit of her stomach. When the chariots stopped just in front of them, one of the scarabs turned its ugly head toward Bree. Its dinner plate-sized eyes looked right at her like she was to be its next meal. It vibrated its razor-sharp pincher jaws then snapped them together. *Oh god, I am going to pass out.* Abruptly she went down. Aston caught her before she fully collapsed onto the sandy ground. He desperately tried to hold her up as if nothing were amiss, but everyone in the group noticed and was overly concerned. All in the group had a look of astonishment on their faces that a goddess would faint at all, but others had a look of skepticism. Thema had an evil smirk on her mouth and her snout pulled up as she watched Aston struggling to hold up Bree's dead weight. Aston looked around and realized this may have blown their cover. He rasped angrily into Bree's ear, "Get ahold of yourself for Christ's sake!" Derrick jumped forward to try to save the situation Bree's passing out had caused. "Your Eminence, I apologize for Neferneferuaten's weakened state. The dimensional travel has exhausted us all to the point of collapsing. We must excuse ourselves to assist our goddess with her ailment."

The two men tried to pull Bree away and exit the area as fast as they could, but Thema's voice stopped them in their tracks. "How is it that a goddess, who has lived for over a millennium, have such weak mortal reaction such as this?"

The king stormed over to Thema and slapped her hard enough that she fell to the ground on her side. She sat up with her hand against her face, and her snout was bleeding slightly. The king stood above his first wife and glared down at her. "You dare doubt our beloved Neferneferuaten? Your jealousy has gone too far this time, wife. She…is…your…goddess! Go to the temple. Bow on your knees till they bleed for your blasphemy. I have spoiled you too long as first wife. You have become repulsive to me. Get out of my sight before I cannot hold back my rage against you any longer."

Thema arose from the ground with a look of death shot in the direction of Bree, Aston, and Derrick. "Husband, take heed, she…is…an…imposter."

The king rose his hand to strike her again, but before he could land his fist on her muzzle again, Thema fled back into the palace hall and disappeared. The bull king heavily snorted a couple of times as he collected himself before he turned back to the still unconscious Bree and her companions.

The king stood for a moment as he looked upon the goddess's unconscious form, and suddenly a strange look crossed the king's face. Aston and Derrick noticed this. They both definitely did not like what they saw in the king's eyes. The king snorted heavily once more. Without a word to them, he turned to his guards. "The tour is off. Take them all to their separate quarters and lock them in. Guard the doors. No one enters their quarters unless it is me." The guards nodded as the king stormed away back into the palace. Without hesitation, the guards grabbed the men and forced them back into the palace. Aston did not like the look King Senepol had given them before he turned away. Nor did he like his response. He was definitely contemplating what Thema had declared. *Damn her, damn them both.* When Aston and his group had first arrived, he had made the mistake of assuming these creatures to be less intelligent than they were. Now he had to reconsider his assumptions. They were close to having their lie exposed, thanks to Bree. He and Derrick would have to put their plan they concocted the night before into action sooner than he thought they would have to. It would even have to be this very night.

As they holed up in their quarters the night before, both had decided to not include Bree when they conducted their dubious plan. She had become a liability, especially since she had threatened to expose them if they touched anything of value from these creatures. Unfortunately, Bree had to stay. Aston and Derrick argued about this decision for over an hour until Aston realized that Derrick was right this time. At first, he argued with Derrick how he did not want to leave Bree behind. She was an asset. These beasts would execute her as fast as they did the interpreter. In the end, Derrick said that it was usually himself that followed his dick, but now it was Aston. Aston realized as soon as that comment came from Derrick of all people's mouths that it was true. Aston did want Bree, and he was wanting to bed her more than he had ever wanted to bed a woman in his life. Bree would just have to become collateral damage; he had to leave his "*dick*" out of it from now on. Considering the payout of being able to achieve what they had come here to do, it would be worth losing this beauty he had developed slight emotions for. He could always find another woman to pacify him after they got back to their realm; it was just too bad that it would not be Bree. He did want her very much. She was a beautiful spitfire, with strength and intelligence. He sighed and followed the guards that shuffled them hurriedly back to their quarters. The guards separated Derrick and Aston from Bree, and the guards shoved them back into their room. After the doors locked behind them, Aston and Derrick looked at each other and nodded, silently understanding that they would be conducting their plan very soon.

*****

The guard placed Bree gently on the bed. The guard that placed her on the bed was not sure what was happening all of sudden. He heard their queen accuse this beautiful goddess of being an imposter. Then he noticed the king's expression when he looked back at the unconscious Neferneferuaten after his queen fled back into the palace. He knew his king was doubting this deity's identity now as well. At this moment, though, he was still gentle. He just could not make himself fully believe that she may be an imposter of their goddess. If they were wrong, he did not want to see her wrath. If his king and queen were correct, well, he did not want to think about executing this magnificent female. She was a remarkable sight. All the guards talked about her beauty since she showed up that strange day. He had been one of the privileged. He was one of the guards in the throne room on the day her entourage arrived.

If she was an imposter, did she not still have knowledge of great magic in order for her to be able to open a crack within their two realms? Then again, it could have been the obelisk that she held on to her person that held all the magic. The guard heaved his big frame with a snort. *It would be as it would be.* He would follow his king's orders no matter what he commanded them to do. The guard lowered his massive frame above the woman unconscious on the bed; he reached out and gently lifted a stray strand of hair from her beautiful face, and then he shook his head. He stood his massive frame away from her, as yet undecided, turned quickly, and left the room only to shut the door and stand guard in front of it as ordered.

Bree awoke from her passing out from fear with the sounds of yelling and stomping coming from outside her quarters. How she got back on her bed bewildered her for a moment until her memory came flooding back to her. Images of those disgusting giant beetles looking at her while they snapped their pincers made her body jolt with a full-body shiver, and she gagged. Abruptly she realized what must have ensued. *Seeing those monsters made me black out. I must have blown our cover. Goddesses do not faint. Damn your ridiculous fear, Bree! What are you going to do now?* Fear for her safety crept up her spine, but she became distracted again by the clamoring and shouting in the hall beyond her room.

Forgetting about her fear for the moment, she removed herself from the bed and went up to the doors. She tried the door and to find it locked. She placed her ear upon the cold wooden panel to get a better idea of what was happening through the thick door. She could hear heavy hooves running on the marble hall coming from a stampeding herd. She could make out bits and pieces of the shouting, as they passed. "They are attacking the royal food stores…fires on the north side…every guard needs to assist…doors are locked, they are fine for now…bastard slaves…save a couple for interrogation…king's orders, kill on sight." Bree stepped back from the door as the yelling, shouting, clamoring, and chaos began to fade down the hallway. For a brief moment, she stared at the door to make sure a guard did not burst in as she tried to understand what may be happening outside the walls of the palace.

A thought popped into her brain to go to the opening in her wall to see if there was anything she could make out. Bree went over to the wall. She leaned out and stuck her body as far as was safe through the opening by holding on to one of the marble pillars. In the distance, she could see the glow of flames and smoke rising to the northeast of the palace. As she listened, she could hear the sounds of combat, swords hit shields, chariots pulled at high speeds, and she could swear she heard those disgusting scarabs hissing and snapping their jaws as they were pulling the chariots. A chilling thought crossed her mind as she imagined the scarabs trained as giant monstrous battle beetles tearing people apart with their oversized pinchers and jaws. Bree shivered once more. She had to find a way out of this chamber and find a way back to the temple so she could try to figure out how to get the obelisks to open the portal to get home fast. This world was not hers, Derrick's, or Aston's world to be in. They had to leave, and they had to leave now.

Combined with the sounds of battle, she cringed as she could also hear the cries of the wounded and the dying. She watched the fires gain height and strength, and she could now smell the smoke as the wind had shifted, bringing the smell of the smoke to now enter her chambers. It was not enough to choke on, but it smelled dreadful—burning flesh mixed with terror, blood, wood, wheat, and such.

It was not a pleasant smell. Bree retched a couple of times and placed her hand over her nose. She began to anxiously pace back and forth in her locked quarters. She tried to forge a plan, but nothing was forthcoming at the moment. Her fear began to fester as her brain just would not function with any critical thoughts of how to save herself or Aston and Derrick at the moment.

8

King Senepol was in his splendor as he arced his gigantic weapon down hard on a smaller raider, slashing him completely in half with it. Then his chariot bounced over the still spasming corpse as he continued for more carnage. Blood splattered, dripping from his armor like a full can of paint that had splattered onto a canvas. He tilted his head and breathed deeply, filling his lungs with the smoke-filled air and bellowed out a loud brutal battle roar. The smell of death and fear excited him, but his bloodlust had yet to be satisfied. He looked like the devil himself who had risen from the bowels of hell. The fire outlined his oversized horns, massive frame, and sword raised in the air for another kill. His mane looked like a mass of snakes thrashing behind him. He rode across the battle on his chariot pulled by the largest and cruelest of his scarabs. He chopped and slashed at fleeing raiders. Mucus flew from his nostrils. Spit foamed around his entire mouth, and sweat soaked his hide. Steam rose from his hot body, as the chill of the night sands was cooler than the heat pouring from his pores.

Bodies of jackal raiders were piling up along the royal stores, now completely consumed by the flames that had been lit during the raid. The king and his giant bull soldiers were taking easy lead of the battle. This was not just due to their size and skill; the raiders did not have the proper armor, weapons, training, or chariots to successfully compete with the king and his royal guards. Bodies, heads, and limbs were sliced off with such force that they were flung through the chilly night air. Body pieces were piling up everywhere over the battlefield. Blood of the dead and dying stained the sands with streaks and pools of red. The remaining raiders were beginning to turn and abandon the fight, desperate to escape in fear for their lives. The royal guards' arrows and spears took care of the ones running away. The mighty force of the spears thrown slammed into the fleeing bodies of the raiders so brutally they entered their backs and exited the bodies' fronts, piercing them like puppets on a stick to the ground with a sickening thud. The arrows tore through all parts of the body, ripping chunks of flesh as they exited through them, killing them instantly.

When the battle ended, King Senepol rode up onto a small hill and dismounted from his chariot with the massive scarab clicking its jaws behind him. He stood proud on the hill that was a small ways distance from where the battle had taken place. The king felt exhilarated. Death, carnage, and the ability to spill so much blood were extremely intoxicating. He breathed in deeply once again. The smell of death was pleasant as it passed into his mucus-covered nostrils. It had been too long between battles. Too long that he had not swung his sword. Too long since he had killed en masse. He was becoming soft in the last while. He puffed his chest to its fullest, flexed his bulging muscles, and stood to his full height as he watched his soldiers put out the remaining fires that were burning the royal food stores. The king snorted. Anger brewed and festered just under the surface. Other soldiers were picking up the bodies of the dead and wounded raiders, throwing them carelessly into a pile. Then the soldier lit the piles of bodies on fire.

The king smiled with enjoyment when he heard the agonized cries ripped from the wounded as the fire slowly burned away at their flesh. The king's own dead only numbered in the dozen. The soldiers carefully placed their own on death carts. Unlike the raiders, the king's soldiers would have a proper burial that was due to them. He filled his lungs with the smell of the burning flesh once more and snorted with pleasure. He roared suddenly. As it echoed through the valley, the royal guards stopped what they were doing, rose their heads in the air, and roared back a victory bellow to their king. With that, the king turned away and lifted his massive frame back up onto the giant chariot. He grabbed the reins away from his driver and oversaw the scarab himself as he rode back to the palace. He had other business to address now. They had kept a couple of the pathetic raiders alive for him to interrogate. He was looking forward to hearing the reasons for this raid. He was also looking forward to torturing it out of them. He would squeeze the answers out of the survivors with his own hands. They would beg for death before he was finished with them.

*****

The three raiders were on their knees all bloody and in intense agony from the torture the king had made them endure. The king paced back and forth in front of them, taking a moment to rest himself from all the pain he had inflicted on these poor souls. One of the raiders began to plead for him to just kill him. The bull king lashed out at this sniveling traitor, and he flew backward from the force of the hit and landed on the floor without moving again. He was out cold. The king snorted angrily. "I will ask you both one more time. Why did you raid my royal food stores?"

Both of the jackal raiders continued to stare at the ground with their hands tightly tied behind their backs, and blood dripped from both of their snouts down their sharp canine teeth, but neither would speak. They both knew they were going to die anyways, so telling the king the truth would not matter at this point. It would not save them. The king squatted in front of the remaining two raiders and snorted mucus from his snout in their faces. "I see you are strong. I admire this trait." Senepol laughed cruelly. "Even though I admire your strength, I will take pleasure in breaking you." Senepol stood back up and motioned to his guards as he said, "Bring her in." The guards left and soon returned, dragging with them an Anubi servant girl who was whimpering in her terror.

The guard carried the terrified servant girl and tossed her roughly to the ground in front of the two Anubi raiders. They both looked up, and one of the jackal raiders gasped and tried to crawl toward her as he yelled out her name. "Safiya!"

The terrified servant girl looked up and saw her young lover before her, bloody and torn, with terrible wounds all over his body. Her heart shattered. "Baahir?" They tried to both crawl to each other, but Senepol grabbed the servant girl ruthlessly, lifted her struggling body up in the air, and held her off her feet with one massive arm by her neck. Safiya gagged and struggled as she clawed at his arm. He grabbed the front of her clothing and tore them off; she screamed with fright, pain, and embarrassment as her nakedness was exposed to all in the room. The bull king plucked a dagger from inside his armor and sliced it down her middle, carving a large gash from her shoulder all the way down to the opposite hip.

Safiya screamed in agony, and Baahir shrieked back in despair and struggled to crawl a little closer. "Don't hurt her! Please, I beg of you!" Safiya sobbed in pain and despair as she saw and heard the agony from Baahir voice as he watched the king cut her open. Seeing the pain in his entire body by her being tortured by Senepol made her realize she would never see her lover again after this terrible night. The king cut her torso again. She tried not to scream, but the pain was so terrible she was unable to hold it back. Baahir cried again, "I will tell you everything you need to know. Just let her go. She has nothing to do with this. You must believe me. Just let her go."

Safiya cried out bravely to Baahir, "No, my love, you cannot."

The bull king cut her again, only this time it was across her eye, down her muzzle, and across her mouth. Blood splattered on Baahir, and he shrieked, "Please! Enough! I will tell you everything. Please stop!" Safiya passed out due to the pain the king had inflicted upon her body; she suddenly went limp in his massive hand. Baahir begged again.

Senepol tossed her none too gently onto the floor and turned his attention back on the raider named Baahir. "I am ready to hear what you have to say. Lie to me, hold back anything, and I promise you she will die an agonizing death along with you and your pathetic partners here. Tell me the whole truth, and I will only kill you two." King Senepol pointed at Baahir and his jackal partner in crime. "Only then will I let your precious Safiya live." Baahir closed his eyes for a moment, but then with a racking sob, he nodded. He understood the danger in his choice of joining the raid on the king's royal stores.

Baahir knew they were all dead once the soldiers captured them. Never in his worst nightmare did he ever think the king would find and torture the only light in his life, the woman he wanted to marry and bear him his children. He would do anything to keep her alive. He would tell the king everything. Senepol was about to kick Safiya's limp body but only stopped when Baahir cried out, "It was the goddess Neferneferuaten. She gave us the courage to burn the royal stores."

The king picked Baahir up with both hands and slammed him against the dungeon wall. "You lie. The goddess has never left my palace since she has arrived." He was about to break Baahir's neck and move on to the other raider, but Baahir choked out, "It was when Safiya tended to her earlier today."

Senepol glared at Baahir but stopped choking him. "Explain."

Baahir stopped struggling and let his hands go limp from the arms of the king. "The goddess let the women eat with her during her morning meal. Safiya told how the goddess became truly angry when she saw how skinny and undernourished the servant women appeared. Goddess Neferneferuaten told Safiya and the other servants that you, as king, had no right to starve those that serve you. That you and your own were sitting well-fed and lazy while your servants starved as they toiled for you. She told Safiya that if she, as a servant, was treated so poorly, she would start an uprising. She would no longer serve those that mistreated her in that way. She would demand to have equal rights that we all deserve. Neferneferuaten told Safiya that no king has the right to treat his people the way you have treated us. When Safiya told me what the goddess had said to her, she did so in the center square of the town. Everyone heard what the goddess had told Safiya. This news traveled to all within our town within minutes. We gathered as townspeople fueled with fury and anger. We feel that the goddess is evaluating us. We decided that if the goddess said this, then it must be a command for us to stand up for what is just for all. The men of town assembled within the hour. That was when we developed a plan to destroy the royal coffers. We did this to make a point against your treatment of us, to show you we will no longer accept being slaves."

Baahir was becoming more courageous as he spoke the words of what the goddess had said to Safiya. He knew he would die at any moment, but the king needed to know that his people would not stand for this any longer. "This is not the end of the attacks. It will continue as the goddess would have us do—to gain back our lives and our rights that you have taken away from us since our rivers and lands have been dying. The harder we work, the more you take away, yet here you are not lacking anything, your bellies are full, and your soldiers are content. Yet we, the Anubi, who toil day in and day out, starve." Just as Baahir had made the last comment, the king became so incensed that he did not even realize that he had snapped Baahir's neck. Baahir's body went limp as his last breath squeaked out of his crushed windpipe. The king scowled at the now dead raider's body.

With a new rage, the king threw Baahir's body hard against the opposite wall. Without warning, he stormed over to the remaining raider and plunged his dagger right through the top of his head. The raider dropped instantly. Senepol panted as he looked toward the guards seeing their king's brutal cruelty. With the raider's body still twitching beneath his feet, the king pulled out the dagger from his head and wiped the blood and brain matter onto his bared chest not covered by armor. Then Senepol demanded that his guards bring the imposter goddess and her entourage down to the dungeon at once. He looked back at the unconscious and bleeding Safiya. "And take this thing out of my sight. Do not kill it. Let its bleeding lacerations be a warning to all the other Anubi that this is what happens when one goes against their king."

9

Four gigantic guards suddenly stormed into Bree's chambers. Bree was ready for this as she knew that her dramatic reaction to the monstrous scarabs had given them all away. She just did not know what to expect when they did come for her. *They may even execute me.* She was so terrified at this moment. The only thing she could do was listen to the demands of the guards and go with them. There was nowhere she could run. There was nowhere she could hide. Bree even contemplated jumping out of the wall opening in her quarters after she had seen that the fires were out and the screams of battle had diminished. She knew at once that she would be jumping to her abrupt death when she realized how far up her chambers were from the hard-packed sandy ground below. Plus, she had no idea where to go, and she did not have any gear or provisions for her to survive in a desert alone.

She simply nodded at the guards and followed them out of her room. Two guards led her down the hall, and the other two guards went across the hall to the other chambers to collect Aston and Derrick. They led her down halls and then down large deep steps to what she understood to be the dungeon area. Then they led her to an undeveloped area surrounded by cells. A couple cells seemed occupied, but she did not pay attention to them as she was worried about herself. She noticed that the floor in this area was smeared with blood. So much blood. The blood was still fresh, and the room reeked of copper. It took willpower on her part not to gag. Just as she swallowed the bile rising in her throat, King Senepol entered from a door opposite the door she had entered in. *He is seething mad. He is going to rip me apart right here. Oh god, I never got to say goodbye to Lisa.* With that thought, she closed her eyes and let a tear fall as her heart hammered in her chest. She could hear the king stomping toward her. She kept her eyes closed, and another tear fell. *I am going to die, and no one will even know.*

She could tell that the gigantic king had stopped directly in front of her. One, she could smell his strong sweat mixed with smoke from the fires. Two, she could feel the air move and change with his movement as he lowered his massive head to match her height. Suddenly she felt his cold wet snout just at the end of her own nose. *Pshht*. Bree's hair blew backward as well; she had grotesque moisture over her entire face. She was so startled that she opened her eyes right after he snorted into her face. There he was directly in front of her, staring menacingly, with a snarl across his bull features. "You dare cry?" He reached up with a sudden movement, and Bree flinched. He did not hit her, though; he flicked one of her tears from her cheek and began to laugh.

"A goddess, crying! A goddess, fainting! You are no goddess of mine. My goddess is strong and taught us by her words that there is to always be a leader who can control and rule over the lesser minions." Senepol continued to chuckle, but as suddenly as he started laughing, his mood changed, and he grabbed Bree by both shoulders and raised her with him as he stood at his full height. Bree's feet were at least two feet off the floor. He squeezed so hard on her arms that tears fell due to the pain. *Now comes the tearing apart,* Bree thought. She squeezed her eyes shut tight and said a silent prayer. She waited for the pain, the tearing, the tugging. She waited for something, but after a moment, when all he did was hold her up by her shoulders, she peeked her eyes open a little. He was staring at her breasts, and he was smelling her at the same time. Bree could see something else in his eyes, other than rage and loathing. What she saw in his eyes frightened her much more than his wrath did. Now his emotions had a different gnawing desire. With this new growing emotion entering his thoughts, Bree knew this meant only one thing for her. Torture! Demoralizing, drawn-out, agonizing torture. Only depraved, evil beings chose to inflict this kind of torture onto another before they killed them in order to prove strength, dominance, control, and power on the poor soul they brutalized. Her blood turned to ice.

There was no way in hell she would endure that kind of torture. He would rip her in half if he tried to bed her just by his size alone. She decided if she died by ripping in half, it would be by his arms, not his member. Out of nowhere, she spat in his face and screamed, "Kill me, you son of a useless cow tit. I deceived you. I lied to you. You bowed down to me. You hit your Thema because of me, and yet she was right about me. Thema will never forgive you. Your men will think you are weak and pathetic because we duped you so easily." Bree screamed out all she could in order to raise his brutal anger so he would just do it. Just kill her at once so there would only be a second of pain and then she would be gone. This way it would be over, not go one for days and nights till he tired of her and then killed her slowly. If she was going to die, then she was going to die her way.

Senepol licked the spittle off his face with his own tongue and then surprised Bree by putting her down gently as he started laughing again. When he finished his rumbling chuckle, he said, "I know what you are trying to do, my false goddess." He reached out to stroke her breast, but she jumped back before he could make contact. The king continued ignoring Bree's recoil. "You will amuse me in my bed. You will pay, with your body, for your deception. You will please me in every way I desire." Bree was so disgusted she tried to spit in his face again. This time he did stop her by smacking her across the face. It was a light tap from the king, but she fell to the floor by its force, and her lip split open and began bleeding as well. Senepol stalked up and squatted his mass beside her. He placed his finger under her chin, making her raise it to look directly at him. "You are a brave little one. You have spirit. You are beautiful beyond compare. I shall enjoy breaking you, small one. You heat my blood, woman, more so than even killing my enemy does. Oh yes, I will enjoy destroying your spirit. I will enjoy it indeed. When I tire of you, and I will tire of you, then I will kill you slowly." Suddenly his large bull-sized tongue exited his mouth and licked her from the bottom of her chin right up the side of her face. The king snorted loudly. "You taste good, my little imposter. I have decided on the course of action I am to take with you and your companions. When your lovers arrive shortly, I will make them watch as I mount and ravage you. When you are full of my seed, I will then make you watch me enjoy killing your lovers slowly with my bare hands." Bree choked and began to gag on her bile rising in her throat again. She was about to beg him to slit her throat (*she really was*), but as she contemplated how she was going to convince him to kill her fast, the dungeon door to the main room slammed forcibly open, and two guards stumbled as they entered in their haste to get to the king.

"My king, the woman's men are missing. They are no longer within their chambers." The speed at which the immense bull king could move still astounded Bree as well as terrified her. He was up and had the first guard pinned against the wall so fast that it seemed like a blur of forward movement. The king slammed the guard into the wall. "What do you mean they are missing?" The king snarled this out with such disgust directed toward his guard that the small bull began to urinate down his leg. Without waiting for an answer, the guard slammed against the wall again, and the mortar on the wall began to crack. "Find them within the hour, or I will skin you both alive, and as you die slowly, I will use your hides as rags to wipe off my pet scarab's shit from in between the cracks of my hooves." Senepol let the terrified guard loose from the wall; both guards never said a word as they scrambled as fast as they could out of the dungeon to search for the escapees. The king stood for a moment and looked out after his guards. His shoulders heaved up and down a couple of times as he calmed himself before he turned back to Bree so he would not kill her in his newfound rage from the news he had just received. Bree began to slowly back up to a set of cell bars, trying to take in what she had heard about Aston and Derrick being missing. *Missing! Where the hell are they, and most importantly, did they escape without me, or were they trying to figure out a way to rescue me?* Hope crept into her heart.

Senepol calmed himself enough to turn back to the woman on the floor. He became enraged that he had to leave her. He wanted to start his delicious torture on her at once. He was looking very forward to releasing his pent-up anger on her beautiful body. He did not trust his guards to find the two missing deceivers, though. Right now, his revengeful lust would have to wait. The king stormed back to Bree, picked her up, and tossed her into one of the cells. As he slammed and locked the barred door, he snorted, "We will continue where we left off very soon, little imposter. Let your mind grasp what I will enjoy doing to your body every night in my chambers." With an evil chuckle, he left for a new quest to find the missing members of her entourage. Bree slammed against the back wall of the cell. She barely heard what the king had said before he left from the ringing in her ears as her head had smacked quite hard against the back wall of the cell. She moaned and grabbed the back of her head. She whistled when her fingers found the open wound that was bleeding through her hair. "Asshole" was all she could think of saying at the moment.

"I thought I was the king's number one enemy." *Cough, cough.* "Looks like I'm mistaken."

Bree's head snapped up when she heard a deep, quiet voice speaking from the cell connected to hers. She peered through the bars to see a large shadow of a man or beast huddled in the far back corner of its cell. It was too dark to see except for the man's size. Despite herself, she smiled at the comment. "I don't want that title. You can have it back if you wish."

There was another coughing spell as the man in the corner tried to laugh, and then a slight groan came from him as he shifted his weight before he spoke again, "May I inquire what earned you Senepol's wrath?" The man's voice was deep and smooth. He sounded very tired and in pain, but he kept his voice even and calm in between his slight groans and coughing spells.

Bree sighed, and she crawled herself over to the cell's connecting bars to sit closer to the voice in the opposite corner. "It's a long story. I don't think I have enough time to explain before they come back for me."

The large figure shifted again as he painfully pulled his massive body closer to the bars to be closer for the conversation. Bree gasped when he came into the dim light of the dungeon. She almost backed away but held still so as not to offend him. He was the largest lion she had ever seen. He was a hybrid of human and lion melded together like the other hybrids here. His main had blood matted with dirt and grim mixed in. He had a large slash across his muzzle that looked to soon be infected. He was also heavily favoring his left side. Bree could see that there was a massive wound there just below his ribs; it looked deep and was bleeding through the scraps he had torn off his clothing to tie around it. He had other deep cuts and wounds all over his body as well. Senepol or the soldiers had tortured him severely to have such wounds. Bree could not help it; she reached through the bars and lightly stroked the beast's left arm that was holding the large wound under his ribs. "What happened to you?"

He tried to chuckle and shrug it off, but the pain caused him to choke and wince. The lion man looked down at Bree's tiny hand as it gently stroked his arm. He looked up at her right in the eye as he said, "This is what happens when King Senepol thinks you are trying to take what he believes to be his."

Bree shivered. His eyes were still very bright with life and humor, even though he was in intense pain and beaten to a pulp. Bree instantly felt a connection to this lion man. There was something about this beast that made her feel that she could trust him. She felt like she actually knew him, which was very strange. "My name is Bree."

The lion man lowered his head in respect. "That is a beautiful and unique name." He coughed again before he continued, "Bree, I'm Jabar. I would say it was nice to meet you, but considering the circumstances..." Jabar trailed off with another cough followed by a hiss.

Bree frowned. "You need immediate medical attention. Your wounds are bad."

Jabar's chuckle rumbled low in his chest. "I am going to die here, so my wounds matter not."

Bree had to turn away for a moment as a tear sprang to her eye. Jabar was so calm talking about his death. It hurt her heart terribly. She just wanted to give the big guy a hug. "I will find a way out of here, and when I do, I will get you out as well."

Jabar shook his head. "There is no dungeon more secure than this one. No one has ever escaped. My people tell tales of this dungeon. We tell the young ones that we will bring them here and leave them in this dungeon if they misbehave. One goes in alive and comes out when they are dead. However, I do admire your enthusiasm." Jabar leaned back against the wall and sighed. They both sat in silence for a moment, and then Jabar quietly inquired, "I must ask, my curiosity is getting the better of me. I would normally not be so forward, but since I am dying, I do not feel so hesitant." Bree turned to him fully so he could see that she was open to whatever question it was that he was about to ask. "What are you? I have never seen the likes of one such as yourself before. I have only seen one such as yourself as a sculpture, in a painting, or described in our ancient tales."

Bree hesitated before she answered. She got up and began to wander around the cell trying to find a loose brick or rusted bar on the cell walls in order to try to escape. Jabar sighed and apologized, "I did not mean to make you uncomfortable. I am sorry."

Bree turned back to Jabar, and it was her turn to apologize. "No, no, you do not have to apologize. I am trying to figure out how to explain what I am for you to make it not sound like a tall tale." Jabar nodded, then sat silent as he waited for her to continue.

Bree was in a conundrum. Should she tell him the truth or make up a lie? If she lied, she may say the wrong thing. If she told the truth, he may not believe her. Then again, he was dying. He may not make it out of this dungeon alive. She decided to tell him the truth. Why not give him an amazing story and let him decide whether or not to believe what she was about to tell him? She turned back to Jabar with her decision made. She sat as close to the bars near him as she could and started her tale. Jabar sat and listened to her the entire time without one interruption. She had to stop a couple times during her tale to make sure that he was still breathing. After she finished describing her last few days, they sat silent again for a moment as Jabar digested her tale. Bree was actually starting to feel nervous that he would not believe her words. Why did it matter if he believed her or not, she did not know, but she realized it did matter to her.

Jabar suddenly rumbled out, "So it is true! Senepol has a second obelisk in his possession. Our mole was telling the truth. You are the one that brought it to him, and this is why I sit here dying in this dungeon!" The look of malice that Jabar turned on Bree shocked and scared her. She scurried away from the bars frightened that he would swipe his clawed hand at her. It disturbed her that he now despised her. This was not the scenario that Bree imagined in her head when she decided to tell him her tale. He blamed her when it was not her fault.

"Jabar, for what it is worth, I am a victim here as well. I told you that I had drugs tricked into me and then forced to open the portal by horrible men. I tried to stop them, but it was too late. The portal opened, and we ended up here. Senepol took the obelisk from me. I did not give it to the king by choice." Bree did not realize that she was sobbing. Why did she feel that she even had to explain herself to the beast in the next cell? Jabar growled low in his throat. For a moment she thought it was at her, but then she heard a soft whisper coming from outside her cell.

"Goddess, it is I, Eman."

Bree sucked in her breath and crawled over to Eman. "Eman, you can't be here. If they find you, they will kill you. You must leave."

Eman stood to her full height as best she could for her age and her crooked overworked spine. "I saw what Senepol did to Safiya. She will never be the same. Her face has been mutilated so horrendously that she will never regain her beauty to find a mate. Safiya's young lover Baahir is dead. There is nothing left for me. I am too old to serve a family that I loathe. They torture, starve, and kill my people. I can no longer sit back and do nothing."

Bree grabbed Eman's hands through the bars and squeezed them tight. "I am not a goddess, Eman. I am an imposter. I cannot let you risk your life for me. My appearing here with Aston and Derrick is what caused all this to happen. All this is our fault. Please, Eman, you must leave here before the king or the guards return."

Eman shook her head and pulled her hands away from Bree's grasp. She took out a key from her apron and opened Bree's cell. As Eman opened the cell door the entire way, she turned back to Bree. "You showed me and the other ladies such kindness that no one has ever shown us before. I know you are not Goddess Neferneferuaten, but you are still a savior and a goddess to me and my people. For that, we will forever be grateful. My people's rebellion began long before you came. It was brewing under the surface. Your appearance and your kindness only gave us the strength to finally stand up and act. This should have happened decades ago."

Bree exited the cell and gave Eman a hug. The old woman embraced Bree in the warmth of her body like a mother would a child for only a moment. "You must go now. There is a—" Bree interrupted Eman as she was about to tell her how to escape the dungeon. "Wait, Eman, please, can you open the next cell. I have to get Jabar out of here as well, or he will die. He, too, is an enemy of Senepol. This will be one life saved from the grips of the king."

Eman hesitated when she looked in the other cell. She realized that the being in the cell that Bree was referring to was one of the Maahes tribe. Her people had battled against the Maahes for centuries. Then Eman decided something. "You there, the one the goddess calls Jabar. I will release you on one condition. You must inform your Jendayi of the Sakhmet tribe that the Anubi are going to rise up against King Senepol and the Apis tribe. Your people have been at war with Senepol and the Apis for too long. My tribe was forced to fight against your tribes for far too long. We can finally fight together. Do you agree, Jabar?"

Jabar stood up with slow, deliberate, yet careful movement as he favored his left side. He held his head high and growled out his reply. "It would be a privilege and an honor to inform Jendayi of this rebellion against Senepol. Eman of the Anubi, may this day prove fruitful for our three tribes to work together to dethrone Senepol. You have my word."

Eman nodded her head in one sharp agreed movement. Then she opened Jabar's cell, turned back to Bree, and said. "Follow me." Bree stepped into Jabar's cell and warily eyed him to see if he would accept her help. He hissed slightly at her, so she stopped. As he tried to step forward, though, he almost collapsed. Bree shook her head and went to him. "Stupid, stubborn man." She tucked herself under his arm by his injured side for support. She then placed his large muscular arm on top of her head. "I may be small, but I am stronger than I look. Lean your weight on my head, and we will get our asses out of here together." Jabar growled low but did as she said. They both slowly exited the cell and followed Eman as she led them down deeper into the dungeon and out a back passageway that had not seen any use in over a decade.

They walked for what seemed like quite a way as they traversed gingerly down the dark narrow tunnel. Jabar had to stop a couple times in order to regain his strength. Bree's neck was sore from Jabar's massive weight pushing down on it, but she ignored it as best she could so they could get out of the dungeon before someone discovered them missing. When they reached the exit, Eman turned to them both. "I have arranged transport for you. You must hurry back to your tribe, Jabar. Take diligent care of the goddess for me." Eman leaned in on Jabar's right side and said for his ears only, "She is the key." Then as quickly as she leaned in, she turned to Bree. "I must go now." Bree hugged Eman, and then Eman rushed away back down the tunnel without looking back. Bree then walked toward the angled wooden doors and forced them open. The dusty doors reminded her of tornado bunker doors. When the sand and dust cleared, Bree helped Jabar stumble out. As they stepped out into the bright early morning sun, they came face-to-face with Bree's worst fear. There, just outside of the hidden doors waiting for them, was a young jackal. He had control of the reins of two horse-sized scarabs that had reins and saddles on them. Bree froze. *Ride on the backs of these mutations? Fuck no!*

Jabar abruptly realized that the strange tiny woman was no longer supporting his left side under his arm. She was unexpectedly gone. He saw the young jackal rush toward him with a look of concern on his face as he was looking at the ground by his feet. Jabar looked down. Bree was lying at his feet, fully passed out, cold. The first thought that Jabar contemplated was just to leave her where she had fallen. He would demand the scarabs from the young Anubi and charge away alone. He hesitated and looked back down at the woman again. He growled to himself a couple of times. There was something he could not put his claw on about this female. He realized that he believed every word of her tale that she had told him earlier. He also realized that this terrible scenario was not her fault. He believed this to be so when Eman came to rescue her. This woman had helped the servants and treated them as equals. It impressed him. What was the turning factor for him was watching her easily convince an old Anubi servant, who had lived through wars with his tribe, to release him. He was actually in awe for a moment when he realized that she was indeed releasing him. He would tell the elder Jendayi everything. He had given Eman his word. Maahes never broke a promise or went back on their word. This woman that Eman called goddess was the key.

With the decision made to follow what he had promised to Eman, he stepped over the woman's body carefully so he would not step on her. He directed the young Anubi to pick the woman up gently and place her on the front of the scarab that Jabar was to ride. The young jackal did as instructed. The Maahe was severely injured, but the young jackal still felt extremely intimidated by the giant. He was shocked when the Maahe male was with the woman. He had volunteered to help the goddess when he found out what the king had done to his sister Safiya. He was too young to go to battle, but he had to do something to appease his anger at the king. He may have hesitated in volunteering for this mission if he knew about the Maahe male. He was glad that he decided to come, though. The Maahe did not seem to be interested in a fight or in the condition for one either. He would have an amazing story to tell his friends when he returned. He did as the Maahe instructed and placed the woman on the scarab that the Maahe was to ride. They had everything ready, so they quickly began to head in the southwest direction, away from Senepol's palace, unnoticed over the dunes of blowing sands.

10

King Senepol and his guards tore apart the entire chamber that Aston and Derrick stayed in. The guards were becoming incredibly nervous as they traversed throughout the palace looking for the two missing culprits. They knew their king's temper; it would fall on one or all their heads (literally) if they did not apprehend them. As Senepol rounded one of the hallways to search in the treasure room, Thema ran up to them in a frantic huff. She stopped in front of her king and burst into tears. The king had no sympathy for her at the moment and demanded, "Get out of my way, woman."

Thema fell to her knees in front of Senepol and choked out through her tears, "The temple…the obelisks…they have been stolen." Without a second thought, the king shoved Thema out of the way as he and the guards stormed toward the temple.

King Senepol glared at the two empty spaces below the golden statue of the goddess. The obelisks were indeed missing. His anger boiled to the surface. He bellowed an angry roar. In his rage, he marched up to the statue. He placed his hands around the edges, and with a mighty shove, the statue shifted then tilted enough that the weight of it slid off its pillar and collapsed severely on the fountain's edge below, which in turn crushed the complete far side of the fountain. Water splattered and gushed everywhere. All the servants had already scurried out of the main temple hall so the only group to see the excessive destruction of their sacred temple was the king, the kings' guards, and Thema, who was hovering in the back. Senepol turned and stood on the platform. He looked down upon his guards, only deeply rumbling out one sentence. His words were calm, which made the guards scatter in fear. When the king was angry enough to sound calm, shit was about to hit the fan. "Find them. Kill them."

Thema took this opportunity to get her jealous revenge she wanted on Bree expressed to the king. She loved seeing Senepol this way. He was all powerful. It had been far too long since she saw her husband in this way, and it was breathtaking. Her king was finally back. She found out that her husband was going to keep the imposter goddess as a concubine slave. This was never going to happen. Thema was going to wait for an opportunity when she entered his bedchamber and then have her poisoned, but torture from the king was much better. Poisoning was far too good for that woman. "That imposter bitch in the dungeon knows where her lovers are with your property. She planned all of this. Torture it out of her, my king. Break her till she confesses. Show her that no one cheats you, my mighty king." Senepol began breathing heavily. He clenched his jaw as his massive shoulders rose up and down, and his chest seemed to grow in size as he stood at his full height. Swiftly he growled and snorted then stormed out of the temple, heading down toward the dungeon. His first wife was right. His petty lust for the imposter goddess could not take precedence over getting the obelisks back. He would indeed torture her now with pain and agony instead. He would get his property back at all costs. His plan to completely dominate the entire realm demanded it.

The king entered the dungeon alone. He immediately noticed the cell he left the woman in had its door ajar. For a second, he was confused. He then noted that the cell that held Jabar was wide open. "No…no…" He scrambled up to the cells and grabbed the bars. They were both empty. Senepol's brow furrowed in anger. He tried to conceive how the cells had opened. Did the woman's companions somehow obtain the cell key and let the woman out? This did not explain how Jabar had gotten out as well. Why would they release someone that was so injured and would hinder their escape? Senepol's brain clicked and clicked. All of a sudden, the clicking in his head stopped. He pushed himself away from the cells.

I have a criminal worthy of imminent death in my midst!

With a low long growl, Senepol exited the dungeon swiftly with yet another mission on his ever-growing plate. He pushed his inner voice aside that twigged at his semiconsciousness. *You are losing con-*

trol. Your kingdom is in jeopardy! The woman and her companion's appearance triggered all this. They were the cause of all the sudden decline of his kingdom. He would make them pay dearly for all this. He had to find his first wife. He had an idea of where the traitor came from; he just did not know which one it would be. His Thema would find out for him.

Thema was delighted to serve her king after he explained to her what he was looking for. They both entered the female servants' quarters with a couple of guards. Thema knew what she was looking for as well. She walked into the dim area of the servant quarters. Everyone she walked by bowed without any eye contact. They even lowered their entire bodies to the floor with their eyes looking at the floor. Not one servant looked at any of the group in the eye except one. Thema walked by the old head servant Eman, who was treating the wounds on poor Safiya. When Thema closely walked by, Eman stood up by Safiya's bed. She did not bow, nor did she turn her eyes away to show her respect. Thema stopped and turned directly in front of Eman and stepped right up to her so she was only an inch away to show dominance. This was usually all it took to have a servant cower, but Eman stood tall and strong and did not step back. Thema found out who the traitor was, and it did not even take one word. She turned to her husband and pointed to Eman. "This one here, she is the one."

All the servants gasped and cried as the guards took their beloved Eman away. They all understood why. They were all aware of what was happening and why. They all had to keep their mouths shut and try to keep trudging along with the usual routine. The king and his people could not discover what was happening underground among the Anubi tribe. Eman had volunteered to be the scapegoat. She volunteered to take the fall for the missing prisoners so the others of their tribe could organize a revolt. Eman walked out of the servants' quarters with her head held high. She did not look left or right, just straight ahead with a small grin on her face. Everything was going according to plan. The king had to fall, and fall he would.

Senepol did not waste any time; in his anger, he felt he had to reestablish his superior dominance by having a public execution. This way, he would prove to all others of the Anubi tribe that going against his rule would have their lives end swiftly. He had his guards round up all the servants and commoners from the palace and the surrounding area as they could find within such a brief time. His guards led Eman up onto the outside platform they used for speeches, announcements, and special rituals. All the Anubians that the guards had gathered had spears at their backs, and they had to stand at the front of the platform to see the execution of one of their beloved elders.

    The guards circled around the crowd so no one would leave or revolt. The king stepped forward and aggressively addressed the crowd with his deep, booming voice, "Take heed, this servant has turned against her king and the laws of the goddess." King Senepol pounded his chest and snorted at the crowd. "Today is an example of what will occur if any other Anubi conspires against myself or the royal family, without trial and by my hand." Senepol turned to one of the guards, who handed him a sharp large blade. The guard standing behind Eman forced Eman onto her knees by kicking out her knee. She almost fell over with her hands tied, and the kick at her knee for her to kneel was not gentle. The witnesses all snapped and growled in unison and surged forward slightly. All the guards pointed their spears at them and forced the crowd back. The king stepped toward the left side of Eman. He raised the large blade to his left. Without hesitation, he swung down in a sharp straight slash directed at Eman's neck. Just as the king slashed down his blade to end the old servant's life, Eman yelled out, "Avenge me!"

11

Bree aroused to find herself slumped over a horse that was riding at a fast pace. She bounced around uncomfortably as she lay on her stomach across the beast's back. She could sense that someone was keeping her from slipping off by holding on to her. Dust and sand were flying in her hair and face, entering every orifice that was open. She coughed and sputtered as she tried to cover her face with her hands to keep the sand from scraping at her face and choking her when she breathed. She felt strong arms raise her up and position her upright so she was riding sidesaddle. Bree, confused for a moment, tried to clear the cobwebs from her mind. Like a lightbulb turning on, she quickly remembered exiting the dungeon tunnel and then… It was like she had been struck by lightning by how fast she jumped off the mount. Jabar did not have time to catch her in his shock at how fast she moved. Meanwhile, Bree was tumbling hard through the sand after her unexpected bail, as they were moving at quite a fast speed. Jabar yelled ahead for the young Anubi to stop as he, too, pulled on the reins of his mount. As Jabar dismounted and turned to see what had happened to Bree, she shocked him when he saw her up and running the opposite direction of them. The young Anubi ran up to Jabar and laughed. "What in the goddess's name is she doing?"

Jabar shrugged and sighed; they needed to get a move on and put miles between them and Senepol's soldiers before nightfall. "Go get her, please."

The young Anubi nodded and then ran after the woman. When he caught up to her, he did not try to stop her; instead he jogged beside her easily as she struggled through the sand. "Why are you running back in the direction of the palace that you just escaped from?"

Bree stopped in her tracks and quickly turned to the young Anubi. "Keep those disgusting atrocities away from me." Bree shivered and started scratching all over her skin as if she had bugs crawling on her.

The young Anubi laughed and pointed at the scarabs. "Who? Oh, do you mean, Pepi and Azizi? Those two are gentle giants, they are. Had a hand in raising them myself with my Siido before he died. They won't hurt you."

Bree scoffed. "Don't care. Don't believe you, and don't even think that I will be getting back on one of those nasty beasts, hand raised or not."

Jabar called out to them about what was taking them so long. The young Anubi raised his hands up in the air and pointed to their mounts then pointed back at the woman, shaking his head vigorously. Jabar breathed in deeply, trying to be patient. He understood by the Anubi's sign language that Bree had an issue with their mounts. Jabar shook his head in frustration as they could not lose any more time. He grabbed a rope from out of the side bags attached to the saddle. He tied a lasso loop on one end, and the other end he tied to the saddle. He did not want to do this, but he felt he had no choice especially with the sun getting higher in the sky.

Bree noticed Jabar mount back up on the giant beetle, turn it, and head their way. She started to hyperventilate. All she could see was the beasts' beady eyes staring at her and its snapping pinchers coming directly toward her. She screamed and started to slowly run in the other direction again. She struggled as she hit a deeper part of a sand dune, but she kept trying. She suddenly saw a loop of rope fall over her head, and then she instantly stopped. She tripped backward slightly as the beast stopped in its tracks. She knew what Jabar had done; he lassoed her like she was cattle. She was not going back near or on those brutes no matter what. She refused to turn around, too terrified to find out if the monster was close to her or not. Jabar spoke up, "Are you going to be civil about this, or am I going to have to drag you? We are wasting time."

Bree shrugged. "You are going to have to drag me."

Without hesitation, she felt a sudden tug as she dragged back against the sand. She screamed in disgust. She did not think Jabar would actually do as he had threatened.

The young Anubi mounted his scarab and followed Jabar, laughing the entire time as he watched the woman struggle to stay above the sand as she skidded like a broken sled none too gently. This was such a hoot. He had not had this much entertainment since he had terrified Safiya with a mouse. The Maahe proved to be one with whom you did not mess with. Bree screamed and yelled curses in Jabar's name until he finally stopped. He turned on the saddle and shouted, "Are you willing to mount up, or are you wasting my time?" Before Bree could answer, the young Anubi rode up close to Bree with his scarab, not thinking that this would disturb her. Bree turned toward the noise, and out she went. It was now Jabar's turn to curse a little. "Bring her here, young one. I will tie her to the saddle so she can't jump off again." As the Anubi brought the woman's limp form to Jabar, he said to him as he handed her up. "I'm Darius, by the way."

Jabar nodded. "I am Jabar."

Darius gasped. "No way. You're the great Jabar? You're lying to me!"

Jabar raised his brow and rumbled out. "Darius, I never lie."

Darius jumped excitedly up and down a couple times. "I can't believe I am on a mission with the great warrior Jabar. Wait till my friends hear about this."

Jabar chuckled. "I am not so great at the moment with these wounds. Let's be off, young Darius. The day is getting away from us. We have to get to one of my secluded hideouts for the night."

Darius hooted, "Jabar's secret hiding spots! No one is going to believe this!" Darius vaulted back onto Azizi. "Lead the way, great warrior Jabar." Jabar chuckled; never in his wildest dreams did he ever think he would have a young Anubi admirer. He tied Bree tightly to the saddle so she was close to the right side of his chest so she couldn't jump off again or lean on his wound. They headed off in the direction of the secluded area that he had used before on his raids. He needed to get to it fast; his wound on the left side was causing him pain, and he was losing a vast amount of blood from all his movements. He needed rest desperately. He was fading fast. He never let on to Darius how bad off he was so the poor boy would not panic or, worse, insist on heading back for help.

Just as he was forcing himself to stay awake, he felt a sudden jerk coming from Bree. He wrapped his good right arm around her so she wouldn't struggle too much and whispered in her ear, "Please don't struggle. I've got you and you're safe. If you struggle any more, I will fall off, and you will be tied to the scarab all alone."

Bree instantly stopped moving. There was no way she would be alone on this beast while tied to it. Bree felt warm wetness on her left side and turned her head to see why. She gasped when she realized it was blood, and it was so bad that she had it all over her. "Jabar, your wound, it's bleeding really bad. We have to stop and patch you up. You need rest."

A soft rumble came from Jabar's chest. "It's only a ways farther, and then we can hide for the night. Then I will rest." Bree nodded and closed her eyes. She had fainted twice already today, and that was very embarrassing. She did not want to see what it was she was riding on, so she focused on the strong warm arm wrapped around her and pretended that she was on a large horse with a prince in shining armor behind her. It seemed to work; she did not black out a third time.

"We're here," Jabar said quietly as they came to a stop by an outcropping of large rocks. Jabar slid off slowly and groaned. He had Darius come over and untie Bree as he just didn't have the energy to do it. She kept her eyes closed as Darius helped her off the mount. Just as she stepped her feet on the ground, she heard something heavy fall onto the sand. Darius released Bree and expressed concern. "Jabar, Jabar, are you okay?"

Bree realized that it had been Jabar's falling body that had made the heavy falling sound. Her eyes flew open, and suddenly she was not worried about the giant scarab standing right beside her; all she focused on now was Jabar. "Jabar, tell me where we are to go! You can't die on us now. We are so close to the spot for us to hide. Jabar, please." She bent low to his face and listened to feel and hear if he was still breathing. Darius was pacing beside them back and forth with his hand on his forehead. When she could feel that Jabar was still breathing, she exhaled, not realizing that she had been holding her breath. Jabar's large hand gently clasped onto Bree's forearm as he weakly said, "The rocks, large crack, tunnel." Then it was Jabar's turn to pass out.

"Jackal boy, help me. Go to the rocks. Find a big crack behind them. Jabar said there is a tunnel under there. When you find it, then you have to come back and help me get Jabar inside."

Darius nodded, happy to have a distraction by doing something. Within minutes, he came back with a big smile on his face. "I found it. It's amazing. If I didn't know what to look for, I would have never seen it. It's a great hiding place for the night. I took a lamp down there already so we can see where we are going." She just nodded and directed the young Anubi to help her drag Jabar to the rocks. It took them a while with careful maneuvering to get him, as muscular and heavy as he was, into the large crack in the rocks. Bree would have never been able to move him if she had been alone, and she could not stop thanking the Anubi the whole time. Each time she did thank him, he blushed. After they entered the cracks in the rocks to the left, there was a crawl space just big enough for one as large as Jabar to crawl through. On the other side of the small tunnel, the floor began to slope down quite a bit, which made it easier for the two to slide Jabar instead of having to pull him. At the bottom, it opened up into a large cave. It was obvious that someone had stayed in the cave before, as there were a couple of bedrolls, a fire pit, utensils, and tools lying about. Darius whistled as he inspected the cave. "This is amazing. No one will find us here."

Suddenly Bree had a startling thought. "What about the mounts? If they are seen, we will surely be found."

Darius laughed. "Oh right, I almost forgot about my pets. I'll deal with them right away. You can stop calling me Anubi. My name is Darius." Then Darius disappeared back up the tunnel chuckling to himself as he heard the woman saying to herself, "Stupid, stupid, of course he has a name."

They had placed Jabar on one of the bedrolls, and Bree used the other bedroll for a pillow under his head. He groaned a bit but still never woke up. After Bree made sure he was comfortable, she went in search of something to clean his wound with and something to bind them with. She had to stop the flow of blood and try to clean up the wound so it would not become infected. Bree found a canteen that thankfully was still almost full of water. She also found a bag full of long bandages. Luckily, Jabar had left all this stuff behind, thinking he may need to use it again. *Smart man to be so prepared for the potential future,* she thought to herself. She cleaned up his wound as good as she could and then wrapped a fresh binding around his abdomen. He was so wide and so muscular it was a workout, but she made it happen. As she finished binding Jabar's major wound and cleaned up more, Darius came back down with a couple more packs. "Azizi and Pepi are down for the night. They're trained to burrow deep into the sand until needed. No one will find them. I'm starving. I'll make us a fire, and then we can eat." Bree nodded again and took the time to sit back and observe Jabar.

It seemed surreal how easy it had been for her to become relaxed around all these hybrid beasts. If someone would have told her a week ago that she was going to experience all this in detail, she would have driven them to the loony bin herself and had 'em locked up with the key thrown away forever. Here she was living in that very bizarre, unbelievable mess. Bree snapped out of her thoughts when Jabar groaned and then hissed in his sleep. She moved closer to his head and put her hand on his massive chest. "Jabar, it's Bree. We are in your hideout. We are safe. You are safe." She did not even realize that she was gently stroking his mane with her other hand. In his coma, he slightly turned his head toward her comforting strokes.

Bree took this time to really study Jabar. His mane was thick as it covered his entire head and around his neck and partially on his shoulders. He had the front of his mane below his ears braided and held together with beaded leather straps. His mane also traversed partially down the center of his back in a thin strip to his tail. His ears were that of a lion, but his entire body was that of a human; however, there was a soft short fur covering his entire body. His hands were human shaped with five fingers, but he had claws that could retract and extract when he needed. He also had thicker longer fur on the backs of his elbows and down the back of his forearms. His legs were human until the upper ankle; here is where they turned more into elongated paws with sharp claws at the end of his toes. His coat color was a silky fawn, and his mane, elbows, and tuff on his tail were a shade darker, like a milk-chocolate shade. His chin and around his mouth were lighter in a cream tone, and his whiskers were on the shorter side. He was massive in size comparison to herself, but he was not anywhere near the gigantic size as King Senepol. Jabar had a leaner musculature that was not as bulky. His physic was more to the likes of an MMA fighter's build than a bodybuilder. Bree noted scars he had under his thin fur. Now he would be adding more to that number from all his new wounds if he survived.

Bree was just thinking how beautiful Jabar was when Darius cleared his throat. "I hate to interrupt your staring at the warrior, but the meal is ready." Was that a slight tone of jealousy Bree heard in the young jackal's voice? She turned and smiled at Darius, wondering if he was jealous of her or of Jabar. The smile she gave Darius made him blush again and look away, which made her realize he was smitten with her. She shook her head in wonder at how these creatures found her attractive in any way since she looked nothing like them. *Was it the human side coming out in them?* she wondered. Now it was her time to blush. Wasn't she just thinking how beautiful Jabar was? It suddenly dawned on her; she found an attraction to Jabar physically. *How very strange.* She accepted a large chunk of meat and flatbread from Darius and ate as she sat in deep thought about this. She liked what she saw in Jabar. This was strange, as she never felt this way about Derrick at all, and he was absolutely gorgeous. Aston was extremely attractive as well, but as soon as she realized what he was, that attraction died instantly.

"How is the meat? Did I cook it too much?" Darius was staring at her, and she again snapped out of her deep thoughts. She was mindlessly munching on the meat without even thinking about it. She looked down at the meat she held in her hands and realized that it was rare, exceedingly rare. She much preferred medium rare but would never insult Darius this way since he went through all the trouble to make them a meal. "Darius, right now this is the best hunk of meat I have ever tasted. Thank you."

Darius seemed delighted and moved closer to her, and as they ate, the young Anubi entertained her with stories of how his Sitto taught him how to cook before she passed away, which led to more tales of his life. Bree sat and listened to Darius and watched him as he spoke and reached a conclusion—Darius was a delight. He had an amazing sense of humor and was a wonderful storyteller. He had a knack for keeping you hanging on till the end of his conversations and leaving you wanting him to tell you more. He was easy to talk to and open to questions. He had a habit of shrugging his shoulders and talking with his hands as he shifted his pointed ears flat, up, or forward depending on what it was he was talking about. He was cheerful as he smiled and laughed often. His eyes sparkled whenever he talked about his family and his friends or something that interested him. Through the conversation, Darius informed Bree that he would be eighteen soon. He was excited to celebrate his maturity ceremony at the end of the season. Finally, Bree realized she had never told him her name and interrupted him. "Darius, I am so sorry for earlier with your pets. My name is Bree." Darius's ears pointed straight up when she reached out her hand. He was about to hand her more meat when she stopped him with a giggle. "Give me your hand. This is how my people introduce us." Darius took her hand, and she shook it with a steady pump as she said, "It is very nice to meet you, Darius."

Bree had to giggle to herself after her introduction. Darius started back into his story about his maturity ceremony. He made sure she was very aware that this meant he was able to mate and take on the responsibilities of a meaningful relationship all the while shifting closer to her as he spoke. Bree slapped the boy on his shoulders and stood up when he got a little too close with his thigh touching her crossed knee. "Excellent meal, Darius. I need to see if Jabar will drink a bit of water. Do you mind if I take the rest of the broth? This may help Jabar's healing if he will be able to swallow it."

Darius's ears flattened, and he shrugged his shoulders. "Sure." He then moved over to the opposite side of the fire and sulked a little. Bree shook her head and smiled to herself. *Oh, the woes and hormones of a teenager. Poor kid. If I am here long enough, I will have to find him a pretty young jackal to take his mind off me.*

12

They ended up staying in the cave for six days. The first two nights were touch-and-go with Jabar. He developed a terrible fever. They listened to him yell out names with immense emotions. He jabbered and moaned for two days and nights, which broke Bree's heart. Darius was concerned for him as well. He left the cave on occasions to get away for a breather. It disturbed Darius to see such a strong warrior fighting for his life and being entirely vulnerable. Bree thought they were going to lose him. She stayed up both nights trying to keep him cool with a damp rag and dripping what water and broth they could down his throat without choking him. Bree cleaned and redressed his wounds as gently as she could without moving him too much. He was a fighter and a survivor. His fever broke by the third night, with herself and Darius taking shifts caring for Jabar so each of them could receive well-deserved rest in between. On the fourth day, Jabar awoke from his fevered coma.

He was able to take in larger amounts of water and broth on his own. All his wounds were healing well except the one under his left rib cage. This needed medication and medical attention. It was just too deep to heal on its own. The fifth day, Darius was getting stir-crazy, and Jabar was getting slightly upset at all Bree's fawning over him. Normally he did not have to have anyone take care of him but himself. Darius had the energy of an Energizer Bunny, so Bree had to continuously send him out of the cave on scouting missions to see if anyone was around or coming near to finding them. She would ask him to go take care of Pepi and Azizi or to gather wood, food, and water just so they would have a break from his continuous pacing, chattering, and more pacing. During the times that Darius was out of the cave, Bree and Jabar talked, learning about each other's stories and lives.

Jabar asked Bree to tell him in detail her story of how she came to be in his dimension again. Bree told him everything in minute detail compared to the first time. She left nothing out. She told him her story right from the moment Derrick picked her up for their date at the museum up till the moment she was in the cell beside him. After her tale was complete, Jabar contemplated for a while about all he had heard. For a strange reason, no matter how irrational her story seemed, he believed every word of it. He now realized that Bree was a tragic victim in their tale as well. He didn't genuinely believe her full innocence at first when she tried to convince him she was innocent in the dungeon, but he believed her now. His warrior's heart was softening toward her. He was extremely grateful for her saving his life and for all her dedicated attention she dispensed to him these last days, keeping him alive.

He knew not why, but it disturbed Jabar how men had used Bree recently. He thought how the men that forced her here as well as her brutal treatment from King Senepol. He watched her closely when she was telling him about what had occurred the last few days. He had come to admire Bree for not losing her faculties with all that happened to her. He understood why men lost their reasoning after being around her. Even poor Darius panted like a pet begging for attention whenever he was around her. It was amusing at first, but now he wanted to swipe the teen away whenever he came near her. She was unbelievably beautiful. Sometimes he would catch himself staring at her when she was busy doing something around the cave, even as dirty as they all were. Her hair was eye-catching. It was long with soft wavy black flowing locks. He had never seen hair such as hers. Mind you he had never seen anyone such as her before.

He wanted nothing more than to run his hands through her hair when she bent over caring for his wounds. She smelled wonderful to him too. He would catch himself breathing in deep when she was near and her hair fell on his face. Her eyes were her best feature. They were the most beautiful dark blue that sometimes they seemed purple. He had never seen eyes of such color before. When he was in his cell in the king's dungeon and he saw her brought in, her beauty amazed him every time he looked at her, even though he was near dying. She instantly reminded him of the statue in his village's small shrine of the goddess Neferneferuaten. He could completely understand why King Senepol and his people believed the tale about her being the goddess returned, especially since they had a fifth obelisk with them.

If he had been in better shape, he would have tried to distract Senepol from hurting her. When he heard how Senepol was planning to torture her, he about vomited with deep-seeded anger and disgust. His battle with the king had been long. This last encounter with Senepol had almost killed him. Senepol had been obsessed for years trying to get his hand on the other obelisks. This obsession had caused battles between all the tribes. So many lives were lost for Senepol's desire to dominate all the tribes. Senepol repulsed Jabar. He had lost his entire family and hunting village for the reason that Senepol attacked in his search to obtain an obelisk. Senepol and his soldiers violated his temporary hunting village, thinking one of the obelisks was hidden there. It was a sudden raid; not one in the village was prepared when the soldiers stormed in. They demolished the village and murdered every being within it, even the livestock. Jabar had been away on a lone hunting excursion the day his village was attacked. He returned from his successful hunt with a fallow deer, a couple of antelope, and a gazelle tied to his mount, only to find everything burning and all the death and destruction the soldiers and Senepol had left.

His entire village was completely destroyed. For half a day he stumbled around looking for any survivors. There was no one left alive. He found his entire family in their temporary hut, their throats cut. He sat on the floor in the middle of his deceased family holding the lifeless body of his little baby sister in his arms. He cried; he screamed and roared in sorrow for the rest of the day and throughout the night. Deprived of any rest, he spent the next few days burying the dead alone. After he buried his friends and villagers, he saved the burial of his family for last. He buried his father, mother, his two younger brothers, and lastly his, tiny baby sister. After the burials, he allowed himself time to mourn for them for days. This was when Jabar transformed. He became savage, full of hatred. He cursed Senepol's name over and over. He had no hopes or dreams for his life anymore except vengeance. So, for the last five years of his life, he became a vigilante assassin. He slaughtered Senepol's soldiers as they performed the king's dirty deeds in the dead of the night silently. He killed countless amounts of Senepol's spies, soldiers, and followers over the years.

Jabar had become a severe thorn in the side of King Senepol, thus becoming his number one enemy. Due to Jabar's interference, he thwarted Senepol's raids before they could happen. Jabar obtained followers that believed in his cause, as they had also lost loved ones by Senepol's orders. They were willing to help spy for him and help him with whatever it was they could. What had landed him in Senepol's dungeon was hearing about strange visitors and another obelisk. A spy he had trusted for years had communicated to him about how Senepol had gotten ahold of an unknown obelisk and that it had been delivered to him by the goddess Neferneferuaten herself. Jabar had to find out the truth himself. If this information his spy had given him, he desperately had to get that obelisk away from Senepol.

The spy Jabar had trusted revealed himself to be a double agent. This Jabar found out too late. His spy had explained how one could slip into the temple secretly. Jabar set out alone with minimal preparations with the information his spy had given him. Sadly, when he crept to the area the spy had said to enter, ten soldiers were lying in ambush. Jabar was able to kill three of the soldiers before a sword gravely wounded him in his side. The soldiers dragged him into the dungeon, and then Senepol beat him to a pulp with his own hands. Then Senepol warned him with intense pleasure that he would face execution after he had another beating within an inch of death again. To Jabar's luck, Senepol had to deal with an urgent matter and left before he could follow through with his last threat. The Anubi began their attack on the royal food stores. The Anubi had saved his life for the moment.

When Jabar completed telling Bree about his village, his quest, and why he ended up in the dungeon, she was fuming, so she said,

"I want to join you. To help you. I want to find the missing obelisks that Aston and Derrick stole. I know they are planning something diabolical and evil. Aston and Derrick are in search of the other obelisks too, I am sure of it. You mentioned obelisks, as in more than one. I know of two. You mentioned Senepol thought your village had another obelisk as well. I saw two more spaces indented beside the two obelisks in Senepol's temple. Are there actually two more besides the one Senepol thought your village had?"

Jabar nodded. "Yes, there are four in total. Well, at least that is what I understood. Now, there seems to be five."

Bree frowned and moved closer to Jabar. In her wanting to learn about the obelisks, she placed her hand on his arm and began softly stroking it. Jabar realized that she didn't realize what she was doing as she asked in thought, "Where are the other three?"

Jabar creased his forehead in thought for a moment. Her touch was very distracting, but he did not want her to stop. He took a deep breath in and told himself to concentrate. He had to describe this carefully so she could understand his people's history as he had learned it. "Our land split into four realms eons ago. It was not this way in the beginning. All eight tribes lived in peace and harmony together. There was one central city with all the surrounding lands shared for hunting and gathering equally. Over time, the Apis tribe began to believe they were more significant, more valuable than the other seven tribes.

"The Apis felt they should be ruling overall. The Anubi tribe had joined with Apis as Apis had convinced the Anubi that they would split the ruling together. This was a falsehood, but at the time, the Anubi believed they would rule side by side with Apis. Apis developed a belief that it was their birthright to be the rulers. Apis also demanded control of the 'keeping of the sacred obelisks.' They tried but did not convince the other tribes that they were the strongest and most capable tribe to govern everyone. All the tribes always shared the energy of the obelisks. Of course, the other six tribes became enraged.

"The Apis and the Anubi were two of the strongest tribes physically, other than my tribe. It was six against two. No side was victorious, only death and destruction occurred for years. The six tribes against Apis and Anubi ruling decided it was best to separate. This occurred when other tribes within the six began to inquire why they should not be leaders too. Before everything turned into greater chaos, the elders of the tribes decided for all tribes to survive, then separation it must be. Two tribes were sent to the north, two to the west, two to the east, and two to the south. The drawn-out battle had virtually destroyed the city. When the tribes separated and went their own ways, the city was deserted and in ruins.

"The elders decided one tribe that was strong and could hunt and protect would merge with one tribe that was intelligent, wise, and spiritual. The elders decided each two tribes would have one obelisk. This was so one tribe would not be able to have total control over another. So, Senepol's tribe, the Apis (bull) and the Anubi (jackal), which Darius is born to, have obelisk number one. The Sakhmets (cat) and my tribe, Maahe (lion), we have the second. The Sobek (crocodile) tribe and the Aspis (snake) have the third. Finally, the Heru (falcon) tribe and the Ibis (crane) have the fourth." Jabar stopped Bree's fingers from trialing up and down his arm and held her hand in his as he thought for a moment and then continued.

"Every tribe has their obelisk secretly hidden. Only certain few individuals within each tribe know where their obelisk is. No tribe knows where the other tribes have theirs hidden. When Senepol came to power, he decided to brag of his strength and told all the tribes that his obelisk would from now on remain in his temple. He challenged anyone who dared to come and take it if one could. He specified that he was going to seek out the other obelisks and finish what his ancestors had started." Jabar squeezed Bree's fingers, and she looked at their very two different hands. It mesmerized her for a while as she noted the size difference and the shapes of his fingers with the claws. His were terribly like human hands, but there were claws where nails should have been, which fascinated her. She came out of her trance when he began talking again.

"I don't know where my tribe's obelisk is hidden or where to even begin. We will have to take a trek to the village of Khemi. This is where the eldest of our tribe lives. They can entrust us with the knowledge of who knows the whereabouts of the obelisk. We will have to explain to them what has transpired with Senepol and your arrival. I know from experience that Senepol cannot obtain more than the one obelisk he already has. He is powerful enough with the one. With that kind of power within the obelisks together, anyone who does not bow down to his rule he will deal with by using swift, malevolent violence, more so than he already has. For all the tribe's sake, I must stop him."

Bree was about to ask Jabar a question when Darius burst into the cave at that moment out of breath. "I spotted six of Senepol's soldiers just south of here. It looks as if they are coming this way. The mounts are under the sand in wait. I tried to get rid of any prints I could find if they get too close." Darius began to pace in worried anxiety. "What should we do if they discover us?"

Jabar winced as he sat up straight and tried to get up, but he wavered with dizziness. Bree was instantly in front of him and demanded that he sit back down. "What do you think you are doing? You are in no condition get up to even think about trying to protect us." Jabar was about to retaliate but saw the look of utter determination in Bree's eyes, so he sat back down with a growl. Bree turned to Darius. "Find dead dense brush to cover the hole to the cave. Cover the entrance fully so even if one enters the crack and under the rock shelf, they will think it is just dead brush against the cave wall." Darius just stared at her for a moment. "Go, go, go, Darius! Get it done." He looked over to Jabar, who nodded. Darius nodded back and spun on his heels to complete the task Bree had given him. Bree put out the small fire and brought anything they needed near Jabar's bedding so they would not have to search for it when the cave became too dark to see anything. She handed Jabar a small ax. When Jabar grabbed the tiny ax in his large hands, he tilted his head toward Bree and raised his brows. Bree half smiled in apology and shrugged her shoulders. "This is all we have for a weapon other than Darius's spear and this knife. Let us pray we do not need them."

Jabar growled in frustration but shook his head as he silently chuckled to himself. He saw the humor in their dilemma too. One tiny female with a knife, a teenage Anubi with a spear, and an injured

Maahe with a small ax. This is what they had to protect themselves against deadly Apis soldiers. If he didn't chuckle, he would be extremely concerned right now. With his injury, he could not defend his little group like he wanted to, but if the soldiers did find them, he would die trying.

Darius came back down to the cave in a rush with his finger in front of his mouth. For an instant, Bree reflected on how the *sshh* sign seemed universal. Then suddenly, they could hear deep voices talking. Along with the voices, they could hear sounds of setting up camp right under the outcropping of the rock shelf just beside the crack where the mouth of the cave hid from view. Bree scrambled to Jabar with Darius right beside her. Jabar put out the one torch that remained lit. They all huddled together in complete darkness, silent and in immense trepidation. Bree was even scared to breathe and was sure that anyone in the near vicinity could hear the pounding fear coming from her heart. The talking from the soldiers echoed loudly down into the cave as if the soldiers were standing right beside the group of escapees huddled in silence.

One of the soldiers must have dropped something heavy onto the side of the rock shelf near the entrance of the cave opening, as it sounded as if a large boulder was coming down the small descent of the cave entrance. Bree managed not to scream, but her entire body convulsed, and a small whimper snuck out of her lungs. Suddenly strong warm arms grabbed her around her torso and brought her closer to a large warm body. The arms held her tight as she leaned into Jabar. He rested his chin on top of her head, and he started to purr deep in his chest ever so slightly. This calmed Bree instantly, making her feel safe. She curled up quietly into the warmth of Jabar's body without pushing onto his wound. Bree could feel Darius trembling beside her as he sat a little off to her left. His breathing sounded like a strangled cat. Her heart reached out to him as she remembered that he was still so noticeably young. Her motherly instinct kicked in, and without a second thought, she reached over with her hand and gently pulled him into her body like Jabar had done with her. He accepted this without hesitation. He rested his large jackal head on her lap. As she stroked the soft fur on his neck, his trembling lessened, and his strangled breathing stopped. There the three huddled in deathly silence, comforting each other with their embraces as they waited for the worst scenario to occur.

*****

Ignorant of the three stowaways only a meter or so below them, Senepol's soldiers set up camp after a long day of scouting for Jabar's group as well as for Derrick and Aston, who stole the king's obelisks. Senepol's soldiers were exhausted. The last five days of nonstop searching depleted their energy. Tonight, they decided to relax. They set up camp in a secluded area in the middle of the desert at an outcropping of rocks, planning on a relaxing night since the entirety of Senepol's kingdom was out searching for the thieves and the escapees. This was the first night the soldiers decided that they would take a night to regenerate. It had been a week of continuous searching with only an hour here and an hour there to rest. They figured without Senepol close, they deserved one night off. Then they would continue with the search in the morning.

The soldiers lit a large fire and began roasting up large desert locusts they had hunted earlier. If Bree had seen the size of these locusts, she would have fainted on sight again, as they were as big as a medium-sized dog. The soldiers laid out their bedding and then sat around the fire to eat their meal. As they ate, they talked, joked, and boasted with each other, not knowing that there were three sets of ears listening to everything. When the soldiers ate their fill, they began to talk about the next day's plans. They argued among themselves on where they would go next to continue their search. Finally, the leader of their small group roared above the rest of the group, "Enough, you idiots. We will head to the forgotten city. They may be there if they aren't dead already. Jabar's wounds were great after Senepol had his way with him. I was surprised he was even breathing after we threw him into the dungeon. The imposter goddess would not be able to survive out here alone without help. She may even be dead already."

One of the other soldiers interrupted the lead soldier, "I would help the imposter goddess survive, at least for one night, in order to have her warm my bed." All the soldiers roared with agreement and slapped each other on their backs as they all began to speak about what they would do to Bree if they had her for a night.

Down in the cave, Bree began to tremble again as she listened to the literal bullshit about her that was coming out of the soldiers' mouths, but it was more out of anger than fear. She felt like a piece of meat only there to entertain the male species in her own world. She fought against that her entire life since she turned sixteen. Now she felt the same in this realm. What was it with the male population and one-track minds? *Sex, violence, dominance, control, sex, violence, dominance, control. Rinse and repeat,* Bree thought as she shrunk deeper into Jabar's warmth a little more. Jabar became infuriated as he listened to the disgusting banter of the soldiers above. He wanted nothing more than to run them all through and cut out all their tongues for their mindless conversations about the woman he now considered a close friend. She had saved his life when she told the servant to open his cell so she could take him with her. He owed this woman his life. He felt extremely protective of her now as well as for the young Anubi that was traveling with them. They had developed a special bond together trying to survive in this little cave while he healed.

After the bantering had died down, the lead soldier began to speak again. He told the other soldiers that he decided for them to head to the forgotten city and search there for Aston, Derrick, and the obelisks. Then they would head south toward Sakhmet's and Maahe's land, as the head soldier figured if Jabar were still alive, he would try to go back to his own people and his own territory to be able to heal and get recruits. As Jabar listen to the Apis soldier, he growled low in his chest. Bree shifted her head to look up at him as she wondered what had triggered the growl, but Jabar just shook his head silently as he thought to himself. *Damn it, that was exactly what I was going to do. I have to figure somewhere else for us to hide out and recover before we try to find the obelisks.*

When the soldiers' voices all died down, the group of three hiding in the cave all dozed off, exhausted with the fear of discovery. The soldiers were up early before the sun rose and woke the three in the cave. Darius slowly snuck up to the mouth of the cave to listen. He was slightly braver now that no one had discovered them yet, and he wanted to make sure that the brush was still covering the entrance. As he crawled closer to the opening, the head of his spear knocked against the side of the rock wall and made a loud scraping sound that echoed down to Jabar and Bree. Outside the cave, one of the soldiers was hanging back from the rest as he relieved himself close to the cave entrance. He, too, heard the sound but was not sure what it was. He adjusted his armor and made his way closer to the brush at the mouth of the cave and began moving aside the dead growth. Darius cursed himself as he braced for the worst. Jabar moved as fast as he was able and was standing at the lower edge of the cave descent waiting for the worst to happen. He was still in pain, but when he heard the weapon resonate on the rock wall, he got up, grabbed the ax, and stood in wait. Bree stood behind Jabar with her knife in hand, not breathing or moving an inch as she thought, *We are so dead!*

Just as the soldier was about to move a thicker piece of dead brush aside that would have exposed the opening of the cave, another soldier called out to him, telling him to hurry up as they were all waiting for him. The soldier snorted out his muzzle and chalked the noise to a rodent or animal for making the noise he had heard coming from behind the dead brush, so he shrugged his shoulders as he turned back toward the others and walked off to his mount. Darius felt relieved; he had almost given them away with his stupid curiosity. He made his way back down to the cave, and Jabar smacked him upside the back of his head when he stood up. Bree came up to him and did the same thing, only on his arm, as he was too tall for her to reach his head. Darius shrugged his shoulders in an apologetic way as he pointed to his spear still strapped to his back. Not a word was said as they gathered what belongings they could. Before they left, they wanted to make sure that the soldiers were far enough ahead that they would not worry about coming up on them. Jabar took the time to explain the plan that he had concocted while the other two slept. He could not sleep well anyways with his mortal enemy's soldiers just meters away.

Jabar sat them all down and explained, "I was going to take us back to my tribe members so I could heal and speak to the elder. We must change plans a bit as Senepol's soldiers said last night that they are heading the way that we were to go. Now we must head west to the lands of the Heru and Ibis tribes. The Ibis tribe are extremely wise, and the Heru are sky-flying warriors that always watch their lands from the sky above. They live in the forest region, west of the forgotten city. I worry as these two tribes have no faith in any other tribe. They have kept themselves segregated from all the other tribes. Darius, I am sorry. I must demand that you stay hidden somewhere close to the edge of their forest, and Bree and I are the only ones going in."

Darius growled out as he pouted, "Why do I have to stay hidden and not Bree? Why is she allowed to go?"

Bree shoved him slightly like she would a younger brother that was not getting his way. Jabar continued, "Because, my young warrior, the Heru and the Ibis detest and kill on sight any Anubi or Apis if they are in a small group or alone that come anywhere near their lands. Your tribes are their mortal enemy, young friend.

"The predecessor before Senepol's reign declared war on the Heru and Ibis tribes because the mountains behind their forests they inhabit are ladened with gold. The king of the Apis wanted to obtain all of it. There has been war over their territory for years. Senepol has lessened the harassment and attacks on the Heru's land since he developed his obsession with collecting the obelisks, but they still detest your two tribes." Darius nodded in understanding but still pouted. Jabar slapped him gently on his back like an old friend. "Besides, I am starting to like having you around and don't want to lose you just yet."

Darius's smile was so brilliant after hearing Jabar's comment that it warmed Bree's heart, so she stood up and leaned into Darius, and before she gave him a kiss on the side of his long snout, she said, "That goes for me too, Darius. I like our little family we have created." Darius touched the area where Bree had kissed him and blushed.

The group of three slowly and carefully snuck out of the cave and had Darius scout the area before they aroused their mounts from under the sand. It amazed Bree to see the two giant scarabs greet Darius as would a dog to its master in her realm. If the scarabs had tails, they would be wagging. This show of affection made Bree swallow her fear. They did not seem anywhere near as frightening anymore. Bree still did not like them or like the fact that she had to ride on them, but it wasn't the same as it was before; she didn't feel dizzy or sick to her stomach when she had to have Darius help her up onto the back of Azizi. She did hold her breath for a while until Jabar was safely behind her. He was still stiff and slow as his wound was holding him back because of the pain, but he was in far better shape than he had been a week ago. The three of them were off and traveling away from their hiding place in the westward direction. Bree was not going to miss the confines of that cave and really hoped that she would never have to see it again. She leaned into Jabar, who placed his right arm around her so she would not slide off the mount; he even gave her a piece of cloth to tie around her nose and face like a mask to keep her from breathing in and eating all the sand that the scarabs were disturbing as they rode fast in the direction of the mountains.

13

As they traveled west, Bree was able to take in all the scenery. At first, there was not much to see but sand and outcroppings of rocks, bushes, and shrubs. Nothing too exciting. She did notice that the more they headed west, the cooler the air became. The sun was still ridiculously hot, but there was a cooler wind the closer they got to the mountains in the far distance. The landscape was slowly changing as well. There started to be more rocks and more hard-packed dirt instead of sand, and cacti were scattered everywhere. She noticed that there were sporadic clumps of grass growth as well. As Bree was blissfully taking in her surroundings out of the corner of her eye, she noticed a movement jumping toward them. Reflexes kicked in, and she automatically flinched, ducked, and closed her eyes for a moment. Jabar jolted as well. He had fallen asleep for a minute as he leaned into Bree's body with the sway of the scarab's movements. When Bree flinched and moved quickly, he did too. He was on immediate alert for danger.

Whatever it was that lunged at them landed on the other side of the scarab, at once turned its body, and launched back toward them. Jabar realized what it was. He saw that it was about to lunge again, so he raised his arm to deflect the blow that aimed to hit Bree in the head. After the second attack, Bree saw what was attacking them, and she screamed. Was everything in this damn place oversized? It jumped at her again, but this time Jabar was ready, and as it sailed past Bree's head, he managed to slice one of its legs off with the knife they had found in the cave. The leg landed in Bree's lap. The damn thing was still moving as it spasmed back and forth like it was still running. Bree didn't dare touch it as it had solid sharp spikes on the leg, and with its spasms, it was tearing into her dress and her leg.

Jabar reached around, and with his clawed hand, he grabbed it and removed it from her lap. The damn thing, even though it had lost a leg, jumped again and landed on the back of the scarab head, right in front of Bree.

Oh shit, oh shit, don't faint, Bree. Looking her straight in the face was the ugliest largest locust she had ever seen. One of its antennae was close to poking her in the eye. Its brown beady eyes bulged at the side of its head. It had a hairy face and plated exoskeleton. The worst part of it, though, was the mouth. As it stared at her, she could see the front of the mouth. It was flat like a spatula but the under jaw moved outward in two separate pieces, and in between the mandible out came the maxilla that had three finger-like attachments on each side; they were waving at her hungrily. Time seemed to stop as the locust and Bree stared at each other. As time stood still, there was a brief whistling sound followed by a crunching thwack. The locust blew off the back of the scarab, landing on the ground with a spear stuck in its side. Darius hooted with joy as Jabar stopped their mount and congratulated Darius. "Great aim, Darius, thank you for acting so fast. I don't think I could have aimed better myself."

Darius jumped off Pepi and ran toward the dead locust. "Woohoo, lunch. I haven't had a locust in a long time. Haven't seen any lately."

Bree cringed. "You're telling me that you are going to eat that."

Jabar slid off the back of the scarab and helped Bree down gingerly, protecting his side still, and then turned to Bree with a smile. "No, we are going to eat that."

*****

When the locust was on a makeshift spit, roasting over a fire, Bree went over to Darius and sat down. "I want to thank you for saving my life. That beast was going to eat me."

Darius looked at Bree strangely and then laughed heartily. "Locusts only eat plants, Bree. It wasn't going to eat you."

Bree frowned slightly. "Then why did it attack me?"

Jabar noticed the conversation and interjected, "I was wondering that myself. It was your long hair that attracted it to us. The wind had your hair blowing and the locust must have thought of your long hair as grass."

Darius laughed at Jabar's comment, so Bree slugged him in the arm. "So you think that's funny, do you! Do you know that where I come from, locusts are only the size of my pinky? Your mounts are only the size of the palm of my hand at their largest! All this is very new and foreign to me. In the last few weeks, I've been torn from my life, my job, my friends. Drugged, kidnapped, forced to open a portal, and thrown into a realm I never knew existed. I was handed over to an evil bull king. I had to lie about who I was to stay alive. Met beings that are only mythical creatures in my world, saw a battle. Betrayed by the men that forced me here in the first place. I took a beating. Then I was assaulted, thrown in a dungeon, aided to escape from said dungeon. I was dragged in the sand, made to ride on the back of a monster, hid in a cave with two male strangers who happen to be half man, half lion and the other half jackal that are both twice my size. I nursed you, Jabar, back to the living. I hid from Senepol's soldiers. Attacked by a giant locust. And now, here I am, about to eat the damn thing. I deserve just a little compassion from the both of you right now." Suddenly Bree jumped up and stormed away.

Darius and Jabar both felt guilty for trying to tease Bree. They had both become close to her and had momentarily forgotten that she wasn't from their realm. Darius went to follow Bree, but Jabar held him back. "Let me go talk to her." Jabar found Bree off by a large cactus with her arms folded across her chest with her back turned to him. When Jabar was close enough, he could hear that she was crying. Jabar's ears flattened against his head in shame. "Bree?" She jumped, startled, and spun around. Jabar was half lion and was very silent, even being the size he was. Bree quickly tried to turn away again, rubbing her tears frantically as she tried to hide that she had been crying. The stress of everything had finally gotten to her. She had been so strong until now. She hated crying, and she hated crying even more when caught doing so. Jabar came remarkably close to her back and just turned her around gently and enveloped her whole body into his as he wrapped his large arms around her, and even his tail wrapped around her legs to hold her close. He never said anything except to purr low in his chest again. The warmth of his hug had Bree outright sobbing. They stood there for a good five minutes with her bawling into his lower chest. She had cried so much that the bandaging on his wound became quite wet from her tears.

As Jabar let Bree cry out her stress, he felt a small burning sensation begin at the top of his wound, but he ignored it. He had moved this day more than he had in the last week. The burning sensation began to become stronger and more intense the longer he stood there. Bree cried on. He winced slightly, wanting to move due to the intense burning of his wound, but he held fast. He was there to comfort his friend if she needed for as long as she needed. Suddenly he could not hold back, and he hissed, causing Bree to pull away. "Oh god, did I lean on your wound?"

Instead of answering, Jabar hissed again, only this time it brought him to his knees. Bree screamed out for Darius, who was there in an instant. "What is it, Jabar? Did your wound open again?" Bree was very worried; Jabar's wound had become infected from the inside. Darius and Bree were about to try to help Jabar up when he suddenly stood up by himself with a strange look upon his face. Bree and Darius backed off a little when Jabar started to peel away his wound dressings.

"Jabar, I don't think that is a clever idea. You haven't healed and we have no more dressings." Bree was now concerned about Jabar's sudden loss of sanity, but he just kept undoing the dressing in haste. When he had all the dressing off, they all gasped in unison. The wound was completely gone, not even a scar remained, and his fur had grown back. They all stood in shock and stared at Jabar's wound sight for a good minute before Darius spoke. "It's a damn miracle!"

Jabar touched the site where the wound had been, and there was no pain; he stretched gingerly at first and then with more vigor. Still no pain. He then crouched on all fours and bolted into a fast run as a lion would in the African safari shows, chasing down prey. He was a beautiful, remarkable sight as he bolted with a speed that was inhuman. He spun back around and stopped back by the fire, where the locust was still roasting on the spit. When Darius and Bree made it back to the fire, Jabar was just standing there staring at the fire, breathing heavily from his exhilarating run. Darius again was the one that spoke first. "What the hell, Jabar? How can this be? Wounds don't just heal like that!"

Jabar kept his gaze on the fire for a moment in deep concentration. He, too, was trying to figure out how his wound had suddenly healed. He also felt in perfect health. He wasn't stiff, sore, or wounded anywhere anymore. He noticed, too, all the scabs from the beating Senepol had given him that were healing under his fur were also gone. In fact, he had never felt so healthy and fit in his life as he did right now.

Suddenly, a thought processed to completion in Jabar's mind, and it thrilled and chilled him to his bones all at the same time. If he was correct, they had to get Bree to safety and fast. If anyone else knew or found out about this, especially Senepol, everyone would then be after her. The look of concern on Jabar's face when he turned his eyes on Bree scared both Darius and Bree. Without a word, Jabar jumped toward Bree, grabbed her, and was on the mount, willing it to go as fast as he could make it go off again to the west. Darius was in shock, and all he could yell out to Jabar was "What about our lunch?"

Jabar threw a comment over his shoulder, "Bring it! We'll eat it on the way." Darius shrugged his shoulders and quickly put the cooked locus carcass in a bag and kicked dirt and sand on the fire, then he, too, jumped on his mount and rushed to catch up to Jabar.

Bree was angry as well as concerned. "What is going through that head of yours, Jabar? You're scaring me! Are the soldiers behind us? Did you catch their scent?" Jabar didn't answer at first, so Bree scrambled herself around so she was sitting on the saddle facing Jabar, who did try to stop her, but she squirmed so much he allowed her to turn when he realized she wasn't trying to jump off the mount again. Bree stared at him right in the eye with hands rested on her hips and the wind blowing her hair all around her face. For a moment Jabar thought, *Damn, she's beautiful even when she's mad.* She looked stunning. The direct sun from the east was just above their head, and it was directly on her face, making her violet eyes seem transparent. Her black hair sparkled with high lights of blue as it blew around in a wild disarray. Jabar did not let up on the speed he was making their mount travel. He was trying to ignore the gorgeous woman staring angrily at him, but he just couldn't keep the strong, silent type of facade up any longer. She deserved more than that. She deserved to hear what it was that he was thinking. Bree knew that she was going to win this battle of wits to get him to speak. She could tell by his posture as he sighed and then sagged his shoulders. His ears rounded out and became smaller in size. His beautiful amber eyes softened a little, and his cat-eyed pupils dilated slightly. When he growled at her then sighed again, she knew he would speak. "I know what healed my wounds."

"Well, don't keep me waiting. What healed your wounds?" Bree said excitedly, wanting to hear what the sudden miracle cure was.

"It was you, Bree, you healed me."

Bree frowned in frustration. *What an excuse,* she thought. *He just feels bad for teasing me.* Then she burst out laughing. "You do know how ridiculous that sounds. I did nothing of the sort, and now, I think you're crazy."

Jabar shook his head in frustration. "Bree, just hear why I have come to this conclusion."

Bree shrugged her shoulders and rolled her eyes at the same time as she sat backward on their mount, staring at him still. "Okay, Jabar, why do you think it was me that healed you?"

By this time, Darius had caught up to them. He was able to overhear what the last few comments were as he rode his mount closer beside them. "This should be good. I want to hear this too."

Jabar growled slightly, but the boy should know as well. This way they would both be vigilant in caring for Bree's safety. Now it was more important than ever.

"When we were in the cave, you told me everything about how you got here." Bree nodded and encouraged him to continue using her hands in a circular motion in front of her. "I found it interesting when you told me that the men that abducted you said they specifically needed you to open the portal while holding the obelisk." Bree rose her eyebrows and waited for Jabar to continue. He slowed the mount up a little. "Why did it have to be you?"

Bree tilted her head and thought for a moment. "They said it was my family history, supposedly being a direct bloodline to the ancient Anunnaki."

Jabar also nodded as he continued, "Exactly, these ancient Anunnaki are the same ones that taught the ancient pharaohs of Egypt how to create my people. Our goddess Neferneferuaten used that magic of ancient knowledge to create the obelisks and a portal to open a new plane of existence so our tribes could survive. Something changed her when she used that magic. It somehow changed her on the inside. When she used so much magic to get the portal created, she must have absorbed that magic into her. I don't know how to explain this in greater detail, as I am not an intelligent Maahe. This is why we must get you to the Ibis."

Jabar continued as they rode farther west, "This magic must be in your blood or your body fluids or both since you are a direct relation to the Anunnaki. Or it may be the whole of you that contains this same magic that Goddess Neferneferuaten dabbled with."

Bree shook her head. "I don't understand your logic, Jabar."

Jabar shrugged. "It may be that everyone in your family bloodline has this magic in them as well. It must be that the Anunnaki had this magical blood, and it regenerated somehow when Neferneferuaten used the magic and entered the portal. That or she had this in her all along, being a descendant of the Anunnaki herself. All this sounds crazy, but all I know is I only healed when your tears soaked my bandage, soaking into my wound. How else can you explain my sudden healing? Only when your tears touched my flesh did I heal. Not only did I heal Bree, but I have also never felt better in my entire life."

Bree leaned back a little and could see that Jabar really believed that it had been her tears that had healed him. "Well, if your theory is to be believed, the only way to prove it is to evaluate it."

Darius let out a whoop as he understood what Bree meant. "Can it be me? I will volunteer. I want to feel what you feel, Jabar."

Jabar was about to refuse, but Bree chimed in, "Great, then it's settled. We need to stop for this." Jabar sighed but did as Bree requested. He was also wanting to see if his assumption was correct.

They stood in a small circle beside the mounts when Bree reached for the knife in Jabar's belt and pulled it out. "Darius, give me your hand."

Darius was vibrating; he was so excited and held his hand out eagerly.

"This is going to hurt, as I need to cut you enough that we can see if it heals." Darius nodded quickly. "How am I going to cry, though? I need to have tears," Bree questioned.

Jabar pointed at the sun. "I know my eyes water when I stare at the sun too long." Bree realized that this happened to her as well, nodded, and turned to look up at the sun. After a second of not blinking, she began to feel like she had to sneeze. "Jabar, take the knife. I need you to do it!"

Jabar took the knife and quickly cut Darius's palm without warning him first. Darius hissed, "Oh man, did you have to cut me so deep?"

Jabar just shrugged with a smile. "You're the one that volunteered."

Bree was still looking at the sun, and her eyes were beginning to water. "Achoo!" Bree sneezed a couple more times then turned. "Darius, give me your hand." She only had one tear, but she made sure that it landed right on the center of Darius's bloody palm. They all watched and waited as they held their breath. Nothing happened. Bree was about to dismiss Jabar's idea when Darius hissed, "Oh damn, that stings, wow! Oh damn! It burns."

Darius began jumping around and waving his hand in the air when Bree scolded him, "Suck it up, Darius. We have to see if it is healing your wound. Give us your hand."

Darius reluctantly gave up his hand, and Jabar held him still as he rocked back and forth on his feet in pain.

"*Holy shit!*" Bree stood, flabbergasted. Before their eyes, the wound on Darius's hand had ceased bleeding and was mending itself back together. Darius stopped struggling, and his eyes bulged out in awe at what he was seeing. He, too, had figured that Jabar's story was just his imagination, but now he had seen it with his own eyes. Darius looked at Bree and could swear he saw an aura of light surrounding her, and suddenly he fell to his knees and bowed low to the ground with his arms out in front of him. "Goddess Neferneferuaten, it is you! You have returned to us."

Bree groaned in disgust and bent down to Darius with her hands pulling him under his arms. "Get up, you buffoon. I am no more your goddess than that cactus over there. I am just Bree Sabry from New York City who happens to have freakish healing tears, but that is it."

Darius stood up but still felt like he should be bowing or worshipping her. It was a miracle, and she had done it with a single tear. "You aren't assessing me, are you? I mean my loyalty to you!"

Bree smacked him on the chest. "Snap out of it, Darius."

Jabar watched, slightly humored, but with his suspicion confirmed, they had to get to the Ibis tribe as fast as they could. He had to keep Bree safe and as far away from Senepol as possible. "Let me talk some sense into him, Bree." Jabar grabbed Darius and forced him to walk with him just far enough that Bree would not hear the conversation he needed to have with Darius. He did not want this burden loaded onto Bree just yet. He didn't want her to be more stressed and scared than she already was.

Darius kept looking back at Bree with awe and wonder still in his expression. Jabar shook it out of him, though, physically. "Listen to me, young blood. No one, and I mean no one, can find out about Bree's healing magic. Do you understand me?" Darius nodded slightly still staring in Bree's direction. This is when Jabar forcibly shook Darius. "*No one can know!* If anyone finds out about this, they will take her from us. They may harm her or even kill her to use her blood and fluids for their own agenda. Do you want that?"

Darius snapped out of his trance-like state when he heard Jabar say that harm may come to Bree. He, too, suddenly realized with Jabar's stressing the seriousness of the matter at hand, that this was crucial to keep his new precious friend alive and safe. "I understand, Jabar. I will take this secret to my grave if it protects our Bree."

Jabar chuckled to himself. *Our Bree.* He liked the sound of that—too much.

14

The next four days and nights were simply travel and sleep. They decided to stay low by sleeping during the day and traveling in the darkness of night in order to stay as unseen as possible. They never came upon any soldiers or danger along their way, and Jabar thanked the goddess for that at least. They were all exhausted, hungry, and in great need of a bath and a change of clothing. Finally, on the fourth midmorning of arduous travel, Jabar informed them that they were closing in on the Heru and Ibis land borders. "That tree line ahead is the edge of the Heru and Ibis border. Darius, I am afraid it is time to get you hidden in a place that you may have to stay for a couple of days alone." Darius frowned but nodded. Along the way, they had hunted and roasted extra beasts so Darius would have food for the days alone without having to start a fire. Jabar pointed to their left. "See that rise over there with the large jutting ledge of rock just before the border of trees? It should suffice for you to hunker down under to stay undetected."

Darius started to head over slowly when Bree called out to him. "Darius!" Bree jumped off Azizi and ran to him. When she approached Darius, he, too, slid off his mount. Bree grabbed his large hand. "Stay hidden. I will not be able to endure it if you become captured or hurt. We will be back for you soon. I will miss you, Darius. Please stay safe for me." She then reached up, and he lowered his face to her height. She gave him a gentle kiss on his cheek. "Promise me." Darius gave her a brilliant smile. "Anything for you, Bree. I promise."

Bree smiled back and reluctantly let go of his hand and then jogged back to Jabar, who stopped the mount a little way back from them to let them have privacy. He nodded to Darius and waved as Bree mounted Azizi. "That goes for me also, young one. Stay safe."

As Darius watched the two ride away, he called out, "Take care of my Azizi." When they were out of sight as they entered the thick forest edge, Darius turned to Pepi with tears in his eyes. He realized then just how he had come to care for Jabar and especially Bree. Jabar was his hero, and Bree was more than a friend; she was an enigma to him. Darius sighed and wiped a tear away as he thought, *If only I was older. I would woo her to be my life mate.* He shook that thought out of his head and instead prayed to the goddess. *Please, keep them safe.* He already missed them, and it had only been a couple minutes. He grabbed Pepi's reins and led her to the rocks ledge and began to take off her saddle and gear so she could go underground to hide. Then he, too, hunkered down and began to wait for the return of the first best friends he had ever had.

*****

The forest was cool, dim, and shadowed compared to the glaring sun from the desert and plains. It was slightly intimidating, as anything could be hiding behind the next tree or under a fallen log. The vast difference of the land change was intense too. The openness of the lands that they just exited from into the sudden line of the forest was like a different world altogether. Bree found herself leaning back into Jabar for security. Jabar felt her anxiety, so he slid his arm around her waist firmly. Jabar's senses were all on high alert. Every opening in the trees had him looking up for anything in the sky, and his ears were constantly shifting in all directions, listening for any unusual sounds. Bree instinctively knew to stay quiet. Azizi seemed to tread on lighter footing as well. They maneuvered in and around the trees. They had to backtrack on more than one occasion, as the forest was too dense in places to accommodate Azizi's size. A couple of times they even had to dismount and have Azizi follow so they would not break branches or make too much noise by squeezing through denser areas.

They had stopped for a break in the later afternoon to have a small precooked meal of roasted locust that Bree had actually come to really like. It took her a full day to even try the roasted locust after they had killed the one that had tried to attack her hair. She had only broken down and eaten because her stomach had begun to talk to her backbone; it was that empty. She was desperately hungry. Turned out that roasted locust tasted like duck. It was oily but had a tender dark meat that had a full robust duck flavor. Bree decided that if she didn't look at what she was eating after Jabar or Darius cracked the outer shell and demembraned it for her and she closed her eyes, she could imagine that it was duck that she was eating, and she was able to stomach it. Now she really enjoyed roasted locust and could eat it without her eyes closed. Jabar and Darius had found this extremely amusing when she took her first bite, but they held in the amusement in order not to embarrass her.

While they ate, Jabar suddenly crooked his ears backward, and in an instant, he was up on all fours, crouched low with muscles bulging, ready to pounce on anything that came near if needed. A low quiet growl exited his throat. Bree instantly put her locust part down and quietly slunk in behind a tree with low branches and did not move or breathe. Then Bree heard what Jabar had heard. It was a low beating sound. As it came closer, it sounded like a large bird flapping its wings as it flew. The sound grew louder as the bird flew closer above them. Bree kept her eyes on the sky, as did Jabar, who had also hidden his large body under a tree opposite to her. Bree had to place her hand over her mouth when she suddenly spotted the bird. It was a bird, or better yet, it was an exceptionally large bird man, and not just one, but three of them. Bree could not look away as she watched as they flew overhead slightly higher than the treetops.

Bree realized they were watching three of the Heru tribe. They were in a V formation. The front flyer had black wings while the two flanking a little to the left and right of the first were brown. They all had armor on their bodies, and the span of their wings must have been at least sixteen feet across. They were massive and yet absolutely beautiful. They all flew as if attached to each other, mimicking each movement the lead flyer made as if it were their own and in exact timing. Bree watched as they disappeared out of sight along the trees, and the sound of their beating wings diminished as they flew farther away.

ARTIFACTS ALIVE

"That was border patrol." Bree squealed when Jabar spoke just off from her right ear. She hadn't even noticed him slink up beside her when the flyers passed out of sight. She turned and smacked Jabar in the chest. "Don't sneak up on me like that. Make some kind of noise so I know you are there, damn it. I almost peed a little."

Jabar chuckled at Bree's statement. "Sorry, I can't help it. It's my nature. We have to stay within the cover of the trees. There will be more patrols as we get closer to a village. I have to remind you, if they find us, do not run. Do not show any aggression. Raise your hands to show we have no weapons and get onto your knees. I hope we can make it to a village. If they find us, just do as I have instructed. We need their help, not their animosity."

"I am glad you have no weapons," a deep voice said from behind Jabar. They both spun around so fast that Bree fell into Jabar's side and knocked him over slightly. Jabar regained his ground as fast as a small cat would. He attacked in an instant as he sprang into action and leaped. But in midair, he realized who was standing there and instantly changed direction, turned his body in a spinning summersault, and landed just at their feet. Bree went face-first into the forest floor and came up sputtering rotting leaves when Jabar launched his leap attack. Then Jabar backed up slowly and placed himself in front of Bree to protect her. He knelt with his hands up and open to show that indeed he did not have any weapons. Bree peeked out from behind Jabar, still pulling leaves out of her mouth to see the three Heru that they had just watched fly over them, standing in front of Jabar with their swords pointed at them. Jabar lowered his gaze to make sure he did not look intimidating and spoke, "We come seeking an audience with your elder. We have extremely essential information to tell them about Senepol and the obelisks."

None of the Heru moved for a couple of minutes while they continued to glare at them silently. The leader never moved a muscle or his eyes from Jabar. He was the same height as Jabar but not as largely muscled. He had a sleeker toned body with tattoos of lines on his shoulders, across his midsection, down under his armor. His head had dark feathers that Bree could see under the helmet, and his eyes were like looking into a falcon that was ready to attack, with its pupils dilated to their fullest. Around his eyes was a bright yellow color that also surrounded his beak where it attached to his face as well as down half his beak. The end of his beak was black and wickedly curved. His feathers ended at his neck just above his collar bones, and that is where the man part took over until one got down to below his knees. Feathers began again as the lower leg changed back to a falcon again. His feet were taloned. He had three front talons and one in the back. His lower legs after the feathers ended were bright yellow like his eyes, and his beak with deadly sharp. He had shiny black talons that looked at least eight inches in length, if not more. All three Heru soldiers had on matching dull golden helmets and brown leather chest pieces that crossed in an X covering their pectorals. In the center of the leather straps was a large oblong golden medallion with a flying falcon supporting a red circle over its head. They all had metal bicep bands and metal bracers on their wrists. They wore large golden belts and had the same type of pleated skirt that all the other beasts wore in this realm, and they all had lower leg armor starting just below their knees to their ankles. The most impressive of all were their gigantic wings. At the moment they were folded neatly back, tucked away. The tops of the wings were over the sides of the helmets, with the end tips of the wings seen at their feet.

The leader of the three Heru finally spoke, "Move, out to the clearing." Without hesitation, Jabar slowly stood up with his hands still up at shoulder level. He turned and had Bree walk in front of him out of the trees and into a small flat field full of flowers and grass. If Bree were in a romantic mood, she would have thought how lovely this spot would have been for a picnic. When they entered near the center of the small field, the leader spoke again, "Stop. Turn around." Jabar turned but lowered his arms and reached behind him to hold Bree and keep her at his back so she wasn't in full view of the soldiers. "You have come at a very perilous time, Maahe. Why have you really come?"

Something wasn't right with the question the Heru soldier just asked Jabar. He could tell that the soldiers were on edge. So, Jabar spoke quietly and with caution, "As I stated earlier, we need to speak to your elder. It is of the utmost importance."

The head soldier pointed at Jabar and crooked his head to the right, telling him to step aside. Jabar hesitated. "Move aside, Maahe." Jabar did not move. The two smaller Heru flyers readied their swords and took a battle stance, and once more the leader said, "Move aside, Maahe, or we will make you."

Jabar's hackles rose, and he crouched slightly, baring his teeth. His ears went flat against his head, and he hissed menacingly. Bree didn't understand why Jabar was taking a defensive stance, so she grabbed on to his belt at his waist. "Jabar?" The three Heru spread out around the two, which caused Jabar to speak. "Since when have the Heru been suspicious of a Maahe?"

The lead flyer stepped back and raised his sword slightly. "Since two small men, like the woman behind you, came to our lands also saying that they have information about obelisks and Senepol. After we invited them into our homes, they attacked and gravely injured one of the elders then fled, escaping into the night like rats."

Jabar growled low; he knew something was off, and now he knew why. "A Maahe would never attack an elder of the Ibis. Our people are allies."

The lead flyer spoke just before he swung his sword and charged at Jabar. "We have no allies anymore." Jabar dodged the first deadly swing of the sword, but this caused him to trip over Bree. As Bree tried to get out of the way to give Jabar more room, Jabar realized that he could not fight them off with Bree around. He could not protect her and fight the three skilled soldiers. They also had the upper hand with weapons. He quickly planned. With the speed of light, he swung Bree onto his back as he went down on all fours, only saying, "Hang on," and then bolted with all his might back to the tree line.

Bree hung on for dear life. She grabbed ahold of his mane and entwined her fingers in tight. She could feel his muscles bunching under her thighs as he ran using every muscle he could to move as fast as he could. He was large enough that her feet didn't drag on either side of him, but even so, she ducked right down on his back with her hands in either side of his mane and her legs tucked up and back toward his haunches so she wouldn't slow him down with wind drag. She luckily had ridden horses bareback in her lifetime. It wasn't really that much different except for the massive flying falcon men that were in hot pursuit above them. As they were about to enter the trees again, one of the Heru thwarted their direction by flying over and then blocking their way to the trees. Jabar without hesitation curved sharply to his left and plowed through a mass number of tall wildflowers and petals scattered and floated everywhere. The second brown-winged soldier swooped in front of Jabar, trying to slash him with his sword in midflight, but Jabar turned a 180 on a dime once again. The soldier screeched in anger, and the echo was haunting as it bounced off the trees.

As Jabar was trying to find a way back to the trees, Bree just happened to look up, only to scream out Jabar's name just as the leader of the flyers swooped down and grabbed on to Bree's arms with his talons. With a swift tug, Bree was off Jabar's back. Jabar twisted in midrun as he felt Bree's weight leave him, and he tried to grab her legs to pull her back down to him, but he was a split second too slow. He slammed into the hard ground on his back, but in an instant, he was up again and running after Bree as the falcon climbed higher into the air with Bree dangling below him. The last thing Jabar heard was Bree screaming for him to "look out," and then there was only darkness as the hilt of a sword slammed hard against the back of his head. The brown-winged Heru picked Jabar up and flew into the air with a flyer wrapping his talons around both Jabar's arms and the other flyer on his ankles. It took them longer to gain height as Jabar was much heavier than Bree. They flew toward the mountains to the village that housed the dying elder of the Ibis.

*****

Meanwhile, Darius sat under the rock ledge, gnawing on a leg bone of an antelope they had caught earlier that week. He wasn't really hungry, but he was severely bored. He also felt uneasy. Something was gnawing at the back of his brain just like his lunch. He could not quiet his brain. He tried to have a nap, but again his mind would not shut off. He kept having flashes of Bree and Jabar getting into trouble or caught in a trap of some kind. He wondered how they were faring in the trees and what kind of wildlife was in there that he could one day hunt. He had never been this far west. Actually, he had never left the land that he had been born in. He had heard stories told by the travelers that came to his village, but he had never left himself. Trees fascinated him. He had never seen trees like this, only a couple of palm trees here and there. These ones were so big and tall. He wanted so much to climb one to see if he could see for miles around at the tops.

He had to talk himself out of leaving his hiding spot a couple times already. *I promised Bree that I would stay hidden and stay safe. Just a couple of days. You can do this, Dar! Prove to Jabar that you are an adult now, who listens. You are not a kid who thinks he knows better anymore.* Darius got up and did on-the-spot jumping and then began to run on the spot till he began to sweat. Sitting around was never a highlight in his life. He was always doing something, like getting himself into mischief, teasing his siblings if he wasn't helping on the farm, training Pepi and Azizi, or learning how to be a great hunter.

Running on the spot for a while had him sweating good now. He was about to lie down to try to snooze again when he heard quite a ruckus coming from the forest area in the same spot that Bree and Jabar had faded into. Darius's heart began to pound, and he lay low on the ground behind tall grass by the rock shelf. The noise was becoming louder. It sounded as if something large was crashing through the trees, coming closer to the spot he was hiding. Random thoughts were popping into Darius's head as he tried to figure out what could be making such a noise. Was it a large beast he had never seen before? His Giddu used to tell him that there were large deer in the forests as well as massive rats bigger than the locusts they hunted. *It's a deer or one of the big rats.* He sure hoped so. Deep down he knew this was not so. Deer were incredibly quiet. Suddenly Darius could see the smaller trees moving, and then what was causing all the noise burst out of the forest, coming directly toward Darius's direction fast.

"Azizi!" Darius forgot all about staying hidden as he jumped up and ran towards his beloved pet mount as he barreled toward him. The sound of Azizi caused Pepi to rise up out of her hiding spot behind the rock shelf, and she, too, trotted over to her mate. When

Darius was able to get Azizi to stop, the large scarab clattered his pinchers together in constant agitation. Darius didn't even hesitate. He mounted Azizi, whistled for Pepi to follow, and headed back in the direction that Azizi had come from. Azizi was moving at high speed, and Pepi followed close behind. Darius was devastated. *Please, goddess, I can't lose them,* he prayed continuously as he and his pet scarabs crashed through the forest, completely forgetting that the Ibis and Heru killed his kind on sight, no questions asked.

*****

Bree struggled to crank her neck around to try and see Jabar; she called out too late for him to watch out as she watched the brown-winged Heru attack Jabar with their sword. She screamed out to him as she saw him go down. "Noooo, noooo, *Jabar*!" She began to struggle, and all the Heru did was squeeze tighter on her arms with his talons. The curved ends of his talons cut into her underarm flesh, and she hissed out. Now she was mad; she was never so mad in her life as she was at this very moment. Her emotions were running rampant, but instead of being devastated watching her friend get attacked, she boiled over. She began to swing her legs backward and forward to get momentum to kick up and forward to hit the Heru in the chest enough to make him land or drop her before they got too high. Other than the danger of the fall, she never thought it through. She just needed to get back to Jabar. The flyer squeezed again, but she didn't stop; her momentum was beginning to sway the Heru, so he dove straight down to frighten her as her legs scraped the top of the tree line. "Bastard!" Bree yelled, and she heard him laugh. This time, instead of getting momentum, she just flexed her arms, pulled up her knees, curled her back, and let her feet fly upward in one swift movement. Just as she did that, the Heru looked down at her to see what she was up to and received a good forced left foot right into the end of his beak.

The piercing shriek that came out of him was frightening, and right as she landed the kick, he let go of one of her arms. She dangled precariously from one arm. Her heart jumped into her throat as she thought she was going to fall, but that didn't stop her from trying to get him to let her go. They had plummeted down closer to the trees again as his eyes were watering fiercely from the blow to his beak. He was cursing at her and telling her to stop moving, but she cursed back. He was trying to fly, clear his eyes, and hold her with his one leg as well as trying to grab with his other talons to get her other arm back. It was quite the aerial show if someone had been watching. "Woman, I will drop you!" he yelled at her when she reached with her free hand and started digging into his leg that was holding her arm with her nails.

"Good, you feathered freak, drop me then!"

He scowled at her as he thought about doing just that. He was finding it hard to fly with all her struggling even for her tiny stature. She was not cooperating in any way. "Damn it, woman, stop that!" Instead of stopping, Bree continued and pulled out more feathers that were popping out from under his shin armor. "I will pluck you like a chicken, you son of a vulture's ass. Let me go!"

If her ripping out his feathers wasn't so painful, then he may have found this highly amusing. She was spunky, that was for sure, but as it was, he was getting terribly angry and frustrated with his load at the moment.

He spotted a high tree and headed for it. Just before he flew into it, he tossed her none too gently into the top of the tree. Bree hit the branches hard and began to fall. She didn't really think he was going to let her go. She just wanted him to land or drop her as he tried to land, but here, she was flying into a tree, and now she was falling fast. She frantically reached out and managed to grab ahold of a branch, but it snapped. The next few branches she tried to snag broke as well. As she fell closer and closer to the ground, she was finally able to snatch onto a larger branch that was able to take her weight. She hauled herself in closer to the trunk of the tree and managed to get her footing firmly planted on another branch below the one that she was holding on to.

She was hurting, with the multitude of cuts and scrapes all over her now as well as the talon holes she had on her arms, but that did not stop her from quickly descending down the tree. The falcon soldier flew around the tree a couple of times and watched as she was able to catch herself before she fell to her death. He knew she wouldn't fall, but he was glad that he was right. He was, however, quite shocked at her ability to move so quickly and began to descend the tree. For such a tiny thing, she was quite strong and brave. "Where do you think to go once you get to the ground, woman?"

Bree never stopped when she answered, "Anywhere away from you, you filthy turkey."

The falcon soldier instinctively knew she was insulting him by the silly words she tossed his way; he had no idea what a vulture, chicken, or turkey was. He could not help himself as he replied, still circling the tree, "Well, at least I am not a tiny naked monkey baby."

This had Bree hesitate, and she slipped a little on one of the branches, so she stopped and turned out as the falcon soldier flew by again. "I am not naked, nor am I a monkey baby. You, sir, are a murderer and a worthless turkey vulture."

The flyer flew past once again. "I did not murder anyone." Bree threw a sharp branch at him and missed. "You attacked us for no reason. You are no better than Senepol. If my friend Jabar is dead, I swear I will kill you myself."

The Heru hesitated in the air. He stopped flying and held himself in one spot in front of Bree, flapping his wings up and down without moving away. "Did you say Jabar? The Maahe with you is Jabar?" The Heru did not wait for an answer as he cussed and quickly flew away, back toward where they had come from. He met up with the other flyers soon enough, and Bree could see them in the distance discussing something together while still in the air. The brown Heru flew away with Jabar fast, and the leader flew back to Bree, who was halfway down the tree now. "Your Maahe is not dead. He is only unconscious. My men are taking him for medical attention to our village. Come, I will fly you there as well."

Bree did not stop. "I am not going anywhere with you, turkey man, especially in the air. You should have asked who we were before you attacked us for no reason."

The Heru became agitated again when he replied, "We had good reason to attack you without question."

Bree kept climbing down the tree. "Oh really? That is not good enough, filthy chicken man."

The insulted Heru was frustrated. "Would you stop insulting me? I was only doing my duty to protect my land from attack. If you let me fly to my village, I will explain why on the way." Bree was about to yell at him again when suddenly there was a massive ruckus coming from the forest where the Heru soldiers had first attacked them

"What now?" The soldier flew higher into the air and then cursed aloud. A falcon screech pierced the sky loud and long as the soldier dived down fast toward where the sound had come from. Bree cursed too. She was too scared now to go onto the ground in case it was a giant monster bear or something worse. If it bothered the soldier, then she was better to remain in the safety of the large tree. She decided to climb higher to see if she could make out what had caused all the noise. When she was able to see over the tops of the trees to the field where they met the soldiers, she instantly screamed out. "Oh god no!" Bree had never descended a tree so fast in her life. She hit the ground running as fast as she could as branches, and stumps impeded her way. *Please no, please don't attack*, Bree thought as she stumbled over a fallen tree. Jabar's warning played in her mind as she picked herself up and tried to untangle her skirt but ended up ripping it off. Bree did not have time to remove it from the snaggled tree branch. She had to get to the field fast. *The Heru and the Ibis detest and kill on sight any Anubi or Apis if they are in a small group or alone that come anywhere near their lands. Your tribes are their mortal enemy.*

As she ran, she did not realize that she was crying. She was running out of steam. Suddenly she heard pounding wings fly over the trees, and she slowed enough to look up and saw six or more Heru heading in the direction of the field. This gave her newfound energy, and she pushed on. It felt like forever, but she finally broke through the edge of the forest and into the field. The sight before her gave her hope as she ran. Darius, Azizi, and Pepi were still alive. Azizi and Pepi were doing their best to keep the flying Heru away from Darius, who had his spear at ready. Four flyers were surrounding them, and three more were flying around, trying to distract the scarabs away from the Anubi. Bree screamed out as she ran closer "Stop! Don't hurt him." No one paid the half-naked woman any attention. She burst into the center of the surrounding soldiers and jumped into Darius's arms. Darius staggered off balance when she vaulted herself right at him that he fell to the ground with Bree straddling on top of him. Darius hit the ground hard. When he realized it was Bree that had toppled him over, he started to laugh as he said, "I think my dreams have come true."

The soldier that had carried Bree away motioned the others to back off as they began to close in with the Anubi down. Bree scrambled to remove herself from atop Darius and spun around to the head flyer. "He is with me and Jabar! He is a friend. If you harm one hair on his head, I swear to you..."

The head flyer snickered slightly as he watched the tiny woman stalk up to him. "You swear what, tiny one?"

Bree was lucky if she came up to just above his ribs in height, but that did not stop her from raising her fist and hitting him with all her might in his stomach. This did not even faze him, and the group of the flying soldiers laughed heartedly as they began to tease their leader with "You have met your match, Sethos, usually you do well with the ladies" and "Sethos, you've lost your touch." If Bree had not been so scared for Darius and so damn mad, she would have realized that the danger was over for now, but she was pumped with adrenaline. So just for good measure, she hit him again, but this only ended with her hurting her hand. "Damn you all, why do you have to be so damn big!" Darius, too, was laughing, so she spun her anger at him. "And you!" She stormed over to him. "You promised me that you would stay hidden and safe. What are you thinking, Darius? They could have killed you." She then hit him in the stomach as well. "Damn all of you."

Darius at least had the sense to stop laughing and look guilty. "I am terribly sorry, Bree. When Azizi came running out of the forest without you, I feared the worst. I did not think about my safety. All I could think about was getting to you and Jabar. Wait, where is Jabar?"

Bree swept her arm back at the group of Heru flyers. "These oversized turkeys tried to kill him, and now he is on his way to their village to get medical attention."

The leader could not take the insults anymore without knowing what it was that she was insulting him with, so he asked, "What the hell is a turkey anyway?"

Bree glared at him as she sneered. "It's a bird that my people eat."

All the Heru flyers burst into laughter except for the leader, who, if he could blush, would have. Bree simply refused to fly even though she knew it would be much faster. She did want to get to Jabar as fast as she could to make sure that he was okay, but she would not fly with the one they called Sethos. The flyers still did not trust them to follow, so half flew to the village while the other half stayed with Bree and Darius after they took his spear. Luckily, they had a better way to get to their village than through the dense forest. On the ride to the tree village, Sethos explained why they had attacked Bree and Jabar without them asking questions first. It turned out that only three days before, two men that looked like Bree had wandered into their forest. When they took them into custody, they had sweet-talked their way into the village and had convinced the Ibis and Heru that they had especially important news about Senepol and the obelisks. When they got to the village, the Ibis priests confiscated the obelisks, and the tiny men went into custody. The tiny men had told them that they knew how to release the power that the obelisks held. They requested a meeting with the leaders of the village, and after council, the men then had audience with all the elders, especially after they said they had stolen the obelisks from Senepol and they knew how to get rid of him. When the tiny men met with the elders of the village, they continuously asked to see the other obelisk and that they needed to see it to be able to make sure that it was the same as the two they had as well as help keep it from Senepol's clutches.

The Heru and Ibis elders denied their request to see the obelisk. The elders hid the obelisk, and it will stay hidden. The men tried to convince the elders to see the obelisk for the rest of the night, trying different tactics. They went to their quarters, frustrated. That night they snuck into one of the Ibis elder's huts, who happened to have the two confiscated obelisks in his room. They attacked him and left him for dead. The elder that they had attacked happened to be the oldest and the wisest of all the Ibis. He was their high priest, and the village was devastated. They have been hunting for the men since, and therefore they attacked Bree and Jabar thinking that since she looked like the two men, she must be conspiring with them.

Sethos finished his explanation, and the group rode in silence for a while. Bree was deep in thought, and Darius looked at her with a worried expression. One of the flyers was leading Pepi just in case they tried to get away. Darius leaned in and whispered in her ear since they were both riding on Azizi, "I am guessing the two tiny men were the ones that kidnapped you and then abandoned you to Senepol."

Bree nodded. "Seems to me they are trying to get their dirty hand on all the obelisks, just like we are. Only they are going to perform evil with it so they can get back to my realm and live like kings." Darius sat back, and Bree went back into deep thought. After a moment, Bree called out to Sethos, "Sethos. Fly down here. I need to talk to you about something particularly important."

Darius looked nervous, and then he pulled Bree into his chest and again whispered into her ear as he squeezed her arms tight, "Bree, I know what you are thinking. This is an unbelievably bad idea. Jabar warned me that if they find out, they will find a way to hurt you or use you for their benefit."

Bree turned to Darius before Sethos flew back to them. "Darius, I understand your concern, but if I can do this, we can get their trust and have them collaborate with us instead of against us. We need all the help that we can get if we are going to do this. Just the three of us isn't enough to overthrow Senepol."

Darius frowned, but after a moment he nodded and let Bree go just as Sethos flew down to them after he made sure he had a watch cover him in the air. "So, this turkey vulture is good enough to talk to now?" Darius snickered, and Sethos glared at him. "Watch it, Anubi. I can still kill you." Darius just shook his head but stopped laughing.

Bree patted Darius on the leg. "Just trust me, okay?" Darius just nodded.

"This elder of yours. He is extremely important to your tribes, am I right?"

Sethos drew his brows together as he nodded. "What are you getting at, tiny woman?"

Bree cleared her throat and began, "I know this is going to be hard to believe, but I can help this elder of yours."

Sethos flew lower and closer to the ground so he could be near Bree as she was speaking quietly. He flew only a foot off the ground. "Yes, he is the most important person in our entire tribe. We do not even know how old he is. He just is and always has been. Our best healers have tried everything in their power to heal him to no avail. He is only just barely hanging on. How do you think that you can help him? I am listening."

Bree sat up straighter and cleared her throat again. "I must get a promise from you before I help you and your elder. If I can heal your elder, then you and the entire Heru army will join Jabar, Darius, and I in our search for all the obelisks and take down Senepol."

Now it was Sethos's turn to snicker. "You are in no position to make demands, tiny one. What you tell me is the same tale that the two tiny men made to us. I am now suspicious of you and your little group. I think I will throw you into our jail when we get to the village."

Darius groaned just as Sethos began to fly away. "I told you, Bree."

Bree screamed out to Sethos, "What if I could prove it to you?"

Sethos stopped in midair and turned back and glared at her for a moment. He cherished his elder and really wanted what Bree was saying to be true. He decided to hear her out and flew back down to the two mounted on Azizi. "This should be interesting. Fine. Prove it to me, and I will think about what you have demanded."

Bree stopped Azizi, and the whole group turned to see why they had stopped. "Why have you stopped, woman?"

Bree slid off Azizi. "Because I need to show you this alone, and no one else can know about it." Sethos frowned, wondering if the tiny woman had a trick up her sleeve but then scoffed at himself. *She is so tiny. What damage could she do to me?* Sethos thought and then nodded. "We will be right back. The lady needs privacy for a personal matter."

Bree rolled her eyes, but no one questioned what Sethos said as they all thought that she had to pee. Darius began to dismount, and Bree stopped him. "Darius, you need to stay."

Darius moaned but got back up on Azizi. "Are you sure you want to show this one your secret?" Bree nodded with a curt nod and turned and entered the trees. Sethos grinned at Darius with a mocking smile then followed Bree close behind with his sword at ready. Darius sneered back. He did not like this Sethos. Jealousy rose in his chest quickly.

When Bree figured they were in the forest deep enough that no one could see them, she turned to Sethos. "Okay, this is going to sound crazy, but I need you to cut your hand."

Sethos stepped back slightly. "Now why would I want to do such a thing?"

Bree inhaled deeply, losing her patience slightly. Something about Sethos just made her lash out at him with insults, which was so unlike her. "What, do you think a tiny little woman like me will hurt you? Or is it that you are too chicken to cut your hand?"

Sethos stepped forward and bent his massive height down to her level. "I do not like how insults fly from your mouth at me. I will not cut my hand without an explanation, woman."

Bree sighed. "I can't show you how I can heal your elder if you will not cut your hand. Just trust me, big bird. It will only sting for a minute."

Sethos grunted in frustration but took out the knife he had taken from Jabar, and he stabbed into his hand without taking his eyes off Bree. "Now you have to make me cry." Without hesitation, he lashed out and smacked her right on the nose. *Wow, that was satisfying,* he thought as he watched Bree grab her nose as it started to bleed, and she screeched. "What the hell was that for? Oh shit, that was perfect." Bree's eyes were watering nonstop, and she smiled with a giggle even though her nose hurt like hell. "That was brilliant. Give me your hand."

Sethos did so skeptically, and Bree let tears fall onto his palm. For a second, they stood there. "Well, I sure am impressed."

Bree shushed up at him. "Give it a second."

All of a sudden, Sethos hissed. "Damn it, woman, what have you done to me?" Sethos hissed again, and Bree grabbed his hand and held it as tight as her tiny grip would let her.

"Oh, grow up, you sissy, and just watch your hand." Sethos hissed again as the sting became near unbearable, but he could not show this tiny woman how much it hurt. He was a strong warrior, and she took his hit in her face like a champion. He did not pull away as much as he wanted to and watched his hand. *Sissy? I'll show her.* As Sethos watched his stinging hand, he gasped and stumbled backward as he saw it begin to heal. As he stumbled back, he tripped on a fallen log and landed hard on his ass and wings while still looking at his hand. Bree kneeled beside him with a huge grin on her face. "Pretty cool, huh?"

Sethos took a moment to tear his eyes away from his hand and then stared at the tiny woman before him. "How? How did you do that?"

Bree grabbed Sethos's hand as she said, "You can't tell anyone. Only Jabar, Darius, and you know about my secret ability. I do not understand how I can do it either. Jabar has an idea about how I can, but it is crazy. If you let me, I think I can heal your elder. If I do, I desperately need you and your army's help to take down Senepol and keep the obelisks away from him. He cannot get his filthy hand on any of them. He will destroy this entire land, including yours, in his quest to obtain all the obelisks and the power within them. If Senepol finds out I can heal like this, he will use me in his desire to control everyone. If he gets injured, he will force me to heal him. Do you see why no one can know about this?"

Sethos nodded still in shock. He looked back at his hand, and it healed completely without even a scar. There was a call out to Sethos by one of his soldiers to see if he was okay since they had been gone for longer than necessary. It took him a moment to respond and only when Bree slapped him. He stared at the tiny woman for a split second, considering hitting her back but quickly changed his mind and then called back, "We are coming."

Sethos stood back up, and Bree grabbed his wrist. "Do we have a deal?"

Sethos turned slightly and nodded. "If you heal my elder, my people will be in your debt, and you can ask anything of me."

The smile that lit Bree's face was magical. "Thanks, big bird. I guess you aren't a turkey vulture after all." At that, she raced ahead of Sethos and exited the trees. Sethos looked at his hand for a moment again and shook his head. He had meant every word he had said just now. The elder that needed saving was like a father to him. Zosar had raised him right out of the egg after his mother died and his father soon thereafter. He would do anything to have him healed, and if that meant lending the entire Heru army to conquer Senepol and his evil terror over their lands, then he was up to the challenge. He followed Bree out of the trees, and they continued their way to the village. Sethos flew back into the sky but could not help constantly looking back at Bree with a strange expression on his face. Darius watched him, and he whispered to Bree, "Can we trust him with your secret, Bree?"

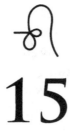

15

Even with Azizi and Pepi, it took them a little over an hour to make it to the Ibis and Heru village. Why they called it a village was beyond Bree. It was more like hundreds of the coolest tree forts connected by bridges high up in the gigantic trees. It was one of the most impressive things that Bree had ever seen. Darius was amazed as well. He had wanted to climb the trees, but this was even better. He was not only going to climb the trees, but he was going to be able to sleep in the trees too. He had an air of a child on Christmas morning, and it made Bree smile. The whole entire village seemed to come out of the woodworks. Bree felt very self-conscious with everyone staring at her and Darius, so she sunk into Darius a little. Darius threw his arm around her protectively but did not seem to mind everyone staring at him. He was looking around in awe. A group of Heru soldiers flew down in front of Sethos with anger all over their faces and in their body language. The largest of them stepped forward. He was furious and spoke to Sethos as he pointed in the direction of Bree and Darius. "What is the meaning of this, Sethos? You bring more enemies to our camp. Wasn't almost losing our elder enough for you?"

Sethos stood proud and stepped closer to the soldier that spoke. "Do not question your commander, Darthos. I bring someone that can help Zosar. This young Anubi is no threat to us. He is not like the others. He has defected from Senepol's grasp."

Darthos scowled at Sethos. "Those tiny men look exactly like her kind. They conned you, and now you put our village in danger again. We can no longer trust your leadership, Sethos. It is time for you to step down as Heru commander."

Sethos chuckled. "I have no time for this, Darthos. Your constant trivial desire to take over my command will have to wait another day. I have more important things to deal with right now."

Darthos unsheathed his sword and stepped forward. "I think not. We will deal with this now. I demand it on the law of the goddess. I challenge you here and now. It is my right as a Heru. I feel you have jeopardized our people yet again and only days apart from each."

Sethos sighed. "Do you really want to do this again, Darthos?"

Darthos did not answer; he only stepped closer and readied his sword in a defensive stance. "All right, I will humor you, but I claim the right that if I win against you once again, you no longer can claim leadership of the Heru army. This is my demand on the law of the goddess. You can only challenge three times. This will be your third time, Darthos. Are you ready to stand down if I win?" Sethos unsheathed his sword as well.

Darthos hesitated slightly, but his scowl returned. "Agreed." Sethos shook his head and sighed. Suddenly Darthos attacked with the speed of an arrow.

Everyone scattered up into the trees to watch the battle and give the two space to fight. Bree, Darius, Azizi, and Pepi scurried back to safety on the outer area by the trees they had entered the village from. Bree feared for Sethos. If he died, then she would lose out on his promise to help them defeat Senepol. Darius, on the other hand, was thrilled. "Oh, this should be good. Hope Sethos gets his ass kicked. I don't like how he looks at you, Bree."

Bree turned to Darius and smacked him on the arm. "Don't be stupid. We need him. He promised me the help of the Heru army if I heal their elder. If he dies, we lose too. Don't you get it? We could become arrested, or worse, if Sethos loses! Use that teenage brain of yours."

Darius scowled and pouted. He realized that Bree was right, and now he, too, was worried for Sethos, even though it would have been very satisfying to see Sethos taken down a notch. Bree watched with her heart in her throat. Darthos was much larger than Sethos, but as Bree watched, she realized that his size slowed him down, and he did not seem as skilled. Sethos was dodging each aerial attack with ease. Not one of Darthos's attacks landed, but every one of Sethos's did. It was embarrassing to watch, where Darthos was concerned. Everyone knew it except Darthos. He had already lost before the battle had even begun. The fight was a remarkable sight, though. Sethos was like a dancer in the sky deflecting everything that Darthos was throwing at him.

Darthos knew he was losing, and to look for a way to distract Sethos, he dove at him but then swerved at the last moment and came at Bree and Darius. The look of hatred across Darthos's face as he came for them scared Bree so much that she froze in place and could not move. Darius did move, however, and leaped up from behind Bree, jumped in the air off Azizi's back, and sucker punched the giant Darthos square in the beak before he could swing his sword. Darius hissed as his hand sliced open on the end of his beak, and Darthos whirled off to the side and slammed into the ground beside Azizi, with Darius landing on his feet in front of Bree, who is still mounted. Sethos was there in an instant and grabbed the larger Heru from behind and held his sword to his neck. "It is over, Darthos. Sheath your sword." Darthos struggled slightly, and Sethos cut into his neck slightly. "I said it is over." Darthos threw a deadly scowl directed at Bree and Darius before he threw his sword down. When Sethos released him, Darthos stood and at once shot up into the air and flew away. Sethos watched Darthos retreat, and then he turned to Bree and Darius. "I am impressed young one. That was fast thinking on your part. You just saved your friend's life."

Even though Darius did not like Sethos, the compliment had him beaming from ear to ear. "No one tries to hurt my friends."

Sethos laughed. "Remind me to befriend you then."

Darius realized that this was an extreme compliment coming from Sethos. He had watched the battle, and he knew that Sethos's abilities at fighting were great. *He isn't such a bad guy,* Darius thought. *If he keeps his eyes and his hands away from Bree.* But of course, he did not say that aloud.

Bree regained her composure and turned to Darius with a big hug around his shoulder as that is all she could reach with him on the ground and her still mounted. "Thank you, Darius! This is the second time you have saved my life. If I am not careful, I am going to owe you."

Darius just smiled down at Bree and cherished her hug with a quick "You promise." And then Bree hit him in the shoulder before she turned her attention back to Sethos. "Can I see Jabar now, please? I want to make sure he is okay."

Sethos nodded and led them to a ladder. "I will meet you up there." He pointed to a large hut in the trees and flew up. Bree needed help from Darius to climb the ladder as the rungs were far apart and too big for her. Sethos disappeared for a bit, and when they were at the top, he showed back up in time to help her over the ledge to the platform. They entered the large hut, and Bree gasped along with Darius. Inside looked nothing like the mud and grass on the outside. Inside was exceptionally clean, spacious, and quite luxurious in an extremely comfortable way. In the center of what seemed like the living area were three of the Ibis tribe priests. Bree realized that these were the crane people. They were the same as all the others except they had crane features with long thin beaks and small feathered heads. They were tall and very slim. Their flying feathers were white, sleek, and not as large and domineering as their falcon counterparts. They all wore long flowing white robes with hoods, and they stood with their arms folded inside large sleeves. Bree would be fascinated if she were not so worried about Jabar. "Where is Jabar? Is he here?"

Sethos stepped forward. "No, Jabar is not here. Not in this hut, anyways."

Bree stepped back into Darius. "Well, then take me to Jabar."

Sethos stepped forward. "You need to heal Zosar first, then I will take you to Jabar."

She frowned at Sethos and then at the Ibis priests, who just stood there silently staring at her. "No, I want to make sure Jabar is okay, then I will heal your elder."

Sethos stepped even closer with his hand on the hilt of his sword. "No. Zosar first. He may not have any time left. It needs to be now."

Bree became suspicious. "Sethos, what are you not telling me?"

Sethos grimaced but held his own and said again. "Zosar first."

Her heart began to pound in her chest, and she tried to turn and run out of the hut. Sethos stopped her with the point of his sword at her neck before she was able to get out the door. Bree instantly started to cry. "Tell me Jabar isn't dead. Just tell me that."

Sethos sighed. "He's injured more severely than we first thought. I will take you to him at once. Right after you heal Zosar."

Bree sobbed and glared at Sethos. "You son of a bitch. If Jabar dies, I will find a way to kill you."

Darius spoke up as well. "I second that, Sethos."

Sethos sighed. "I understand. I am willing to take that chance. Zosar is in the back room. Come."

Thankfully, Bree was already in tears, and she did not have to have someone or something force her to cry. What she saw in front of her on the bed was a sad sight as well. There on the bedding was a withered old body feebly lying on his back with a mass of pillows propping him up. His breathing was very shallow, and he had cuts everywhere that Bree could see. His feathers were dull and sagged without life, and they were no longer white. All the feathers had blood splatter on them, and they had pink stains where someone had tried to clean off the blood. Bree grimaced. *How could Derrick and Aston have done this to someone so old. How evil.* It made her sick to her stomach. There were more Ibis priests around the bed, and they backed off when Sethos, Bree, and Darius entered the room. Sethos in a commanding but respectful voice asked everyone to leave. No one moved as they looked at Bree with heavy suspicion. "She is here to help. Believe me. Would I bring someone in to kill my father?"

The priests looked from one to another. One of the priestesses approached Bree, and without saying anything, she gently took Bree's hands in hers and then stared in her eyes for a moment before she closed hers. The priestess did this for only a second. Then she opened her eyes and dropped Bree's hand with a nod. Then they all left without a word. Bree looked over at Sethos, and he held his hand out toward Zosar. Bree slowly went over to the side of the bed. She was scared to sit on the edge in case she disturbed the elder or hurt him. Tears afresh spilled down her cheek. This poor man. Bree was shocked that he was still alive. She prayed to herself that this would work as he was in such a bad way. All she knew is that she could heal a single wound, not an entire body and internal injuries that she was sure he had. Bree hesitated a little while longer when she heard Darius whisper, "You must do this, then we can take care of Jabar. He needs you too."

With this reminder, Bree knelt on the side of the bed. She thought of every sad thing she could think of to keep the tears flowing, and the last thought was of Jabar lying on a cold slab, dead because they had not gotten to him fast enough. Fresh hot tears flooded down her nose and cheeks, so she leaned over the old feeble elder and just let all her tears land on his face over the lacerations. She went a step farther and pulled the sheet off his chest, gently opened his robe, and let tears fall where the wounds were deep and angry. *Please let this work, please*, Bree whispered to herself. They all waited, holding their breaths. After ten seconds with no movement, Bree stood up and backed over to Darius and grabbed his hand. They watched for thirty seconds more without a sign. Bree turned to Darius with a very worried look on her face that matched his look also. "Maybe I can only heal small wounds." Darius scoffed at Bree as she said this and quietly reminded her that Jabar's wound was massive and infected and she was able to heal him. "Yes, Darius, but it was only one wound, and he's young and wasn't on his deathbed."

Still nothing. Sethos slowly went over and kneeled beside the bed. "Father, you must try. You must live." When there was absolutely no movement from the elder, Sethos placed his head on his chest to see if he could hear if his heart was still beating.

Slowly Zosar's hand moved up and caressed Sethos's feathered head, and the elder spoke, "My Sethos."

Sethos head came up fast, and he laughed and cried at the same time; he was so relieved. "Father?" As they watched, wounds began to heal and disappear on Zosar's face and chest. Zosar coughed with a slight grimace and sat up in bed. "No, Father, you must rest."

Sethos tried to stop Zosar and stay in bed, but Zosar scolded him gently. "I have never felt this well in years. Let me up, son." Zosar patted Sethos on the cheek beside his beak, and he looked over to Bree and Darius. Suddenly he stood up with the ease of a young man and walked over to Bree with a look of startled awe on his face. "It cannot be! Neferneferuaten? You have returned! I have waited eons for this moment. I thank you. You healed me. You could not have picked a more proper time to return. The vials of your lifeblood you left us have depleted."

Bree sighed sadly at the joy she saw in the old crane's eye. It was going to break his heart when he realized that she was not Nefertiti. Bree reached out and gently took the elder Zosar's hand. "I am sorry, sir. I am not Nefertiti. My name is Bree Sabry."

Zosar laughed gently and squeezed her hand. "Ah, Bree, you are Nefertiti, just in a new life is all."

Darius jumped up and down. "I knew it! I knew you were someone special."

Bree rolled her eyes and looked at Sethos. "I can't do this right now. I must get to Jabar."

Sethos was still looking at Zosar with concern. "Father, I insist that you rest now. I must keep my promise to Bree and take her to heal her friend."

Zosar nodded and said something very strange as he set himself down on a comfortable chair beside his bed. "Jabar needs to heal. He also plays a vital role in what is to come." The three of them stared at Zosar, confused. Zosar waved them away. "It is all right. Go now. We will talk in detail later." Bree was the first to move out of the room, followed by Darius. Zosar stopped Sethos as he was turning to leave the room. "Take great care of her and her friends, my son. They are more important than you know. I will explain later. Go and watch over her."

Sethos bowed his head toward the man that raised him and exited the room. Sethos directed Bree and Darius to another hut that was at the other end of the trees. It was the hut they used as a healing hut. Hut was the wrong word to call it, as it was massive. It covered over twenty giant trees in length. It was laid out like a hospital with cots laid out in lines. Beds had occupants with the sick and injured. Bree spotted Jabar instantly and ran over to his bedside with Darius close behind. Sethos stayed near the doorway in respect of their privacy but watched Bree closely as he wondered what Zosar had meant about the group of three before him. *They all play a key role in what is to come.* Sethos pondered, *What is to come?* Sethos shook his head. Zosar had never led him astray before. He would have to be patient to find out what Zosar meant with the rest of them later.

Bree gently picked up Jabar's hand and held it tight. "Jabar, we are here. Darius and Bree. I am going to take care of you." Looking at Jabar lying limp on the cot had tears pouring out of Bree. She frantically looked for a wound but could not find any. She panicked. "How will I heal him if there's no open wound for my tears? Darius, help. I can't find any injuries."

An Ibis priestess moved closer as she overheard Bree's distress. "He has no external injuries. He had brain damage from the extreme blow to his head. He has bleeding on his brain. He is comatose from the pressure."

Bree inhaled deeply and looked at the priestess with pleading eyes. "How can I heal him then? You must help me." Bree was desperate, and Darius started to pace up and down the aisle of cots. Bree crawled onto the cot beside Jabar and lay beside him with sobs wracking her body. *Think, think, think, Bree. There must be a way in, to heal him. He is counting on you.* All of a sudden, it was as if someone had flashed a picture directly into her brain. She saw a vial full of blood floating in the air, and then it was gone as fast as it had come. She sat up quickly remembering what Zosar had said while he was holding her hand. *The vials of your lifeblood you left us are depleted.*

Bree whooped aloud, and Darius rushed forward. "What is it, Bree? Did you find a way to heal, Jabar?"

Bree shook her head. "I don't know, but I must try. Get me a knife, and be quick about it." Darius searched but could not find one, so he went off in his search. The Ibis priestess stepped forward and handed Bree an intricately carved knife without saying a word. Bree took the knife from the slim hand. "Thank you." The priestess moved away without a sound.

Sethos stepped deeper into the healing hut toward Bree. He did not hear the conversation, and when he saw Bree with a knife, he was worried that Bree was so upset that she may consider harming herself. When she raised the knife and thrust it into her hand, he leaped over cots to stop her. "Bree, no! Don't harm yourself. You are too important." Before he could get to her, she had turned Jabar's face to her and opened his mouth. When he reached her, she was already squeezing her palm and letting her blood drip directly onto Jabar's tongue. Sethos stopped just in front of the cot in shock. "What are you doing?"

Before Bree could answer, Darius ran back with a knife in his hand. "I found one! Sorry it took so... Oh, you got one." Bree lay back down half on top of Jabar and half on the cot with her head resting on his chest. "Bree, what—?" Sethos grabbed hold of Darius and shook his head at him. Darius understood, and they stood watching silently.

Bree raised slightly up and down from Jabar's breathing. She could hear his lungs getting stronger by the second. She could also hear his heartbeat gain strength and thump louder. In her excitement, she wrapped her arms around his shoulders. "That's good, Jabar, heal. Come back to me."

Suddenly a loud purring came from Jabar, and to everyone's surprise, he yawned. In his sleep, he wrapped his large arms around Bree with a smile growing on his lips. He began gently stroking Bree's hair and back with one hand in a loving manner. Bree sat up looking at Jabar as he stared back at her. "Am I dreaming, or are you an angel?"

Bree laughed aloud and grabbed Jabar by his face and kissed him square on the mouth, then she jumped up off the cot excitedly so Jabar could sit up. The priestess's eyes grew wide, and she quietly slipped away. Sethos stepped back in amazement, and Darius was patting Bree on the back, repeating, "You did it!" over and over. Sethos now understood what Zosar meant. He had to keep her safe at all costs. She was their goddess returned. She was Nefertiti, and he would give his life for her.

When Jabar sat up, he looked confused, so Bree filled him in on what had occurred. When Bree had finished her explanation, Jabar looked over at Sethos. Sethos could not tell if he was angry or not. Then Jabar stood. He was close to Sethos's height, but he was far more muscular. Jabar stepped toward Sethos, looking him straight in the eye. Sethos stood his ground, and then Jabar slowly held out his hand to him. Sethos inwardly sighed in relief. He wanted to be Jabar's friend, not his foe. Sethos reached out and took the hand that Jabar offered, and they clasped onto each other forearms with their other hand in a friendly manner. Jabar stated, "I understand why you felt you had to attack us. I would have done the same if it was my tribe. I am sorry it had to come to this, though, and cause stress to my friends." Jabar pulled Sethos closer, and he stepped into him as well and quietly said for only Sethos's ear, "Next time you place my friends in danger, though, I will not hesitate to kill for them as I did this last time."

Sethos stepped back with a curt nod. "I would not want it any other way. Bree is special, and I will stand beside you with the Heru army to protect her at all costs."

Jabar nodded with a grunt. With that understanding between the two warriors, Jabar turned back to Bree and gave her a giant bear hug. "Thank you again, my lady. I would have died twice over if not for you." He released Bree reluctantly and looked down at her lack of garment. "Why are you half dressed? Never mind, come here. He grabbed a small towel and wrapped it around Bree's waist and tied it securely. "That's better. Now no one can ogle you anymore." As he said that, he turned to Sethos, who looked away quickly, and then Darius, who blushed and shrugged his shoulders. Jabar then said to him with his deep voice, "You disobeyed me, young one."

Darius laid his ears flat against his head, and the smile wiped from his face into a frown. "But if you had obeyed me, we may all not be here, standing together right now. Thank you for keeping Bree safe. You are one I am proud to have by my side." Darius lifted his head proudly and beamed with a wondrous smile at Jabar. This coming from Jabar was even a bigger compliment than that of Sethos's earlier when Darthos tried to attack Bree.

*****

The priestess that saw the miracle of Bree healing Jabar was shocked. Never had she even heard of such a thing and just with her blood. When the woman and the young Anubi entered the healing hut, she instantly saw her exact likeness to their goddess statues, but when she saw the miracle, she had to go speak with the other priests and priestesses about what she had seen. If this woman could heal the Maahe, then she could do the same for their beloved Zosar. She flew up to Zosar's hut and entered reverently but quickly. She stopped short only two paces into the hut when her eyes caught sight of Zosar standing in the center of the living space, healthy and healed, conversing with a couple of priests. Her beak fell open, and her knees wobbled. Two miracles in one day. She went down on her knees and called out, "Elder Zosar, how is it that you have healed? I was coming to tell the priestesses caring for you that you could become healed. I just saw a miracle by our strange visitors with the Maahe in the healing tent. She healed him with her blood. It took only moments, and he healed completely."

Zosar went over to the priestess and helped her stand up. "Yes, Sister Panya. It is our goddess returned. Therefore, I stand before you. She is the one that healed me also."

Panya's eyes grew large, and her beak fell open again. "The woman in the healing hut is our goddess Neferneferuaten?" The priestess Panya became even more shocked than before. "I just stood there unable to help her. All I did was hand her my ritual knife. I did not bow. I treated her like a commoner. Oh, Elder, forgive me."

Zosar smiled gently. "My dear Panya, even she is unaware that she is our goddess. She calls herself Bree. I am sure she is not angry with you. She healed the Maahe. That is great news. Please, Panya, I need you to gather the other elders and all the priests and priestesses to the sacred hut. Tell Sethos that he is to bring our goddess, the Maahe, and the Anubi to the sacred hut at sunset. There will be much to discuss. Now go, do as I ask, Sister. I will see you in the meeting as well."

Panya nodded and hurriedly exited Zosar's quarters to do his bidding. Zosar turned back to the other priests and finished the conversation that he was having with them. "Now, as I was saying earlier, tell them that this is to be a feast to be remembered. It is not every day we have a goddess in our midst."

16

Jabar, Bree, and Darius experienced a tour of the village by Sethos after they left the healing hut. The village was amazing. Even their markets and shops were in the trees. Sethos explained that the ladders lifted if there was any trouble coming near the village or if anyone attacked. They also had nurseries; this fascinated Bree and Darius. Both the Heru and the Ibis were born naturally like a human baby but encased in an egg still. There they had incubators for another month until they hatched. Bree was thrilled to be able to hold and play with all the baby Ibis and Heru. Darius thought they were cute, but he wasn't interested at all when he heard Heru warriors practicing and left the nursery to go watch the warriors practice. Bree had to smile when she turned back to the babies and found older ones climbing all over Jabar and pulling on his mane. He was extremely gentle with the little ones, and it warmed Bree's heart. He was tickling one of the baby chicks and playing peekaboo. This was a completely different Jabar that she had the privilege of seeing earlier, and it was nice to see another side of him. Sethos was trying to stay away from the babies but ended up giving in to their adorability and held a couple as well.

Jabar was finally able to disengage all the little ones, and he also went out to watch the Heru warriors practice, leaving Sethos with Bree. Sethos was distant to her now as he just did not know what to say to a goddess, and Bree called him out on it. "Hey, Sethos, did I suddenly grow two heads?"

Sethos frowned at her, not understanding what she meant. "Ever since we came out of the healing hut, you have treated me as if I have a disease. You haven't talked to me. You have stayed behind me, and every time I catch you looking at me, you look away or have a weird expression on your face. Did I do something wrong?"

Sethos looked down in embarrassment and apologized. "I am truly sorry. I just don't know how to talk to you since, well, since you are our goddess."

Bree stormed up to him and hit him in the arm. "Stop it right now, big bird. I want the Sethos who called me names and punched me in the nose back. I am not any kind of goddess, nor am I Nefertiti. Damn it, you turkey vulture, I am just Bree. If you keep acting this way around me, then I don't want you around me. Got it?"

Sethos could not help it. At first, he was horrified when she reminded him that he had indeed punched her in the nose, but as she then called him a turkey vulture, all he could see was the woman Bree, and he burst out laughing. "You are right, tiny woman. I admit that I did not know how to act anymore with all this mumbo jumbo." He reached out and gently smacked her on her shoulder. "From now on, you are just Bree."

Bree stumbled slightly with his shoulder smack and laughed as well. "That's better, big bird." They laughed together aloud. Jabar and Darius were just below them on the ground watching the training, so they looked up to see Sethos and Bree laughing together.

Jabar frowned, and jealousy flared in his gut. He did not like seeing Bree getting on so well with the commander of the Heru army. He saw a couple times in the last hour how Sethos looked at her when she was not noticing. He had noticed, and it bothered him. Just as he was thinking, Darius elbowed Jabar in the ribs. "I don't like how he looks at her, Jabar. He follows her around like a lost puppy."

Now it was Jabar's turn to laugh as he looked at Darius. "That's funny 'cause I thought exactly that of you only days ago."

Darius kicked dirt around with his foot and pouted out. "Yeah, but she is our Bree. What if she begins to like him too?"

Jabar grunted, not liking the sound of that question at all. He turned and looked back up at Sethos and Bree, and suddenly Sethos gently picked Bree up and held her close before he lifted off and flew down to the two of them. He landed and gently returned Bree to the ground, letting his hands linger on her waist a little too long for Jabar's liking.

Jabar growled low in his throat, and Sethos heard it, but instead of stepping away from Bree as Jabar's growl warned him to do, he raised his brow in a challenging way and then grabbed Bree's hand, looked straight at Jabar, and spoke, "Come, I've instructions to show you to your sleeping quarters so you all can freshen up and rest for this evening's celebrations. Bree, let me fly you back up, and the others can meet us there."

Bree turned to Sethos and, to his disappointment, declined his invitation to fly. "That's okay, Sethos. I will go up with Jabar and Darius. Just show us the way."

It was Jabar's turn to raise his eyebrows at Sethos as he took Bree's other hand and spoke, "Here, Bree, I will help you up the giant ladder if you would like."

Bree accepted his offer and then looked at Sethos as she dropped his hand and teased him as she said, "Okay, big bird, show us the way."

Darius piped in as they began to walk, "Hey, why does Sethos get a nickname and I don't?"

This eased the tension, and everyone laughed.

Bree had never enjoyed a bath as the one she just exited out of. The tub, for one, was gigantic as it needed to fit the Heru. It was like bathing in a large hot tub, and she was in it long enough for the water to become cool. When she stepped out of the bath, she was alone, for which she was extremely thankful. She hadn't been alone in so long. She took advantage of her empty quarters and walked around naked, letting the air dry her skin instead of a towel. She went over to the massive bed and longed to just fall into it and sleep at least twelve hours, but Sethos had said there was going to be a feast in their honor that evening, and she was ravenous. Sleep would have to wait for now. She raised her knee up onto the bed and threw her wet hair over her shoulder and started to comb her fingers through it to detangle it. There was no hair conditioner here. Her hair was long and thick; luckily it wasn't prone to oiliness. She closed her eyes and hummed to herself as she preened.

*****

Jabar was in a private quarter and enjoyed his cleaning. He had never felt better. Bree's healing had fixed him up completely. He felt as if he had the energy of a young cub. After he dried his mane, he donned the outfit that Sethos had lent him from one of the Heru warriors close to his size. It fit well. The half-length pleated sari was a dark brown that matched the chest straps. The outfit came with matching armbands, shin pads, and bracers. One of the priests brought in a medallion and gave it to Jabar to wear for the evening that he had bought from an old Maahe. It had the Maahe symbol of family unity engraved into it. It was quite a beautiful piece, so Jabar thanked the priest and agreed to wear it. He left his quarters when he finished in search of Darius. An Ibis priest directed Jabar to the room beside him. He entered and found Darius admiring himself in the mirror. He also had Sethos lend him Heru clothing, and he looked very dashing, all cleaned and dressed. "Looking good, young one. You will have the younger ladies turning their heads tonight."

Darius grinned from ear to ear. "You really think so? Wow, you look good too, old man." They grasped each other on the shoulders in a friendly way, appreciating each other's outfits.

"Have you seen Bree yet?" Jabar questioned the Anubi.

Darius shook his head. "Not yet. I just finished dressing myself. If we look this good, I can't wait to see what Bree looks like dressed up."

Jabar smiled, saying that he was going to see if she were ready yet and they would meet up soon. A priestess pointed him down the hall to the end. Jabar thanked her and wandered to her room. He entered the room quietly in case she decided to lie down for a snooze. The view that greeted him had him instantly heated with the hottest desire he had ever felt in his life. His loins tightened painfully right up into his stomach. Standing in front of a long oval mirror with her hair cascading over her right shoulder and her one leg up on the bed was Bree gloriously naked. The mirror was at an angle that she could not see who was entering the room, but Jabar could see her entire front and back. She had her eyes closed, and she was humming to herself as her fingers slowly combed the tangles out of her hair. *Oh, goddess, she is perfect.* Even though he knew it was wrong, he just could not make himself look away. She was the most beautiful creature he had ever had the opportunity to lay his eyes upon. He almost went over to her; his desire to take over running his hands through her hair and caressing her smooth perfect skin with his hands was so overwhelming he found himself moving forward without even realizing it. When he was about halfway into her room, he snapped out of it. He took one last longing glance at the perfection before him then quietly turned and left the room without her realizing that he had entered her quarters. When he exited the room, he at once went outside for fresh air and let his body return to normal and his blood pressure decrease. He inhaled and exhaled deeply. Then he closed his eyes, and all he could envision was Bree behind his eyelids. "Damn it," he said to himself aloud. He hit the railing with his fist as his desire flared again. His member throbbed painfully as if begging him to go back to Bree's room. His eyes flared open when he heard Sethos's voice behind him. "You seem irritated, Maahe. Is everything all right?" Jabar sighed then growled out with slight annoyance. This was the last person he wanted to see right now. "I'm fine. I was just remembering something."

"Whatever it is, I am here for all of you. Is this something I can help you with?"

Jabar turned slowly toward Sethos. He wondered if the Heru was baiting him. They were equals, and it seemed that they both had an eye for Bree. Jealousy flared in Jabar's chest. He had to calm himself down before he spoke. Sethos may be trying to help, but he doubted it. "Thank you, but no, Sethos. This is a personal matter."

Sethos nodded once. "I was just on my way to see if Bree needed anything. I will be going then."

Jabar rushed up to Sethos and grabbed his arm. "No, wait." He could not let Sethos walk in and see Bree in her glorious state as he did. He had to stop him without letting on that he had accidentally walked in on her. Sethos stopped and looked at Jabar's hand that was holding his arm a little too firmly. "Um, what I mean is, Darius is young and raging with hormones. I do need help keeping an eye on him so he stays out of trouble and doesn't try to infringe on anyone's lady tonight. Everyone is on edge with him being an Anubi. I don't want to have any trouble with the kid. I would really appreciate your help." Jabar dropped his hand away from Sethos.

Sethos chuckled as he nodded. "I agree. I remember how I acted around beautiful women when I was his age. I wonder, how is he around Bree?" Without waiting for an answer, Sethos, still chuckling, entered the rooming hut with Jabar close on his heels.

Jabar made sure Sethos knocked and wait for Bree to say enter before they just barge in this time. It wasn't Bree that answered the door, however. It was an Ibis woman. "No visitors right now, Sethos. Us ladies have volunteered to get the lady ready for the feast tonight. Leave us now so we can get her dressed. We will escort her to the hall when she is ready." Without waiting, she shut the door and left Heru and Maahe standing in the hallway staring at the door that closed on their faces. Sethos looked behind him, and the two men just shrugged their shoulders. They walked away and went to find Darius to make sure he wasn't getting into any trouble. They finally found him in a room with noisy voices coming from it. There he was sitting at a table playing mehen with Heru and Ibis youngsters around the same age as Darius. It was a type of board game whose board depicted a coiled snake divided into squares. One needed to protect the deity who wrapped around the sun god Re during his journey through the night to steal the snake's eggs using three lions, three lionesses, and six sets of six marbles. Poor Darius was at a loss as he had just learned the ins of the game and still had no real understanding of the rules.

When Darius spotted Jabar and Sethos at the door, he politely excused himself, and the other youngsters teased him for leaving as he was losing hopelessly. When he joined the two men at the door, he quietly thanked them for rescuing him. "I always spent my time hunting or training my scarabs. I never understood the draw to these kinds of games."

The men raised their eyebrows at him, but Jabar chimed in, "Do not worry, youngster, I never understood those either."

Sethos just chuckled with his little tidbit of commentary. "It takes intelligence and skill, but we were meant for bigger and better things like protecting the ones we love." Darius beamed and then waved goodbye to the others still playing the game. They all waved back saying that they would see him at the feast.

Jabar slapped Darius on the back. "It is good to see you making friends."

Darius shrugged, and then with a sly grin, he whispered, "They told me the names of some girls that wished to meet me. They are Heru girls."

Sethos tsk'd. "Watch it, boy, you are not here to dally with girls. You are here to make sure Bree and Jabar complete an especially important mission, which my army is going to support. No late night for you. It is eating and then rest. We rise early on the new sunrise. Remember that."

Darius pouted slightly but then smiled. "Yeah, the mission is more important than girls. Bree is the only girl for me right now."

Jabar and Sethos looked at each other and shrugged their shoulders. Sethos pointed in the direction of the outer doors. "Come, both of you. It is soon time for the feast."

*****

"Who was that at the door?" Bree asked when the Ibis woman came back to see how the outfit was working.

"Just you do not worry about that. We are here to make you shine tonight." Just when Bree had finished pulling out all the tangles in her hair, she thought she heard someone at the door. She quickly donned a towel and wrapped it around her, and she went to the door to see if there was anyone there. She thought she saw the tail end of Jabar exiting the door to the balcony only to be run over by a group of Ibis ladies, all excited, carrying clothing and makeup. Bree backed up into her room to allow all the ladies entrance and could not help feeling the excitement that the ladies were exuding. They all introduced themselves and then promptly set to work on Bree. They began fixing her hair and her face and tried to find something suitable for her to wear. Her size was an issue as everything they had was gigantic compared to her small stature.

The ladies had to improvise, and the ladies all were up to the challenge. Since Bree was so small without any wings, they had to cut and sew everything that they had brought in for her to try. In the end, they fixed Bree up in a simple white loose-fitting dress that went to the floor. They cut off the arms and sewed sheer indigo fabric to golden armbands that attached at the back to the other arm. They sewed a belt of sheer indigo fabric around her waist to sinch the loose dress in. Then the ladies added the same indigo fabric on the collar and around the neckline. For accents to highlight the dress, they quickly sewed in decorative beads to the center of the belt to loop down on each side of the hip and joined in the back of the belt at her lower back with a split in the front of the dress to the top of her thighs. They finished off the piece with a golden headband that when placed on her head rested midbrow with designs of the eye of Ra on each side just by her temples. The ladies kept Bree's hair straight but braided three small braids on each side of Bree's hair with indigo beads woven in that matched perfectly with the color of the sheer fabric. To end the attire, they fitted her with flat leather footwear cut just for her and wrapped in golden fabric up her legs to her knees.

When they finished with her hair and dress, they sat her down and began on her face. They completed her makeup and let her look in the mirror. It was impressive, to see the woman that looked back at her. Never would she have thought that she could pull off blue eyeshadow and black kohl eyeliner, but damn, she looked good. She thanked the ladies for all their challenging work even though it was a whirlwind and only took the ladies a brief time to complete everything. They were miracle workers in Bree's eyes. Bree felt beautiful and could not wait to see her friends finally see her cleaned up. After the ladies left her room, she sat on the edge of her bed when again there was a knock on her door. When she answered it, there on the other side was Zosar and a couple of Ibis priests at his back. "We have come to personally escort you to the feast." Then Zosar stepped closer and admired the view before him as he looked at Bree. "May I say that you look wonderful tonight, my lady."

Bree bowed her head slightly in acknowledgment. "Thank you, Zosar. The ladies were amazing to me. Thank you for sending them. They were the ones that put this all together."

Zosar smiled. "Well, my child, they had a perfect canvas on which to work."

Bree blushed at the compliment, and in her embarrassment, she blurted, "Shall we go then?"

As they walked to the feast hut, Bree had her arm draped through Zosar's, so she quietly whispered to him, "Please, may I ask one favor from you about tonight?"

Zosar leaned in with a nod. "Anything, my dear."

Bree whispered even lower, "I don't want you to mention that you think that I am Nefertiti. I am a normal person. I don't want anyone to feel uncomfortable or think that they need to pray, bow, or throw themselves at my feet. I am just Bree. Okay?"

Zosar patted Bree's hand gently and chuckled. "Of course, my dear. We will talk about that after the feast. I have so much to tell you afterward, but for now, I will keep our little secret."

Bree was going to correct Zosar again that there was no secret but let it go. They were about to enter the hall, and the delicious smells wafting their way distracted Bree, making her realize how hungry she truly was.

When they entered the hall, it was completely full of everyone from the village attending, and they all stood up from their seats. Zosar led Bree over to a platform in the middle of the hall surrounded by all the long tables full of food. "You all may sit. Tonight, we feast in welcome of our guests, who not only healed me but will join us in the fight against Senepol. The Heru army will join our guests on a mission back to the Maahe and Sakhmet tribe to see if they will join the battle. Then we will all travel and ask the same of the Sobek and Aspis tribe if they will join. With the six tribes reunited as one again, we may stand a chance in overthrowing Senepol and have our tribes at peace once more after hundreds of years at war." The audience cheered in unison when Zosar paused. Zosar introduced Bree to everyone without saying that he thought her to be Neferneferuaten, to Bree's relief.

As Zosar continued talking a bit more to his tribe, Bree scanned the room to find her friends. When she laid her eyes on Jabar, she sucked in her breath at how handsome he was. He cleaned up well. They were standing along the back wall with Sethos. Darius looked very dashing too, but Bree could not take her eyes off Jabar. Her heart began to pound, and her stomach fluttered. She smiled brilliantly at them all.

Jabar felt the same way. When he noticed Bree enter, his breath caught in his throat also. He knew she was beautiful, but now that she was clean and dressed nice, her hair done, and her face touched with color, she was a true vision. Sethos was having the same thoughts in his mind. He found her extremely attractive. At first, he wanted to tease Jabar and Darius about their feelings for the tiny female. He knew they both wanted to be more than friends with her, but now, he, too, was under her spell and could not take his eyes off her. Darius was in the middle of Sethos and Jabar, and at the same time she entered the room, Darius elbowed them both in the ribs with the comment. "Wow, she looks amazing. Now tell me she is not a goddess, Jabar." Jabar wasn't sure she wasn't a goddess anymore, either.

Sethos leaned over with a whisper directed at Jabar: "Maahe, you are going to have competition. I am stepping in the ring."

Jabar stood straight, and his mane bristled as he growled low. Sethos did one better. "May the best warrior win her heart."

Just as Jabar was going to tell Sethos to back off, Zosar summoned him and Darius to the center of the room. There he introduced them to his tribe saying they were like one of their own, including the Anubi, who was safe. Bree stood in the middle of her friends and grabbed both their hands when Zosar finished his speech. He led them to the front table with him. Zosar was in the middle with Darius and Sethos on one side and Bree and Jabar on the other. Jabar looked over the table at Sethos and raised his brow with a grin. Sethos frowned. He would be patient. He would woo Bree on his own time even though he would have loved to sit beside her tonight. He started to really like her nickname for him. He wanted to hear her call him big bird at least once more tonight.

The meal had been fantastic. Jabar was extremely impressed with the amount of food the tiny Bree packed away. She ate as much as he did. She even burped quietly. He was the only one that heard it, but she looked over at him, and they both burst out laughing, to which everyone looked over to see what had been so humorous. "Oh my, I think that is my cue to stop eating before I explode. It is all so delicious."

Jabar, still chuckling, let out a larger belch, to which they giggled again. "Oh, that's better. I agree I should stop too."

Just as everyone was finishing the meal, beating wings and a thump in the center of the room drew everyone's sudden attention. Darthos flew down to the center of the feeding hut from the opening on the top of the ceiling. Sethos stood at once in a defensive mode, as did Jabar and Darius. Darthos flared his wings before he spoke. The room became silent with anticipation of what was happening. Darthos had been missing since he had his defeat earlier that afternoon. "Is everyone enjoying themselves? Are you all taken in with by this alien woman and Zosar?"

Sethos stepped forward. "Enough, Darthos! Is your ego so big that now you question our elder?"

Darthos laughed in his response. "Am I to understand you all"—Darthos swept his hand out as he spun once around the center of the room—"gather tonight, blindly letting our entire tribe of Heru warriors follow the word of Zosar and this strange woman, who is accompanied by a nomad Maahe and an enemy Anubi, just because Zosar's has a delusion? You all, sitting here tonight, cheering on, asking for not one shred of evidence or reasons as to why? Do you all march thoughtlessly without concern for your own because one of our elders tells you to? I want to know why! I demand an explanation!"

The whispers began as soon as Darthos finished. A couple of Heru and Ibis called out in agreement, wanting an explanation too. The room became noisy and unsettled with tension rising.

Zosar calmly stood and leaned over to Jabar with his hand gently on his arm. "Please be seated, Maahe and young Anubi." Jabar did not hesitate to listen to the elder and sat down at once. Darius hesitated and growled menacingly at Darthos before he sat down. Zosar then leaned over a little so Bree, who sat wide-eyed at Darthos, could hear him state, "I apologize that this has happened, Bree. I was hoping I would have been able to talk to you and your group before this happened in private. It is time to explain to all what is happening after tonight and why. Darthos is correct. Everyone needs to know." Zosar stood up from his chair and walked behind Sethos, telling him all was well and to have a seat. He approached Darthos serenely with his hands moving gently up and down to quieten the room. "My tribespeople, Darthos is correct. Everyone should not follow blindly into danger without knowing why. I must ask forgiveness for my assumption and for using the influence of my status to think that I did not have to explain. After I make clear the reasons, I give everyone of both our tribes the choice to join in the fight against Sethos or to step back and stay without judgment."

Darthos smugly glared at Sethos as Zosar spoke. Sethos glared back along with Jabar and Darius. Bree kept her eyes on Zosar because Darthos scared her as much as Senepol did. There was an evil aura surrounding this Heru. It sent shivers down her spine.

17

Zosar sighed; Darthos was forcing him into this precarious position, and in turn, Bree's secret could not stay a secret any longer. For everyone to agree to help stop Senepol, the tribe had a right to know. Zosar turned to Bree. "Come down to me, my dear."

Jabar stood quickly. "No. Zosar?"

Bree placed her hand gently on Jabar's arm. "It's okay. They will find out eventually anyway. We need them, Jabar. If my ability will convince the Heru warriors to join us, then this is what I must do." Jabar was angry, but he also understood. If Bree was willing, then she was a grown woman and could make her own decisions, but he still worried for her safety. He did not like Darthos one bit. He felt that he had an underlying reason for his actions, whether it was to rile Sethos or for another dark reason. He knew they would find out soon. He was not looking forward to that day. Darius whined as Bree went behind him, and she stroked his shoulders, whispering, "It's okay, my friend." Bree walked to the center of the feeding hall with her head held high and her back straight. Jabar tapped Darius, and they both went over and stood by Sethos. Jabar commented to them both, "We need to keep a close eye on Darthos. Something is brewing in that one." Sethos and Darius nodded curtly in agreement.

When Bree stood beside Zosar, the room became completely silent. Zosar turned to Darthos and told him to hold out his arm. Darthos laughed. "What do you have up your sleeve, old man?"

The crowd all sucked in their breath at Darthos's direct insult to Zosar. Now it was Zosar's turn to chuckle at Darthos's behavior as he tsk'ed before he responded, as if talking to a child, "You asked me to give the tribes a reason to stand up to Senepol. In doing so, I need you to hold out your arm."

Darthos growled but did as Zosar requested. Zosar gently held Bree's arm that was closest to him, then without warning, he took out a hidden blade from his robe and sliced open Darthos's arm. Darthos, at once, jumped back with a hiss. "What is the meaning of this?"

Without answering him, Zosar quickly cut Bree's arm just enough so it bled then turned to Darthos. "Give me your arm." The strong command coming from Zosar stopped Darthos from arguing, and he gave him his bleeding arm. Zosar placed Bree's arm just above Darthos and let a small drop of blood drip on Darthos's open wound.

Darthos lunged back once more just after he saw her blood mingle into his. "You dare taint my blood with—" Darthos hissed in pain during midspeech and grabbed his arm. "What have you done to me?" The entire hall was on its feet, leaning in to get a better look, whispering and guessing. Zosar did not give an explanation as he waited. Bree went back over to stand with Jabar, Darius, and Sethos. Jabar grabbed Bree's arm and looked at it to make sure it wasn't a bad cut and then held her hand within his when he noted it was more of a little prick than a wound. Darthos held his arm in a rage. He fell to one knee as the sting intensified. "You've poisoned me!" hissed Darthos.

Sethos barked out over the table, "Shut up and look at your arm, you idiot." The look on Darthos face when he noticed that his deep wound was healing was comical indeed. Everyone was now on their feet and was even crawling over the tables to get a better look. Darthos gaped at his arm. "What sorcery is this?" The noise in the hall was overwhelming when they realized his arm completely healed. There was clapping, hooting, whispering, yelling, and whispering from the crowd until Zosar yelled out, "Quiet!" It took a moment for the noise to settle in the feeding hall. Darthos was still looking at his arm in utter confusion. The pain was gone. He began rubbing the area repeatedly.

Zosar addressed the crowd once more, "This young lady, whom we have the privilege to have in our midst, is extremely special." Zosar motioned for the crowd to sit again, which everyone did so quickly. They knew he was leading into an explanation that was sure to be amazing in the telling. Everyone's eyes were on him, and they hushed, leaning forward in anticipation of a great tale.

"As you know, I am one of the last three surviving originals. Staying is, of course, myself, Jendayi (elder of the Sakhmet tribe), and Cepos (elder of the Sobek tribe). In the beginning, there were thirty-two originals that survived the culling ordered by Pharaoh Akhenaten in our birthland of Egypt. Our beloved Neferneferuaten was our salvation. Her love for our kind saved us. She is our goddess and our queen." Everyone in the hall bowed their heads in respect at the mention of Nefertiti for a moment, except Darthos, who had backed off the center platform and silently slipped away unnoticed by the crowd as they focused on Zosar and the tale he was telling. As Zosar began speaking, the tribes focused on him, Darthos took the opportunity to slip away, flying north with concentrated deliberate speed.

Zosar also bowed his head out of respect for a moment and then continued, "What I am about to reveal to you will explain as to how I have survived so many eons. What I am about to tell you all tonight may come as a shock." With this explanation, whispers of oohs and aahs sounded throughout the hall. Zosar continued, "Only the originals were privileged with this knowledge, but tonight, I gift you all with this ancient knowledge too." The room shattered with excited whispers and tense interest. All the tribes knew the old tales of Egypt and their goddess and how they arrived, but they never understood why the elders had survived for so long. It just was. Now they were going to be privy with the secret. Excitement grew within the room. One could cut the air with a knife; it was so thick.

"In my youth, Neferneferuaten chose me as her favorite. Why, you may ask? I do not know. It may have been our similar interests in science, learning, and expanding our knowledge. I never went a day without being by her side. I remember those days with our goddess fondly, filled with peace, love, laughter, and friendship until darkness plagued us. Akhenaten, the pharaoh of Egypt, grew envious of how his people of Egypt began to think of us as magical beings, heaven-sent, and then over time as gods. He ordered our destruction due to his possessiveness of his reign. We lost our brothers, sisters, friends, and comrades, slain in the name of Akhenaten's hatred of our kind worshipped by his people. Neferneferuaten, I, and four of her smartest and wisest scientific priests delved into creating a portal to enable us to escape our genocide. Her Anunnaki ancestors had passed down knowledge of the existence of different planes that we could not see within our own world. The Anunnaki expressed in their teachings that there were ways to generate fractures between our plane into others. My queen decided to try to save us by stealing ancient papyrus and scrolls depicting how one could conduct the opening of a portal. The papyrus and scrolls had complex codes. Only the Anunnaki bloodlines would be able to decipher them. It took us moons to figure out how to decipher these written clues to conduct the creation of the fissure or portal to a new realm.

"We were able to decode from the scrolls that we needed to create five obelisks with the ancient codes carved into them from top to bottom. We also translated that the key to the obelisks was blood. Specifically, Anunnaki blood. Neferneferuaten was a direct bloodline of the Anunnaki. Her blood was the final crucial key. Inside all the obelisks we sealed a vial of our goddess's blood into the bottom of each. This is what gave them their power. When they were close together, they become stronger. Separated, they were weaker. We were stronger and healthier around all five of the obelisks together. With trial and error, we finally were able to fracture the planes, and the portal began to open. With more trials, we were able to stabilize the portal to stay open. Neferneferuaten sent in her loyal guards to search the area we opened. They were the only ones allowed to enter the fissure between the two planes to make sure it was safe to do so. They entered, and we waited with anticipation of what they would find. The guards came back describing a land exactly like Egypt, but it was void of life. For weeks after the first entrance into the portal, Neferneferuaten had her guards round up Egyptian beasts, fowls, insects, and reptiles from their land and moved them secretly through the portal into the new land so they would fill our land with food, life, so we would prosper. The guards also took in supplies, weapons, clothing, and building materials that the eight separate species created needed to survive and generate a new life within this new plane. Everything was set for us to move to our new realm.

"The day we were entering the portal, Akhenaten soldiers came in full force. This was a sad day for all who were entering the portal. Thirty-nine of us entered along with our queen. We did so without knowing that Akhenaten's soldiers had found our secret crypt just as we entered. Suddenly spears and arrows flew through the portal as we entered. The arrows hit us, including myself. An arrow entered through my back, narrowly missing my heart, and pierced out the front of my chest. Six of us perished instantly. My queen took an arrow in her shoulder. We fell together. As I lay there dying, my queen raised herself and was sitting above me, crying. Luckily, the soldiers that remained on the other side of the portal were able to kill the Akhenaten's soldiers that had entered the crypt. They were able to hold off the rest of Akhenaten's soldiers from entering the crypt, but..." You could hear a pin drop in the hall when Zosar paused as they waited for him to continue with his tale.

"I remember my queen sitting beside me, ignoring the arrow in her own shoulder. With painful effort, I placed my weakening hand on her cheek, thanking her for trying to save us all. Ignoring her pain, she lifted my head, placing me in her arms. My queen grabbed the spear penetrating my body and pulled it free, then she hugged me. We embraced one last time, whispering our goodbyes into each other's ears. Then I died."

The crowd gasped, confusion plain on everyone's faces. One of the Ibis priests spoke out, "But, Elder, you are here with us now. You couldn't have died."

Zosar smiled. He was a wonderful storyteller as he had everyone on the edge of their seats, including Bree, Darius, Jabar, and Sethos. Somewhere in the telling of the tale, Bree had reached out with her other hand and ended up embracing Jabar's hand with both of hers. Without question, Jabar held both her hands gently. Sethos noticed, as did Darius, and they both frowned for a moment but then became distracted again by Zosar as he continued his tale.

"I was at the brink of death, and then suddenly I came back with a penetrating, scorching pain within my torso. When I came back to the living, my grievous wound was healing before my eyes. I watched in awe as the wound sealed itself to nothing but healthy revitalized flesh without a scare. Neferneferuaten had left back through the portal, thinking that I had perished, as she was no longer by my side and the portal had disappeared. I did not know if our queen had survived or if she had succumbed to her wounds or further attacks by Akhenaten soldiers when she had exited the portal. Scattered beside me were four of the five obelisks we had created to open the portal. Someone must have thrown them into the portal. The portal must have been sealed before the fifth made it through. For a moment, I thought that our new realm held a great magic. My sudden healing was attributed to our new lands that healed me. I realized I was wrong about my idea when I looked around me. My dear friends that had succumbed to their injuries were still deceased. They had not healed from their grievous wounds. As the rest of my comrades gathered and began to collect our lifeless comrades, I wondered if I had been healed by the magic of the obelisks strewn at my feet. With this thought, I roused myself and at once took the obelisks and placed them by my closest fallen comrade and waited and waited. Yet there was nothing."

"We all marveled at how I had healed. After we had prepared our friends for burial, we pondered on what could have healed me. I began reflecting on our conversations that Neferneferuaten and I had over the times we had spent together learning. Our quest for gaining more intelligence led us into conversations about the Anunnaki and their vast intelligence about space, planets, technology, and how it was that they never seemed to age or to die. I recalled one of our conversations about why the Anunnaki had come to earth in the first place. This question led us to ancient papyrus in the royal library. They told us of the Anunnaki's extreme interest in gold. They were trying desperately to find a way to create gold instead of having to mine for it. How were the two linked—eternal life and the need for gold? We investigated deeper. Recorded in the papyrus said the Anunnaki came to earth because of the vast amount of gold in the planet's ground. They settled here for this one reason. Gold! They had depleted the gold on their planet. They needed to find more.

"They had learned over time that if they melted down the gold, separated the compounds, and then ingested them, it changed their aging process. This breakdown of the gold compounds and ingesting them had given them immortality. After the Anunnaki traveled through space to earth, the papyrus said, this is when the Anunnaki discovered by chance that ingesting the gold compounds and adding high-speed space travel had caused a change in their molecular makeup. They now had the ability to heal each other with their body fluids—their blood being the strongest of their fluids. Needless to say, we were overly excited to find out this secret information."

Zosar stopped his story and walked over to a table and took a drink of wine. He noticed how everyone was beginning to peek in Bree's direction—with reverence, with fear, with confusion, and others with enlightenment. Zosar cleared his throat, starting again where he had left off.

"After creating lower intellectual beings to work their gold mines, the Anunnaki dreamed of returning to their home planet. They had to figure out how they were going to gather enough gold to take back with them. The amount they needed to keep their race ageless was vast indeed. Space travel took time, and they could only come and go from earth to their planet Nibiru every three thousand years as their planet came back around its directory closer to earth. They started to delve into alchemy. After a thousand years, they had found out how to create gold by reverse engineering the compounds that made gold. Now with this discovery, they no longer needed to remain here on earth. They could safely go back to their planet and continue being immortal without having to take any gold back with them. Soon after their breakthrough discovery, Nibiru was coming close to earth again. This is when the Anunnaki picked up and left Neferneferuaten's ancestors back on their own planet.

"When we finished reading all the papyrus, Neferneferuaten picked up a knife and cut my finger and then her own to see if her blood could heal us since she was of Anunnaki lineage."

Sethos interrupted Zosar. He noticed how the people were looking at Bree, and it made him uncomfortable. Bree didn't notice yet, but she soon would. "Did Nefertiti's blood heal you like Bree's did?"

Everyone turned back from staring at Bree and focused on Zosar, awaiting his answer. Zosar sighed deeply. "No, it did not."

Everyone in the crowd moaned, and others called out, "Then what healed you?" "How did you heal then?"

Zosar calmed the crowd, with his hands calmly waving up and down. "For a long time, we tried to figure it out. I could not stop thinking that it was our goddess's blood that had healed me, but I did not know how. It had to be the blood. We had needed her blood to power the obelisks, so it had to have been in her blood.

"After years, the other originals did not remember about my healing and moved on to more important things. We began to procreate, survive, raise families, and build a city. I, however, could not stop thinking about finding the solution. After more years, our population was thriving. The city was coming along beautifully. We had built a life in our new lands. We placed the obelisks in the temple that we had built in our goddess's name. Having them together kept us healthy, strong, and prosperous as long as every individual visited the obelisks at least once a week in the temple. Even the land and the wildlife changed slowly for the better, growing larger over time with the obelisks in our new realm. I was beginning to slowly ignore how I had healed from death as well. Then tragedy came upon us. One of the Maahe originals named Andre received severe injuries by a crocodile while hunting at the river. All the originals gathered and watched him in agonizing pain, slowly dying. His wounds were grievous. Bringing him to the obelisks did not help him. His wounds seemed far too great for even the power of the obelisks.

"When the other originals took him back to his home to die, I stayed behind in the temple. I have no idea why, but Neferneferuaten's voice as clear as day entered my head. The voice said only two words: 'The blood.' Before I knew it, I had picked up one of the obelisks. With my knife I had built into my walking stick, I pried open the bottom of one. There was the vial of blood that we had encapsulated so many years before. I was the only original that knew the blood was in the obelisks. I placed the obelisk back into its position, and with the vial, I ran to Andre's home. I prayed that he was still holding on. When I reached Andre's room, I knelt beside his bed and opened the vial. I poured a miniscule drop of Neferneferuaten's blood on his wound and waited."

Now it was Darius's turn to interrupt Zosar. "Wait, but if the goddess's blood didn't heal you, why would you think it would heal Andre?"

This was the question that Zosar was hoping for, and he said two words: "Space travel."

Everyone in the feeding hall was confused. They had no idea where Zosar was taking his narrative. Space travel came only in ancient stories by the elders. It was a myth, a fantasy. It was only in make-believe. They all still happily lived a primitive life, and that was how they wanted it. There was no need for space travel or even a want to.

Jabar couldn't wait; he was bursting at the seams with the need to know how all this linked in with Bree. "I remember this legend from my Maahe elders. Andre healed. The legend never said it was from the blood of the goddess, though. Everyone assumed that it was the goddess answering prayers."

Zosar nodded toward Jabar. "Yes, Maahe, you are correct. But only because we made sure the legends would never tell the complete truth. You see, after Andre was healed by the blood of our goddess, I explained to the originals about the blood. They also questioned me about the space travel theory, and this is what I told them.

"The portal we opened consisted of just that, space. We don't know where our realm is in space, even to this day. We only know that the portal was a doorway from our old land to here, our new land. For all we know, this realm we exist in could be halfway across the universe from earth. Stepping through the portal was, in a unique way, a kind of space travel. I realized that Neferneferuaten's blood healed me only after we entered the portal. So, if this was true, then her blood in the obelisks would have changed as well. I had proof that it was indeed her blood that had healed me, and now her blood had healed Andre."

Jabar interrupted again, "But why change the legends? Why not just tell us what really happened?"

Zosar swept around the room and pointed to a Heru. "What if I gave you and only you the ability to see the future and no one else could? Would you share this ability to everyone, or would you keep it to yourself?"

The Heru laughed and then said, "I would share it, of course."

Zosar nodded his head. "Ahh, would you? Everyone here tonight finds out that you have this talent. The whole tribe begs you to tell them their future. Soon they want you to tell them what their day-to-day future is. Now no one has the will to do anything without you looking into their daily future in case something bad is to happen to them or their family, and they think with your ability, you will be able to change their future if you predict something bad. This way they can avoid any danger. Now your talent has become widespread. Other tribes hear of your ability. They come from all ends of the lands, every day a new group, to demand of you to tell them their future. You still have everyone in your tribe relying on you for this too. One day, your mother asks you to tell her what her future is. You see that she will die in a tragic accident and there is no way anyone can stop it."

Zosar is in his element with keeping everyone in suspense. He continued, with his face close to the Heru he was questioning, "You try in every way possible for this to not be as you have visioned, but it does. Your mother's demise happens exactly as predicted. Your family blames you. They insist that you should have been able to prevent this tragedy. Everyone begins to want you to tell them about other people's futures, to look into their private lives to find out if they can manipulate their foes if they know what to look for. Every day you receive bombardment, pestering, followed everywhere you venture. You never rest, you never sleep. Your life is no longer yours. The visions you see in other futures make you sick, angry, sad, or disgusted. This ability makes you change the way you see and feel about loved ones and friends. Tell me, Heru, would you share your gift now? Would you share it with only a trusted few who swear an oath to never reveal your secret, or would you keep your ability to yourself?"

The Heru in question gulped. He looked around the room with embarrassment, looking to see if anyone had an answer before he spoke, "I would keep it to myself, Zosar, now that I have heard how it could ruin me."

Zosar smiled and backed away to the center of the circle. "Ahh yes. I did not have this opportunity to keep the secret of the blood to myself since all the originals were there to see the miracle. We all swore an oath that very day. No one, except the elders, would know of the secret of the blood. We went back to the temple to retrieve the other three vials of blood. One was given to the Apis, who would share it with the Anubi. One to the Ibis, who would share it with the Heru. One to the Sakhmet, who would share it with the Maahe, and the last went to the Sobek, who also shared theirs with the Aspis. Over time, each vial was depleted. Mine was the last to remain. Our city thrived for a time until conflict between the tribes began to stir and the Apis leader wanted to take my remaining vial and control of the obelisks. War ensued, and we separated after the city was in ruins. With the tribes separated and the vials of blood gone, the originals began to age and die. I decided when there was only myself and two originals left that I would share what remained with only them. My vial ran out a decade ago. Now the last remaining three are aging, and we will soon die too. I was in the afterlife's door until this beautiful creature saved me with her blood." He pointed in Bree's direction, and everyone stared at her in awe. Zosar directed his next comment to Bree. "Your blood activated when you came through the portal. I know you are not our goddess returned now, but you are a direct descendant of Nefertiti. Your blood is her blood."

Zosar held his arms out and slowly spun around the room, gaining everyone's attention back to him. "Imagine the power that King Senepol will have if he gets this miracle that sits before you. Imagine if he obtains the obelisks and Bree together in his grasp. He will be unstoppable. He will reign havoc on us all. We will not survive. He will enslave us. This is why we must stop Senepol. This is why we go to the Sakhmet, Maahe, Sobek, and Aspis so they will join us in stopping Senepol before he can ruin life as we all know it." Zosar stood as tall as his ancient back would let him with his head held high and his voice strong. "My Ibis. My Heru. *Are you with me?*" Everyone stood on their feet and cheered, clapped, and hooted their acceptance to join in the quest that was upon them. Not one declined. Zosar swept his eyes across the room, seeking out Darthos, only to not find him. Zosar frowned but addressed the crowd once more. "Be ready, we leave at the next full moon."

18

Darthos landed in a dark, swampy spot deep in the lands ruled by the Sobek and Aspis tribes. The land was wet, with untold creatures waiting in the sludge of the swamp in ambush to become a beast's next meal. He was careful. He had been at this meeting spot before. He folded in his wings and hunkered down. He used the secret signal special for these kinds of meetings. Darthos waited to hear the signal response. The signal returned just as he thought he wouldn't receive a response. Slinking out of the darkness on his belly, Sa'd glided into view. Darthos entered into the moonlight for Sa'd to see him and that he was alone. Sa'd slithered closer to Darthos, letting his legs and arms exit from their hiding pods within the length of his snakelike body. When his legs fully exited his sleek, scaley body, he stood tall, matching Darthos in height. "What do I owe for thissss unexpected visssit to me, Heru?" Sa'd spoke with extenuated *s*'s as his forked tongue flicked in and out of his mouth, evaluating the air for any other scents other than Darthos.

"I come requesting a meeting with Senepol. I have current information that will be beneficial to him. Take me to him at once."

Sa'd tucked his legs back in to his body and started to slither around Darthos slowly with a chuckle. "Why ssshould I? Tell me thisss information you believe to be detrimental. I will decccide if it'sss important enough to take you to Sssenepol."

Darthos stamped down his building irritation. Sa'd wasn't just anyone to have mad at you. He was cunning and deviant. He always looked after himself first. "I brought you the two escapees with the two stolen artifacts, did I not?"

Sa'd continued to slither around Darthos with his length coiling closer around his feet. "Yesss, yesss. Senepol was delighted, but you did not complete your end of the agreement. Zosssar, I hear, is sssstill alive and well."

Darthos scowled at Sa'd for reminding him of that failed part of the plan. "This is the important news I bring for Senepol and the reason Zosar still lives. He should have died, but he healed."

Sa'd's coiling body began to wrap around his lower legs and the lower tips of his wings. "Healed, you sssay. You were sssupposed to end him. You left him alive. Tell me, how did he heal?"

By now Sa'd had the length of his body half coiled, tightening around Darthos, who was beginning to panic. "If you kill me now, you will never find out. Zosar, the Ibis, and the Heru army have a new weapon that could damage Senepol's plans. If you do not release me, it will be your fault the table will be turned against Senepol."

The speed of Sa'd's coiling around Darthos increased till he starved him of breath. "You dare threaten me, Heru. I am Sssenepol's messssenger. I will decccide if the newsss you bring isss worth hisss knowing or not. I could kill you. No one would know."

Darthos choked as he gasped for breath with Sa'd squeezing tightly against his chest. "Zosar…has…the…woman."

Sa'd suddenly release his hold slightly, so Darthos was able to gulp in a small breath before he continued. "Her blood…can heal injuries…even ones…on the bridge to the afterlife." Sa'd released his squeeze on Darthos a little again. "I have witnessed this myself. She healed Zosar. When I challenged him tonight, he cut me! She healed me with a small drop of her blood."

Sa's released Darthos; he fell to his knees, gasping for breath as Sa'd uncoiled himself entirely from around him. Sa'd unsheathed his legs, walking away from Darthos as he clutched at his burning chest. "Sssooo you do bring good newsss. Come, Senepol awaits.

*****

Laughter erupted from the dining hall as Darthos and Sa'd followed Senepol's guards to the dining hall door. When they entered, Darthos was confused as he noted the two small men he had handed over to Senepol the night he had thought he'd murdered Zosar.

There they sat, uninjured and laughing at something that Senepol had just said. There they sat, dining with the king, stuffing their faces with delectable food and drink, having a grand time. The guards announced to the king their arrival as they stood, waiting acknowledgment. Senepol took another guzzle of his wine before he raised his hand, waving it in a gesture for his new visitors to come around for him to see. As Darthos walked to the side of the table, Derrick and Aston tipped their glasses to him. Darthos frowned and turned his head slowly away from the tiny men to look at Senepol. King Senepol's deep chuckle resonated through the entire hall. "My friend, you look somewhat confused. Sit, have a drink with us."

An Anubi servant pulled out a chair for Darthos. Another of the Anubi servants poured him a drink and backed away to stand against the wall to await any other demands. Darthos didn't pick up his drink as he stared over at the two tiny men he'd handed over to Senepol as prisoners only a week before. Senepol growled out, "You do not drink, Darthos. Is the wine not to your liking?"

Darthos shifted uncomfortably in his seat. Sa'd slithered up beside Senepol, answering for him, "It seems Darthos is at a loss, seeing the gentlemen he captured dining at your table, my liege."

Senepol burst into laughter and leaned forward toward Darthos. "You are not the only one who can bargain with a king."

Darthos frowned again, regaining his voice. "King Senepol, I must admit, seeing these two sitting at your table comes as a surprise. Did they not steal from you your most precious possessions?"

Derrick and Aston sat in silence as they watched the conversation with wicked smiles plastered upon both of their faces. "They have discussed with me as to why they stole my property and have in return explained to me why I should let them live—as you did when you first flew to me, begging for my help in your scheme to assassinate your precious elder Zosar and the leader of the Heru warriors in order for you to take over leadership of your tribes. You did not follow through with your end of our bargain, Darthos. A little snake told me that Zosar still lives as does Sethos."

Darthos growled at Sa'd, who grinned and shrugged his shoulders. Darthos picked up his goblet, draining a heavy part of it before he placed it back down on the table. "This is why I have come, my king. The woman that you look for throughout the lands—I know where she is." Now Darthos had Senepol's complete attention. "She is with Zosar and Sethos as we speak. She also brought with her the Maahe, Jabar." Without warning, food, plates, and drink were scattered everywhere that lay in front of Senepol as he stood up with a roar, clearing everything with his mighty fist before him. Servants darted forward to pick up the mess. Darthos continued, "I do, however, have great news you want to hear of."

Senepol was standing in front of the table and slammed his fists down upon it, shaking the entire marble table, with all those around fearing it was about to break. Senepol snorted out his snout with a growl following, "Your news better please me, Darthos, or you will not live to see the next rising."

Now it was Darthos's turn to smile as he gulped down more wine, signaling the servant to pour him some more. "Her blood is magic. The tiniest drop can heal the most grievous of wounds, even if one is close to crossing over to the afterlife. I have seen it. She healed me in front of everyone in the Heru and Ibis tribe with one of Zosar's famous demonstrations. This is when I left, flying to tell you. The woman and all the obelisks together in your possession would surely make you the greatest king that ever was, my liege. All the lands and tribes will easily be yours for the taking, excluding, of course, my portion, to which I negotiated."

Instead of Senepol shouting out with joy, he angrily looked over at Derrick and Aston and snorted menacingly, slowly stomping in their direction. "Why have you two not informed me of this magic blood the woman possesses?"

Derrick and Aston scrambled out of their seats, realizing Senepol was seething mad. Aston spoke as he tried to stand his ground with the hulking king stomping toward him, "This is information that we knew nothing of. We only knew that she was of your goddess's bloodline. She was the key that could open the portal from our world to yours. We have told you of all we knew. We knew nothing of her ability to heal with her blood. You would have been the first to know this. We would have definitely disclosed this information to you. You must believe us. You are too wise and powerful to keep this kind of information secret from you. You would have found out just as you have tonight and killed us without a second thought. My king, I value my head where it is right now."

Senepol had reached Aston by this time and towered over him as he snorted with his fist raising to bash in Aston's face. "I know what they are trying to do." Senepol hesitated and lowered his angry face so he was only an inch away from Aston's.

This time it was Derrick who spoke up calmly, sitting back down and even placing his feet crossed at the ankles upon the table as he leaned back with a drink in hand. "They are going to try to find the other obelisks. All we have to do is have them find them all and gather them together. We let them do all the work at finding the other three obelisks. Then we take Bree and what is rightfully yours and kill all that oppose you. It's simple really."

Senepol lowered his fist with a sudden burst of laughter. He reached around Aston, shoving him aside in doing so to slap Derrick on the shoulder. Derrick flew forward, barely stopping his head from slamming into his legs that still rested on the table. Senepol walked back to his place at the head of the table, laughing in amusement. A servant picked up his chair that had tipped over from Senepol's rage just before he sat back down without waiting to see if the chair was indeed there. The Anubi servant stepped back with a huge sigh of relief in that he was able to raise the chair in time, or he would have surely met his end.

Senepol grabbed a large haunch of meat, biting off a large chunk as he directed his word, chewing still as he spoke to Aston and Derrick, "I knew I liked the two of you. Your determination for power almost matches mine. I like this plan, tiny monkey. When the girl and the obelisks are in my clutches, we will open a portal. You both will bring me back the weapons of destruction described to me. These guns, these bombs. When you deliver, I will supply you with all the jewels and gold you need to take over your realm as I will take over mine. I, however, am changing our agreement. Jabar, Sethos, the three remaining originals will die, and the girl, well, she will remain with me."

Derrick jumped up in anger. "You promised if we found her, she would be given to me."

Senepol just chuckled deeply at Derrick. "Shut up, tiny monkey, this is not negotiable."

Derrick was about to retort, but Aston grabbed his sleeve and pulled him forcibly back down to his chair and whispered, "Bree is not worth our deaths. Drop this obsession with her now." Derrick did as Aston demanded, but the scowl did not leave his handsome face.

Senepol stood and insisted that Sa'd take a seat. A servant rushed over, pouring him a drink. Senepol raised his goblet, "Gentlemen, tonight we drink. Tomorrow, we prepare for war."

*****

The next evening, Bree sat in her room with Jabar, Sethos, and Darius. All three insisted they stay with her when an Ibis priestess told them to relax, rest, and eat, as Zosar was in the temple praying to the goddess and would be a while. They readily agreed, completely depleted from the long dramatic days before. Bree was lying on her bed napping. Jabar watched her sleep as he carved a spear. Sethos was standing at the window looking at the sky and listening for any sign or suspicious sounds, while Darius snored loudly in the corner on a hammock. A knock on the door awoke Bree and Darius. Sethos and Jabar jumped up with weapons drawn. Sethos answered the door with caution. When he saw who it was, he backed into the room, giving Zosar space to enter. Even though he was old and feeble, his presence commanded respect. "I must apologize for all my theatrics the other night, Bree. I thank you for your courage. Without it, I dare say we would have Heru following Darthos and backing out in the fight against Senepol."

Bree only nodded, but it was Sethos that spoke, "Darthos is missing. I fear he has something diabolical planned. I understand why you had to do what you did the other night, Father, but with doing so, Bree is now in even greater danger than before."

Zosar nodded to his adopted son. "I agree. After you left the dining hall, I had an urgent sense to enter the temple. As I began to pray, I heard a name—a name so ancient. I in my arrogance forgot about our most powerful god. The name Heka screamed in my head. I have meditated for a couple of days and realized I had no choice. I invoked the god of all tonight. I have never before tried to beg for help from the creator of gods until now. Heka's power, his magic, is everywhere and is everything. I prepared myself as one so powerful demands. I humbled myself before I prayed to him for answers. I washed myself in the sacred pool, dressed in fresh linens, placed food offerings, and burned incense. I washed the golden statue of our goddess with sacred oils before delving myself in deep meditation. I come to you tonight with a message from Heka. He graciously bestowed upon me a vision."

No one spoke; Sethos's, Jabar's, and Darius's mouths hung open in understanding. One having a vision provided by Heka, who was only described in ancient tales of the old gods, was fascinating and terrifying at the same time. They had a new respect for Zosar right now. Bree had heard of the god Heka briefly in her studies. If he had a vision given to him by this ancient god such as Heka, she had seen more unbelievable things of late including what her own blood could do. She, too, listened intently as Zosar continued quietly.

"I see giant flames on the horizon. Out of the flames, charging toward me is a flying Heru warrior wielding a blade. He slashed it down on me. I feel pain and death approaching. The flying Heru fades into a dark mist. My pain eases as I can now see two silhouettes, one of a Heru struggling within the coils of an Aspis. I suddenly cannot breathe. As soon as I think I will suffocate, I can breathe again. Misty images change into themselves, swirling and rolling in space, and now I see a Heru receiving a crown upon his head. Our people cry in anguish upon their knees. This image fades as Senepol bursts out from the flames on a chariot pulled by monstrous red-eyed scarabs. In one arm he holds five glowing obelisks. In the other he holds a woman who is bound and gagged. Riding on each of Senepol's shoulders controlling the reins of the scarabs are two men. As they control the chariot's reins, one grabs for the obelisks, and the other grabs for the bound woman, but they are just out of their reach. As they come closer, a portal opens above their heads, our goddess's face manifests in a white smoky vapor, dominating the entirety of the inner part of the portal. She opens her mouth to scream but instead spews a river of blood, drowning Senepol and his chariot. The flames wash away. Smoke rises, and blood soaks into the sands.

"The sun appears on the horizon bright and beautiful. On the horizon stands all tribes united together. They stare down at a sparkling portal as it grows and opens on the sands. Above the united tribes swirl wispy images in the stars of a Heru, an Anubi, a Maahe, and a woman with long flowing hair. In front of the portal in a semicircle are the five obelisks. A dark figure of a Maahe walks out of the sun toward the portal as the line of all the tribes disappeared up into the misty figures floating in the stars. Our goddess appears from the portal with her arms outstretched. The Maahe and our goddess embrace as lovers. As they separate, the Maahe shoves the goddess back into the portal as the obelisks rip from the sands, following the goddess as the portal seals forever. All is black. I can only hear a mournful cry. This is where my vision ends."

Darius couldn't wait as the room fell silent. "Zosar, what does the vision mean?"

Zosar sighed heavily. "Darthos is the one that tried to end my life. He took the men. They did not escape. He took the obelisks. Darthos is in league with our enemies. He has flown to Senepol informing him of Bree's power. Senepol will be coming for Bree. He will stop at nothing to get Bree and the remaining obelisks into his clutches with the help of Darthos and the men that came with Bree. If Senepol is victorious, our defector will be dictator over the Heru and Ibis. For the unity of all the tribes, we must overthrow Senepol. Bree must return to her own realm and take the obelisks with her. The magic of the obelisks is too great for just one. If they stay in our realm, there will always be another power-hungry Senepol waiting in the wings. The vision tells of heroes." Zosar points at Sethos, Darius, Jabar, and then to Bree. "You were the four in the stars. You are the ones the goddess chose to prevent Senepol's destruction on our people and lands. Our goddess is guiding you. She will take care of you if your hearts are pure."

*****

When the door closed behind Aston and Derrick as they entered their chamber, Aston grabbed Derrick and punched him right in the mouth. Derrick stumbled back with a look of surprise and then anger as he regained his balance and touched his bleeding lip. "What the fuck was that for?"

Aston was seething. "You are one stupid son of a bitch. You do realize we are trying to keep ourselves alive by aligning ourselves with an unstable lunatic, which is three times our size and thinks nothing of torture and murder on a whim."

Derrick licked the blood from his lip. "What does that have to do with you punching me in the face?"

Aston shook his head in disgust. "You just can't stand her not worshipping you as every other woman in your presence has before, can you?"

Derrick frowned at Aston in confusion. "Who the hell are you talking about?"

Aston threw his hands up in the air. "Bree! I am talking about Bree. I, for one, am not going to die because your brain is in your cock."

Derrick sluffed at Aston's comment. "Bree is mine until I am finished with her. Senepol can have my sloppy seconds when I'm done."

Aston's face went bright purple, and the veins popped out of his forehead with rage. He launched himself at Derrick. The two smashed to the floor. Aston was much stronger than heartbreaker Derrick and had him pinned while he punched him in the face. When Derrick had enough and lay limp in Aston's grip, Aston let Derrick's head drop to the floor and pushed himself off. "So, help me God, Derrick, if I have to cut off that dick of yours to get what we came here for, then I won't hesitate for a second. Do you understand me? We came for the obelisks. If you can keep your dick in your pants and your mouth shut, we will get them. When we are back home, you can have all the damn pussy you want. Forget about Bree. She is dead anyway."

Derrick dragged himself up and swept his unkempt hair away from his eyes as he spat blood onto the floor. He headed over to a lounger, poured himself a drink, and slugged it back with a hiss as the alcohol burned the inside cuts of his mouth. With a smug look on his face, he turned back to Aston. "Fine, Senepol can have her." He spat once more on the floor and then flopped into the lounger, continuing to drink the entire urn of wine. Aston wrapped his knuckles with linen, as they had sliced open on Derrick's teeth. He sat on the edge of the bed watching the spoiled brat get drunk and realized that Derrick would have to disappear. He was becoming a detriment to his mission. All that mattered were the obelisks. When he had them in hand, he would make Derrick vanish. His uncle Vincent would understand. All Victor ever cared about was money and power. If he brought the obelisks back to him, the sorrow of losing Derrick would not last. They would move on to improved things. Aston thought about slicing Derrick's throat as he passed out drunk on the lounger but turned away in disgust. Tomorrow would be a busy day; Derrick may still be of use to him. Senepol seemed to like him for now, so maybe he would keep him around as a distraction to entertain Senepol. With that in mind, Aston crawled under the covers on the large bed and promptly fell to sleep.

*****

As everyone was settling down for the evening in the Senepol's palace, a figure of an Anubi popped up in the darkened window of the servant quarters for a moment. A homing pigeon flew quickly out of the servant's hands as it was released into the air. "Fly to Jendayi, little bird." Then the Anubi figure disappeared unnoticed. The pigeon flew quickly in the direction of the planes to which one of the last three originals lived, with a crucial message tied securely to one of its legs.

19

The full moon was a week in coming before they were to leave on their quest to find the obelisks. They decided half of the Heru army was to stay behind to protect the village. With the warriors that were going on the mission, they were focusing on training. With the reduction of warriors, everyone in the village helped secure the village in case of attacks. They beefed up the border patrols and watches, added traps within the surrounding forest of the village, and built a tall security wall around the outer edges of the village as well. Jabar, Darius, and Sethos were in constant training during the day, so Bree decided to join the training. She needed to at least try to defend herself. She didn't need to be such a burden to the ones trying to protect her. Every night she collapsed in her bed exhausted from the day of vigorous training. She loved it, though. She spent the day with her friends as they taught her all they knew. The best part of her day was her time alone with Jabar. They would go off to a quiet field where Jabar taught her hand-to-hand combat with a sword and daggers. He showed her both offense and defense moves as well as how to slip out of certain holds and knots. They laughed together and teased each other constantly in between the focused training. Bree found that Jabar was an amazing, patient teacher. Jabar found that Bree was a devoted and an extremely adaptive person. They impressed each other on a daily basis and never tired of each other's company. They had become inseparable. They had become best friends.

At first, Sethos was quite upset at the growing relationship between Jabar and Bree. He also liked Bree very much, but he realized after a week of trying to pursue her that it was a lost cause. He watched them together every day with envy at their growing friendship and decided he would lose if he continued, so he backed off. He was also developing a strong bond with Jabar. He was a great warrior, hunter, planner. He was intelligent, brave, and honest as the day was long. Sethos had never had a good friend, but Jabar was becoming just that. However, he never told Jabar that he was backing off his pursuit of Bree. It was much too entertaining seeing how jealous and frustrated Jabar would get when he flirted with Bree. Darius still adored Bree too, but the relationship had turned into a brotherly adoration. Plus, there were flirtatious Heru girls around the same age as Darius that had caught his eye. There were also young Heru males that really liked Darius's company. They all became fast friends, so he was usually training, eating, and hanging out with them during the day. At night, they all still gathered and slept in Bree's hut. They felt the need to be as close to her as possible in case of an ambush. Their little circle was developing into a tight unit that not one of them had expected. Their friendships developed as naturally as breathing without having to think about it.

The morning before they were to leave, they are awakened by a loud knock at their door. A priest was on the other side and stated, "A large group of Sakhmet and Maahe are en route to the village. Zosar has asked to prepare yourselves for their arrival." Without another word, the priest turned and left, disappearing down the hall. Sethos left the room to his own hut, but before he did, he gave Bree a kiss on the cheek, which had Jabar growling quietly so only he could hear. Darius jumped out of his hammock, blurting out that he was going to get ready with his friends for the visitors' arrival, leaving Jabar and Bree alone in the hut. Bree was still wiping sleep from her eyes, still foggy, not quite awake. Jabar, though, was wide awake and began pacing the room. He was worried. It had been years since he had seen his own tribes. He had been a nomad since the destruction of his village and the murder of his family. Would the Maahe feel that he had abandoned them? Would they accept him back? Did he want them to?

Bree sat on the edge of her bed and watched Jabar for a full five minutes as he paced, muttering to himself then stopping to listen out the window then pacing again. He looked nervous. This was unlike him. "Jabar, are you okay? You're acting like a kid on the first day of school."

Jabar stopped and sighed heavily. "Seeing my people again after so many years is troubling."

Bree stood up from her bed and walked over to Jabar, wrapping her arms as far around his large torso as his size would allow. "You are worried for no reason, my friend. I bet they will be overjoyed to see you."

Jabar returned the embrace. "I have been without my kind for so long. Since the murder of my family and my village, I have had a one-track mind. All I have thought about was destroying Senepol. I fear the worst. What if they think I deserted them?"

Bree felt his sorrow and hugged him tighter. "I bet they've missed you. Jabar, you dedicated your life to preventing Senepol from destroying more villages. You are a hero, Jabar—a vigilante hero, but a hero nonetheless. They will be delighted to see you."

Jabar turned and collected Bree into a bear hug. "What would I do without you, Bree? You are right. I shouldn't be nervous about seeing my own tribes. Thank you."

Bree had just enough time to dress, run a brush through her hair, and pinch her cheeks to add color before they left the room. They waited with all the others as the visitors entered the newly built defense gate. Bree squeezed Jabar's hand reassuringly. He took a deep breath and then exhaled. Zosar was at the front of the tribe to greet them. Bree was amazed at the amount that had come. There were over a hundred of them. Bree was fascinated. The Sakhmets' mounts were gigantic rats. Bree found this humorous because of the irony of it. The giant rats were horrifying, but she was becoming used to the strange and unusual by now. The Maahe mounts were simply large elephants. They weren't mutants or terribly oversized. They were just large elephants with saddles that could carry two or three Maahe at one time. In the center of the large group was an elegant covered chariot. Instead of standing in it, there were seats piled with cushions. Upon the cushions sat the Sakhmet elder Jendayi. Bree looked at the visitors and marveled at how beautiful they were. The Maahe were powerful like Jabar, and the Sakhmet were sleek, elegant cat people. She looked back at Jendayi and couldn't tear her eyes away. She was stunning to look at.

The only catlike attributes about the Sakhmets were their faces, ears, paw-like feet, and a strip of fur down the center of their spines that connected to their long swinging tales. Everything else about them was completely humanlike. They moved like cats though with precise, effortless flowing movements. It was enchanting to watch them. Suddenly out of the crowd of newcomers, a female voice was yelling out Jabar's name. A tall gorgeous Sakhmet burst from the crowd, running toward Jabar. Jabar released Bree's hand instantly when he spied the woman calling out to him. When she closed in, she leaped through the air, into Jabar's arms, embracing him, followed by a kiss that made Bree blush in embarrassment. She had never felt so awkward in her life as she did at this moment. When the beautiful Sakhmet finally pulled away, she had tears in her eyes. "I can't believe it's really you. I have missed you so."

Jabar had to pry the woman off him before he could put her down. He cleared his throat before he responded, "I have missed you too, Zahra. You look absolutely beautiful."

Bree quietly walked away to give Jabar and his past lover privacy. Why her heart was breaking was beyond her. He had never in any way expressed anything but friendship, but it still hurt nonetheless. Sethos was at once by Bree's side with a concerned look on his face. "Sometimes the forgotten past can come back to haunt one's new life."

Bree only nodded and blinked back tears that were about to flow. There was no way she was going to cry. She was acting ridiculous. Bree changed the subject. "Do the Sakhmets and Maahe make it a habit visiting with such a large entourage as there is today?"

Sethos shook his head. "To tell you the truth, this is the first time I can remember them ever visiting our village. Jabar was the first Maahe I have seen within our borders for more years than I can count. Zosar always traveled to a central meeting place when the elders of each tribe got together for their yearly council gatherings. Their timing is uncanny. We were heading to see them after we spoke with the Sobek and Aspis tribes. Something is amiss. This visit is not a coincidence. Let's go to Zosar. He will be summoning you shortly anyway." Bree nodded, and Sethos grabbed ahold of Bree's hand. Bree looked back toward Jabar and noticed that he was also watching her with Sethos with a strange look on his face as the beautiful Sakhmet still chatted to him. Childishly Bree held fast on to Sethos's hand a little friendlier than she should have. *Take that, Jabar. Hope you feel as hurt as I do.* The moment the thought entered her brain, she felt guilty.

Jendayi gracefully exited the chariot and approached Zosar. Behind her was a distinguished yet seasoned Maahe warrior. Zosar bowed to them both, and they returned the gesture. "Jendayi, Montu, this is an unexpected surprise. Our tribes were coming to see you very soon to ask of you an incredibly special favor."

Jendayi smiled. "A little bird informed me trouble, once again, is brewing within the Apis tribe. I ventured to our temple to meditate on this issue. I had a troubling vision shown to me by the god that I had forgotten about for eons. It was a vision from Heka." Zosar stood fast with no emotion upon his face as he heard Jendayi speak. "After the vision, Montu and I discussed it in detail. We both concluded we needed to come and assist in any way possible."

Zosar sighed, and his shoulders seemed to have weight removed from them. "I believe we both have experienced the same vision from Heka. We had forgotten him, but he never forgot about us. Your presence is most welcome. You have saved us time in travel and discussion. I also want to introduce you both to the special guests that I believe are the center of our vision." Zosar turned to Sethos and Bree, beckoning them both forward. He searched the crowd for Jabar and Darius and bid them forward as well. When they all approached, Zosar introduced the group to Jendayi and Montu.

Jendayi tried not to be surprised when introduced to Bree; she stepped up close to her and stroked her face gently with her hand. "The resemblance is uncanny. How strong her bloodline is! You healed Zosar! I thank you with all the eons of my life." Bree nodded slightly; she was still in awe of Jendayi. Her beauty, poise, grace, and intelligence exuded from her like a glowing aura. Jendayi walked over to Jabar, who was looking at the ground, too embarrassed to look her in the eye. Jendayi also stroked her hand on his face. "My vigilante warrior. It saddened us so to hear of your hunting village and the loss of so many of your loved ones' lives. We hold a vigil each year for all who died that day. Sweet warrior, Montu and I understand why you felt you needed to stay away. Just know we will always love and support you as well as what you have done. You alone have saved an untold amount of lives. Hold your head high, Jabar. Never be ashamed of following the call of the goddess." Jabar fell to one knee and kissed Jendayi's hands. The elder Montu stepped forward as Jabar arose. They embraced each other with heavy slaps to each other's backs. Montu never said a word. He just nodded to his long-lost warrior. Jendayi gently reached out, taking Jabar's hand as well as Bree's, and placed them together. "Your souls entangle one another. Take care of each other. Protect each other. One without the other will only cause unbalance."

Jendayi moved to Sethos and took his hand in hers. "You must be the flying warrior they call Sethos? You, too, play a particularly significant role in all this. Protect these three with your life, Sethos. Without you, this will all fall apart."

Sethos bowed and thumped his hand in a fist against his chest. "I will do as you say, Elder Jendayi."

Montu returned the symbol of strength and promise by thumping his fist against his chest back to Sethos. Jendayi and Montu turned lastly to Darius, who stood with his head bowed and his shoulders slumped. Overwhelmed in the presence of the two elders, his heart began to race uncontrollably, especially with Jendayi. She was a deity onto herself. "Come to me, young Anubi." Darius gulped as he stepped forward and fell to one knee, keeping his head low and his eyes to the ground. "Do not kneel, young one. You are an equal here." Darius looked around and then up at Jendayi, who had a gentle smile directed at him. He stood slowly, and Jendayi stepped forward, grasping his upper arms. "One so young yet so brave. Without your sacrifice of leaving your family behind to help save Bree and Jabar, none of this would have happened. Your family bloodline is strong, courageous, and noble. Stand proud, young Anubi, you complete this pod of heroes." Darius stood tall and puffed out his chest from the praise he received from the elder. Montu repeated the first pound to his chest, and Darius reciprocated. The elders moved back toward Zosar, who requested they all join him in his private quarters to divulge and discuss information and implement a plan to move forward.

The Maahe and Sakhmet visitors that came with Jendayi and Montu pitched tents within the Heru and Ibis borders. They stayed within the protection of the newly constructed border wall. As everyone set up camp, Zosar, Jendayi, Montu, Bree, Jabar, Sethos, and Darius gathered in Zosar's private chambers. Jendayi did not waste any time. As everyone sat down, Jendayi had Montu open a trunk that they had brought up from the chariot that had traveled with them for their visit. Everyone went silent. Jendayi lifted out something covered in a deep blue-colored throw. Montu took the covered object and placed it on the center table where everyone congregated. Jendayi pointed to Zosar and asked him to do the favor of taking the cover off to reveal the object underneath.

There in shock sat everyone, looking upon the uncovered once hidden obelisk that Jendayi had kept hidden for eons. Even Zosar was speechless as they all sat staring at the obelisk. In the dimly lit chamber filled with cascading smoke billowing from incense burners, Jabar spoke first, "How did you know?"

Finally, Montu spoke. "To conquer Senepol, this was the only option."

Suddenly Zosar stood up and moved to his private room. Within minutes he returned with a large *Phalaenopsis* orchid in a large vase and placed it in the center of the table beside the obelisk. Everyone looked at Zosar with confusion. Bree perked up, "I have never seen a more beautiful orchid. You must have groomed this beauty for years. What does this have to do with the obelisk?"

Zosar just smiled as he leaned over the table and pulled hard on the roots of the orchid with one hand as he placed the other on the vase. As everyone watched Zosar, the plant was released from the vase and pulled up, with the roots entangled around an object. Everyone sucked in their breaths and waited. They all knew what the roots entangled, but they stayed silent until Zosar cleaned the roots of the orchid and the dirt away from the sacred obelisk. After

Zosar completed the dramatic reveal of the second obelisk, everyone just sat in silence, contemplating the two sacred pieces sitting side by side together on the table, watching them as they began to glow and slightly vibrate. Sethos was impressed how Zosar had been able to keep the secret of having the obelisk right beneath all their noses. He was sure someone had buried it within the mountains. He had admired that very orchid every time he had come to converse with his adoptive father. Not once had he ever thought that within the vase it held the ancient artifact.

Bree watched to see if anything else happened before she spoke. "When Senepol placed the two obelisks together, he transformed. He grew bigger, stronger. Why is this not happening with any of us right now?"

Montu responded to Bree's question. "Did Senepol place the obelisks together in the temple?"

Bree nodded.

"The obelisks connect to the temples, but they also associate what one most desires from them. The obelisks are neither good nor evil. They only respond to the need of those who have them. When we had them all together in the forgotten city, the need was for life, growth, food, and healing. Then individuals in the tribes realized that they wanted them for possession and power. The obelisks were divided between the tribes so no one had the potential to use the obelisks for evil. Senepol is evil. Senepol wants power, control, dominance overall. We all, sitting here tonight, want peace, unity, oneness. The obelisks know this, and the obelisks provide what is the desires and needs of the people or person in possession of them."

Jendayi stood up, walking herself around the table. She stopped just behind Bree and began to gently string her fingers through Bree's long black hair for a moment, then she spoke, "Senepol has two. We have two. Ours are stronger than his, if you are willing, Bree. Your blood will rejuvenate the power within these two obelisks before us. They can be more powerful than Senepol's. This, of course, is only if you agree to bless the obelisks with the power of your essence that is within you."

Zosar reached for the obelisks and turned them over. He pulled out a wooden plug, revealing a small space in the center starting at the base of the obelisk. "We will do the same thing as Nefertiti did with her blood so many millennia ago. We will place a small amount of your blood into a cleaned intestine, then we will seal them and place them within specially made goatskin containers that we have then put into the base of the obelisk and cap them off once more. We will make five skin vessels with your blood. If by miracle we are able to obtain the other three, we will have them already at our disposal to place in the remaining obelisks. We need to defeat Senepol. Once we have defeated the bull king and have all the obelisks in our possession, we will need to go to the most sacred of temples that we sadly abandoned so long ago. We need to go to the forgotten city and perform a ritual there to open a portal. Then Bree, you and the obelisks must go back to your plane. If the obelisks stay here, we will only have another rise up and become another Senepol. Once you get them to your home, it is up to you."

Bree looked over at Jabar as he sadly looked back at her. *Do I want to go back to my home?* Bree thought to herself as she looked at Jabar. The thought of leaving brought her more pain than she ever imagined it would. Without expecting such emotion, she started to cry. To lighten the mood in the room, she spoke up, "What a waste, no one here that needs healing." Everyone laughed, which improved everyone's demeanor. With the tension broken, Bree agreed to fill the tiny intestinal tubes. With the task complete, two of the five blood vials went in the base of the obelisks. The power that emanated from the obelisks changed. They were now humming softly, and the glow coming out of the hieroglyphs pulsated a soft blue. Everyone in the room felt peace and knowledge of what they must do flow through them. Bree felt clearheaded; Jabar felt bravery coursing through his blood. Sethos could feel his wings strengthen and grow strong. Darius felt indestructible, while the three elders felt wisdom and intelligence like they had never known before. Even the four tribes gathered within the village could feel a change in the atmosphere. They were all calm and ready to end Senepol's constant bombardment of their lands and their people. There was a halo of blue aura encasing the large village. The glow softly pulsed and moved like one would see if looking at the aurora borealis from a distance.

20

It was an impressive sight, seeing the large congregation of travelers as they were close to entering the swamplands of the Sobek and Aspis. The Heru warriors all flew above protecting the entire line of travelers from the air. The front of the pack were half the Maahe warriors, and the back of the pack were the rest in case of a forward or back attack. The second in line and the second last were the Sakhmet tribe armed with their bows and arrows. The third were the Ibis priests as they surrounded the center of the traveling group, which were the two Elders and Montu in possession of the two obelisks. It had taken the large entourage over a week to travel to the outer rim of the swamplands. The Sobek and Aspis were already aware of their coming. Runners had traveled ahead to tell them of their arrival. They needed guides from the swamp tribes to direct them through the perilously difficult terrain. There were sinkholes; deep, dark, chilly waters; dead trees; rotten stumps; weeds; and hidden deadly creatures at every turn. There was quicksand in the most unexpected places, and to top it off, they were fighting off the gigantic mosquitoes, flies, and horrendous toads that could gulp down a small child. The smell of the lands was that of rot, mildew, and mold. Steam rose from within the reeds at all times, making it hard to see, as the thick, foggy mist only allowed one to see a limited amount in front of them at any given time. The worst of it for ones not from the swamplands was the missing view of the sun. It was always twilight during the day and extremely dark at night.

Jabar was becoming uneasy the closer they came to the swamp region. His last dealing with the Aspis had landed him in Senepol's dungeon, beaten within an inch of his life. Sa'd, the Aspis spy he had used for years for information on Senepol, had bitten him in the ass.

If he saw Sa'd, he would kill him instantly. He worked for both sides at that time, and now Jabar assumed that Sa'd had fully crossed over to the Apis side. Had others followed him was what Jabar thought about now. Were the Sobeks on Senepol's side now? They were soon to find out. There was a lengthy line of Sobek soldiers standing along the swamp border. They stood two feet apart with their spears at their sides, ready to use, but not at the moment in an aggressive manner. The weapons were there if needed. Bree was enthralled with what she took in from the Sobeks' appearance as she sat on Pepi with Jabar right behind her. She noted that they looked deadly, each one of them. Their crocodile heads were shorter snouted than an actual full Nile crocodile. Their teeth were the scary part. They were long and had a zipper effect with one on the top jaw fitting in with one on the bottom jaw. It looked like they had a constant evil grin on their faces. Their eyes were slitted with heavy brows over the top. Their entire bodies, even the human parts, were covered entirely in crocodile skin. The muscles in their necks bulged out snakelike, connecting to massive shoulders and chest, corded with bulky muscles. Their hands and feet were webbed for faster travel in the water. They had strong massive thick tails that reached the ground behind their feet that helped counterbalance their bodies for better footing. Bree would never want to come up to one of these creatures in a lonely darkened alley.

Jabar felt Bree shiver and wrapped his arms around her waist and placed his large maned head on her shoulder and began to quietly purr. He knew this would calm her. Jabar found this to be his favorite go-to method to help Bree calm down. It worked at once. Sethos flew down with Heru warriors, greeting the head guard. They had a brief discussion that no one could hear. After a minute, Sethos turned and walked to Jabar, Bree, and Darius. They waited for Zosar, Jendayi, and Montu to approach them before Sethos spoke, "We have come at a troubled time. Their original elder, Cepos, has fallen terribly ill. They do not think he will survive through the night. They are very wary right now. They suspect foul play within their ranks. They do not think this is a coincidence that he has fallen ill as our runners showed up informing them of our arrival. They have our runners in custody. They are suspects in the possible poisoning of their elder."

Jabar growled out one name: "Sa'd." Everyone turned to Jabar with confused expressions. Jabar explained to them briefly what had occurred between himself and Sa'd only a month earlier that had landed him in Senepol's dungeon.

Zosar, Jendayi, and Montu gathered together for a couple of minutes to confer between themselves. They all agreed on their idea and turned back to the small group, explaining what they had decided. Bree sighed. Her arm had yet to heal from the bloodletting a week ago to fill the vials for the obelisks. She was full of wounds on her arms from healing so many as well as Sethos's talon punctures. She was able to bring the near dead back to life, but she was unable to heal herself, but again they asked her to demonstrate her special ability. She readily agreed for the good of the group. Jabar volunteered to be the one cut open for them to show the Sobek soldiers Bree's ability to prove to them that she could heal Cepos. Sethos flew back over to the Sobek soldiers. They laughed and looked extremely speculative. They agreed purely out of curiosity. They only allowed Jabar and Bree to join Sethos. Jabar handed the head Sobek soldier his blade and asked him to cut him deep on his chest. The Sobek soldier accepted the blade all the while smiling at the other soldiers around him. Without warning, he viciously slashed Jabar deeply across his chest. Jabar groaned and staggered back a little but stood his ground as blood poured from his chest wound. Bree was startled at the Sobek soldier's unnecessary violence with the cutting of Jabar. She stalked up to the giant crocodile man, grabbed the blade away from him, and quickly cut her own arm. "Pray you do not need me to heal you because I would leave you to die." She didn't wait for a comment as she turned and quickly but gently smeared her bloody arm against Jabar's chest.

Jabar braced himself for the immense stinging he knew was about to come. It would be as bad as the wound pain itself. The head guard was about to scoff at them when suddenly Jabar went down on one knee, gritting his teeth with a loud hiss. To the amazement of the Sobek soldier, he could see the blood flow slowing and the wound beginning to heal underneath all the blood. He gasped loud and long, to which other Sobeks closed in to watch the show. They all stood agape with their toothy mouths hanging open. The head soldier helped Jabar to his feet. "I would have never believed if I did not see. You say this tiny female can heal our Cepos."

Sethos only nodded. "The sooner the better. She healed Zosar, who was at the edge of the afterlife, and look at him now." The Sobek soldier looked over Sethos to see Zosar, who was watching, and he waved back with his beak and wings. Jendayi and Montu just bowed their heads once.

Jabar stood up fully healed; the burning had subsided. The head Sobek soldier once again looked at Jabar's chest; he even reached out and touched the now completely healed wound. "Not even a scar. I must do one more thing to be convinced this is not a trick." The soldier took out his own blade and sliced open his own chest. "I must see if her blood heals a Sobek."

Luckily, Bree's cut was still bleeding, and she hadn't wrapped it yet. So without hesitation, she smeared her bloody arm across his chest too. All the soldiers waited. The Sobek soldier groaned loudly and fell to his knees then gurgled as if he was choking when the healing pain commenced. They all calmly waited. "Oh, goddess, it's working. I feel my wound healing from within." When the wound healed on the soldier's chest, they were convinced without a doubt. With the cutting, healing, and proving Bree's ability finished, the Sobeks agreed to let only the elders, Jabar, Sethos, Darius, and Bree enter their swamps. Everyone else stayed on the outside of the swamplands just on the border and set up camp.

They had to go on foot; the mounts would only slow them down to traverse the swamps. They did not have time to have the mounts, who were unfamiliar with the territory, get stuck or sink in quicksand, as time was of the essence. The land they traversed was dark, wet, and gloomy. A couple of times they had to hunker down while the Sobek soldiers dealt with nasty beasts and bugs. You could hear one of the large mosquitoes coming from quite the distance; they were that big. Bree was sure if they sucked her blood, it would only take two of them to suck her dry. She could not wait till they were as far away as possible from these swamplands. Everywhere she looked she could see glowing eyes and beasts behind every dead stump or branch or leering up from just below the murky waters. The sounds were just as spooky, and she felt as if she was in an episode of *Haunted* or *Paranormal*. After an hour of careful walking and stepping, they came to a massive dead tree that looked ancient and evil. Its branches were barren of leaves, with sticky moss and vines hanging lifelessly to the ground. If it were dark, one could easily mistake it for a giant monster with terrifying arms rearing out of the ground to snatch up anything close and eat them whole. The hollow knots in the tree housed owls and other unseen creatures. Bree was afraid to approach it, but with Jabar holding her hand securely, she was able to quickly enter the side of the tree that had a hidden entrance to the bowels of the earth below. The entrance of the tree quickly led down underground, deep under the swamps.

Sethos helped Zosar, and Darius was honored to help Jendayi with the descent into what seemed to Bree like entering hell. The more they descended, the more she noticed tunnels heading off into other directions. If they had not a guide, they would forever wander aimlessly, lost within the dark maze under the swamp. After uncountable twists, turns, cutbacks, and constant avoidance of rotting roots, they finally turned into a massive opening. They entered into a hall that was actually a total contradiction to the tunnels they had traveled through. The ceiling appeared constructed from massive boulders. The walls were set in a concrete type of hardener, and the floor was solid stone. Bree realized that this must be a throne room and a gathering spot for meetings, festivals, and large meals with huge solid wood tables and benches covering the floor and a throne at the far end that made Senepol's throne look small. At the moment, the throne was empty, as was the hall. They passed through the throne room and down dark halls designed to withstand pressure and seepage of water from the above swamps. They were all led to the private chambers of Cepos. The room was sparsely, furnished with a large canopy bed in the center of the room, one grand wardrobe, and a bedside table full of candles, but nothing else.

In the center of the bed lay Cepos. He lay propped up with pillows, his eyes closed. His scaly skin was pallid and gray. His breathing was labored. Bree would have thought him dead if it weren't for the occasional hard rise and gurgled breathing coming from the elder. The room smelled of death. Bree had to force herself to not be rude and place her hand over her mouth and nose. She noted that everyone in the party was desperately trying to do the same. Everyone was silent as they looked upon one of the last of the three originals dying before their eyes. Jendayi sobbed sadly, and Zosar looked extremely upset. Bree took this as a sign to step up. She went over to the head soldier that she had healed earlier. "Is he able to drink?"

The soldier nodded slightly. "Just barely."

Bree placed her tiny hand on his scaly arm. "Can you bring me a goblet, and may I borrow your dagger please." The soldier snapped his fingers at someone sitting at the elder's bedside that Bree had missed earlier. She startled as she watched a large female snake hybrid slither forward. Bree had to suppress a scream. She did choke on her own spit again though when the long slithering creature was in full view and then popped her legs and arms out of body sheaths and flared out her neck like a cobra would when threatened. She opened her mouth, flicking a dark-red forked tongue which displayed her long sharp fangs in the process. Bree wanted to flee. Why did this creature make her want to bolt in the opposite direction as fast as she could? Even the sight of Senepol as frighteningly large and beastly as he was didn't make her want to turn tail and run. Bree felt weakness enter her knees and dark spots closed in on her vision. *Don't pass out, don't pass out, don't pass out* was all she could think of until she felt Jabar at her back. He encased her within his massive warm arms and pressed her tiny frame into his chest as his gentle purring vibrated through her to calm her soul.

The head soldier said something quietly to the female serpent, and she slithered away to do his bidding. Jabar leaned down to whisper into Bree's ear, "That is one of the Aspis tribe members. Not only are they amazing with herbs and healing, but they make incredible assassins. They are cunning, sneaky, and sly. Aspis are highly intelligent. Never underestimate the Aspis. You never truly know which side they are on at any given time. Stay away from them if you can, Bree."

Bree turned to Jabar. "What is it about a serpent that causes such fear?"

Jabar chuckled quietly. "I think it may be their hypnotic movements and their eyes. I, too, am uncomfortable around them." The serpent healer returned and handed the goblet to the head Sobek guard, then without a word, she gave the visitors a look that sent shivers up all their spines, then she turned, slithering back to her spot by the bed, becoming almost undetectable once again.

The head soldier handed Bree the goblet. Jabar hated this part. He hated seeing Bree in pain. He noticed she was appearing weaker, paler, and more tired. When he looked at her arm littered with wounds, old and new, it broke his heart. She could not heal herself, which seemed extremely unfair. He leaned down once more to whisper into Bree's ear. "Are you well enough for this, Bree? You have spilled much of your lifeblood in the last couple of days. You should wait a day. Let you gain your strength back."

Bree turned, faced her best friend, and placed her small hand against his furred cheek. "This will be the last time for a while, Jabar. We need the Sobeks to join us. Saving Cepos will gain their loyalty and respect. He is near death. I can feel it. If I don't do this now, the elder will be gone by tomorrow. I must do this now."

Jabar nodded and backed away from Bree after he handed her his dagger. Bree found humor in this. There was still Jabar's blood and the soldier's blood dried on the blade. Well, thank God for no blood-borne diseases like AIDS or hepatitis on this plane, or they would all be in grave danger. Bree took in a deep breath and quickly reopened the wound from earlier on her arm. She cringed slightly, but when she saw the blood begin to flow, she held her arm over the top of the goblet.

After the blood was draining down Cepos's throat, he began to cough and sputter. The female serpent slithered back and forth beside the bed, extremely worried, and she voiced her concern, "What isss thisss? How will her blood heal the elder? What demon magic isss..." Before she finished her sentence, a loud hiss emanated out of Cepos, and then he groaned deeply, turning into a snarl and then another deep cough. The coughing stopped, and Cepos gulped in a deep breath as his body went into an epileptic-type spasming. Suddenly he sat up; his eyes popped open, with his hands flying to his chest. "Oh my" was all he said as he looked around the room. The color of his skin was returning to a natural dark green, and his slit eyes looked bright and rejuvenated. He turned to the Aspis beside him. "What did you give to me, Tiye? I'm healed. I feel renewed."

All the visitors within the room were silent. Tiye looked over at Bree with a very strange look, then she turned back to look at Cepos. "Cccepos, I did all within my power to heal you. I mussst tell you your recovery was not of my ability. It was that ssstrange tiny woman'sss magic. Ssshe brought you back from entering the afterlife. It'sss sssomething I have never witnessssed before."

Cepos suddenly realized that it was not just Tiye in his chambers. He looked beyond his immense bed into the darkness of his room. He slowly climbed his mass out of bed, gingerly at first, not truly trusting how well he felt. The Sobek soldier bowed low as Cepos came close to him. "It is good to see you well again, Cepos. We feared the worst." Cepos slapped his soldier on the shoulder in response and moved closer to the group in the center of his chamber. Jendayi, Zosar, and Montu stepped forward.

The surprise in Cepos's eyes seeing the elders gathered in his chambers shocked him. "I truly must have been entering the afterlife if you have all gathered. How many days was I sick to be able to have you all here at one time together?"

Zosar looked tiny beside Cepos as he chuckled. "We only found out an hour or so ago of your illness. Truly we came together to talk to you for an entirely different reason. It happened to be good timing on our part, coming when we did and with who we did."

Cepos frowned at Zosar and turned to Jendayi and Montu. "Is this true, my dear friends? This is all just a coincidence?" Jendayi and Montu nodded. "Well then, please let me freshen up, and I will meet you all in the throne room within the hour. There is much to discuss."

Cepos entered the throne room as promised within the hour. He walked right to Bree, and without waiting for her to adjust to his

ARTIFACTS ALIVE

massive size, he grabbed her in a full-on bear hug and enveloped her within his scaly body. Bree couldn't breathe until her release from the hug. She was amazed to see the kindness within Cepos's crocodile eyes as he looked down upon her after the hug. "I have been informed that you are the one I must pour my thanks on for saving me from the afterlife." Cepos actually got down on both knees and held on to Bree's hands, which looked so small in his massive webbed ones. "I thank you sincerely. I may be millennia old, but I am not yet ready to enter the afterlife. I must say, as I look at you now, you are the exact image of our goddess. Are you our Nefertiti finally returned?"

Bree had to stop herself from rolling her eyes before she smiled and answered, "No, Cepos, I am not Nefertiti, but I have been told that I am of her direct bloodline."

Cepos remained on his knees. "Ahh yes, this makes sense to me. Again, little one, I thank you. I hear you have come with a purpose. I am your servant. Ask me what it is you desire, and I will repay you in full." Jendayi stepped forward and helped Cepos rise from the floor. When Cepos sat at his throne, he urged Bree to sit beside him so he could keep his savior close. He felt comforted with her near him at the moment. Bree did so and sat on the enormous armrest of the throne, and Jabar stood close beside her. When everyone settled, Zosar told the tale of his vision, and then Jendayi added hers. They reviewed their plan against Senepol and the need to retrieve all the obelisks to Cepos and why it would be good for him to join with them to take Senepol down.

Cepos listened intently without interruption until they asked him to join them. He cleared his throat. "I have never had the problem with Senepol that you all have had. Senepol has no interest in the swamplands. There is nothing here for him to take except mud, slough water, quicksand, dead stumps, mosquitoes, and vicious beasts. Should I send my soldiers in to help just to have them killed or injured for a fight that isn't even ours?"

Jabar spoke up on this one. "If I may, Cepos, I fear that your illness was not natural. Your own soldiers feel the same."

Cepos's eyes scoured the room until they came upon his head soldier. "Is this true, Taafeef?"

The head soldier stepped forward. "I wanted to discuss this with you in private, Elder, but yes, I fear, as Tiye does, you ingested poison during supper for the Sobek and Aspis general meeting. You had fallen ill post supper that very night. Your symptoms resembled poisoning. Tiye couldn't heal you. She didn't know the type of poison you ingested. It was a poison that was unknown to her. She used everything in her arsenal to try to cure you. Nothing worked until they all arrived with the woman."

Cepos patted Bree's lap as if seeking comfort. "Explain."

Jabar stepped forward a little and described how the Aspis named Sa'd sold him out to Senepol and what had occurred. Jabar asked if Sa'd had been present at the general meeting. Cepos frowned as he thought about this question. "You know, I do not recall. He has always attended the general meetings before, for he is Abasi's second in command. Taafeef, I need you to question all the cooks and servants. See if they remember anything slightly suspicious about the actions of Sa'd that night, even if it is something as small as him tripping on a root." Taafeef removed himself after a bow to Cepos to begin his mission of questioning. The conversation in the throne room continued. "Why do you think Senepol wants to assassinate me? I have nothing he would need."

Montu joined in the conversation with this question by Cepos. "My friend, it is not what Senepol needs from you but what he needs from the one that would gain from your death. He needs support and help to find and obtain the obelisks. The ones helping him are as greedy and power hungry as Senepol is. He must have promised the swamplands to Sa'd or whoever Sa'd is working for in exchange for their support."

Sethos spoke up as well, "Yes, I agree with Montu. One of my own warriors who has been a thorn in my side, always nipping at my heels to take over leadership of the Heru warriors, named Darthos, has turned to Senepol. I am quite sure he has fled to Senepol with the news of what Bree's blood can do. I also am convinced that he has a deal for control of the Heru and Ibis tribe if he helps and supports Senepol with classified information and obtaining the obelisks. Darthos attacked Zosar. He was near death just as you were only weeks ago. He, too, was lucky enough to have Bree arrive at just the right time."

Jabar piped back into the conversation to add, "I have personally witnessed Senepol desire for the obelisks. He will stop at nothing to obtain what he desires. He killed my entire hunting village, including my entire family, in his search for the obelisks. He cares not of anything but himself and power. The ones helping him right now should be on their guard. Once Senepol gains what he needs from those who aid him, he will kill them. If he gets ahold of all the obelisks, he will be unstoppable. Do not think he has not come for you. It has already happened."

Just as Jendayi was going to ask Cepos about the Sobek's hidden obelisk, Taafeef ran back into the throne room, very disturbed. "Sire, there is something very foul amiss. I went to find Tiye to help me question everyone about Sa'd. I can't find her anywhere. Her chambers are in a mess. Her personal items and clothing are gone. She left in a rush. I can't find any Aspis within our tunnels either. They are all gone. I fear our visitors are correct. There is something deadly brewing. We must evacuate at once."

Just as everyone in the throne room understood what Taafeef had conveyed, there was a loud booming sound that shook the throne room ceiling, causing large chunks of rock and dirt to come loose and fall to the floor. Right behind the first surge, there was another and then another. Everyone in the throne room dodged debris falling in mass all around. Just as Taafeef was running to protect Cepos, a massive boulder fell from the ceiling, crushing Taafeef beneath its heavy weight. Jabar grabbed Bree and yelled for everyone to follow him, but his line of exit became blocked by another huge boulder falling in front of the tunnel exit. Dirty water began to spew through openings in the ceiling, and the throne room began to fill up with swamp water.

Sethos had Zosar on his back, and Darius did the same with Jendayi. Montu moved quickly to assist Cepos, who still sat upon his throne looking, completely stunned that someone would actually attack his domain. For an original, Montu realized that he was not the smartest brick in the pile. Montu pulled hard on his arm to get him to move just in time as a gigantic boulder smashed down and destroyed the throne. Montu yelled at Cepos, "Show us a way out!"

Cepos snapped out of his being stunned but never made it any farther. A large boulder fell upon him and Montu, crushing them both instantly where they stood. Both bodies twitched then ceased to move. Jendayi screamed out Montu's name, but it was too late. Jabar roared in misery when he saw Montu and Cepos go down, but he quickly looked for the rest of his friends. He would mourn later; right now he had to save his friends. He saw Sethos pinned under a boulder by his wings, and Zosar flew from off his back just in time, barely missing the crushing weight. Darius called out to Sethos, who yelled, "Leave me. Get your asses out of here, now!" Darius stopped and looked over at Jabar, unsure of what to do. Jabar placed Bree down. "I will be back in a moment. Stay under this ledge. It seems stable right now. I will be right back. I promise."

Bree nodded; she was so frightened she couldn't move anyway. She watched as Jabar gracefully dodged all the falling debris and leaped over large boulders in a single pounce to get to Sethos as he yelled over the noise, "Darius, take Zosar and Jendayi. Head to Bree. I will get Sethos out safe. You do the same." Darius nodded as he grabbed Zosar in one arm, and Jendayi was still clinging for dear life on his back. He wasn't near as graceful as Jabar, but he made it to where Jabar had left Bree with both elders, scraped up but still standing. When he got to the area where Bree was supposed to be, she wasn't there. Darius panicked. When he looked back at Jabar, he could see them both struggling with the large boulder that had Sethos pinned. The water level was up to their waists now. Darius could only pray Sethos and Jabar would make it out. He had two originals counting on him to get them out. He prayed to the goddess that Bree had found a way up the underpass. He decided. He squeezed through the slightly blocked tunnel and ran with Zosar in one arm and Jendayi desperately clutching his back as he rushed up the collapsing mud-filled tunnel.

*****

That voice, so calming, those eyes, so hypnotic. "Follow me," the beautiful voice said over and over. "Yes, good, follow me." She slipped at times, but gentle hands would help her back up, and those eyes would look deep into her soul, keeping her calm and her breathing relaxed. "Follow me." She could no longer hear screams or the sound of falling rocks or the cascading rush of water anymore. She was entering a drier area. She no longer felt mud under her sandaled feet, only packed solid ground. "A little farther, tiny one, follow me." The voice sounded like music in her head. All she wanted to do was follow that voice forever. In a trance, she walked and walked, following those hypnotic eyes and that angelic voice. Up and up, they climbed; tunnel after tunnel they turned and wove through. Then she was out of the dark abyss, into the coolness of the late afternoon mist of the swamp. "Stop, little one. You did well." Then a sharp pain radiated from the back of her head. Now there was only blissful darkness.

*****

Darius was exhausted. He gently placed Zosar on the wet spongy ground, and Jendayi slid off his back. She lowered herself beside Zosar, sobbing for the loss of her dearest friend, Montu, and Cepos. They were all soaking wet and covered in mud. Zosar's leg and forehead both had deep ugly gashes, but he was conscious and alert. Jendayi's wounds were less severe. She was okay physically other than that. Darius had a large wound on his left thigh that came from the same boulder that had hit Zosar. He, too, was also full of scratches and cuts over his face, arms, chest, and legs. They all waited on the soggy ground for any signs of life coming from the tunnel from which they had exited. This tunnel was just a hole in the ground. No big ominous tree for this one. They waited and they waited. Nothing. Now Darius worried even more. *Did Jabar and Sethos survive? Did he make the right choice? Where was Bree?* He was about to burst into tears when he felt a gentle hand stroke his bloody face. "You saved us, young one. Thank you." Darius looked up into Jendayi's soft gray eyes and sniffled back a choked sob. He would not cry. He was an adult now; he was a warrior. He would wait until they got back to camp when he was alone to release his emotions. Right now, he had to stay strong and keep the two remaining originals alive. He slowly stood and raised his hand to his lips and release a long loud whistle a couple of times and then sat back down and waited. It only took a brief time for them to hear crashing and splashing in the swamp coming toward them at high speed. Darius sighed; the sounds coming their way was a huge relief, or so he hoped. Soon out of the mist charged Darius's faithful mounts. He stood to meet them and gave them both a warm greeting with a soothing voice. He placed Zosar on Pepi, making sure he was able to hang on. He then helped Jendayi sit in front of him on Azizi. Darius knew the scarabs would keep them safe now. Darius let his pets pick their way through the dangerous swamps without his guidance. He trusted his pets more than he trusted himself right now. They had made it safely to him, so he trusted they would safely lead them out of this dangerous, unpredictable swampland.

21

Bree awoke with a splitting headache and to voices arguing just beyond her sight when she tried opening her eyes. She tried to feel the back of her head and realized that her hands, tightly tied, were starting to go numb. She noted her legs were also bound, and she had a gag over her mouth. She tried to figure out how she wound up in this predicament but could not recall a thing. Her head pounded aggressively, and she squeezed her eyes shut from the pain, trying to will it away. This didn't help. She decided to focus her attention away from the pain in her head and try to listen to the ones that were arguing. She opened her eyes again but saw only cracks of light coming through. She realized she was bound, gagged, and stuffed into a wooden crate. The voices were becoming heated, so she refocused her thoughts and concentrated on listening.

The female voice in the argument rose chillingly, "I could have died. You didn't wait for my sssignal."

The male voice chuckled. "You ssstill live. We have the package. Everything worked out asss planned. Why are you ssso upssset?"

The female scoffed. "Sssometimes I don't think you really love me! I almossst died becaussse you are too impatient to follow ordersss."

The male voice, angered, now spat out, "Ssshut up, you are making my head pound, woman." Bree was terrified. She realized by the voices and the overaccentuated *s*'s that she was a captive of a couple of Aspis. She even could guess who they were. It was Tiye and the mystery Sa'd. She could even guess where they were taking her, and it made her heart pound in cold terror. They were taking her back to Senepol.

She checked her bondages, but they were secure. Her hands were numb, and her feet were becoming that way. No amount of pulling was helping. The bonds had been wet down. The more she moved, the tighter the ropes became. Hot, searing pain was radiating up her arms from the ropes rubbing on her wounds. The couple of Aspis were silent. They were traveling fast and on rough terrain. Bree felt sick to her stomach with the unstable swaying of the crate. She also gave up on trying to free herself from the bonds. *What happened to Jabar and the others? Were they safe?* Bree closed her eyes trying to remember her last memory. Loud booms, shaking, boulders falling, water pouring in all cracks and crevices. Cepos and Montu crumbling under the weight of a large boulder. Jabar leaving her to help Sethos trapped under debris. Darius scrambling to help Zosar and Jendayi. Then, Bree remembered the voice. She remembered looking into the dark tunnel and seeing the eyes. Then nothing except the words, "Follow me."

Were her friends safe or dead in the chaos of the collapsing throne room? Tears burned her eyes, causing her head to feel like it was about to split in half. "No, they are fine. This is not what Zosar and Jendayi's visions predicted." She had to hold on to that to keep her sanity. She sucked back her agony, tears, and fears so she could produce a way to save herself when she was back in Senepol's grasp. *Focus, Bree, be smart with this. Use your gift for you to stay alive. Woo Senepol to trust you enough that you can slip away.* Bree breathed in deeply. She kept her eyes closed, focused her thoughts, and began to meditate with a quiet soothing hum.

*****

The Sobek soldiers holding the line at the swamp border all suddenly turned around with spears at ready when they heard loud crashing coming from within the swamp. When they recognized the ones mounted on the scarabs charging toward them, they still kept their weapons ready but relaxed a little until they noticed the terrible state of the passengers. Pepi had a large dead toad locked in her jaws, and she was full of weeds, branches, and mud. Azizi did not look any better. A large chunk of his exoskeleton had torn off just below the left side of the saddle, and he was missing half of his front pincher. The Sobek soldiers had to circle around the agitated scarabs to help Darius gain control and slow them to a stop. He jumped off, helping Jendayi down. Sobek soldiers came forward and did the same for Zosar.

Hearing all the commotion, everyone in camp stood to see the scarabs charge out of the swamp. Suddenly everyone was running or flying to meet up with the injured. Darius and the elders couldn't keep up with all questions thrown at them to the point where Darius had to hold up his hands and yell, "Stop, all of you! Take Zosar and Jendayi to the medical tent. Take Pepi and Azizi and give them a well-deserved treat and a wash. Sobek, Heru, Maahe, Sakhmet warriors, follow me." No one questioned the young Anubi or his orders. Zosar and Jendayi went for medical attention with Ibis priests. Others took the scarabs' reins and led them away as all the warriors followed Darius to the center of the camp. They gather around the large fire. Darius cleared his throat, trying to figure out how to explain what had happened in the swamp.

Darius gazed upon all the warriors waiting for him to start. He owed it to the Sobeks to know that their beloved original had perished in the attack. Darius took a deep breath and stood tall and proud, standing his ears to a full point before he spoke. "It saddens me to have to bear such terrible news. After Bree healed Cepos, there was an attack. We gathered in the throne room to discuss critical issues when the ceiling of the throne room began to collapse. I again am sorry. Sobeks, Cepos and Taafeef didn't make it." The Sobek warriors just stared at Darius, stunned. He turned to the Maahe warriors next. "My friends, Montu is also gone." The Maahe all turned their heads to the sky, roaring their sorrow at the loss of their leader. Suddenly Sobek warriors were in an uproar. One stormed right up to Darius with his spear pointed at his throat. "You lie, there was no attack. Your people killed them when you had the chance. It was your people that poisoned Cepos, wasn't it? You will die right here, right now, Anubi."

Just as the Sobek warrior raised his spear to thrust it through Darius, Jendayi yelled out from the doorway of the medical tent. She limped toward the group. "Stop! It is true what Darius tells you. I, Jendayi, the last of the two originals, watched as Montu, Cepos, and Taafeef fell with my own eyes. No one could have saved them. It all happened so fast. Darius risked his life to save myself and Zosar. If it weren't for this brave young Anubi, we, too, would be dead." The Sobek warrior holding the spear hesitated, then he stood down and backed away from Darius slowly to let Jendayi into the center of the large group of warriors to speak.

Jendayi made it to the center of the warriors just as it started to rain heavily. Her large tears, mixed with raindrops, cascaded down her beautiful face; her whiskers lay flat to her muzzle, her ears flat against her head, expressing her immense sadness. Jendayi looked at the mass amount of gathered warriors from their five tribes. She realized they needed strength at this moment of shock and disbelief. She was an original. They needed her right now just as she needed all of them. She stood tall and proud, speaking with renewed strength of an original. She had to convince the Sobek tribe to join their cause. "We lost one of the last originals today when Cepos fell. We also lost a great Sobek warrior, and..." Jendayi choked on her next words. "We lost Montu, leader of the Maahe tribe too." New tears flowed down Jendayi's cheeks. Darius had to look away and bite his tongue for him to hold back his tears. The pain from her words exuded sadness like an aura all around the camp. Jendayi continued as the rain poured down, "The throne room was a setup. The sabotage to the tunnels had organization. There is deep, underlying evil going on. It all leads back to Senepol.

"We came to you today to ask Cepos for his aide, not to assassinate him. We needed him. We needed him to help us in the fight to stop Senepol from taking over all our tribes and all our lands. Senepol has pledged a select few certain amenities if they aid him in his deviant plot. The Heru lost one of their own warriors to Senepol's charms. He tried to eliminate Zosar but failed. Now he has come to you Sobeks. Now he has attacked you in your own home. Senepol wants the obelisks, and he wants Bree. You all saw she is the real thing. Sobeks, she healed Cepos. He was whole again and rid of the poison when we congregated in the throne room with him. Taafeef was trying to save Cepos just as the large boulders began to fall from the ceiling and swamp water poured in. You must always remember Taafeef as a hero. He died trying to save your elder today. Montu stayed true to his vigilant leadership to the very end. He never faltered, he was brave. May they all cross over to the afterlife in peace."

Jendayi let this sink in, and they all bowed their heads in respect for their fallen. Jendayi continued, "We have other losses. Bree is missing. The last we saw of Sethos and Jabar was within the throne room desperately trying to shift a large boulder off Sethos as it had pinned him down by his wings. We do not know if they made it out alive. The rising swamp water was up to their waists. We must organize a search party and make our way back to your tunnels to see the damage and to recover the bodies of our leaders, loved ones, and friends for a proper burial. I know our arrival is much too coincidental for the tragedy that has just befallen us, and I agree. I beg of you as an original to believe me. It wasn't us. I have to admit that there are ones among us that want to cause us harm. Just before the collapse of the throne room, Taafeef set out to look for Tiye. Cepos wanted to question Sa'd in suspicion of his poisoning. When Taafeef returned, he was very troubled. He said Tiye was missing. Her chambers were cleared out of her belongings. He also noted that not one Aspis was around either. They had all cleared out of the tunnels just before they collapsed."

The Sobek warriors were incredibly angry as well as disturbed. Their partner tribe for eons had turned against them. The Aspis murdered their beloved Cepos and one of the last three surviving originals and destroyed their home all in support of Senepol. The news was devastating, but they believed every word that was spoken by Jendayi. They had all tried to stay out of Senepol's sight. They thought he would leave them alone. They had heard the stories. Now Senepol's war had come to them. Senepol would pay for this with his life. The second in command of the Sobek warriors stepped forward and bowed in respect to Jendayi. "I am Waaiz. I am now commander of the warriors, if what you say is true and Taafeef is no longer with us. I will speak on behalf of the Sobeks. You have us. We will not stop until Senepol is dead."

Immediately after Waaiz made his statement, the Sobek warriors dropped to all fours, growling with menace as they opened their mouths wide. They snapped their jaws shut and began shaking their heads back and forth ferociously. Then in unison, as if to music, they all turned over and over, simulating a death roll. With a couple of death rolls complete, they returned to all fours, forming a large circle. The Sobek warriors began running around in the circle they had formed, snapping and growling at the tail of the soldier in front of them. Suddenly, they all jumped up on two legs, raised their weapons into the air, and simultaneously bellowed a loud war cry that echoed far into the swamp, then they stood stalk still, staring into the fire.

Darius bent down to Jendayi with fear in his voice. "Does this mean they agree with Waaiz?"

Jendayi nodded when she turned to Darius. "Yes, young Anubi, they agree. What you just witnessed is the Sobeks' war dance."

*****

Bree was dying of thirst, as she dehydrated like a prune from all the sweat that was pouring out of her. It was burning hot as a dry sauna in the little crate. She was so hungry that scabs on her wounds were starting to look like bacon. She hadn't been able to feel any of her limbs for the last day and wondered if they were about to fall off from lack of blood flow. The most embarrassing thing, though, was they never fed her, never gave her any water, and never let her out of the crate, which meant she had not the courtesy of relieving herself. She hadn't peed herself since she was a young child. Thank God her bowels weren't full, or she would have really been devastated. Every muscle in her body besides her numb hands and feet was screaming at her. She couldn't shift herself or turn, so she had lain in one spot and one position the entire time. It felt like something was chewing the bones in her hip and her shoulder. Her head never stopped pounding either. Now she understood when people would say they prayed for death. She caught herself at times praying for just that.

Sa'd and Tiye never watched what they said as they traveled. Bree had learned that most of the Aspis had abandoned the swampland and were now temporarily set up in Senepol's palace. She also heard Sa'd brag how Senepol had promised the swamplands to him and Darthos was to get the forest region as long as Senepol had the rights to the gold from the mountains. Tiye revealed in conversation that Senepol was again in possession of two obelisks, which meant the fifth obelisk was safe for now. This at least was good news. With nothing to do but listen to the idiots that were transporting her either argue or spilling all, she tried drowning them out at times by thinking of her friends, especially Jabar, to keep from going crazy. She missed him so much; her soul ached. Lately she had been privileged to fall asleep in his arms as he purred her off to sleep. Since they had met, they had barely been apart.

Bree had come to the realization that she had deep feelings for her lion man. It was strange to her at first when she thought about it. Her being human and him being half lion. She realized, though, she just didn't care about their differences. All that mattered was their friendship and how he made her feel. He was strong, kind, patient, funny, honest, and intelligent. He was always warm when she snuggled into him to sleep. He never scolded her or scoffed at her. He always had her safety at the forefront of his mind and knew how to calm her with a hug and his soft purr. Every time she was with him, she was at peace. She was where she was supposed to be, and that was by his side. Bree convinced herself that Jabar, Sethos, Darius, Zosar, and Jendayi had all made it out of the throne room. She promised herself that she would see them all again, and when she did, she would tell them how important and special they were to her, especially Jabar. This is what kept her going—her new friends that she would die for if it meant saving them all from Senepol.

Bree snapped out of her inner thoughts when they suddenly stopped. She could hear Sa'd talking to someone, and then within a couple of minutes, they were moving again. Bree realized quickly that it wasn't them moving. It was just the crate she was in that was moving. The crate lifted away from the mounts. *Oh shit, we've reached the palace. They're taking me inside.* She braced herself for what was to come by breathing deep and repeating over and over *"he needs you, he won't kill you, he needs you"* to herself. The movement stopped, and she felt the crate placed on the floor carefully and then nothing. She heard whoever had carried her in leave the room and close the door behind them. Her heart began to pound so hard she could feel her entire body moving to the beat of it. All she could hear was her breathing. She feared she would hyperventilate. *Nothing like a little suspense, Bree. They're making you wait on purpose. They want you good and scared. Don't give them the satisfaction. Stay strong, girl. You've got this.* She didn't have to wait too long, though, as the door crashed open. Her whole body jumped with fear at the loud sound. There was definitely more than one person entering the room, but they were dead silent verbally. Something banged on the top of the crate; she realized that they were opening the sealed lid. With a loud crack, light shone in. She had to close her eyes from the brightness, being in the dark crate for so long. She blinked a couple of times, and when her eyes adjusted, she looked up. "Fuck!" she groaned aloud. Leering down at her were Senepol, Derrick, Aston, and Darthos with wicked grins plastered on their faces. After her explicit language, they burst into laughter as they reached in and lifted her out of her temporary prison.

*****

It had taken a full day with everyone from the Heru, Ibis, Maahe, Sobek and Sakhmets' tribes cleaning away debris, stumps, boulders, and thick mud to reach the tunnels that led to the throne room underground. It took the next day till afternoon to find Taafeef and Cepos's bodies crushed by large boulders. With the discoveries of the Sobek bodies, the Sobek tribe left the site with their kin's bodies to mourn. Everyone else understood, for they would have done the same for their tribe members. After they paid their respects, the Sobek soldiers were going to travel to the Aspis underground village to see if anyone were still there. When the Maahe obtained the body of their leader, they, too, took him off to mourn away from the site. The rest kept digging. Darius kept calling out Jabar's and Sethos's names, continuously hoping for an answer. He kept his hopes up. They had not found their bodies yet, so maybe, just maybe, they were somehow still alive. Suddenly Darius thought he heard something. He stopped to listen, perking his ears in the direction he thought he heard the sound from. *There.* He heard it again. "Everyone, stop! I heard something. No one move." Everyone froze in their spots. He heard it again. "There, over there. I think I can hear Jabar." Darius jumped with such speed he slipped and fell but regained his footing instantly. "Here, we need to dig here." Darius was frantic as he clawed with his own hands at the mud and debris.

They dug for an hour and came upon large boulders stacked upon each other. With the harnesses strapped to the elephants, they were able to slowly move the boulders aside. Darius paced in the mud as he mentally urged the elephant to move faster. He was terrified that the boulders would slip from the ropes. When they moved two of the large boulders, suddenly Jabar's clawed hand reached up through a muddy crack. Darius had never been happier and more relieved in his life. He pounced on Jabar's hand, lying on his stomach, grasping it for dear life as he yelled out, "Jabar? Oh goddess, Jabar!" He didn't even realize he was bawling until a Heru warrior pulled him away so they could dig the other boulders out safely. It turned out that as Jabar was trying to help release Sethos, three large boulders collapsed just above their heads, one behind them, one in front, and the other on top. The water stopped when it got to their stomachs and never reached any higher. They were able to breathe by the mud sealing in air between the pocket of the large boulders. This created enough air for them to survive for a couple of days.

They removed Jabar first. It took longer to release Sethos's wings. When the boulders were all cleared, they discovered one of Sethos's wings was badly broken and the other was badly bruised, missing important flying feathers. Both men were soaking wet, dehydrated, starving, and sick in their lungs from the dirty bacteria-infested swamp water. Bree's world called it pneumonia. The minute Jabar was free, he began asking to see Bree and where she was. Jendayi stated that they would talk when he got back to the medical tent and he rested. Jabar was having nothing of that. He jumped up and wobbled a bit but tried to keep his balance. "Tell me where Bree is. Is she okay? She made it out. I know she did. Jendayi, where is Bree?"

Jendayi bowed her head and took a moment to answer. Jabar started to walk toward an elephant. "Jabar! She is missing. No one has seen her since the collapse. We didn't find her body in the rubble. She must have gotten out, but no one knows where she is." Jabar fell to his knees. Jendayi was about to run to him when suddenly Zahra ran out from the helpers covered in mud to Jabar's side.

She reached out to him gently and helped him up from his knees. "Dear friend, you aren't going to do the lady any justice with the condition you are in right now. How far do you think you will get? Please, you need medical attention, a bath, hot food, and a good rest before you can be of help to anyone. Come, let us get you fixed up. You need your health if you are to find your friend." Jendayi listened for a moment and then backed away, frowning slightly. Zahra had always had a soft spot for Jabar. She had pined for him all the years he had not come back. She was the most beautiful Sakhmet of the entire tribe. Zahra always had suitors and was pursued by both the Maahe and Sakhmet males, though she turned all her suitors down when asked to marry. She was trying to weasel her way back into Jabar's affections. Jendayi prayed to the goddess that this would not interfere with their quest, nor with Jabar and Bree's special bond. She loved Zahra, and long ago she had hoped Jabar and she would have mated. Now she thought differently, understanding Jabar had a different path to take in life that did not include Zahra. She would keep an eye on her, but for now, Jabar needed a woman's touch and a woman's care. She let her suspicions be for now, but she would intervene if necessary.

Jabar realized that Zahra was right. He was in no condition to help anyone. He would give it one day and one night, but no matter what anyone said, he would be leaving with the sunrise alone, if he had to, to find his Bree. His heart seemed hollow the minute he heard Bree was missing. He knew Senepol had her. How he got her, he did not know. He would find her, and he would save her even if it meant his life, but he would make sure Senepol joined him in the afterlife. Bree was the key to all their lives being peaceful. He shoved other thoughts of Bree out of his head. He started thinking of her: her laughter, smile, hair, eyes, even her voice. He physically shook his head and forced himself to stop. If he continued, he would be jumping on the back of one of the elephants, and well, he would surely die. His emotions were dictating his action. Not being prepared was the worst thing he could do. He had to be smart. He would think of Bree tomorrow. Right now, he had to heal.

Sethos was extremely depressed. He couldn't fly. He was very thankful for being alive, but it would be a long time till he was able to lead his warriors in any aerial battle. He refused a stretcher; his pride would not allow himself the courtesy. He had to show strength at this perilous time. He could feel the misery and defeat of the tribes right now, and showing weakness was not an option. He had to keep up morale. His heart was also torn when he heard Bree was missing. He thought he was over her and gave his heart to her as a friend, but he realized this was not true. He, too, wanted to climb onto a mount and charge in to rescue her. It was Darius that broke into his thoughts. "How pathetic." Sethos looked over at Darius, who was walking toward him with a very confused look on his face. Darius pointed toward Zahra aiding Jabar.

"That! Her! Look. Jabar just crawled out of a death pit, and she is already making her moves on him."

Sethos choked on laughter as he looked over to where Darius was pointing *Oh, thank the goddess for Darius and his ability to take my mind off my own painful thoughts*. He watched with Darius as Zahra tried to bear Jabar's massive weight and how she stroked his back with one hand and batted her eyelashes up at him under his armpit. "Maybe she is just being kind and is trying to help him," Sethos stated.

Darius huffed and shook his head. "It's obvious is it not."

Sethos teased Darius. "Are you jealous, my boy?"

Darius jumped back, truly offended, and Sethos laughed aloud, which made everyone turn his way and smile, happy to see his injuries were not wearing him down. "No. I'm not jealous. I am upset for Bree. Jabar better not fall for that, or I will have to punch him in his face."

Sethos laughed again. *Yes, thank goddess for Darius.*

*****

If Bree weren't so sore, she would be terrified, but as it was when they lifted her out of the small crate, she couldn't straighten out her limbs. Derrick piped up when they lifted her out, "Holy shit, what in God's name is that smell?"

Bree was instantly embarrassed but quickly turned into anger. "It's piss and sweat, you moron. You'd smell like that too without the courtesy to relieve yourself for two days combined with the desert heat." Senepol burst into laughter. Derrick backed away in disgust but didn't say anything more.

Aston was holding on to her arms when he said, "If you don't stand up, Bree, we are going to drop you."

Bree was not impressed. "Do you think I want to look like a pretzel and smell like piss? I'm seized up. I couldn't move in that tiny box."

Senepol placed his massive bull head close to hers and asked her calmly, "You are saying you were kept in the box the entire time."

Bree opened her eyes wide and glared at Senepol. She didn't care; right now death would be merciful from all her pain. If she offended him and he killed her right now, she just didn't care. "Duhhhhhh!"

Senepol snorted in her face and then turned to Aston. "What does 'duh' mean?"

Now it was Aston's turn to laugh. "I'm assuming she hasn't been out of the box since she was stuffed into it."

Now Senepol seemed to be getting angry. Bree did not care. Still curled into the fetal position, they placed her on a cushioned ottoman that was big enough for her to sleep on. She groaned in pain. Senepol ordered Derrick to fetch a servant to bring her a pillow, which he resented. Senepol turned back to Bree. "Did they not feed or water you?"

Bree answered with sarcasm, "I am not a pet, but duh!"

Senepol stood and bellowed out to one of his guards, who entered the room quickly, "Bring me Sa'd and Tiye immediately!"

Bree realized that Senepol must have ordered them to treat her well. He needed her, and now he was angry that they did not follow his orders. *Oh goodie*, she thought. *I hope Senepol lets me watch them reprimanded. Tit for tat, I say.* A wave of pain broke through her thoughts as Aston cut off the bonds from her ankles and hissed at the sight. Her ankles rubbed completely raw; the ropes were actually stuck to her skin. The same was for her wrists. When he cut and peeled off the rope, Bree swore like a sailor. Aston, acting like he cared, said, "I am sorry they hurt you, Bree."

Bree snorted and met his gaze with one of pure disbelief. "You can take your bullshit and shove it up your ass. You left me here to die, you son of a bitch."

Senepol burst into laughter and slapped Aston on his back. "I think I'm starting to like her."

22

Jabar and Sethos were both checked over by the Ibis priests. Sethos's wing was set, but there was nothing they could do for the lost feathers. They were both dehydrated and ordered to drink fluids. They took herbal medication for their lungs, bathed, ate, and then ordered to also rest. Zahra fawned over Jabar in the med tent. She insisted on her feeding him and helping him to the bath. She applied ointment on all his cuts and then brushed out his mane. When Jabar just wanted to sleep, Zahra insisted on staying with him. He wanted to be alone, but he was too tired to argue. He flopped onto his cot and passed out. Sethos stayed in the med tent for observation. The priests had given him a very potent medical herb for pain. They wanted to make sure he stayed put, not moving his wings too much.

Darius stayed with Sethos as well, to keep him company and his spirits up, or so he told the priests. They scolded him and told him to sit and not bother Sethos as he needed his rest. Of course, the two didn't listen; they discussed quietly when the priests weren't close. They tried to figure out how the Aspis knew they were coming and figured that there were a couple more moles in their midst. Sethos whispered to Darius, "Darthos had awfully close friends in the tribe that always backed him whenever he tried to challenge me. They must have slipped Darthos the information that we were coming. This must have been how the Aspis had been able to develop their plan."

Darius nodded and whispered back, "That makes total sense, Sethos, but then Senepol is already aware we are coming in for battle."

Sethos thought for a moment. "Then we will have to change our strategy. We can get Senepol to come to us. Keep this to yourself, Darius. I need to talk to Zosar and Jendayi about this, but tomorrow we head to the forgotten city." Sethos was frustrated, angry, but more so, hurt. How could any of their own side with Senepol?

Waaiz entered the tent and at once came over to Sethos. He was upset when had stood beside Sethos and Darius. "It looks like there was quite a fight at the Aspis village as well. They just left their dead where they fell. Never even gave them a decent burial. Their leader, Bassel, is also dead. Looks like they poisoned him as Cepos had been. We assume not all the Aspis wanted to go over to Senepol's side, and they died because of it. There is one good piece of news for you. As we were cleaning up the dead, I was moving Bassel's body away from his throne. When I did this, I had to bend low and got a really good look at the throne's legs. I had never looked before, but there it was right in front of my eyes. Bassel's throne was built upon four replica obelisks, like the ones you are looking for. I thought to myself. I wonder if one of these could be the real one."

Waaiz paused, making Darius jump up impatiently. "Well, was one the real one or what?"

An exceptionally large smile spread across Waaiz's face. "I think so, but I carried the throne here and gave it to Zosar and Jendayi for inspection to make sure."

Sethos and Darius were thunderstruck. How amazing was this? If it turned out that one of the legs of the throne was authentic, then they had three of the five. Sethos thanked Waaiz for his quick thinking and how amazed he was. Then he told him to ready the Sobek tribe for the trip to the forgotten city. Waaiz pounded his chest in acknowledgment and turned to leave the tent when Sethos called him back, "I know this is a strange request. Please only tell your tribe about heading to the forgotten city and tell them to tell no one else."

Waaiz cleared his throat before speaking again. "I thought we were going right to Senepol to battle."

Sethos grinned and nodded. "Yes, I have concluded that we have traitors in my tribe. I need to turn the tale on them, and this way, Senepol will not be ready. They will now come to us. These traitors will have to scramble to get the latest information to Senepol and, with their attempt, I will know exactly who they are."

Waaiz nodded his head in agreement. "That is a spectacular tactic, Sethos."

Sethos made his next statement truly clear. "Tell no one else but your warriors. I don't know who I can trust, but I do trust your tribe. It is my tribe about which I am concerned." Waaiz thumped his chest once again and quickly left the medical tent.

*****

Jabar felt a soft warm body beside him as he awoke slowly. He snuggled Bree closer to him and began to purr the way she liked. She rolled to face him as she snuggled in for his affection. Suddenly she was kissing him and caressing his face with her hands. Oh, how had he dreamed of this. He kept his eyes closed as he kissed her back. Whiskers rubbed his face, and for a moment, he hesitated. *Whiskers? Bree doesn't have whiskers!* Jabar's eyes flew open, and his immediate reaction was to push Zahra away from him as fast as he could. She fell with a thump onto the floor as she slipped off the cot. "Zahra? What do you think you're doing?"

Zahra at once teared up. "I have missed you so much, Jabar. Do you know all the requests I've turned down to marry because I was waiting for you to return so we could pick up where we left off?"

Jabar sighed heavily and helped Zahra up from the floor and sat her on the side of his cot, sitting next to her. "Zahra, I never promised you anything. You should never have waited for me. We had one summer together so many years ago. It was wonderful, and I will always remember it fondly. We were young and daring. I am no longer the Jabar you remember, Zahra. I could never make you happy."

Zahra jumped up, furious. "It's because of that strange furless woman, isn't it? What magic has she weaved you into, Jabar?"

Jabar shook his head sadly. "If you must know, she hasn't put a spell on me. That woman and I have an incredibly special friendship. She saved my life more than once. It changes one's relationship when you have been through the shit that Bree and I have been through in such a brief time."

Zahra's lip quivered. "You're choosing her over me?" Jabar sighed as Zahra stomped her foot like a child. "Every single unmarried Maahe and Sakhmet warrior and even a couple of the married ones would kill to have me as their mate. You dare turn me away. You are no one within the tribe anymore. Mating with me would raise your status again, with everyone welcoming you back with open arms. You may even become leader because of the death of Montu. I'm giving you one chance, Jabar. Are you willing to turn me away for that witch whore?"

Zahra's true colors were blaring in Jabar's face right now. She was so jealous of Bree that she was green with it. Jabar stood to his full height and stepped close to Zahra and quietly said, "Yes, I pick the witch whore, as you so kindly call her." He stepped around her to leave the tent. He couldn't even stand to look at her or be in her presence for a moment more.

Zahra grabbed his arm as she dropped to her knees. She was shocked that he would turn her down. Everyone wanted her. She was the most beautiful of her tribe. She could not understand how Jabar could turn her away. "Please, Jabar, I didn't mean it. Don't go. Stay with me. Let me remind you what we had that summer. My body is yours. Lie with me."

Jabar didn't even turn back to look at her. He was so disgusted he had to leave before he smacked her. He shook her off his arm, and as she fell to the ground, he left the tent. Zahra stayed where she fell, sobbing at the entrance of the tent. As Jabar walked away, he heard Darius call out to him. Thankful for the distraction, he changed direction and headed over to Darius. He needed distraction from what had just happened desperately. He hoped Darius and Sethos had developed a plan that involved killing something. He needed to urgently work off a bit of steam.

*****

Soaking in a hot bath never felt so amazing before as did this one. Bree's muscles ached a little less the longer she soaked. An Apis priest had given her an herbal concoction to relieve her pain. It was beginning to kick in. What bliss. Bree was alone in a small room. Senepol had arranged for her to have a bath brought in with a portable tub. She couldn't converse with any servants this go around. This suited her fine. She didn't want anyone pawing over her right now. While in the bath, a priest opened the door without knocking, leaving food on a small table beside the bed, and then left without a word or a look in Bree's direction. Bree sighed. At least no torture, and she thanked God she did not have to stew in her wretched body fluids in a dark spider-infested dungeon. Bree closed her eyes. The food brought in smelled fantastic. Her mouth watered, but the hot water felt too good on her sore muscles to leave the tub just yet. The door opened once again. Bree ignored it, assuming it was the priest bringing in something else. Warm hands eased gently down her shoulders, sliding into the water to cup her breasts. She jolted upright, spinning around in the tub, trying to hide her nakedness with her hands.

Total disgust registered across her face when she recognized Derrick. "You son of a bitch. *Get out!*" Derrick just smiled as he began circling the tub. Around and around, he slowly encircled as he watched her try to hide under the water. She knew he was playing with her, him thinking she was a victim of his. So, to throw him off, she took her power back. She dropped her hands, stood up from the water, exited the tub as she normally would if she were alone, walked over to the bed where the large towel lay, picked it up, and casually wrapped it around her nakedness. Derrick was surprised. She was supposed to be frightened of him. He wanted her terrified. He felt deflated at her reaction. He had to get his control over her back. "You brazen little bitch!" As he said this, he walked right up to her, smacking her hard across her cheek. *How the hell did men know how to hit a woman right where the stars would begin dancing in front of their eyes and sting so bad it made one's eyes water? Did they take a class on this or just instinctively know?* Bree thought to herself. She forced herself not to raise her hand to her cheek. Instead she open-palmed him square in the nose and kicked out hard with her foot right into his groin.

Bree smiled as Derrick stumbled back and grabbed his nose with one hand and his crotch with the other. *Thank you, Jabar, for teaching me that move.* Derrick raged; no woman bested him. He charged at her like a raging bull, knocking her back onto the bed. He was like a demon, ripping at the towel to get it off. He punched her hard this time. She almost blacked out with that one. He may have never worked a grueling day in his life, but he was tall, muscular, and worked out daily in a gym back home. He was overpowering her quickly. She fought like a lioness, screaming and yelling at him the whole while.

The door to her small room slammed open. Senepol's frame filled the doorway for only a split second. He was on Derrick, pulling him off, and without qualms he smashed him up against the opposite wall, choking him. "You knew she was off-limits. Yet here you are accosting what is mine. You are no longer welcome." Derrick struggled uselessly, grabbing at Senepol's one hand that held his throat while Senepol spoke. As soon as Senepol completed his little speech, Bree heard Derrick's neck snap. He slumped to the ground, and Senepol turned around to face Bree, still sitting naked and in shock upon the bed. Senepol appreciated the view before him much more than he wanted to, but now was not the time. "Cover yourself before I finish what Derrick started." Bree broke free from shock and covered herself quickly. "Good girl. Now come here." She hesitated slightly and then slowly slid off the bed and walked over to Senepol. In a flash, he snagged her arm and sliced it open with a dagger. Bree hissed at the pain, but he wouldn't let her go. He maneuvered her to stand beside Derrick's body. "Heal him."

Bree was confused. "He's dead. It doesn't work that way."

Senepol tightened his grip on her arm, bent down, opened Derrick's mouth, and placed her dripping arm over it. They watched as her blood dripped into Derrick's mouth. Senepol waited. "Why isn't it working?" he asked as nothing was happening.

"I told you. He's dead. I can't bring back someone who has passed over. It only works if the person is still alive, Senepol."

Senepol growled, stood up, and pulled her with him out of her little cell room. They went down hallways, and she soon found herself pulled into Aston's room.

Without a word, Senepol approached Aston, who was enjoying a massage from one of the Anubi servants. Without warning, he sliced Aston's bare shoulder. Aston jumped up from the lounger in shock. "Son of a bitch!"

Senepol growled at him to shut up. "Heal him then."

Bree sighed as Senepol shoved her in front of Aston. She couldn't look him in the eye, nor did she want to heal this asshole, but she lifted her arm and smeared her blood onto Aston's shoulder. They stood and waited for a full two minutes and still nothing happened. Senepol looked at Bree in disgust. "Have I been deceived, Bree? I was under the assumption that your blood can heal, and yet it does not."

Bree stood shocked as well. *What if my healing ability isn't working anymore? Has my blood returned to normal? I am so dead.* Bree thought fast to save her own skin. "I healed Jabar, Zosar, Darthos, a Sobek warrior, and Cepos from near death. My ability only works on Nefertiti's creations."

Senepol thought for a moment. He let her go and turned to the Anubi servant. "Come here." The servant lowered her gaze but came over to Senepol without question. He reached for her arm and cut her deeply. She fell to her knees, gasping as she held her arm with a pleading look in her eyes as she looked at Bree. "Do it" was all Senepol said. *Please, please let this work.* Bree thought to herself as she moved toward the servant. Her arm wasn't bleeding as much anymore. She had to squeeze and pull open the wound to start it flowing out again. *Damn it, my arm is starting to look like I self-mutilate.* She bent down to the servant, who looked only to be Darius's age. She gently wiped her blood over the deep wound, praying that it would work as it did for the others. "Don't be scared, but this will hurt a bit." It didn't take long for the servant girl to start groaning and then screaming as she held on to her arm. Before everyone's eyes, her deep wound began to heal. Senepol was in awe, and he began to laugh heartedly. He took his dagger and cut his own arm, grabbing Bree from off the floor beside the servant and smearing the remainder of her blood onto his fresh cut. Senepol didn't scream, but he did whistle a little as her blood began to heal his arm. He stood and stared at the spot the wound no longer was. He laughed and laughed in absolute giddiness. "Oh, woman. I hope you understand how important you are to me now. From now on, you will never be far from my side. You are mine, my enigmatic lady."

Aston stared at Bree with a strange look on his face as he held a cloth to his bleeding shoulder. "Why do you think your blood doesn't work on me?"

Bree just shrugged her shoulders. "I don't know the answer to that. I can't heal myself either. I am as ignorant as you, Aston."

Senepol took Bree back to her little room and pointed at Derrick's body. "A guard will come and dispose of that garbage soon." Senepol bowed slightly. "You may not be the goddess, but I will treat you as one if you obey me, Bree." Without waiting for a response, he exited the room without another word, locking the door behind him. She could hear him chuckling to himself as he walked away. Bree stared at Derrick's limp form; suddenly her bravado evaporated. She began shaking violently. She was not sad in the least that Derrick was dead; in fact she was relieved. She was still trying to recuperate from her travels in the box. Her body and emotions imploded into themselves. Her arm was full of unhealed cuts, and they throbbed painfully. She was becoming anemic from all her blood loss and lack of proper iron in her diet. She was feeling very weak. She wondered about the amount of blood she had actually lost in the week. Did the body replenish right away, or did it take a week, a month, or longer? She sighed. She wasn't a hematologist; she was an archeologist and didn't have those answers for herself. She needed to desperately escape again. She looked around her tiny room. This room, however, only had a small high window, solid walls with a heavy locked door, and no other way in or out. What she would give to be back with Jabar and her friends. Right now, she felt hopeless. She flopped back down on the bed, wrapped her arms around her legs, dropped her head on her pillows, and sobbed.

*****

The next morning Zosar and Jendayi confirmed that Waaiz had been correct in his assumption with one of the throne legs being one of the five obelisks. Now they had three in their possession. What a stress relief for all of them. One less worry of having to search, losing precious time. They all decided to keep the secret about the obelisks. No one knew they had any of them except their little group, and they wanted to keep it this way. Jabar, Sethos, Waaiz, and Darius gathered everyone around after breaking camp, with everyone ready to head out to Senepol's lands. Sethos had explained earlier to his close group of the change in plans to head to the forgotten city instead of to Senepol—have Senepol come to them so they could be prepared instead of the other way around. Zosar and Jendayi agreed that this was a great plan in order to weed out the traitors. Sethos gave an announcement to all the tribes of the change in direction and plan. Everyone cheered and was a little relieved with the change as the forgotten city was closer in distance as well as a better place to set up for battle. They would have been out in the open going to Senepol. Sethos watched Darthos's friends very carefully as he broke the news. As they traveled, himself, Jabar, Darius, and Waaiz kept close eyes on them to see if they broke rank and tried to disappear. At the announcement, Darthos's posse didn't look pleased with the change in plans. Sethos figured they would try to leave after setting up camp that night.

    Sure enough, when the sun went down and everyone was settling for the night after a long sweltering day of traveling, Darthos's clan tried to make their move. They had a tent together, so it was easy enough to keep an eye on them. They weren't the smartest Heru warriors in the tribe, that was for sure. They were about to take flight, but Sethos, Jabar, Darius, Waaiz, and a couple more soldiers were on them. Sethos made sure that as they captured them, he let slip that they had the three obelisks that Senepol was searching for and then conveniently let one of them escape. He did this knowing the Heru traitor would fly to Darthos and Senepol to tell them the new plan, the new destination, and that they had the obelisks. This way Senepol would have to come to them. He wanted the obelisks so badly he would not be able to wait patiently for them to come to him. When tossed into a makeshift jail, Sethos asked Darthos posse one question: "Why?"

Only one spoke, "Darthos is our leader. We only answer to him. He negotiated a good deal with Senepol for us after he conquers the lands. You are all going to die. Why not get a deal when the deal is good?"

Sethos shook his head in dismay before he calmly replied to that comment, "Don't you get it? Senepol never keeps his promise to anyone, ever. If Senepol wins, you are the ones dead when this is over. Darthos too. Senepol has never, nor will he ever, let anyone have what he considers his and survive to tell the tale. It saddens me that you have chosen to go against your own people. I hoped you were better than that."

Three of the four Darthos supporters lowered their heads in shame, but the fourth spat at Sethos. "Darthos will prevail."

Sethos wiped the spit from his armor. Without comment, he turned and walked toward Jabar and Darius. "I grew up with these warriors. How did they turn to hate their own?"

Jabar slapped Sethos on the shoulder. "Greed, power, riches, fear. These spawn from unknown evils. Evil is the easier choice to make. This is not your burden, nor is it your fault, Sethos. They chose their path. What happens to them because of their choices is now in our goddess's hands to judge."

Sethos looked at Jabar and laughed. "When did you become a priest? That was pretty deep stuff right there."

Jabar laughed as well. "Was it? It sounded better in my head. Come, friend, I'm famished. We'll fill our bellies as we figure out how to get our Bree back."

*****

The next morning, Bree found herself escorted to a large dining hall. She seated herself at the table as two guards remained behind her by the wall. The table was ladened with food and drink, but she didn't touch anything; she just sat waiting. She could sense that something bad was about to happen, making the food on the table look unappealing. Through the door of the dining room entered Senepol's first wife, Thema. Bree sighed. This was the last person she wanted to see. She would have preferred it to be Senepol, if she were being honest. Thema sat directly across from her and began helping herself to the choicest morsels of each of the plates. With her plate now loaded, she ate a couple of grapes before she spoke. "Our food is not to your liking?" Bree cleared her throat but said nothing. Thema ate a little more. "I thought you would like to know that we beheaded the old servant Eman. You know the one I speak of. The traitor that helped you escape the dungeon."

Bree gagged; she couldn't help it. *Oh god, poor Eman.* Never in her worst nightmare would she have thought these despicable creatures would stoop as low as murdering an old lady by beheading her. Evil surrounded her. Thema smiled. This was the reaction she had been looking for. She hated the woman sitting across from her. She hated the intense interest her husband had in her. She loathed her beauty, her talent. She despised everything about this tiny woman.

Thema started to toss grapes at Bree as she laughed, recalling the day's events. "Yes, yes, we had a public execution. It was overly exciting, especially when the old woman's head rolled off the platform and landed at the feet of her ten-year-old grandson." Another grape hit Bree right on her face. That was all it took. Bree had never moved so fast in her life, even though every muscle still screamed in pain. She was up and over the table before the guards even realized that she had moved. She grabbed a sharp knife sticking out of a slab of mutton without stopping and dove at Thema, sticking it deep into her right eye. Thema screamed, trying to shove Bree away. Bree was faster. Out and in, out and in the knife plunged into Thema's face, neck, left eye. Anywhere that Bree could stick the knife in before the guards were able to pull her off was good enough. The struggle caused Thema and Bree to fall away from the table. Bree was wildly stabbing anywhere and everywhere she could reach as she dodged Thema's hands. Blood spurted everywhere as the puncture to Thema's jugular erupted. The knife became too slippery to hang on to. Bree didn't even realize she wasn't holding the knife anymore as she continued to hit Thema over and over. When the guards finally reached her and lifted her off Thema, she screamed and roared her frustration. Thema gurgled, grabbing at her neck. Blood sputtered from her mouth as she coughed. The guards stood stunned with Bree struggling between them as they watched their queen bleed out on the dining hall floor. Thema jerked a couple times more, blood spewed from her mouth, and then there was a horrid gurgling sound and a horrible rasp of air. Then nothing. She was dead.

    Senepol, Darthos, and Aston ran through the doorway and stopped. They heard loud screaming as they headed to the dining hall to break their fast, but never in their wildest dreams could they have imagined the scene before them. Thema was lying in a pool of blood, covered in deep wounds from her face to her neck. One of Thema's eyes lay beside her on the floor, still attached to the optic nerve, staring in their direction. Bree was struggling as the guards held her still, roaring down at Thema's corpse, spewing every obscenity that she had ever heard while she struggled with the guards to let her go. Senepol walked over to his first wife's corpse and looked down at her. He bent down to inspect the damage but did not touch her. He slowly stood back up. No emotion showed on his face when he turned to look at Bree. Darthos still stood at the door, looking quite amused, while Aston ran to stand beside the guards, trying to explain to Senepol why he still needed Bree and to not kill her for this atrocity just yet. Bree did not hear or see any of this. She remained fixated on Thema. Flashes of Eman's head rolling over the platform and down onto the feet of her family and friends played over and over in her mind, with Thema's smiling face in the background. Everything around her was in slow motion. Even her struggling felt like she was underwater. The voices in the dining room sounded far off in the distance. Aston stepped in front of her and suddenly smacked her hard enough to shake her from her manic state.

    "What the fuck, Bree?" Aston said in complete shock. Senepol, however, still looked at Bree without emotion. He stood frozen just staring at her. *What the hell was she thinking? Senepol is sure to kill her now*, Aston thought to himself as he watched Senepol watching Bree.

    Suddenly Senepol began to snicker, and a low grumbling sound came out of his chest, which quickly turned into full-blown laughter. "You never cease to amaze me, my tiny beauty. You will fit well by my side nicely. What an asset you are turning out to be. Thema was getting on my nerves with her obsessive jealousies." Senepol ordered the guards to release Bree. They looked confused at first. She had just murdered the queen. They obeyed but eyed Bree warily. When the guards released her, she went over to Thema and spit on her corpse. Senepol burst into laughter once again. "You will make one hell of a wife. These arrangements will commence after I slaughter all who oppose me. You and the obelisks will be my reward. Oh, how I look forward to that." Bree never spoke or moved as Senepol talked; she just stood there, breathing heavy, staring down at the mayhem she had caused. He continued to laugh as he sat at the head of the table and began to eat as if nothing had happened. Darthos joined the table and followed Senepol's actions.

Aston still stood, staring at Bree breathing heavily, staring down at Thema's bloody body. *She snapped. She's lost it. Her mind has finally broken from all this chaos.* Aston wasn't worried about her, but he was now wary. He would have to watch his back at all times when Bree was around. He didn't want to end up like Thema. Aston was shocked, impressed, and a little worried of Bree now. He never expected this from Bree. She was a beautiful face with intelligence to match, but this… He never believed she was capable of such violence.

Senepol informed Aston about Derrick's demise, which relieved him. He even praised Senepol for a job well done. He was trying to figure out how to get Derrick out of the picture for a while now. He figured he now had Senepol right where he wanted him. He just needed to get his firsthand sight on the obelisks again. He was sure the tribes that Bree dabbled with had a couple of obelisks as well. He needed them all. He planned to see for himself once the battle started. He would make sure to lay in wait till the battle and then sneak in to gather them up when everyone was busy in combat. He would have to be fast. Senepol would fall. Aston had no doubt about this. There were five tribes against him now. Six, if the Anubi changed sides like he knew they would. The Anubi despised Senepol and how he treated them as slaves. It was just a matter of time. Senepol's army was vast with two hundred strong, and now he had a little less than a hundred Aspis on his side, but it would still be two tribes against six. Senepol thought high enough in his own ability that the odds didn't faze him. Aston wanted to stay in Senepol's good graces, so he sat down and helped himself to food, joining into the conversation that they were having and acted like nothing was wrong, that this was another typical morning. Senepol had a couple of his priests come in and force Bree to drink a concoction that would have her sleeping in blissful nothingness for the day, then they took her back to her locked room to sleep off the trauma of her morning.

Just as they were finishing their breakfast, two guards stormed into the dining hall, carrying between them an exhausted and injured Heru warrior. Darthos stood and quickly went over to his best friend. "Asim? What has happened? Where are the others?" Senepol and Aston sat watching the Heru warriors, waiting to hear the tale Asim would tell.

Asim was exhausted; he had flown nonstop the entire night to make it to Darthos as quickly as possible. "Sethos discovered us. I was the only one that made it out. Sethos has changed the plan of fighting the battle on Senepol's lands. He is taking up refuge in the forgotten city and will wait for Senepol to come to him."

"*What?*" Senepol was furious; everything was ready for the tribes to come to him. He had Bree; he had two of the obelisks. The traps had been set all around his lands; ambushes were all laid out. He had everything thing lying in wait for the planned battle. Senepol stormed toward the Heru warriors in a rage. "I won't sway my plans. *They will come to me!*"

Asim cleared his throat. "There is more, my king. I overheard it slip that they have found the remaining three obelisks. They have them in their possession as we speak. I assume they will try to trade the woman for them. I escaped before I heard any more so I could bring you this news."

Senepol's demeanor changed in the blink of an eye. He slapped Asim on the back, and he laughed heartedly. "Decent job, Heru. This is good news indeed. The little monkey man Derrick was correct. Let them find all the obelisks. I have changed my mind. We go to them."

Darthos could see through the plot, though, and warned Senepol. "My king. This is a trap. They know of your desire to have the obelisks. Do you think it wise to take this battle to the forgotten city? They will be able to have better defenses set before we make it there. It will be us slaughtered and not them."

Senepol laughed evilly. "Oh, Darthos, you lack vision, my boy. This is why I am king. We will go to the forgotten city. We will function as if we are preparing for battle by the forgotten city's border. This is when I will send Sa'd to find out where the obelisks are. When he returns, a select few of us will sneak into the city to retrieve the obelisks while my army bluffs an attack. We will be in and out with my prize before they will even know I am not in the battle. I will, of course, have a double so they think it is me leading my soldiers to war. This is going to be easier than I anticipated." Senepol was almost salivating as he rubbed his hands together. He yelled out to his head guard and told him to prepare for the battle at the forgotten city. That they would leave in three days' time.

Aston was having a conundrum. Now he would have to figure out how to convince Senepol to bring the other two obelisks with them to the forgotten city. He wanted to have all five to bring back when he opened a portal. He had the sacred scroll memorized by heart now. The first day they came through the portal and Senepol killed the translator, Aston retrieved the scroll where it had fallen before they followed Senepol to the temple. All he needed was five minutes with the obelisks together and Bree for her bloodline. With the portal open, he would slip through with the obelisks, and the rest would be history. *So, what would be a good reason to convince Senepol to bring the obelisks with us to the battle?* he wondered.

23

The five tribes had finally reached the outskirts of the forgotten city. They set up camp on the flat stone slab on the outer rim of the city. Sethos insisted that everyone save strength and recuperate so they could start organizing, build defenses and traps, and figure out strategies for the upcoming battle. Between their five tribes, they were approximately 350 warriors strong. The Ibis priests that came along were for medical and spiritual purposes. They would not fight as they were not skilled in that department. The Heru would be their air defense, as they were skilled with archers and could use the composite bow while in the air. When they ran out of arrows, they were also skilled in hand-to-hand combat. The Maahe and Sobek were the main ground defenses. Both were formidable opponents who were strong, agile, and capable with weapons as well as using their teeth and claws. The Maahe tended to use the Khopesh sword or short sword in battle. The Sobek tended to lean towards the bronze-tipped spears and wooden shields while keeping their mace-axes strapped across their shoulders to finish their opponents off. The Sakhmet were going to be the ambushers. They were skilled in hiding, sneaking, and preying on smaller groups or could sneak in behind the battle and ambush the Apis from behind using their poison-coated daggers. Darius was convinced that what Anubi came with the Senepol and Aspis, they would mutiny to their side and be allies in the battle. Sethos and Jabar sure hoped he was right. There would be at least one hundred Anubi, so if they did, they were very proficient with a javelin and would swell their ground-fighting numbers much higher.

  On the way to the forgotten city, they hunted and gathered herbs, grains, fruits, and vegetables the entire time. They were going to have a feast tonight. One to feed everyone to keep up their strength and morale and the other to honor everyone—tribe members, friends, loved ones who would not be coming back from this battle. Tonight would be a celebration of tribes and unity. Tomorrow they would begin to be ready for battle. Sakhmet rogues, however, spread out around the forgotten city and surrounding areas to make sure there were no ambushes waiting and the Heru scouts took to the skies to make sure Senepol's army was not closing in yet. While the feast was being prepared, Zosar and Jendayi headed off to the center of the city. They headed to the grand temple to see if it were in suitable enough condition for the Ibis priests to set up for deep meditation and prayer so they could call upon the gods to bless them in battle. They had to carefully pick their way through all the debris and overgrowth of plant life within the city streets, but they made it to the temple safely. They were both surprised how well the pyramid-shaped temple had fared. The temple had damage on the outside with trees, grass, and weeds growing through the large stones, but the inside was quite untouched. Even the statue of the goddess was still standing proudly in the center of the temple. The ledge around the goddess was still intact where the four obelisks once sat.

There were vines growing up and wrapping around her, but it made her look even more surreal and otherworldly the more one looked. There were even torches still in place that they were able to light as they entered. Inside was damp and musty with a little debris here and there, with stones that had fallen down from the ceiling and out of the walls strewn around, but it was still impressive. Jendayi and Zosar took out the obelisks from their packs and placed them in their respective places on the ledge encircling the goddess's statue. They glowed light blue and pulsated softly, with a low even hum. Zosar and Jendayi stood back as they both relished in the energy the obelisks radiated around them. They felt focused, strong, healthy, and younger. It felt wonderful to be back home. If only they could keep the obelisks, but alas, they knew that someone else would rise up and try to claim them and their power as their own. They couldn't imagine destroying them, so they would send them back through the portal where they originated from. At least that was the plan. Zosar placed the third blood vial they prepared earlier with Bree and placed it in the Aspis obelisk. Once completed, the color of the obelisks switched from blue to green, and the hum increased with a vibration as well. Zosar and Jendayi smiled to themselves. With the obelisks in place and reactivated with Nefertiti's bloodline, the war would be over soon, and Senepol's fearful reign would crumble.

Zosar and Jendayi made it back just as the feast was starting. Before they joined the feast, they let Sethos, Jabar, Darius, and Waaiz know the obelisks were back in the temple. "I thought I could feel a renewed energy in the air. I knew you were successful," Sethos mentioned as they all walked toward the feast fires. They all agreed. The air felt pure and refreshing; the mood of the tribes was energetic and friendly, with the aura around the city pulsating good vibrations. The mood of the evening was just what everyone needed before the preparations for war began on the next sun rising. Zosar stood on a stone placed before the feast laid out on the walking stones below. He addressed the large group of tribes, "Tonight, we feast and celebrate our advancement as we begin taking back our lands, extinguishing our fears, and coming together as one. It has been too long our tribes have segregated. We are all our goddess's creations. We belong together, not separate. Every one of us adds to the other. We are all important. No one is better or worse than the other you stand beside. Each of us contributes to the safety, growth, development, and happiness of our tribes. One loss is a loss for all. Tonight, I pray we remember this. I want to see the tribes mixing tonight. Introduce yourselves to ones you do not know. Mingle and enjoy our diversities, for tonight is a night for freedom and unity. Think not of the battle ahead, for we worry about this on the new sunrise. Enjoy, mingle, eat. Be as one."

During the feast, Ibis females gathered together with their drums, rattles, sistrums, tambourines, lutes, lyres, oboes, shepherd's pipes, and harps and began to play celebratory music. Sekhmet females also gathered and danced to the music. Everyone was at peace with full bellies and friendly conversations. The night was one to remember for their future. The food created and shared by all tribes was delicious as well as first tries for all. Each tribe had added their own creations to the feast. The dishes also felt like a unity of the tribes as everyone partook of each tribe's different dishes. This night of unified celebration was a success. It strengthened rapport between them all, showing everyone that being together, being unified, was the way of the future.

Before dawn the next morning, Zosar and Jendayi left once again with a couple of high priests from each tribe and took them back to the temple in the center of the city, where they would stay to prepare the temple, meditate, and pray during the battle. As the sun rose on the horizon, casting shadows along the city walls and fallen structures, everyone began to awaken to start preparations for the coming days. Soldiers sharpened weapons; leatherworkers repaired and finished armor, helmets, and shields. Soldiers gathered tallying and counting all weapons, sharpening those that were dull and fixing those broken or about to break. New weapons were crafted where they were lacking. They gathered saps and tore fabric to wrap around arrows' tips and javelins to light anything they hit on fire when deployed from their bows and hands.

They gathered firewood and water and soaked arrows and daggers in poison milked from the Egyptian cobras so if the weapon or fire did not kill, the poison on them would. Others moved and hoisted large stones to create barriers, and they scouted areas that would be best for ambush attacks as well as places to position runners, scouts, and the Sakhmet rogues. They discovered the best places for the archers that didn't fly to be up and within close buildings whose structures were stable enough to hide and hold them as they helped keep close attackers at bay. They shaved down logs into spikes and dug them into the ground or wedged them in between large boulders to help injure or take down their foes' mounts, which included the giant scarabs and the massive hyenas. Their own mounts were armored to the teeth as well. They had twenty-six Maahe elephants with long tusks plated in copper; Azizi and Pepi, Darius's giant scarabs, also had copper plating specially made to attach to their jaws. They would also use the massive rat mounts of the Sakhmet tribe to help chew down and bite ground defenses. They dug deep trenches around the main battle area to slow down advancing mounts as well.

Everyone and everything that was capable in battle would be in the battle.

*****

Bree once again found herself tied and on the back of a giant scarab. Only this time it wasn't with Jabar and Darius. To her misfortune, she was stuck with Aston in a carrier strapped to the back of the scarab. It had a sun cover and a soft bench. It swayed back and forth softly and would have been an enjoyable way to travel if it weren't for the company forced on her to travel with. Senepol rode just in front of them on his giant chariot, leading the pack of soldiers that numbered close to four hundred. The scarabs were frightening enough, but Bree tolerated them. She, however, was not prepared for the sight of all the gargantuan horse-sized hyenas ridden by the Aspis. They drooled, smelled terrible, and were constantly laughing in their high-pitched manner that caused Bree to perpetually be uneasy. Bree hated them instantly. She tried to sit as far away from Aston as the bench allowed. They did not talk as they departed Senepol's palace. Aston made himself comfortable by stretching his long legs across the carrier in front of Bree. Even if she wanted to stretch her legs, she didn't dare, or she would be touching Aston. He wrapped one arm around his side of the carriage and then leaned his other arm closest to Bree right across the back of the bench behind her head. She knew he was doing this on purpose to piss her off, and it was working, especially when he wouldn't wipe a smug look from his face.

Finally, she couldn't hold back any longer. She had to ask why Aston seemed so self-righteous. "What scheme has gone your way that you have that look stuck on your face?"

Aston had been waiting for her to ask and maneuvered himself so they sat closer together so he could talk quietly. "I am glad you asked. I am going to get us out of here."

Bree hmphed. "Us?"

Aston chuckled quietly. "I understand why you think that way. You think I don't like you, but I do like you. You are beautiful, intelligent, and would make a great asset to my plans back home."

She rolled her eyes. "Just get to the point, Aston. I am already getting a headache."

Aston chuckled again. "You are also to the point. You take no shit, and I admire that. I have convinced the narcissistic king to bring along his obelisks."

Bree, despite herself, was now extremely interested in what Aston had to say. If she could figure out a way to get a message to Jabar and the others that the two obelisks were coming to them, they could hatch a plan as to how to steal them from Senepol. "How the hell did you manage that?"

Aston smiled smugly again. "All I had to do was remind Senepol about what had happened in the temple when he first got both obelisks together. If he brought them, imagine how unstoppable he would be if all the obelisks were at his side during this escapade."

Bree raised her eyebrows. "That's all it took?"

Aston nodded. "That's all it took." Aston figured he now had Bree's full attention. He would give her a little tidbit more, and then maybe he could get information out of her. "See that chest at Senepol's feet? That's where he keeps the obelisks, tucked in nice and neat beside him."

Bree looked over at Senepol's feet and noticed the chest. She tucked that information away for later.

Now Aston had to find out if the other tribes had at least one or more of the obelisks. "Imagine if we could have all the obelisks together. We could use them to defeat this monster, save your precious friends, and then open a portal to get home."

She leaned away from Aston to look him square in the face. *He's up to something.* She just knew it, and it had nothing to do with saving her friends or anyone else but himself. She put on her best smile. "Oh god, that would be amazing! If only we knew where the other obelisks were, this would be so much easier."

Now it was Aston's turn to humph. *She's hiding the fact that they have at least one. I will have to be smarter with this chit.* Aston told himself, *She is smarter than I give her credit for.* Aston resumed his previous position with his legs up and crossed over the edge of the carriage and his arm back behind Bree. "Your friends, alive and safe.

We make it home alive and safe. Ah yes, wouldn't that just make it all the easier?"

Sa'd was riding behind the scarabs carrying Aston and the woman. He had to make Senepol trust him again after the beating he and Tiye received when they delivered the woman. He watched them closely. He didn't trust the small man one bit. He knew Aston had his own agenda, and it wasn't helping Senepol. He watched Aston tell the woman about the chest carrying the obelisks, noticing her quickly looking over at Senepol's feet. He also surmised that the woman didn't like Aston or trust him by her body language. He needed to convince Senepol to separate those two. She may not like Aston, but if she thought he could help her escape, she would defiantly utilize their communication and try to get him to help her. She already was aware where the obelisks were on this journey. She could be trouble. He had heard how she decimated Thema. If she were capable of that, then what else could she be capable of? Sa'd would keep his eye on both.

Sa'd waited till they broke for camp that night before he brought up his concerns to his king. "I watched them all day, my king. Sssomething isss brewing between thossse two. They may try to go for the obelisssksss. Didn't you tell me that it was the woman'sss bloodline that enabled them to open the portal to get here in the firssst place?"

Senepol sat up from his lounger, taking notice of Sa'd. At first, he was trying to ignore the Aspis; he was still not pleased with his treatment of his property, but this was something that was plausible. Sa'd could be correct. If they did get ahold of the obelisks, he could lose the woman back to her own plane. This was unacceptable. Not only did he need her blood to keep him healed if wounded, but he figured her blood linked somehow to the obelisks. Having her with him when all the obelisks were in his possession would make them much more powerful. Her escaping was not an option. "Sa'd, I must admit you are working yourself back into my good graces. You were correct with bringing me your concerns."

Sa'd bowed to his king. "Only for you, my liege."

Senepol nodded. "Bring her to me now. I will keep her with me during the night hours. I put you in charge of keeping an eye on them closely during the day, Sa'd. Bring me any information you find out from them during travel. I am placing my trust back in you, Sa'd. No more mistakes. This is your last chance to prove yourself to me. Keep them away from the obelisks. If they try to steal them, kill Aston, but no harm whatsoever is to come to my little lady. Do I make myself clear?"

Sa'd bowed again and left the tent with a satisfied look on his face. He would not fail his king this time. The control of the Aspis tribe was close to being his.

Sa'd led Bree into a tent. When he untied her from the small makeshift cell, she knew Senepol had ordered her brought to him. Where else would he be taking her? She was very relieved when she found out her assumption was correct. Sa'd was evil, and she remembered her trip in the box he made her suffer through. She didn't want to be in his presence at all. This particular Aspis was not to her liking. He was a sniveling snake. He was the one that had Jabar almost killed and thrown into Senepol's dungeon. Sa'd could choke on his own forked tongue and drop dead for all she cared. When she was in Senepol's tent, he instructed she be tied to his bedpost. When Sa'd did as instructed, he smiled evilly at Bree and whispered, "Have a good sssleep, lady." Bree figured that Sa'd assumed Senepol was going to take advantage of her tonight and he was happy about it. She spat in his face. Sa'd was so close to striking her, but Senepol yelled out, "Leave us, Sa'd!" Sa'd turned, bowing slightly to Senepol, but before he left, he flicked his tongue out at Bree with a malevolent glare.

Senepol lounged a little while longer as Bree sat on the edge of the bed watching him. She prayed Sa'd would not be correct in his assumption. Just Senepol's size alone would crush her if he tried anything with her. She was beginning to feel sick to her stomach. Senepol stretched as he stood up from his lounger. Bree's heart jumped into her throat as he untied her and moved her to the top of the bed where he retired her there. "Lie down. Sleep. We have a long day ahead of us." Then he lay beside her and proceeded to fall asleep. Bree was so relieved yet perplexed. She thanked her lucky stars but was still on edge. His massive form was far too close to her. Sleep was very unlikely; her bonds tied in a way that she would not be able to get loose, but she was able to lie on her side with her back to him, as her arms were tied low on the post. She lay as close to her tied wrists on the very edge of the bed as possible. She listened to Senepol's deep exhaling, and soon she fell asleep to the rhythmic breathing of the beast beside her.

24

Bree awoke to a heavy weight across her midsection. It was heavy enough to pin her to her spot and she couldn't move. When she opened her eyes and looked down, she saw that it was Senepol's left arm thrown on top of her. She could feel his hot breath wafting down her neck. Sometime through the night, he must have rolled over, and now she was truly stuck. He must have felt her try to pull herself out from under his arm, which woke him. As if this was a normal morning for him, he snuggled her closer to him and tucked her under his chin and just held her to him. Bree held her breath; she prayed that it was his other arm she could feel pressing against her bottom. It sure felt the size of an arm. She squeezed her eyes shut as he breathed in heavily. "I should take advantage of this opportunity, but again it is not the time." He released her quickly and rose from the bed, leaving her unscathed. Bree's lungs decided to work again as she realized she was starving of breath from holding it in. She sucked in a large lung full of air and willed her heart to return to a normal beat. She lucked out once again. The gods were smiling down upon her this morning. She quickly thanked them. He came around and untied her. He pointed to a large empty pot on the floor. "Relieve yourself. Fresh clothing and water beside it are for your use as well." He removed himself from the bed area, dropping a curtain to give her privacy. *Who is this Senepol, and why is he treating me so well? What is he up to?* Bree was sure something was up, but she quickly used the chamber pot and took advantage of the clothing that was small enough to fit her. They must have been for a child, but they fit, and they were comfortable. She washed herself, quickly realizing she couldn't hide from him forever and stepped out from behind the curtain. He wasn't even in the tent, but there was food left on the rug by his lounger, so she helped herself and ate her fill quickly.

An Anubi servant entered the tent with an Apis guard. The guard stood at the door as the servant began to clean up the morning meal. As the servant turned to take Bree's plate from her, something slipped into her hand. The servant never said a word or looked at Bree as they turned back to gather up the rest of the meal, and then they exited the tent. Bree was smart enough not to react or look at whatever it was that the Anubi servant slipped to her. The guard, however, stayed. "My lady, if you are ready, Senepol has requested that I escort you to your mount for the day's ride."

Bree choked slightly on what the guard had said. *My lady!* The guard was acting as if she was Senepol's lover. *Well of course, you twit, you spent the night in their king's tent. They suspected that I am now his lover.* Bree nodded but politely asked, "Would you mind if I used the chamber pot before we go? It is a long ride. I may not be able to hold it that long, if you know what I mean."

The guard cleared his throat, slightly embarrassed. He nodded. "I will be just outside the tent, my lady." Bree made sure he was completely outside before she ducked behind the curtain. She tore open the small note that said, "All Anubi on your side. None will fight for Senepol." The message came on a small piece of cotton. Bree did not want anyone to find it, so she wadded it up as tight and small as she could, stuffed it in her mouth, and swallowed hard. She gagged a couple of times, managed to get it down, then proceeded to exit the tent, where the guard took her to the carriage mounted to the scarab for the day's travels.

Aston smirked at her as the guard left without tying her to the carriage today. "Looks like your sleepover in Senepol's tent earned you his favor today."

Bree was disgusted that he would even mention that possibility. It seemed like every male in camp saw her go to the king's tent and just assumed he bedded her. So instead of fighting with him, she looked him straight in the eye. "Jealous much?"

Aston burst out laughing. "God, I love your wit."

Bree just shook her head. She would never understand men. He was only a tent away from Senepol's and saw Sa'd take Bree out of her little makeshift cell into the king's tent. He listened for over an hour, waiting to hear screaming or exchanged blows as Bree tried to fight off Senepol's advances. To his dismay, he heard nothing. "So, if you're done with disgusting assumptions, I received a message today."

Aston looked slowly around like he was taking in the activities of the soldiers. He observed when Sa'd had taken Bree to Senepol's tent right after Sa'd talked to the king for a while. He knew Sa'd was a sneaky bastard and didn't trust him as far as he could throw him. He caught him trying to listen in to their conversations yesterday during their travels and knew he would take anything he suspected to Senepol, and he did just that. Sure enough, there was Sa'd mounting up, about to come in behind them. Aston cautioned Bree with a head toss to the direction behind him. "He's Senepol's spy. Watch what you say when he is around, Bree. He knows that you know Senepol has the obelisks. He's ordered to watch us closely. Anything you need to say that is important will have to wait till he is not so close. Sshh, he is coming now."

Bree sighed but nodded slightly, and they both kept silent the entire morning. Tiye rode up to Sa'd after the afternoon break, and Sa'd backed off a little to have a conversation or argument with her for a couple minutes. Bree took advantage of Sa'd's distraction. "The Anubi will not fight with Senepol. They want to defect. I need to get a message to Jabar somehow so they don't attack the Anubi when the battle starts."

Aston smiled to himself as he listened to Bree. "I knew they wouldn't support Senepol. They despise him. Let me see what I can do about the message. Looks like we are on the wrong side of the battle."

Now it was Bree's turn to laugh. "You mean you are on the wrong side. I am not bound to that sociopathic beast like you. I picked my side weeks ago."

Aston sighed, making sure Tiye and Sa'd occupied one another still. "Look, Bree, I meant it when I said all I want is the obelisks. I have no side. I personally do not care in the least what happens as long as we can get home. I tell you what, if I get a message sent to your lion friend that the Anubi are on their side and not to harm them, can I trust you to help me open the portal so I can get home? If you want to stay here, I really don't care, but I want to get back. Do we have a deal? I scratch your back, you scratch mine."

Bree contemplated; she trusted Aston as much as she trusted Derrick. *May he not rest in peace.* What other option did she have right now? Getting a message to Jabar would save a hundred Anubi lives. Giving Aston the option to get back home with the obelisks may cause hundreds of thousands of people's lives. Aston wouldn't have her to help him use the obelisks if she stayed, so maybe he wouldn't be able to take over the world. She already decided she was going to stay here with her new friends, and right now the most important thing was to keep Darius's tribe safe. "Okay, Aston, we have a deal. If you get a message to Jabar, I will help you get home."

Sa'd smacked Tiye's mount away as he was annoyed with her and came back up to be behind the carriage. It was too late; they had discussed all they needed to.

Again that night, she went to Senepol's tent; only this time he wasn't there. A guard stayed in the tent but did not talk to her. When her supper came, she ate alone, asking the guard if he would like to eat, since there was far more than enough to share. He looked around and peeked out of the tent; he shrugged his shoulders and grabbed a leg of meat and a hunk of bread, bowing to her as he devoured it. She took him a large goblet of wine as well, and he accepted that readily too. After eating, Bree was so tired she couldn't keep her eyes open, so she stated to the guard that she was ready to go to sleep. He followed her into the bed area, and she sat near the post waiting for the guard to tie her to it like the night before and waited. The guard never approached her and just stood guard. Bree shrugged her shoulders and crawled on the bed, falling asleep as her head rested on the pillow. Senepol never came until extremely late. He kicked out the guard and lay beside Bree on the bed, who awoke, terrified tonight was the night. He threw his arm around her tiny form, pulling her close to him like one would a teddy bear, and promptly began to snore. She again found herself thanking the gods over and over till she, too, fell back asleep.

The next day was exactly the same as the other two—hot, dusty, traveling toward the forgotten city. Aston talked to an Anubi servant to find a way to send a message to Jabar. He told them what the message should say and that if they received it to have Darius tie a blue cloth to his spear to let the Anubi know that they had received the message and would not harm them if they came over and not fight with Senepol. The Anubi servant was wary at first that it was Aston inquiring about the message and not Bree. But he relaxed when he realized that Bree must have told Aston, as she was unable to be alone. The servant agreed and stated that they knew how to get a message out and would send it immediately. When Aston was able, he told Bree quietly that the message had been sent as promised. Bree was relieved because she could see the forgotten city far in the distance later that afternoon. The battle would be starting soon. Thank God the Anubi would be at least safe from one side. Darius would be thrilled. She wondered if he was nervous about having to fight against his own people. Now he wouldn't be against them; he would be fighting beside them, the way it should be.

*****

A couple of spotters entered the camp in search of Sethos and Jabar. They found them sitting at a makeshift table planning battle strategy. "Senepol and his troops are advancing on the southern borders. Looks like their numbers are—" Suddenly a pigeon landed right in the middle of the table with a note tied to its one leg. They all stared at the pigeon for a moment, not sure what to do. Never had they seen a homing pigeon before. Jabar moved first, very slowly. The pigeon just cooed at him as he gently pulled on the note. When the note was off the pigeon's leg, it instantly flew up and away. Everyone stared at Jabar as he opened and read the note. He jumped up with a whoop as he yelled for Darius. "You are not going to believe this, Darius! Get over here."

Sethos patiently waited for Darius to join the group, and Jabar slapped the young Anubi on the shoulders. "What is it, Jabar? You look as if something has made you really happy. Did you find out something about Bree?"

The mention of Bree agitated Jabar, and he hung his head for a moment. "No, but she was able to send us a message." At this point, everyone stood up saying a unanimous "*What?*" Jabar passed the note to Darius first, who almost began to cry and then whoop for joy before he handed the note to Sethos.

When Sethos read it through, he then read it aloud for all near: "Anubi will join battle against Senepol. Have Darius tie large piece of cotton to spear. A sign for message received." Bree's name was signed at the end of the message.

"I knew it. I knew Bree would help out in any way she could. Now my people will be safe thanks to her. Goddess, that woman is amazing. Now we also know that she is safe." Darius was overjoyed with the message. He immediately went to find the brightest piece of material he could tie to his spear. He would make sure he waved it high when the battle began. Jabar was also extremely relieved, not only because the Anubi tribe was now on their side but mostly he knew that Bree was still okay. He understood that she was in Senepol's hands; he remembered the first time he had seen Senepol's treatment of Bree in the dungeon. He squeezed his eyes shut. When he healed, he tried to go to see if he could get her back, but everyone, including Zosar and Jendayi, held him back. They all reminded him that it would be a suicide mission if he went in to get her back. They reminded him that Senepol would treat her very well as he needed her. It killed him on the inside but knew that they were right. He wanted nothing more than to have her back by his side. She was a grown woman who was very capable of taking care of herself. She had proven that repeatedly since he had met her, but he still missed her so much his soul ached.

Sethos kept reading the note over and over as relief swept over him about the Anubi coming onto their side. He wanted just as much to go with Jabar to save Bree but ended up being one of the ones holding Jabar back from leaving. He had always been the voice of reason. They both did not need to die as they would have if they went in raging with emotions. He was as much in pain as Jabar was, but he could not show it to his friend. He knew he was the odd one out in this situation. Right now, they had to concentrate on the battle ahead. It was soon. Very soon. They would be up to their elbows in blood in the next day or so. They had to keep their focus on the battle ahead and not on a woman that had stolen both their hearts. As hard as that was, it was Sethos's only option. Six tribes were now counting on their leadership. Saving Bree had to be on the back burner right now.

Jabar walked over to Sethos and slapped him on the shoulder. "Bree is okay, but if Senepol touched her in any way, promise me that it is me that gets to end his life."

Sethos smiled at the one that he now considered his best friend. "Get in line, friend. We both want to see her safe." Jabar frowned slightly but then changed his demeanor as he looked over at Darius, who was tying a bright blue piece of cotton to the part of his spear that connected to the shaft, but then frowned again as he turned back to Sethos.

He bent low as he said, "You love her, don't you?"

Sethos looked Jabar straight in the eye. He thought about lying to his friend, but that would get them nowhere, so he answered honestly, "Yes, I do love her. I am sorry, friend. She is infectious. I tried to not care, but she has a way of grabbing your heart and not letting go." Jabar sighed, but Sethos continued, "My love for her is not returned, Jabar. She only has eyes for you. I understand and realize this. It hasn't changed how I feel about her, but I know that it is a lost cause for me, my friend. I promise you that I will not get in your way. I love her, but her happiness and your happiness are more important to me than my feelings. Jabar, she loves you, not me."

Jabar looked and felt stunned. He respected Sethos, but now Sethos was even a better friend to him. His honesty came at an appreciative time. "Thank you, Sethos," was all Jabar could say before he turned and walked away. Jabar had to stop himself from talking about Bree, or he would break. He could not think about her in Senepol's clutches right now. He grabbed the first Maahe warrior and took him with him to spar, hoping this would help him concentrate on anything else but Bree.

*****

Zosar, Jendayi, and the rest of the priests had everything they needed to begin their meditation and prayer. Their three obelisks were set up and humming continuously as they glowed a beautiful blue green, like their sacred lotus. They placed themselves around the golden statue of their goddess and began to meditate. There they sat on weaved mats after they lit incense all around the temple to burn and purify the air. They fasted since the feast to purify their bodies. Zosar passed along *Psilocybin cubensis* (magic mushrooms), grown on barley, to enhance their accessibility to communicate with the gods. "Blessed is the celestial food of the gods so we may set our minds to the vibrations of their communication." All the priests bowed low toward the statue of their goddess and then held up the flesh of the gods to the sky. They all spoke in unison, "Blessed are we, blessed are the gods, blessed is their flesh of life." They all put the *Psilocybin* to their lips, kissed it, and then proceeded to place it in their mouths and chew exactly twenty-one times and then swallowed. Each priest lit white sage around their bodies and then sat with their legs crossed. The priests that did not partake in the *Psilocybin* began playing instruments that promoted calmness and relaxation. The meditation began. As they delved deep into their inner consciousness, the obelisks matched the priests' brain waves and pulsated slowly, picking up with speed and different calming colors as the priests went deeper and deeper into meditation.

*****

Senepol's army finally stopped and broke camp with the forgotten city in their sights. It was still far away, but it loomed in the distance. All Bree could think of was that Jabar and her friends were there. She was so close yet so far away. Bree stood watching the skyline in the direction of the forgotten city. She had the ability to wander wherever she choose but with a guard following her at all times. "What are you looking at?" The guard was curious as they stood there for over twenty minutes.

Bree sighed; she wasn't about to lie to him. She turned to the guard and honestly asked, "Why do you follow Senepol?"

The guard stood silent, taken aback by her question. "He is our king, my lady."

Bree turned back to look at the forgotten city for a moment and then looked at the guard again. "Okay, let me ask you the question in a separate way. Do you think what Senepol is doing is right?"

The Apis guard frowned back at Bree in confusion and answered again in the same way, "He is our king."

Bree sighed in frustration. "So you are saying you would jump off the tallest cliff of a mountain even though you knew that it meant certain death just because your king told you to?"

The guard looked at the ground thinking hard about the question that Bree asked and then hesitated before he answered, "Why would I jump off a cliff if certain death was only what awaited me, even if my king told me to?"

Bree walked over to the tall Apis guard, patting him on the lower arm. "Exactly!" She turned from the guard and walked back to camp.

The guard didn't follow her right away as he stayed looking out at the forgotten city for a couple more moments and then slowly turned to follow. Exasperated, Bree thought about the coming battle. Everyone just aimlessly followed the will of Senepol just because. Did nothing change? Was every realm, plane, country, or planet the same? Was there nowhere in existence that didn't have mindless followers because of one sick individual's lust for power? She already knew the answer, but it still frustrated her. The battle would claim hundreds who would receive grievous injuries or die because of Senepol. Nothing changed, and it was depressing. All she wanted to do was fall asleep in Jabar's arms with him purring her to sleep right now. A couple of tears escaped her as she thought of Jabar and his friendship. She missed him so much. His image flashed before her as she walked back to her tent. She feared for him and all her friends. What if he became injured or, worse, killed in this battle? Would she ever see him again? She wiped the tears from her eyes when the guard caught up to her and quietly asked her, "Would you go against your leader if he gave you an order?"

Bree stopped and looked the guard dead in the eye. "If I knew it was wrong, yes. I would rather die for what was right than conduct an order just because someone in power told me to. I want to go to the afterlife with a clear conscience, wouldn't you?"

*****

Sa'd slithered up to Aston's tent just as he was finishing his supper. He didn't announce his arrival as he slipped into the tent. Aston was startled but didn't show it. "What a pleasure to see you, Sa'd. What do I owe you for this unexpected interruption?"

Behind Sa'd was Tiye. "Our king isss sssending usss on a sssecret misssssion. He hasss ssspecifically asssked that you join usss."

Aston was not pleased; he didn't trust this particular Aspis. Going on a mission with him was something he didn't look forward to. "I take it that this is an order and not a request?"

Sa'd only smiled evilly.

"Can I at least ask what the mission is about?"

All Sa'd responded with was a hissing chuckle.

Aston sighed. "Give me five minutes, and I will be ready. I will meet you at your tent."

Sa'd and Tiye slowly exited the tent with Sa'd commenting, "Five minutesss." Pissed off was an understatement for how Aston felt at the moment. He knew that Sa'd had something up his sleeve, and here he was without a weapon. As Aston thought of this, he spied the sharp two-pronged meat fork lying beside the leftover meat on his platter. *Bree killed Thema with only a small meat knife. This will come in handy.*

Aston was at Sa'd's tent in less than three minutes with the meat fork hidden in his boot. "Ready?" was all he said as he gave Sa'd and Tiye the same courtesy as they gave him as he barged unannounced into their tent. Aston walked in on Sa'd and Tiye coiled in a hideous sexual mess on the floor, and they hastily tried to disconnect while Aston stood there with his own evil grin. Aston bowed to Sa'd and Tiye as they separated. "Shall we?" They all exited the tent and headed off with hyena mounts toward the eastern border of the forgotten city. The sun had set by the time they reached an area where they ditched their mounts and went the rest of the way on foot. Before they went any farther, Aston asked again, "What is this mission, Sa'd. I stress that in order for me to help you, I must insist on knowing what it is we are doing so I don't mess anything up."

Sa'd rolled his slit eyes like a child. "We are trying to find where they have the obelisks."

Aston laughed at Sa'd, and Tiye defended Sa'd, "Why are you laughing, monkey man?"

Aston cleared his throat and put on his best charm for Tiye. "Well, gorgeous, how do we even know that they have any of the obelisks? Last I knew, Senepol had two and was in search of the others."

Tiye puffed up her neck a little at his comment on her looks. "We are a select few to know they have found the other obelisks. Now we need to find out where they are stashing them."

Aston tried not to look surprised. "They have the other three. How does one so beautiful have the ability to keep such secrets, you minx?"

Tiye slithered closer to Aston, flicking her forked tongue at him as she came nearer. "I have many more sssecretsss. Let me know if you would like a sssample later."

Aston held his disgust in as he stroked the scales on her arm. "I would like that."

Sa'd broke up their conversation with an evil hiss as he shoved Tiye aside. "You are such a whore. And, you, stay away from Tiye." Tiye slinked back away from Aston but still had a smile on her mouth, and she winked at Aston. Aston winked back, even though it made him want to vomit. They continued in the dark in silence. Aston had a challenging time keeping up with the two Aspis. They were extremely fast as they slithered in and out of brush and behind trees and boulders. He was very fit, but their movements were unhuman.

They made a wide berth around the east side of the city. They finally entered the city border on the very opposite side from the opposing camp to the north. They dodged detection from scouting parties patrolling the city borders until they were able to find a spot to enter the city itself. Aston thanked God that there wasn't a full moon. He was sure the patrols were going to sniff them out from their scent alone. He wasn't sure if these creatures had the ability to smell better than a human could or not. After a couple of hours of hiding in the shadows, avoiding the patrols, Aston stopped them as they decided on their next hiding spot. He whispered, "Do you have any idea where the obelisks are being kept?" Sa'd just stared at Aston, and Tiye giggled. "Sa'd, do you have any idea, or are we on a scavenger hunt?"

Still Sa'd ignored Aston. Tiye pipped up, "What is a scavenger hunt?"

Aston just rolled his eyes in the dark. "Okay, so I will take that as a no. You have no idea where to start looking. Sa'd, the obelisks are sacred to your tribes, right?"

Sa'd finally responded with a nod.

"Well then, it is my best guess to look for a sacred place like a temple. Is there a temple in this city?"

Sa'd glared at Aston for a moment and then answered, "Yesss, there isss a temple in the cccity cccenter."

Aston nodded. "Good, good, then that is where we need to check first. Boss, lead the way."

The small group were able to make it to the center of the city undetected. There were lots of debris that it was amazingly easy to stay hidden. The temple had loads of entrances, so they picked the one that seemed to have fewer patrols. Sa'd sent Aston in as they stayed hidden. Aston was up to the challenge. He wanted to make sure that the other obelisks were there. Aston had absolutely no respect for Sa'd; he reminded him of a Bronx drug dealer who thought he was a dangerous leader but was only a corrupt sewer rat doing Senepol's dirty work. Aston chose to go up and into an entrance that would be able to look down into the temple he hoped. His choice was correct. As he slipped into the temple shrouded in darkness, he was able to see the entire temple below. The ledge had collapsed dangerously, but he was able to squeeze onto a small shelf that was still intact. There below, he could see twelve priests sitting on mats in meditation circling a large golden statue of Nefertiti. There was an inner circle surrounding the statue with four placements for obelisks to fit into. Three of the four spaces contained the obelisks he sought. Aston was almost salivating. If only he had Bree here with him, he would be able to open a portal now and be back home in a matter of minutes. He cursed under his breath, took one more look, and then exited the temple.

When Aston returned to Sa'd and Tiye, he mentioned quietly, "All three obelisks are there. I counted twelve priests in meditation. I didn't see any guards."

Sa'd rubbed his hands together with a slight hiss. Tiye wrapped her snake body around Aston's legs with a pulsating constriction. It wasn't tight enough for Aston to feel pain, but it wasn't meant to. "I am ssso impressssed I could just sssqueeze you."

Sa'd glared at the two before he shoved Tiye. "Woman, you are tesssting my patienccce. We need to leave. We found what we needed. Let'sss go."

They were able to maneuver out of the city without notice and headed back toward their mounts. Every chance Tiye had she would slither around Aston in a sexual manner. She would touch Aston or flick her forked tongue in his ear shamelessly. About halfway back to their mounts, Sa'd had enough. Instead of blaming the true one at fault, Sa'd turned on Aston. Out of nowhere, with the speed of light, he coiled around Aston, completely constricting tighter with every coil around his body. Aston was unable to grab the pronged fork from within his boot, as like a sausage, his arms were pinned at his sides, unable to move. Sa'd had complete control as he coiled, ending up with his face right in front of Aston's. "I don't like you. You come here ssstiring up problemsss, making sssecrets with Sssenepol'sss whore, sssneaking under Sssenepol's nose. He can't sssee you, but I can. Now you dare make movesss on my woman right in front of me."

Aston couldn't speak if he wanted to. The breath was fast in exiting his body, and he was suffocating. Tiye was thrilled; she loved making Sa'd jealous. This is what she craved from Sa'd. It was exciting. She slithered around excitedly as she watched Sa'd squeeze the life out of the little man, chanting "Do it, kill him. Make his eyeballs pop out of his head" repeatedly.

Aston was starting to black out. He felt a couple of his ribs about to crack also. Suddenly in midsentence, there was a loud thwack sound, and Tiye dropped to the ground, convulsing in her body's final attempt to stay alive. There in the center of her forehead protruded a dagger. Sa'd uncoiled himself from Aston, who collapsed to his knees, sucking in large gulps of precious air. Sa'd was shaking Tiye, demanding that she get up. When he realized that she was dead, he exploded with rage and turned on Aston. Aston had already caught his breath and was ready for him. When Sa'd lunged at him, it only took one stab to the center of his chest to stop him. Sa'd slithered back slightly. He stared at the pronged fork for a moment and then looked up at Aston in confusion. "Who—" He was unable to finish as he, too, dropped to the ground, dead. Aston quickly bent down to retrieve his weapon when someone stepped out of the shadows. "I wouldn't do that if I were you."

Aston froze when he felt a dagger at his throat. "Turn around, slowly." He obeyed and found himself looking at a female Sakhmet rogue casually standing with two daggers pointed at his throat. She was stunning, if you were into cats. "You must be one of the men that brought that witch with you when you came through the portal."

Aston was confused at first but then chuckled when he realized who the witch was that this Sakhmet was talking about. "It sounds to me that you don't like Bree."

The Sakhmet female shrugged. "Let's just say I want her gone." Aston raised his eyebrows at her and then casually pointed to Tiye's body. "By the way, thanks for that. I'm Aston, and yes, I am one of the men that came through the portal with the witch." Aston stuck out his hand and waited for the Sakhmet to take it. She ignored it completely as she went over to Tiye's body and pulled out her dagger, wiped the blood off on her pants, and replaced it into her dagger strap across her chest. "I'm Zahra. I want to discuss a deal with you."

Aston grinned. "A deal you say. Well then, let's hear it."

Zahra got straight to the point. "Are you going to open the portal again?"

Aston tilted his head toward her as he wondered why she was talking to him instead of killing him. She was Senepol's enemy. He knew she knew he came from Senepol's camp with Sa'd and Tiye. *What kind of deal does she want to make with me, and what does the portal and Bree have to do with any of this?* "Why should I tell you anything?"

Zahra laughed lightly. "'Cause I am the one holding daggers at your throat."

Aston raised his eyebrows again. "Fair enough. Yes, I'm going to try to open the portal so I can get back to my home. Why do you ask?"

Zahra didn't hesitate. "I need you to take the witch back to whence she came from, and in return, I will make sure you are able to open the portal."

Aston clicked his tongue as he suddenly understood. Bree was competition to this Sakhmet female, and she wanted that competition gone. He wasn't going to tell her that he needed to have Bree there to open the portal, so this worked in his favor if he had a little help. "Fine. You have yourself a deal."

Zahra smiled brilliantly at Aston. "Good. If you tell anyone about this, I will kill you."

Aston smirked. "I don't doubt you would."

As Zahra walked with Aston back to where Sa'd had left their mounts, they discussed how Zahra would help Aston open the portal. All Aston cared about was getting the portal open and getting the obelisks back with him. He decided to let Zahra in on Senepol's plan. "I don't care what you do with this information as long as we open the portal. Senepol is planning to use a body double when the battle commences. Once I tell him where the obelisks are, he plans on sneaking in and stealing them while you all are in battle. All he cares about is getting ahold of the obelisks. You realize if he accomplishes this, the battle is all but lost. He will rule over all of you."

Zahra frowned. "I'm aware. Lead Senepol to the east side of the temple. I will make sure you get in. Only the priests will be in the temple, so it shouldn't be too hard. I must insist that nothing happens to my priestess. She is one like me. She must survive. I care not about the others."

Aston nodded. "I will take care of it. How will you know when we arrive at the temple?"

Zahra only said, "I will know." She faded back into the darkness, leaving Aston standing alone with three horrid-smelling giant hyenas.

25

Senepol stormed into Aston's tent that morning and yanked Aston out of his cot he only lay down on an hour before. "Did you find where the obelisks are being kept?"

Aston glanced at the floor as he dangled in the air by Senepol still holding him above the ground. "Could you put me down first?"

Senepol just glared at Aston. He sighed. "Very well then. Yes, we found them just before Sa'd turned his coils on me and tried to end my life."

Senepol dropped Aston back on the cot. "Do they have all three?" was all he said, ignoring the second half of what Aston had mentioned.

"Yes." Senepol laughed and then mentioned, "Sa'd and Tiye are missing. Would you know anything about that?"

Aston stood up from the cot and walked over to his jug of wine and drank straight from it without bothering with a goblet. "Like I said earlier, Sa'd tried to kill me, so I ended him and his whore."

Senepol stared at Aston but then burst into laughter. "This is funny to you?"

Senepol grabbed the jug of wine away from Aston and took a deep drink from it before responding. "Between you and Bree taking care of all my loose ends, I may want to keep you around. Sa'd expected I would give him rule over the Aspis when all this is over. What he failed to understand is there can be only one king, and that king is me."

Aston smirked before he took another long swig from the jug. "Poor Darthos. Do you want me to take him out for you as well?"

Senepol chuckled. "Now that you mention it, not yet. I still need him, but who's to say when I get the obelisks that he must remain alive?"

Aston prayed he would not be around much longer when they entered the temple, but he entertained Senepol. "I never liked the guy myself. Consider it done."

Senepol slapped his hammer of a hand on Aston's shoulder, almost knocking him to the ground. "Good. Tomorrow, we fight. Prepare yourself." Then Senepol abruptly left the tent, leaving Aston to think. *This will be my only chance to open the portal. If I lose this opportunity, it is my neck on Senepol's chopping block. Zahra better hold up her end of the deal.*

*****

As Senepol left Aston's tent, he was thinking on the same lines. Aston would have to die. He knew too much, and the promise of weapons beyond his imagination no longer mattered. Why would he need anything more than the obelisks anyway? Aston would show him where the obelisks were, Aston would kill Darthos, and then he himself would kill Aston, claim the obelisks, and rule the entire land. He was chuckling as he entered his tent. His eyes went immediately to Bree still asleep on his bed. He walked over to her side and stood silent as he looked down at her sleeping form. Everything was coming together. He would soon have everything he desired, including a wedding and bedding the tiny beauty lying in his bed. He reached down and swept a lock of hair away from her beautiful face. Yes, everything was coming along genuinely nice indeed. He turned and left the tent. He had orders to relay to his army. Tomorrow he would be supreme ruler of everything. He could not stop smiling.

*****

Bree lay motionless as Senepol entered the tent. All she could do was pretend to still be asleep. She prayed he was just going to grab something and leave again. Nope, he came over to her and stood beside the bed. Her heart pounded, but she remained still. *Just leave, please, just leave,* she prayed the entire time. Suddenly she felt a whisp of her hair removed from her face. She stopped breathing. *No, no, no.*

And then he was gone. She sighed heavily and quickly removed herself from the bed. She had to escape back to Jabar today. Senepol had not yet abused her, but that would not last. She dressed quickly and exited the tent to look for Aston. She had to ditch the guard somehow so she could speak to Aston privately. Just as she exited the tent, she noticed Aston exiting his. They made eye contact. Aston cranked his head in the direction behind his tent. He obviously needed to tell her something too. She turned to the guard that was right on her heels. "I am so embarrassed to have to ask this of you, but my chamber pot broke, and I have nowhere to relieve myself. Would you mind greatly if I went off into the brush over there, you know, so I can pee."

The guard frowned at her. "I must not have you leave my sight."

Bree played it up as she crossed her legs and began to bounce slightly and bite her lip. "Do you think it wise if I tell Senepol that you saw my body, which is his property, all because you would not let me have a moment of privacy?" She saw the guard flinch and look over in the direction of Senepol, who just so happened to start yelling at a group of soldiers as they cowered before him. Bree played it up some more. "I promise that I won't say anything. Besides, how can little ole me be able to escape such a robust, fast, strong soldier as yourself?" It sickened her to have to play a damsel in distress as she caressed the soldier's ego. "Please, I am going to pee myself. Can you just give me a couple of minutes? I promise I won't run away." She reached out and ran her finger down his arm and batted her eyelashes at him.

The guard caved. "A couple of minutes only. Then I come looking, no matter what."

Bree smiled her brilliant smile at him and picked up her long skirt. "Thank you." And then she ran behind Aston's tent. Aston was waiting for her. "I only have a couple of minutes."

Aston nodded. "Last night, Sa'd, Tiye, and I found where they are keeping the obelisks in the forgotten city. Senepol plans on attacking the front lines tomorrow, but he will not be there. He is sending in a body double to function as himself as he takes you and I to the temple to steal the obelisks while everyone focuses on the battle."

Bree cursed. "Shit, that sneaky bastard. Senepol can't get those obelisks, Aston. You want to get the portal open to go home, right?"

Aston snorted. "Yes!"

Bree peeked out from behind the tent, yelling at the guard, "I am almost done!" as she waved hastily to the guard. "You need my cooperation to open the portal. Well, I have decided. I will help you. Just promise me that you will take those damn obelisks with you, but I am staying. I won't be coming with you through the portal."

Aston smiled at Bree. "Suit yourself, if you want to live with these savages. Tomorrow then."

"Tomorrow then." To Aston's surprise, she grabbed and shook his hand then quickly ran out from behind the tent, back to the guard, who was walking over to look for her. He chuckled as he overheard her say, "Thank you so much. I was about to pee myself."

When Bree reentered Senepol's tent, she quickly went over to the chamber pot and wrapped it in a blanket before she broke it to silence the sound from the guard outside. If the guard became suspicious of her and look to see if the pot broke, then he would see that it was. She then paced nervously back and forth in the tent. Senepol was a sneaky bastard. He wasn't even going to battle. He cared nothing about his men or anyone else but himself. How was she going to be able to help Aston with opening the portal when they got to the obelisks? It would take at least five minutes to open one. How was she to get away from Senepol? Where were the obelisks? How could she stop anyone from injury or death? How would she be able to escape to get to Jabar? So many questions ran through her mind with no answers forthcoming. She paced all day, barely touching her lunch. She would grab a small nibble here and there as she paced by her plate but couldn't sit still long enough to actually eat.

Suddenly Senepol entered the tent with one of his soldiers. She quickly yelped at the abrupt entrance of both large beasts and flew onto the bed. Senepol ignored her, but the soldier stared at her for a moment but then looked back at Senepol. Servants came in soon after, and a flurry of activity started. Senepol took off all his armor, his personal jewelry, and his bangles from his arms and horns. The soldier did the same. The servants whisked around, exchanging everything of Senepol's to the soldier without a word. For a couple of minutes, Bree was confused, but as soon as the soldier began putting on Senepol's armor and personal items, she understood. *So this is to be Senepol's double,* she concluded in her head. The soldier was the same size, height, and mass of Senepol. He had the same coloring even.

As Bree watched them, she could see how easy it would be to believe that this soldier was Senepol, even sitting this close to them. *This isn't good. No one will be the wiser in the battle. What can I do? What can I do?* She was beginning to lose hope. The last touch was a large flowing royal robe placed on the back of the soldier, and Senepol suddenly questioned Bree, "What do you think, my lady?"

Bree stood up and walked over. Lying wouldn't work, for Senepol already knew that he was a perfect double, so honesty was the best right now. She sighed. "He looks exactly like you." Suddenly Bree had a thought. She walked around Senepol's doppelganger as she voiced her thought aloud. "What will happen if they don't see me beside you? They know that I am in your possession and that you would want me near you in case you're injured so I can heal you.

Senepol glared down at Bree. She could see the wheels turning in his head. Then he turned abruptly as he growled out, "Fuck," and stormed out of the tent.

Bree cursed herself over and over realizing that she shouldn't have said anything. *What the hell is wrong with you, you idiot!* Bree was disgusted with herself. If she had just left it alone, Jabar and Sethos would have known immediately something was up if Bree wasn't by Senepol's side during the battle, but *nooo,* she had to go ahead and blabber out his mistake. Now she enabled him to fix said mistake. It was her turn to curse aloud, "Fuck! Fuck! Fuck!" Behind her, she heard a deep chuckle. She had forgotten all about the soldier still standing in the tent with her. She turned her anger on him. "What the hell are you laughing about? Get out of my sight before I tell Senepol you tried to assault me in his absence."

The soldier did the exact opposite and sat down on the lounger, still chuckling.

"Did you not hear what I just said?"

The soldier poured himself a large goblet of wine left from Bree's lunch and began munching on the food as well. All Bree could do was watch him in exasperation. Then he spoke, "I'm to stay unseen in this tent by Senepol himself till the battle tomorrow. I'm not going anywhere, little one."

Bree cursed again as she stomped over to the bed, ripped the curtain shut, and threw herself on the bed all the while listening to Senepol's double laughing at her.

Senepol returned to the tent only being gone for a little while. He threw back the curtain with a grin on his face. "I am starting to think you want to stay with me, my lady."

Bree was sitting in the center of the bed with her legs crossed. She was so angry she actually threw a temper tantrum by standing on the bed and stomping her foot. "Go suck an egg" was the only comment she could muster up in her rage.

Senepol raised his brow in humor at Bree's comment. "Thanks to you, I have been able to rectify the problem you pointed out to me. That was one thing I had overlooked. Are you sure you aren't having reconsiderations toward me?" Senepol reached out, grabbing Bree's arms with the speed of a cat, and dragged her to him. "I have been very patient with my need for your body underneath me, woman. Take heed with my patience not to take you right here and now. Your rage excites me."

Bree froze in his grasp, but in spite of herself, she spat in his face. Senepol growled and threw her down on the bed, crawling atop her in an instant, and ripped her dress wide open as she struggled beneath him. He paused as he appreciated her nakedness for only a moment and then groaned as his meaty hands grabbed her breasts and squeezed them painfully. Bree roared in his face as she tried to slap and claw anywhere she could reach. Suddenly a throat cleared loudly behind them.

Senepol sat up, still straddling Bree, but he grabbed and held her hands down as he growled out, "I'm busy."

There was shuffling behind him as whoever it was that interrupted them was trying to figure out if it was worth staying to tell Senepol what it was that was so important he had to interrupt in the first place. "There's a problem in the ranks of the Aspis, my king. They are questioning where Sa'd has disappeared to. They're threatening not to fight."

Senepol lowered his head so his snout was only a centimeter from Bree's face. "Once again, you've lucked out. Take heed, my lovely, you and I will finish this after the battle. Then I will claim you with or without interruptions." He leaned down, dragging his tongue across her breasts, then sat up, purposely licking his lips before he vaulted off the bed. Senepol and the soldier that saved Bree by coincidence left the tent, leaving the doppelganger behind. He sat on the lounger picking at his teeth with a bone staring in Bree's direction. "Well, that was a disappointing interruption, I must say. Best entertainment I've had in years."

Bree covered herself quickly as she spewed out, "Screw you." Senepol's double laughed at her again.

*****

Every single Aspis had gathered at the center of the camp as Senepol stalked without fear right into their midst. "I hear you all have something to say to me."

One of the younger Sa'd followers bravely spoke up, "Where is Sssa'd and Tiye?"

Senepol turned to the young Aspis, pinning him with a malevolent glare. "Who are you to dare ask a king such questions?"

The young Aspis looked around and gained strength from the number of his kin beside him. "You tell usss, or we do not fight for you, Sssenepol. You are not our king yet. Sssa'd isss our leader, and we follow him that followsss you. Only when we win and Sssa'd has leadership of our ssswamps will you be acccepted as our king. Tell usss, or we leave."

Senepol stalked slowly toward the youngling, barely keeping his murderous rage in check. When he reached the one who had spoken, he purposely stomped on his tail as it swished back and forth with his heavy hoof. The young Aspis hissed but tried to stay strong under the pain of Senepol's hoof. "Good to know you have my back, Aspis."

ARTIFACTS ALIVE

Senepol leaned forward, enabling him to press his full weight onto the Aspis's tail as he continued to speak. "Sa'd is on a mission I personally sent him on. Tiye went along for the ride. I trust no one else but Sa'd to do this mission for me that will, in the end, benefit you all nicely. Question me again, young one, and I will kill you for your insubordination. Do you understand?"

Without waiting for an answer, Senepol huffed as he turned and slowly stalked out of the center of the group without looking back. The Aspis respected fear and strength, even though they were ones to hid in the shadows, as they were truly cowards by nature. With Senepol walking into the center of their circle with absolutely no fear gained back all the Aspis's loyalty just for that reason alone. They all hissed violently at the young Aspis that questioned Senepol as soon as he left their circle. The young Aspis knew that he would not be alive in the next couple of minutes. His own kin would now rid themselves of him for his folly since he was the one that ignited the Aspis's agitation that Sa'd was missing in the first place. They now blamed him for angering the king, so he tried to quickly slither away, but the entire group of Aspis soldiers amassed on him, each trying to get a fang into him to end his life.

Senepol was smiling as he entered his tent once more. He was aware that the Aspis that had questioned him would die. That is why he did what he had done. Ignorant Aspis. He was king for a reason, one for which he commanded respect. If one was a smart king like he was, one studied and understood everyone you had in your corner. You figured out what made them tick. He knew the Aspis were cowards. He knew they would be back on his side the moment he walked into the center of almost one hundred Aspis warriors without fear. He chuckled to himself again as he could hear the Aspis tearing apart the one that questioned him. Thankfully for Bree, Senepol no longer was thinking with his second brain. He was now in a very boastful mood and went immediately over to the jug of wine, flopped himself on the lounger beside his body double, and related the tale of what had just transpired. Bree made herself as small as she could on the bed, listening to the tyrant king spew his conceit to the soldier beside him as they recalled past grandiose war tales well into the night.

26

The dreaded day had arrived. Bree awoke by Senepol, reeking of alcohol and sweat, pulling her out of bed. Without any words, Senepol had her by the arm and none too gently dragged her out of the tent and threw her onto the back of a rotten-smelling slobbering hyena. She thanked God she had tied her ripped dress securely enough the night before so her female bits were hidden from exposure, or at least her chest wasn't exposed. Senepol had ripped the entire front of her dress open the previous evening, so she tied it together just at breast level, but her navel and cotton wrap around her nether regions was fully exposed. The early morning was chilly and overcast with a misty rain miserably drizzling down as if as an omen of what was to come. Bree tried not to show any apprehension or wretch at the smell coming off the beast she sat upon. She noticed that Aston was right beside her on a hyena as well. Senepol tied her wrists to the horn of the saddle and then walked away to address the already lined-up soldiers. Senepol's body double was in his personal chariot at the head of the masses of soldiers, with a box built onto the back.

Bree squinted at the crude wooden box fastened to Senepol's chariot. *Who is in there?* The figure in the box wasn't moving. Bree realized that, in fact, there was no one in the box. It looked as if someone was, and it was meant to represent herself. So, this was how Senepol fixed the problem that she had brought up to him the day before. It looked as if someone was in the box. With the battle going on, no one would even suspect that it wasn't herself with all the chaos of battle. *Smart*, Bree thought as she sighed in defeat. What an idiot she was. *Stupid, stupid, stupid idiot,* she repeated over and over to herself. She looked up into the mist, praying that Jabar would see through the ruse, but this meant that he would have to get close enough to Senepol to realize she wasn't in the box. This could mean harm to Jabar or, worse, death. Aston noticed Bree look up into the sky as the rain misted down on her. Her torn white dress plastered against her body and didn't leave anything to the imagination. *God, she's beautiful.* Aston appreciated the view as Senepol growled out orders for his army to advance and line up for battle just before the forgotten city borderlands. He belted out orders, and soon the army was marching out without them.

Senepol mounted behind Bree, which snapped her out of the trance of prayer she had sent up to every deity she could think of for the safety of her friends. Senepol noticed how Darthos, Aston, and his soldiers ogled Bree in her wet outfit. His jealousy threw a cloak around her without speaking and shifted their mount to move. They headed in the direction of the forgotten city opposite the way Senepol's army marched. Aston caught Bree's eye and nodded. Right now, she couldn't care less about what was going through Aston's meaning of the nod. All she could think about was Jabar, Sethos, Darius, and their safety. That was all that mattered at the moment. She looked away from Aston before she burst into tears.

*****

Jabar had waited the last couple of days for another pigeon to fly down with a note attached to its foot from Bree. He prayed every moment one would fly down and deliver just one small message saying that she was okay. This never happened, and his frustration festered. He rose hours before anyone else that morning and prayed to their goddess like he had never prayed before for a sign that everything would be okay, that Bree was okay, and that they would soon be together, safe. He knelt on his knees for the entirety of his prayers until Sethos approached him just before the rain began to fall. Sethos had watched Jabar for a couple of minutes before he approached him. He, too, had prayed the entire night. He had faith in their goddess that it would all be set right. He had to believe. He had to believe in order to function. He placed his hand upon Jabar's shoulder, and the two stayed in that position for a moment.

"It will be as it will be, my friend. The goddess is on our side. She will show herself through Bree, however it is to be," Sethos stated quietly to Jabar.

Jabar raised himself off his knees. "If anything happens to me today, promise you will take care of her with your life."

Sethos grinned sadly at his friend. "Ditto." They both looked off into the direction of Senepol's camp, and with an almost telepathic communication, they both walked away from each other and began to prepare for the imminent battle. Within the hour, the entire five tribes stood, prepared and ready at the front lines and in their designated positions, watching as Senepol and his army approached the forgotten city in the distance. Sethos had informed the entire army to not attack the Anubi when the battle started. Darius climbed upon the massive boulder, with his spear waving high above his head as the bright blue cotton flag flapped back and forth in the misty rain.

*****

Both armies stood facing each other; Darius waved his spear high as he waved it above his head. Senepol's army lined up behind Senepol's body double. The Apis warriors were the first in line behind Senepol's chariot. Behind them lined up were the Anubi with all their scarab mounts, and finishing the line behind the Anubi were all the Aspis mounted on snarling, drooling battle-ready hyenas. Sethos, Jabar, and Darius stood fast. They, too, looked menacing with the lineup that awaited Senepol's army. The front line consisted of a mixture of mounted Sakhmets on their giant rat mounts with their poisoned weapons, mixed with Maahe and Sobek warriors. The second of their line consisted of the rest of the Maahe and Sobek warriors interlocked with spears, swords, and shields. To each side of the Maahe and Sobek line stood thirteen fully armored and mounted elephants. Behind those lines flew the Heru warriors in the air, fully stocked with bows and arrows that could be lit on fire and shot down from above as well as poisoned javelin spears. In the back of the line within the front city fallout were other archers placed to take out any that broke through the front lines. Outlined in the sides of the city intricacy placed and hidden were the Sakhmet rogues that would attack from the sides when the battle commenced. They also knew that the Anubi warriors would turn on their counterparts and join them in this fast bloody battle. Senepol's army did not stand a chance.

*****

Zahra watched Senepol's small group dismount and stash their mounts behind an outcropping of rocks. She stayed hidden for a moment and then rushed back toward the edge of the city line toward the patrols left to guard the unprotected side. She approached the patrol, stopping them. "Sethos has requested that you join in the battle. Senepol's numbers seem greater than expected, and he has asked for full assistance so this battle can end swiftly. He has left me and other hidden rogues to take out anyone that may slip by and try to enter the city from this side."

The patrols were slightly wary but trusted one of their own and without question. They headed off quickly toward the battle, excited that they would see action. *Well, that was easy enough*, thought Zahra as she headed off toward the other patrol to tell them the same. With the side of the city now unprotected, Zahra sighed in relief. Her job was complete. Senepol and Aston now had access to that side of the temple to get in undetected. She made her way back to the small oncoming group as they closed into the side of the city. Soon she would be rid of the witch, and Jabar would be hers once more.

*****

Senepol's body double made sure he stood out at the front of the line as he had his chariot ride up and down in front of the line. Jabar and Sethos immediately noticed the small wooden makeshift cell attached to the back of the chariot. "She's in there. That bastard has her right in the center of battle," Jabar seethed. He climbed on the boulder that Darius stood on and yelled out to his lines of warriors so they could hear him, "Do not attack the wooden cell on the back of Senepol's chariot at all costs. Bree is inside that cell. No harm is to come to her, or you will answer to me. It is imperative that we get Senepol off the chariot and dispose of him so he does not have access to Bree and her healing abilities. Do I make myself clear?" Every warrior thumped their chests in response. "We wait until Senepol charges. We hold position till Senepol and his warriors advance to the center of the battlefield, then we attack. Remember our strategies, and this battle will be in our favor. May the goddess be with us all." Just as Jabar finished his speech, the heavens opened and began to pour down heavy rain. This was like a signal to Senepol's army, as there was a sudden battle cry from Senepol's chariot, and they all started running toward the forgotten city. Sethos climbed onto the boulder beside Jabar and Darius, who was still waving his spear frantically. "Hold your positions. Hold, hold." Senepol's army advanced with speed, and when they reached the center of the battlefield, Sethos yelled out, "*Attack!*"

*****

Zosar and Jendayi with the rest of the priests were deep in meditation. The three obelisks glowed suddenly deep red, as the priests chanted in unison. Rapidly the obelisks began to vibrate and hover slightly above their slots, humming loudly. The priests were aware deep in meditation that the battle had started. Their bodies became ridged, and their heads snapped up with their eyes shooting opening as their irises rolled to the back of their heads so only the whites were exposed. Their arms shot out above them stiffly toward their goddess's statue, and their chanting grew louder and faster. The obelisks pulsated and began to spin in unison as they hovered loudly humming in sequence with the chanting coming from the priests.

*****

Zahra made sure that Aston was able to notice her in her hidden position for a moment as their small group entered the side of the city. She quickly gave him a thumb-up as he led the group slowly and carefully toward the temple. *She came through. Good girl* was all he thought as he quickened his pace without giving away to the group Zahra in her hiding spot. The rain poured down on them, and they were all drenched to the bone. "It's this way, come" was all Aston said. Bree dragged along behind Senepol with a rope tied around her wrists and held to Senepol like a dog leash. He had his two obelisks strapped to his back, and two Apis warriors were right behind her. There was no way she could escape. She did, however, toss off the cloak Senepol had wrapped around her when they left the camp. It was making it impossible to not trip and stumble on it as they snuck to the city center. Senepol was trusting Aston to show them the way and didn't notice anything else as he focused on getting to the temple. He was a beast on a mission, and as soon as Aston said the coast was clear, he became more intense and focused on getting to the temple at a faster pace. He was so close. The obelisks on his back began to vibrate and heat up through the sack on his back. His mission was within his grasp. He would be king of all within the hour, and he was drooling in anticipation. He pulled hard on Bree's bonds, and she fell at times trying to keep up with him in the rain. He didn't even notice as he dragged her along. She had to have the Apis warriors assist her up as he dragged her in his rush to get to the temple.

*****

Just as the two armies were about to clash in the middle of the battlefield, Senepol's chariot swerved off and exited behind the line of warriors behind him. Jabar's only focus was on that chariot. Nothing else mattered but getting to Senepol and getting him off the chariot. Jabar was seething with rage. The time had come for Senepol's end, and if Jabar had his way, it would be his weapon that ended Senepol's life. The two armies met. Roaring, screaming, weapons clashing, arrows flying, blood spilling ensued en mass. True to their word, the Anubi turned and began their attack on the Aspis and Apis warriors. Chaos erupted when Senepol's warriors realized what was happening. Not only were they fighting the front assault, they were now also fighting those within their own ranks. Panic arose within Senepol's army, but it was too late; the battle was full on, and there was no escaping. Blood, death, screams, and horror were all that awaited the warriors that followed the masochistic king, and now they also had the Sakhmet rogues attacking from the sides and from behind. Senepol's ranks were falling at an alarming rate, but they were strong beasts that would not go down as easily as hoped.

*****

The ease at which they were able to enter the temple was laughable. No one suspected Senepol's devious plan. They assumed he would be thirsty for his enemy's blood as he led his army into battle. Never did they think that he cared so little of his own people that he would abandon them just to obtain the obelisks. As they entered the temple, Darthos slowly gained space between him and Aston. He realized as they left the camp that Sa'd was still missing. He instinctively knew that Sa'd and Tiye were dead. This would not be his fate. He now understood that Senepol was going to rid himself of any agreements he had previously agreed to in order for him to be the supreme ruler over all the lands. Darthos was now in a bad predicament. He decided the only way for him to survive was to kill Aston and then get Bree. With this leverage, he would then negotiate his survival with Senepol. Bree in exchange for his rule over the Heru/Ibis lands. He would kill the witch if needed. He had to show Senepol he was a force to be reckoned with. Senepol didn't notice the tension in the air with Darthos or with Aston as they both plotted against him. All Senepol focused on the moment he entered the temple was the spinning, pulsating obelisks surrounding the goddess's statue.

*****

Jabar sliced his way through the throng of battle and closed in on Senepol and his chariot. Senepol was busy as he was slicing his massive sword toward a Sakhmet rogue that saw Jabar headed their way and decided to help him by keeping Senepol distracted. Jabar took out the chariot's scarab first; he rushed toward it, and just before its razor-sharp pinchers sliced into him, he dropped and slid under the scarab with ease from the mud caused by the downpour of the rain. As he slid, he opened up the scarab's underbelly like butter with his sharp sword. He was able to roll out before the chariot ran him over. The scarab collapsed, causing the chariot to shift forward and over the dead beetle. Senepol bailed out of the chariot, and Jabar never gave him a chance to recover. He was on him in an instant. Senepol's head rolled away from his body as Jabar stood above him soaking wet, panting from the exhilarating excursion. He nodded with thanks to the Sakhmet rogues, and they took off to rejoin the remaining battle. Without celebrating the death of Senepol, all that mattered to Jabar now was getting to Bree. He leaped over the flipped chariot, making his way to the wooden cell that prisoned her. It lay on its side with the front smashed open. Jabar yelled out Bree's name as he tore at the wood. He reached for her, praying she was only unconscious as she wasn't answering him. His hand met with wet sandbags dressed in lady's attire. Fear bubbled up in Jabar's heart. Bree wasn't there.

Jabar instantly jumped off the small wooden prison, quickly making his way back to Senepol's body. He passed the heap that used to be Senepol and headed to Senepol's severed head. Looking up at him was a beast that resembled Senepol, but in an instant, Jabar recognized that it wasn't him. A loud angry roar bubbled out of Jabar's throat as he spun back toward the forgotten city limits on all fours as fast as his legs would carry him. He swerved and maneuvered himself through the fighting and raced to Sethos with Darius standing on the boulder shooting arrows at their foes. Jabar slid to a stop. "We've been deceived! Senepol and Bree are not in the battle. He had a double take his place and a dummy of sandbags made to look like Bree. Follow me at once. I know where they are, and we need to get there fast." Sethos and Darius looked confused but didn't question Jabar. Just the look of fury and pain etched on Jabar's face was enough for them to follow their friend. They quickly found mounts and within seconds were following Jabar to the city center toward the temple with a speed as if a demon were biting at their tails.

*****

All the priests were deep in meditation, and without a warning signal coming from any of the outer patrols guarding the temple, they were none the wiser that the temple had uninvited guests. Everything happened at once. Senepol removed his sword from its sheath on his hip and leaped up behind Zosar. Bree realized too late what Senepol was about to do. Just as she screamed out Zosar's name, Senepol's blade sliced completely through Zosar's back to pierce out of his chest and lofted off the meditation mat. Zosar's eyes rolled back to normal, and he looked down at the blade protruding from his chest with shock. Bree roared in anguish as she tried to scramble up to reach Senepol and Zosar. Just as Senepol lifted Zosar high above him, Jabar, Sethos, and Darius entered the opposite side of the temple. They witnessed the horrible scene before them as Senepol laughed and flung Zosar's limp body into another priest as they were coming out of their trances. Sethos roared in agony seeing his father slaughtered and tried to fly over to the chaos but only ended up falling hard as his still broken wing failed him. Darthos took this opportunity and lunged at Sethos as he was down. Darthos was delighted to see his enemy wounded and could not take flight. With sword raised, he slashed down upon Sethos.

A spear blocked Darthos's down-slashing blade. Darius stood just off to the side of Sethos and managed to block Darthos's attack with his long spear. This gave Sethos time to roll away from the assault and enable himself to fight his lifelong nemesis. Darthos growled in anger as his foe escaped and turned on Darius, slashing to the side. Darius just managed to skip away, but the tip of Darthos's sword sliced into the top of his shoulder. Darius stumbled back and fell from the pain, but quick-thinking Sethos had his bow at ready and shot an arrow. The arrow only managed to embed itself in one of Darthos's wings, but it was enough to have him turning away from Darius to focus back on Sethos.

Aston couldn't believe his luck. There on the ground lay the two forgotten obelisks. Without hesitation, he snatched them up and snuck around to the opposite side of the goddess statue. Bree reached Zosar's body, and she crumpled beside him, lowering her head to his chest to see if by chance he was still breathing. All the priests were now screaming and yelling. Most were trying to flee out of the temple. Senepol's soldiers dispatched a couple as they tried to run. Senepol noticed Jendayi and headed for her. The last of the originals. Senepol smiled evilly as he approached her with his bloody sword intent on her being his next victim. Everything would line up nicely with her out of the way. Suddenly, a small freakishly fast body jumped in front of Jendayi, placing themselves in between her and Senepol. Zahra hissed and bared her teeth at Senepol as she told Jendayi to run. Senepol growled in frustration that his prey had protection and slashed down hard toward Zahra.

Jabar followed behind his friends and witnessed the chaos; he immediately jumped in between the two soldiers that were picking off the poor defenseless priest and dispatched them quickly. With the soldiers down, he frantically looked everywhere for Bree and found her just reaching for an obelisk that lay by Zosar's body. He yelled out to her just as he grasped that she was going to try to use the obelisk to try to heal Zosar. The moment her hand touched the obelisks, there was an intense flash of blue light that stopped everyone in their tracks.

The temple shook as the obelisks vibrated with strong shock waves, knocking everyone over where they stood. Debris fell from the ceiling, coating everyone in dust. The obelisks hovered up and high into the air, circling the goddess statue. A strong wind came from within the obelisks, and lightning thundered out of each of them, connecting them together, with fingers of electricity arching each together. Aston had to let go of the obelisks he was holding as they burned his hands and then blew him back as they, too, lifted into the air to join the others. The obelisk that Bree had touched rose with the others as well, only Bree could not let go. She had become somehow attached to it. Her body convulsed as she fell into a trance as it lifted her into the air. The obelisk stopped in place in line with the others as it disconnected from Bree and proceeded to connect itself with the arcing lightning of the others. Bree's body continued floating up and above the head of the goddess's statue. Her body bent backward with her arms flung behind her; her head snapped back facing up to the ceiling. Suddenly her mouth dropped open, and blue light flashed out of her mouth like a protector illuminating everything above her as the wind whipped at her hair and dress.

Everyone in the room froze in their places, shocked at what they were seeing. Aston was the only one not awed at what was happening to the room or to Bree. He picked himself off the floor and immediately began reciting the scroll to open the portal that he had memorized by heart as he held himself in place on a large chunk of ceiling that had fallen long ago so he wouldn't blow away by the intense winds coming from the obelisks. Jabar couldn't take his eyes off Bree as he tried desperately to reach her, but the closer he advanced, the stronger the winds shoved at him, keeping him away. Darthos snapped out of his shock and leaped toward Sethos with his sword raised above his head, but Sethos was ready, and with a quick roll of his neck and a deep breath, he let his readied arrow fly. The arrow pierced threw Darthos directly in the center of his throat as he was only inches from slicing Sethos's head off. His body landed at Sethos's feet. Sethos sighed in relief and then moved to Darius, who was sitting on the floor holding the gaping wound on his shoulder, staring up at Bree. Senepol also regained momentum quickly as he needed to get to the obelisks, and the little Sakhmet flea was in his way. He no longer cared about getting to Jendayi; he needed to get to his destiny and to Bree. She was his meal ticket.

Sadly, Zahra, distracted by the scene in the center of the temple, caused her demise. Senepol's bloody blade sliced across her throat, opening both jugulars, spraying Senepol with her lifeblood. Without waiting, Senepol turned, forcing his large mass into the wind toward Bree and the obelisks. Suddenly the light coming from Bree's mouth pulsated and turned a bright white. A misty form of a woman's face began forming within the light that pulsed from Bree's gaping mouth. It looked exactly like Bree but somehow ancient. A voice boomed from the misty mirage. The voice sounded tired and sad as it spoke, "My precious beings, I was wrong to leave you in the care of the obelisks. I only wanted you to live in harmony and peace, with the obelisks aiding you with growth and prosperity. Alas, nothing changes, human or not, it all ends up the same. For this reason, I must remove the obelisks. To my disappointment, I have watched for eons as you have torn each other apart. My soul has cried out in regret hearing your anguish and your prayers. I've sent this woman of my bloodline I use as my conduit now to intervene. I watched, I heard, I aided, I cried. I love all creations of my forebears. Do not take this as punishment but as enlightenment to survive without aid or false powers that I shouldn't have left with your kind to begin with. I am sorry." The face evaporated in the light, and the goddess was gone as Bree's mouth closed. Within moments of the goddess's disappearance, a fissure began to fizzle and crackle with purple lightning as a space began to open in front of the golden statue in midair.

The obelisks began to lower themselves to the ground, but the vibration of them changed, and they stopped rotating. The wind died down as the obelisks were now just above the ground. The portal was becoming larger as Aston continued chanting out the memorized scroll ritual. In just a minute, he would be home. Bree was beginning to lower back to the floor of the temple as well. Senepol unsheathed as he listened to the words of the goddess; he had to get to the obelisks quickly before they disappeared. The goddess had gone soft. She would no longer receive any prayers or devotion from him. The obelisks were his; he was destined for them to be in his control. Senepol vaulted his powerful frame off the ledge he had just killed Zahra on and slammed his full weight to the main floor as he charged toward the center of the temple. If Bree was to be the destructor of the obelisks, then she would have to die. Senepol's delusion believed that if Bree died, then the power of her bloodline would die with her, and the obelisks would remain intact with him.

When the wind died down, Jabar was also able to charge in toward the center of the temple. He saw the crazed look upon Senepol's face as he charged toward Bree. He intuitively realized that Bree's life was now in jeopardy. He had to get to her first. He had to stop Senepol before he reached her. The portal was growing in size at an increased rate of speed, and Aston finished the recital of the scroll. The portal was suddenly gaping with the center's blackness, escaping into the temple like it would swallow the entirety of the building as it expanded. The obelisks began to vibrate toward the portal, and Senepol roared in frustration. His eyes were only on Bree.

As he neared his target, he vaulted his bulky frame off a giant boulder and jumped into the air to reach Bree faster than running would, with his sword raised above his head to strike her down. At the exact same time, Jabar vaulted himself off the middle ledge and into the air with his sword also above his head aimed toward Senepol. Suddenly there was a giant flash of light and a loud, ear-pounding boom as the portal fully opened. The remaining occupants of the temple temporarily lost the ability to see and hear. Aston was able to maneuver himself over to the portal opening just before the flash and boom escaped from the finalized portal opening. Four of the five obelisks had already vanished into the portal's vortex. Aston realized he was satisfied with the four obelisks and decided staying to see if the fifth obelisk made it through the portal was not worth his life.

Bree floated softly down onto the floor of the temple and was instantly out of her trance, confused and unaware of what had just occurred. A heavy wet weight landed onto her lap as she sat up. Something large landed just off to her left with a grotesque thump, and something large landed just in front of her. Bree looked down at her lap to see what it was that fell on her. Staring up at her was the grimacing head of Senepol, his facial expression glued into a menacing snarl. Bree shoved Senepol's head hard and as far away from her lap as she could. She noticed Senepol's headless body lying just off to her right that barely missed crushing her as he fell dead to the floor. Bree panicked. She had no idea how she had ended up by the goddess's statue on the main floor of the temple and scrambled to rise from the floor. There before her was the most fantastic sight she had ever seen. Jabar was kneeling on one knee holding his sword out and to his right side, panting from his excursion. At the moment he couldn't see and just knelt in front of Bree, trying to collect his surroundings and understand what had happened right after the flash of light. Bree leaped into his arms and kissed him everywhere her lips could reach on his face. She was crying and laughing together at the same time, repeating his name over and over again. Jabar dropped his sword and clung desperately to the woman that had stolen his heart into a full body hug as he stood up.

Jabar still couldn't see anything or hear clearly, but he was so happy to have Bree back and in his embrace. He could hear her muffled voice as she spoke right into his ear, "He's dead! Senepol is dead. You did it." Jabar's eyesight was just coming back, and he was able to see Bree's beautiful face full of tears and smiles. She couldn't stop caressing his face and mane with her hands. Jabar quickly noted Senepol's dead body slumped on the floor behind Bree. He looked back at Bree, and they locked eyes. Jabar swooped his head down and kissed Bree as he did every night in his dreams; she returned his kiss with the passion he felt. When they separated, Bree was breathless. "Do you know how long I have waited for you to kiss me, my love?"

Jabar's heart soared with joy at hearing her say "my love." Just as he was about to confess his undying love to Bree, a hand reached out from the portal, snagging the back of Bree's dress. Jabar felt Bree ripped from his embrace as if in slow motion. He watched as a force drew her backward into the dark portal's abyss as he tried to reach out to save her. Bree disappeared as the portal crackled, fizzled, and unexpectedly closed. Jabar stood for a moment with his arms still outstretched, trying to comprehend what had just happened. When his brain realized Bree was gone and the portal closed, he let out a mournful, agonized cry and fell to his knee's as he screamed out, "*Noooo, nooo, nooo!*"

Epilogue

Jendayi, Darius, and Sethos gathered on the ledge, looking down on Jabar as he screamed out his emotional agony of losing the woman he loved just as he had gotten her back. Sethos felt his heart break for his friend as well as his for himself. The air seemed heavier in his lungs, and the light dimmed deep inside his heart. Darius stood in shock, watching the spot where the portal had closed, not believing his dear friend was gone. Tears welled up and splashed down his young face. Jendayi fell to her knees as she glanced around the carnage left in the temple. They had won with the tyrant Senepol dead below, but at what cost? She was the last surviving original; she, too, began to quietly cry as her gaze fell upon the crumpled body of Zosar. Her heart held mixed emotions on what had occurred. Jabar's head fell to his chest, and as he did, his eyes fell upon the last obelisk that never made it through the portal laying on the temple floor by his feet. Hope flared in his heart as he stood from his knees, moving to the obelisk and gently scooping it up. *She had come through once before. She could do it once again and come back to me. She is trying to get back right now as we stand here.* To keep from succumbing to heartbreak, he held tightly to this hope as he gently cupped the now cold silent obelisk within his bloody, war-torn clawed hands.

End

About the Author

J. T. was always a responsible youth and had to raise herself as her mother worked extensively to support the family. J. T. also married young and found herself divorced at the age of twenty-four. She decided to live on the wild side after adulting at such a youthful age. She joined a country band and toured around Alberta for a little under a year. She realized she couldn't live on the road and quit the band but stayed dating her bass player for another six years. Partied out at the age of thirty-three, she decided it was time to be an adult again by buying a house, having kids, and working in health care, only to find herself a year later a single mom for the next thirteen years. During the COVID pandemic, J. T. took advantage of isolation from main society and decided to follow another one of her dreams and began to write. This time, she took a leap of faith in herself, sending her manuscripts for review with publishers. This is now her third published book since 2020.

CPSIA information can be obtained
at www.ICGtesting.com
Printed in the USA
JSHW020018290423
40808JS00007B/26